THE DRAGON ON THE BORDER

GORDON R. DICKSON

THE DRAGON ON THE BORDER

ACE BOOKS, NEW YORK

THE DRAGON ON THE BORDER

An Ace Book
Published by The Berkley Publishing Group
200 Madison Avenue, New York, New York 10016

Book design by Arnold Vila

First Edition: April 1992

Library of Congress Cataloging-in-Publication Data
Dickson, Gordon R.
The dragon on the border / Gordon R. Dickson.
p. cm.
ISBN 0-441-34233-7
I. Title.
PS3554.I328D73 1992   91-21270
813'.54—dc20   CIP

Printed in the United States of America

10 9 8 7 6 5 4 3 2 1

This book is dedicated to Elizabeth Pearse,
in memoriam,
for a lifetime lived richly, valiantly and well

CHAPTER 1

"Ah, spring," said the good knight Sir Brian Neville-Smythe, "how could it be better, James?"

Sir James Eckert, Baron de Malencontri et Riveroak, riding beside Sir Brian, was caught slightly off guard by the question.

True, the sun was shining beautifully, but it was still a little chilly by his own personal, twentieth-century standards; and he was grateful for the padding underneath his armor. Brian, he was sure, was feeling if anything a little on the warm side—certainly he seemed to find the day balmy—and Dafydd ap Hywel, riding a little behind them, wearing nothing but ordinary archer's clothes, including a leather jerkin studded with metal plates, should by Jim's standards also be feeling chilly. But Jim was ready to bet that he was not, either.

There was, in fact, some reason for Brian's reaction.

Last year it had been good weather for them all, both in France and in England all through the summer. But the fall had made up for that. Autumn had been steady rain; and the winter had been steady snow. But now the winter and the snow had passed; and spring was upon the land even as far north as here in Northumberland, next to the Scottish border.

It was toward this border that Jim, along with Brian and Dafydd, was now riding.

Jim woke suddenly to the fact that he had not answered Brian. An answer would be needed. If he did not echo the other's cheerful sentiments about the weather, Brian would be sure that he was ailing. That was one of the problems that Jim had learned to accustom himself to in this parallel fourteenth-century world, in which he and his wife Angie had found themselves. To people like Sir Brian, either everything couldn't be better, or else you were ailing.

Ailing meant that you should dose yourself with all sorts of noxious concoctions, none of which could do any good at all. It was true that the fourteenth century knew a few things about medicine—though these were usually in the area of surgery. They could, and did, cut off a gangrenous limb—without the use of an anesthetic of course—and they were sensible enough to cauterize any wound that seemed to have infected. Jim lived in dread of getting wounded in some way when he was away from home and could not let Angie (the Lady Angela de Malencontri et Riveroak, his wife) take care of his doctoring.

About the only way he would have of fending off the mistaken help of people like Brian and Dafydd would be to claim that he could take care of the matter with magic. Jim, through no fault of his own, was a magician . . . a very low-rated magician, to be sure, but one who commanded respect for his title among non-magicians, nonetheless.

He still had not answered Brian, who was now looking at him curiously. The next thing Brian would be asking was if Jim had a flux or felt a fever.

"You're absolutely right!" Jim said, as heartily as he could, "marvelous weather. As you say, how could it be better?"

They were riding across a section of flat, treeless, heather moor, thick with cotton grass; and expected soon to be dropping down to sea level as they approached their destination, the Castle de Mer, home of their former friend Sir Giles de Mer, who had been slain in France the year before while heroically defending England's Crown Prince Edward from a number of armed and armored assailants; and who—being of silkie blood—turned into a live seal when his dead body was dropped in the English Channel waters.

Their trip was a usual duty undertaken by knights or other friends under such conditions, to advise the relatives of their former friend of the facts of his death; since news of such, in the fourteenth century, did not always get carried back to those relatives, otherwise. Any more than it had in the fourteenth century on Jim's world—not that this reason had justified making the trip to Jim's wife, Angie, any more than if he had chosen to do so from a whim.

Jim could really not blame her. She had not been happy being left alone most of last summer; with not only the castle and its inhabitants, which were normally her responsibility, but all of Jim's lands with their tenants, men-at-arms and others who lived on them to take care of as well.

As a result, she had been firmly against Jim's going; and it had taken him a solid two weeks to talk her around.

Jim had promised finally that their ride to Giles's family castle would take no more than ten days, they would spend no more than a week with the family, and then another ten-day ride back—so that the trip could take in all no more than a month. She had not even been ready to agree to this; but, happily, their close friend and Jim's tutor in magic—S. Carolinus—had happened to show up about that time; and his arguments in Jim's favor had won the day for him. Angie had finally agreed to let him go; but not with very good grace.

Their destination was on the seashore just below the town of Berwick, which anchored the eastern end of the Scottish/English border—the end of the old Roman wall. The de Mer Castle was supposedly only a few miles south of the town; and built right on the edge of the sea.

The description they had of it was that it was actually a peel tower with a certain amount of extra buildings attached to it, but not a great number. It was also about as far north as it was possible to get in this district of Northumberland, which had once been the old Scottish land of Northumbria, without entering Scotland itself.

"Better, it may hardly be," commented Dafydd ap Hywel, "but not well will it shortly be, as the sun goes down and the land cools for the night. If you'll look, now, the sun is almost on the horizon; and already skeins of mist are beginning to form ahead of us. Let us hope then that we reach de Mer Castle before the daylight is full gone; else we will find ourselves camping out overnight once more."

It was unusual for a mere bowman to speak up so freely in the presence of a couple of knights. But Dafydd, with Jim and Brian, had been Companions in a couple of tussles with the creatures of the Dark Powers, who were always at work in this medieval world to upset the balance between Chance and History.

Because of Jim's being originally from a technological civilization six hundred years in advance, and because he had picked up a certain amount of magical energy in being transported along with Angie back to this world, he seemed to have attracted the particular animosity of the Dark Powers, at work here.

Carolinus, who was one of this world's three AAA+ rated magicians and lived by The Tinkling Water, near Jim's own castle of Malencontri, had warned Jim that the Dark Powers were out to get him, particularly and simply, because he was more difficult to handle than someone native-born to this world and time.

However, all that was beside the point now. The fact was that, almost as soon as Dafydd had spoken up, Jim had begun to feel the bite of the air even more sharply through his armor and padding than he had before. Also, for some reason—emotional, no doubt—the sun seemed closer to the horizon than it had been even a couple of minutes earlier.

Moreover, the wisps of mists over the moorland were indeed thickening, lying like thick threads of smoke here and there some two to six feet above the grass; and now beginning to join up with each other, so that soon all the moor would be cloaked in mist; and it might well be perilous to try to continue riding under those conditions—

"Hah!" said Brian suddenly, "here is something that comes with the night, that we had not counted on!"

Jim and Dafydd followed the line of his pointing finger. Some little distance ahead of them, the mist had thinned to reveal movement beyond it. Movement which now emerged into full view to reveal itself as five horsemen. As they got closer, for they were riding directly toward Jim and his two Companions, something strange about them struck all three men.

"All Saints preserve us!" ejaculated Brian, crossing himself, "They ride either upon air or on invisible horses!"

What he said was beyond dispute.

The five indeed appeared to be riding thin air. From the movement of their bodies and their height above the ground, it was easy to see that they were on horseback and that their phantom steeds were moving; but there was nothing visible between their legs and the ground.

"What unholy thing is this?" demanded Brian. Beneath the up-turned visor of his helmet his face had paled. It was a square-boned, rather lean face with burning blue eyes above a hooked nose; and his chin was square and pugnacious with a slight dent in the middle of it. "James, is it magic of some kind?"

The fact that it might be magic, rather than something unholy, plainly offered to take a great deal of the superstitious awe out of the situation for Brian. But from Jim's point of view it did nothing to render less perilous the physical aspect of it. The three of them; he, Brian and Dafydd, with only two of them in armor, were facing what appeared to be five full-armored knights, their visors down and all holding heavy lances. It was a prospect that made his blood run cold; much more so than anything supernatural would have done. Not so with Brian.

"I think it's magic," answered Jim, more to reassure the other than for any other reason.

There remained the faint hope in Jim that the approach of the five might not be unfriendly. But this was firmly and forbiddingly enough dissipated. As those approaching got closer, a movement by each of them clearly announced their intent.

"They set their lances," commented Brian, the natural color in his face quite back and the tone of his voice almost cheerful, "best we do likewise, James."

This was exactly the kind of situation that Angie had feared for him, when she had objected to his going. In the fourteenth century, as it had been once on their original world, life was uncertain. The wife of a man who had left her with a cartful of produce for a nearby market town, never knew whether she would see him alive again or not.

There were innumerable perils on the way. Not merely robbers and outlaws along the road to the town. But the danger of fights; or even a reasonless arrest and execution of her husband once he was at the town, for his violation of some local edict, or other. Both Angie and Jim had known this of medieval conditions. They had known it intellectually as college instructors in their own twentieth century; and they had known of it as a reality, during their first months here. But it had taken them a little while to know it in their guts, as they did now. Now, Angie worried—and it was no weak worry at that.

But the fact of it was no help to the situation at the moment.

Jim reached for the heavy lance resting butt down and upright in the saddle socket in which it was normally carried; and laid it horizontal, pointing forward across the pommel, or raised forepart, of his saddle, ready to meet the charge. He was also about to lower the visor of his helmet when Dafydd trotted his horse a little ahead of them, stopped it, and swung down from its saddle.

"I would advise the two of you to stand clear," said Dafydd, reaching for his longbow, uncasing it and taking down his capped quiver, "to see first what a clothyard shaft can do to these, whoever they may be. There is no point in closing with them, look you, unless you have to."

Jim did not share Dafydd's coolness. Armored men on invisible horses could well be invulnerable to arrows even from Dafydd's tall bow. But Dafydd showed no sign of fearing this.

Calmly, completely indifferent to the thunder of the invisible, pounding hooves coming rapidly nearer and nearer to them at a canter about to break into a gallop, and to the five brilliant steel points of the spears, each with half a ton in weight of striking power behind it, Dafydd draped the leather strap of his quiver over his right shoulder so that the quiver itself hung comfortably at his left hip, upper-end forward. Tall, athletically slim and handsome, as usual every move of his body could have been a demonstration of how such action should be performed.

Now, he flipped back the weather cover from the quiver, chose an arrow from among those within it, examined its three-foot length and broad metal tip critically, then put it to the bow and pulled the string of the weapon back.

The longbow stave bent, the feathered end of the arrow continued to come back until it was level with Dafydd's ear—and then suddenly the arrow was away, leaping up as it left the bow. Jim was barely able to follow its flight with his eye, before it struck the foremost mounted figure squarely on the breastplate and buried itself in him right to the feathers.

The knight—if that was what he was—fell from the horse; but the rest came on. Almost immediately, there were arrows sprouting from three more of them. All but the one who had fallen turned to run, the three with the arrows in them somehow clinging to their invisible steeds so that they were carried away into the mist and out of sight.

Dafydd recased his bow. Calmly, he put it with his recapped quiver back in their places on his saddle, then remounted his own horse. Together they approached the place where the armored figure first hit had fallen.

He was strangely hard to see; and when they came up to where he should be, they saw why. Brian crossed himself again.

"Would you care to be the one to look more closely at it?" Brian asked Jim hesitantly. "—Seeing it may be magic?"

Jim nodded. Now that his first fear was over, unlike the two with him he was more intrigued than awed by what he had just seen. He swung down from his horse and approached what lay upon the ground, to squat down beside it. It was a combination of chain and steel plate, with padding beneath.

Dafydd's arrow was buried in the chest plate, up to the feathers, and the point stuck out through the back armor. It was much like the armor Jim wore himself; but somewhat old-fashioned. His eye for armor was developing, and he was able to notice that not all of the armor parts matched with each other the way they should. Dafydd pulled his arrow on through the backplate to recover it, and shook his head over the damage this had done to the shaft's feathers. Jim stood up.

"Two things are certain," he said. "One is that the arrow stopped him—it looks, permanently. Secondly, whoever or whatever was in the armor isn't there now."

"Could it be some damned souls from hell," asked Brian, crossing himself again, "sent against us?"

"I doubt it," answered Jim. He came to a sudden decision. "We'll take the armor with us."

He had got into the habit of carrying a coil of light rope, along with the other gear on his horse. It had turned out to be useful a number of times. He used it now to tie together the loose pieces of armor and clothing; and made a bundle which he fastened behind his saddle with the other goods his horse carried there.

Dafydd said nothing.

"Now the mists have thickened," said Brian, looking around them. "Soon it will be thick fog and we'll not see which way to go. What do we now?"

"Let's go on a little farther," said Jim.

They remounted and went on a little way, while the fog—for it was really fog now—thickened. But after a bit, they could feel a damp breeze, cold on the right side of their faces; and they noticed that the ground was beginning to slope in that direction, rather steeply.

They turned their horses to the slope and rode down. After about five minutes they rode out from under the fog, which now became a low-lying cloud bank above their heads, and found themselves on the shingle of a pebble and rock-strewn seashore. The cloud had lifted. Perhaps five hundred yards to their left, up the bank, was a dark peel tower—a common form of fortress to be found on the Scottish border. It rose from the shingle like a single black finger, upright, with some outbuildings attached to its base.

It sat right above the edge of a cliff face falling vertically to the creamy surf that beat on the shore, but some fifty to eighty feet above it; by virtue of being built on a little promontory that grew higher toward the end where the tower was built.

"Castle de Mer, do you think, Brian?" asked Jim.

"I have no doubt of it!" answered Sir Brian merrily, setting his horse into a canter.

The rest did the same; and a few moments later they were riding over the wooden drawbridge that lay down over a deep but dry ditch, to a large, open doorway with two cresset lamps, made of baskets of iron bars forged together to hold fuel, burning on either side of the doorway some ten feet off the ground, to hold back the darkness of the night and the mist.

CHAPTER 2

"James! Brian—and Dafydd!"
    With that shout, a short, luxuriantly mustached figure was running across the hard-packed damp earth surface of the court-yard toward them; a squarely built young man, with a very large hooked nose. He wore only a mail shirt above his hose and his hair, flaxen in color like his mustache, was tousled.

"In God's name!" said Brian, reining up abruptly. "First horses of air; and now dead friends rise again!"

But in a fraction of a second his attitude had changed. He was down off his horse and—fourteenth-century style— kissing and embracing the smaller man in a crushing hug of his metal-clad arms.

"Hah!" he half-shouted. "But it is well to see you, Giles! You were near a week dead, with the best speed we could make when we put your body into the English Channel waters. True, we saw you change to a seal as you entered the water. But after that—no word. Nothing."

More cresset lamps were spaced around the interior of the courtyard, but they were too distant, and not bright enough because of that, to show whether Giles was blushing or not. But on the basis of past evidence; Jim, who was now also dismounting along with Dafydd, was willing to believe he was.

"A silkie cannot die on land," said Giles, "but I own it was a sad time after that. I came back here and my family recognized me, of course, but there was nothing they could do to get me back into man-shape again. Not until a godly abbot came to Berwick and they invited him down here for a few days. In the end, my father talked him into blessing me, so that I became a man again. But my father also warned me then that I will have no second escape from death if I again die as a human on land. After that blessing, I may turn into a silkie in the water, but I cannot escape my fate ashore!—James!"

Now Giles was hugging and kissing Jim. The links of the smaller man's chain mail shirt scratched loudly on Jim's own armor but no more noticeably than the bristles of Giles's beard seemed to rasp and spear into Jim's cheeks.

The kiss was the ordinary handshake-equivalent of the period—everybody kissed everybody. You would conclude a purchase or a deal of some kind with a perfect stranger by kissing him or her—and most people at this time had very bad teeth and therefore rather unsweet breath. You kissed the landlady on leaving an inn after spending the night there.

But Jim had generally managed to avoid this custom, so far. Now, with Giles, it would seem cold of him not to accept it whole-heartedly. Jim wondered how women stood the beard bristles.

He made a mental note—which at the same time he guiltily knew he would have forgotten by the time he was home again—to make sure he was as clean-shaven as possible, next time, before kissing Angie. Jim also winced to think of what it must have been like for Giles, himself, with the solid-metal-clad sleeves of Brian's arms enclosing him, in spite of the chain shirt.

However, Giles had made no protest, and shown no discomfort. Then Giles was hugging Dafydd, who likewise seemed to take it in no other way but with complete happiness, though in this case Giles's chain mail must have bit noticeably even into Dafydd's leather jacket.

"But come inside!" said Giles. He half turned and shouted. "Ho, from the stables! Take the horses of these good gentlemen!"

Half a dozen servants appeared with the same suspicious quickness with which Jim's servants at Malencontri had a tendency to appear, whenever something interesting was going on.

They led off the horses and several of them, two of them wearing kilts of differing colors and patterns, carried the saddles and personal gear inside.

Giles led them forward, and flung open the door of a long wooden building which was obviously the Great Hall; leading to the tower. As a Great Hall, it was noticeably smaller than that of Jim's castle; but it was arranged the same way, with a long table on a lower level stretching the length of the hall; and a shorter one—the "high table"—crosswise on a platform at the far end.

Giles led them eagerly to the table on the platform, which was obviously, by the smells, just in front of the kitchen; which here would be on the ground floor of the tower itself. Not only the doors through which they had entered the hall, but those beyond leading into the kitchen, now propped ajar, were tall and wide enough to ride horses through.

It was plain that this castle, like so many other border castles, was designed with defense first in mind. It had been built for a situation in which everyone could, need came, retreat within the stout, flame-resistant stone walls of the peel tower itself.

This was a wise and standard practice if attackers were too numerous or too strong to fight off in the courtyard; or beyond the front curtain wall that held the main gate, with its two cresset torches.

The high table was deserted; and the air, although heavy with the same smells Jim had encountered from all Great Halls that Jim had had anything to do with, was pleasantly warm after the growing chill of the outside night.

Giles sat them at benches at the table and shouted for wine and cups, which came with the same suspicious quickness that the servants had shown with regard to the horses and the gear outside in the courtyard.

Almost on their heels came an individual from the kitchen doors who dwarfed all of them.

"Father, these are the two noble knights I told you about who were my Companions in France, and the archer of renown who was also with us!" Giles said, beaming. "James—Brian—Dafydd, this is my father Sir Herrac de Mer."

He had not sat down himself; and, next to his father, he looked like a midget.

Herrac de Mer was at least six feet six and muscled in proportion. His face was square and heavy-boned, with close cropped black hair tinged with gray. His shoulders were a good hand span on either side wider than those of Dafydd, which were by no means narrow shoulders.

His face had borne a frown at first, seeing strangers already seated at the top table. But the frown evaporated at the words of Giles's introduction.

"Sit! Sit!" he said waving them back down, for they had all gotten automatically to their feet at his entrance. "—Yes, you too, Giles, if they are friends of yours—"

"Thank you, Father!" Giles slipped eagerly onto a bench several seats away from the rest of them. It was clear that while a seat at the high table might be his by right, not only as a knight but as a member of the family, he could not sit in his father's presence without his father's permission.

The rest sat down as well.

"Father," said Giles, "the gentleman closest to you is Sir James Eckert, Baron de Malencontri et Riveroak, and just beyond him is Sir Brian Neville-Smythe. After Sir Brian, is Master Dafydd ap Hywel—the like of whom, I swear, there is none—as far as men of the longbow are concerned."

"Thank you," murmured Dafydd, "but indeed it is also that no crossbowman has ever outshot me, either, as to distance or target."

Herrac's black eyebrows, which had been shadowed slightly in a frown above his deep-set seal-black eyes, on seeing a seated man in a leather jerkin, abruptly smiled. He was naturally not used to entertaining an archer at his high table. But, of course, this archer was different.

"I had heard of you all before Giles told me about you," he said. He had a resonant bass voice that came rumbling softly out from deep within him. "The Ballad of the Loathly Tower has been sung even in this hall, good sirs—and you, Master archer. You are all welcome. My hospitality is yours for as long as you wish. What brings you?"

And he sat down himself at the table with them.

He was not only tall; but he was one of those men who, like Dafydd, kept his back as straight as an arrow. So, if anything, he seemed to tower even more over them at the table than he had standing up.

Dafydd and Brian waited. It was obviously Jim's position as the ranking member of the three to be first in answering the question.

"We came to bring your family the story of Giles's death," said Jim. "Both Sir Brian and I saw him take to the water—"

This was a delicate way of putting it. He was not sure whether Sir Herrac would have approved of his son letting others know about his silkie blood. But certainly the other could read between the words on a statement like that. Jim went on.

"—but it never occurred to us that he might be back here. Least of all that we should see him as we see him now, in his full strength, well and happy!"

"For that, we give blessings to Holy Church," rumbled Herrac, "but Giles has told us little, beyond the fact that he died at a large battle in France. My other sons will be here soon; and meantime we can set in process a dinner worthy of your company."

He lifted a powerful open hand from the table, slightly, in apology.

"It will take an hour or so. Can I suggest you all have a pitcher or so of wine, and then let Giles show you to your room? So that you can then prepare yourselves as you see fit, to eat and drink properly, if sobeit you think any preparation be needed. That way, when you come down, you can tell all the family at once. Alas"—his face for a moment was shadowed as if by the remembrance of agony—"that my wife is not here to hear it as well; but she died of a great and sudden pain in the chest six years past on the third day before Christmas. It was a sad Christmas in this household that year."

"I can well believe so, Sir Herrac," said Brian, his quick and generous sympathy leaping immediately into response to the word. "How many other children have you?"

"I have five sons," said Herrac, "two older than Giles here, and two younger. The youngest is but sixteen, even now. I also have one daughter, who is visiting neighbors today; but will return tomorrow."

"Surely, that too is an excellent thing, Sir Herrac," said Dafydd in his soft voice, "for a man should have both sons and daughters, look you, if his life is to be truly fulfilled."

"I feel as you do, Master Dafydd," rumbled Herrac.

He seemed to shake emotion from him.

"But," he went on, "we are concerned now with the present and in particular what is to come tonight. It will be interesting to hear you tell of Giles in France. He was never one to tell us much about himself."

And he looked fondly down the table at Giles, who was—Jim thought—most surely blushing now, if only the torches about the hall had thrown light enough to show it.

Herrac rose from the table.

"Giles," he said, "when these good friends have drunk, will you take them to the uppermost chamber; and see that all their wants are satisfied?"

It was a statement, in fact an order, rather than a question to his son. Giles bobbed to his feet.

"I'll take good care of them, Father," he said, "the best care."

"See you do," rumbled Herrac; and strode away from the table to vanish once more into the noise and odors of the kitchen and probably to someplace in the tower above, from which he had undoubtedly been summoned by news of their arrival.

It was up that same tower about twenty minutes later, when the wine jugs had been emptied, that Giles led them to a top-most room. It was obviously normally occupied by Herrac, himself. Giles remarked that it had been a private chamber for his father and mother, when his mother had been alive. A wooden frame with some half-finished needlework on it still stood in one corner. Clearly, Herrac had vacated it for his guests.

"You will stay at least the month, will you not?" said Giles eagerly, as he showed them to this room. He was asking them all; but his eyes were on Jim. "There'll be fine hunting as soon as the weather warms a little; and fishing, if you're interested, such as you never encountered. There's a thousand things I'd wish to show you. You will stay?"

Jim winced internally.

"I'm sorry, Giles," he said, "but business requires a stay of only a week; and then, I, at least, must start home again."

He winced again internally at Giles's suddenly unhappy face.

"You must remember," Jim said, "we thought you dead, or lost forever as a seal in the waters of the English Channel. We hoped to do no more here than tell your family the manner of your death, and then make our decent withdrawal. Had we known differently, possibly we could have planned differently."

"Oh—oh, I understand," said Giles, with an effortful attempt at a smile. "Of course, you wouldn't have expected much more of a stay than was necessary to a family which had lost a son.

I was foolish to think of a longer stay; and wrapped in affairs, both magical and ordinary, as you yourself must be, James . . . It's quite all right. We'll simply make the most of the week."

Jim stood, feeling terrible. It hurt him deeply to see Giles's disappointment. But he could not delay his return, or Angie would immediately begin to assume that something had happened to him. He hesitated, hoping that Brian would speak up and say something to back him up. But Brian stayed silent.

To someone such as Brian, a duty like the trip here to the Castle de Mer could never be thought of as anything that could be put off simply because of wifely fears. It was a custom of the time; and customs of the time were iron laws in many respects.

"I'm sorry, Giles," said Jim, again.

"That's all right, as I say," said Giles.

"Well, well," said Giles, trying to smile. "Still, it will be a week to remember. Now the bed here, though large, may be a little small for the three of you—"

"That's all right," interrupted Jim. "I sleep on the floor. Part of the rules of my magic, you know."

"Oh. Of course!" said Giles, completely satisfied.

Jim's original excuse, that he had made a vow that kept him from sleeping in any bed (which would be invariably populated with vermin), which had worked so well the previous year on their way to France, had become a little worn. Instead, he had come up with an excuse that his apprenticeship in magic required him to sleep on a floor rather than a bed.

This excuse served perfectly well; and it had only been afterwards that Jim realized that almost any excuse served, as long as the word "magic" was uttered in connection with it. Accordingly, he now chose a portion of empty stone floor; and from his gear unrolled the mattresslike quilt that Angie had made for him.

As traveling knights with only themselves and their horses, they did not carry much in the way of possessions. Consequently, there was not much dressing to be done for dinner. Effectively, they took off their armor; and Jim, after persuading Giles to get him some water, used some homemade soap he had brought along and washed his hands and face.

This also he had explained as a necessary magic ritual; and Brian, with Dafydd, had accepted it. Nonetheless, they waited a little impatiently until he was done. He wiped his face with his hands, shook what water remained off his hands, and—leaving these parts of him to air-dry—he went with the others back downstairs to the table, the refilled wine jugs and the waiting cups.

Giles joined them there immediately. They sat talking and drinking; and while they did, one by one, Giles's brothers came home.

It was plain they had already been warned of the fact that there were guests at the high table whom their father did not wish disturbed, so none of them had been seen. But they had most certainly been heard, since their individual returns. Like their father and Giles, they had bass voices. But they did not rumble so much as roar. They could be heard shouting to each other all over the castle.

Finally, with surprising hesitation and bashfulness, one by one, and clearly in planned order, they came to be introduced to the three famous guests.

The first to come, of course, was Alan, the oldest of the family. He—as his brothers were to prove to be also—was cast in the same heroic mold as Herrac. Like Herrac and Giles, they all had the seal-black eyes, large, hooked noses and flaxen hair. None, however, had a nose as large as Giles. Nor were any of them—even Alan—as big, as tall, or as wide-shouldered as their father. But they were all considerably larger than Jim, or even Dafydd; and, like their father, heavily muscled. It was a little, thought Jim, as if he, Brian and Dafydd had been invited to the home of some giants.

However, the giants, particularly these younger ones, were clearly overawed at meeting face to face people of whom they had heard in a ballad. They came up, were introduced, and took their seats at the table. Alan took his as if by right, and then one by one gave the others permission to sit as they appeared. Besides Alan, there was the next oldest brother, who was Hector; then the next youngest after Giles—who was William—and finally, the youngest, sixteen-year-old Christopher. They all spoke in as low voices as it seemed possible for them to speak.

Clearly, Herrac de Mer ran a taut household.

As the wine disappeared down their capacious throats, however, they became bolder; and the three guests were plied with all sorts of questions about knighthood, weapons, armor, people in France, dragons, and just about everything else that the sons' minds could conceive of, and that could legitimately be asked without being considered an uncivil question.

This continued until they all at once fell silent. Looking up, Jim saw the reason for it. Sir Herrac himself had entered the Great Hall from the kitchen and was coming to take his seat at the table.

He did so. For a moment his black eyes frowned at his five noisy sons, who looked guiltily down at the tabletop.

"Giles," he rumbled, "have your brothers been bothering your guests?"

CHAPTER 3

Jim frowned slightly. Was it his imagination that Herrac had put a slight, extra emphasis on the word "*bothered*"—the kind of emphasis with which members of a family send signals to each other?

It would be easy to tell himself he had heard no such thing. But he knew this was not true. Now what was it that Herrac feared his sons might have said or asked that Herrac thought might *bother* Jim, Brian and Dafydd—or any one of them, for that matter?

Whatever the message, Giles had evidently reassured his father by ignoring the implication.

Right now he was visibly swelling simply with pride at the reference to *his* guests. An answer seemed to tremble instantly on his tongue, and then was choked back. When he did speak it was in a milder voice.

"I think they may just have been as excited and happy as I, to see these gentles and Master archer," he said.

"Good," said Herrac. "William, go tell the kitchen that the serving of food can begin. We can talk and drink as we are fed.

"—With your permission, my Lord and Sir Brian?" he added. There was a slight catch in his voice at the end of the sentence. Dafydd smiled reassuringly at him, to show he understood the knight's inability to include even an archer like himself in the formal request.

Again, although the words were a question, an affirmative answer had been practically implied by the tone of Herrac's voice. Both Jim and Brian hurried to express their agreement with the idea that dinner should start. In fact, Jim was very happy that it was starting. He had been put in a position of taking a little more wine before dinner than he liked, considering that there would be more of it both during and after dinner. He could always, of course, magically change it to milk in his cup. But right now he was conserving every scrap of magical energy he possessed.

He had expected that Giles's actions in France would have been the first subject of conversation. However, Herrac was evidently a host who had his own idea of how talk at his table should go. Consequently he engaged the three guests in conversation, himself, while his sons sat silent during the early courses of the meal.

He was a good conversationalist. But to Jim's mild puzzlement, Herrac seemed to want to say little or nothing about himself, his family and lands, or local matters. In fact, when Jim, out of sheer courtesy, ventured on these topics, Herrac deftly returned the subject of their conversation back to that of his guests.

They talked about the weather, both this year and last, about the differences between this part of England and that from which the three of them came, in the south; also, about the various ladies and activities of the guests, and about the ballad version they had heard of the battle of the Loathly Tower. This last topic gave Jim and the others an opportunity for which they were grateful, to point out where the version of the ballad the de Mers had heard was wrong.

The fact was that all the ballad versions were wrong. This, because there had been added to all of them whatever the maker of that particular version had thought would make it most interesting, as well as long and dramatic as possible. Nearly all versions, including the one the de Mers had heard, had Jim going to London and asking permission of King Edward to go out and attack the creatures of the Loathly Tower. Whereupon, the King had graciously given him permission to do so, with the implication that afterwards he would be rewarded.

As it had happened, this particular added part had been heard by the King, himself; and pleased his English Royal Majesty enough to make him convince himself that it was true. A result had been confirmation of Jim's possession of the castle and lands of Le Bois de Malencontri.

Another had been his award of arms to Jim. Though it was true that Jim could have created some arms of his own, on the basis of his claiming to hold the mythical barony of Riveroak, which had been the name of the twentieth-century college at which he and Angie had been graduate students and assistant teachers. But an award of arms from the King was a special honor and much to be preferred.

For this and other reasons, the matter of the King's permission was one part of the ballad that neither Jim, Brian, nor Dafydd bothered to correct. For all Jim knew, Brian and Dafydd might have, like the King, convinced themselves that it was the truth.

But there were other additions and even errors in the reporting of the ballad that could stand correcting; and these the three mentioned.

It was not until at last the food had been cleared away and they were well into the after-dinner drinking—which was beginning to look rather frightening to Jim, since it seemed that both Herrac and his other large sons could outdrink even such a notable imbiber as Giles had shown himself to be, in France. Jim was very glad, consequently, when the question of Giles's actions in France finally came up for discussion, as a result of a direct question from Herrac about them.

"Giles has actually told us nothing but that he was slain at a large battle somewhere in France and that the three of you brought his body back to the sea for burial," said Herrac, looking down the table a little severely at Giles—who avoided the glance. "I understand from what you gentlemen say that there was more to it than that?"

"A great deal more," answered Jim.

"Yes," said Herrac, his deep-set eyes still on the embarrassed Giles, "why did you not tell us the rest of it, Giles? I'm confident that there would be nothing unknightly or shameful about what you did."

"Far from it," murmured Brian.

"Well, Giles?" demanded his father.

"I—" Giles almost stuttered, "I was rather hoping—just hoping, you understand—that some minor balladeer somewhere might just be looking for something to make a new ballad about and choose it. That's all."

Hector let out a hoot of laughter from across the table.

"Giles thought they would make a ballad about him?" boomed Hector. "That would be something to tell the crows! Giles in a ballad!"

"Indeed," said the soft voice of Dafydd, "I know of many ballads made with less cause and with less of a subject to sing about."

"By Saint Dunstan!" said Brian, bringing his fist down upon the table with a crash. "And that is so! More so than most of the pretty songs sung about the land!"

"Hector," said Herrac, "leave the table."

"Father—" cried Hector, already crushed by Dafydd's and Brian's retorts; and now further stricken at facing the prospect of not hearing what the others would hear.

"As a favor to us," said Jim quickly to Herrac, "perhaps you would forgive Hector, this one time. It's difficult to realize that someone you grew up with can do mighty things in the eyes of the world. It is not easy for anyone to face such a fact, though often we all must come to it."

Herrac looked grimly at Jim, then twice as grimly at Hector.

"Very well," he said, "you may stay, Hector—but only because our guest requests it. Watch your tongue from now on!"

"Yes, Father," muttered the second oldest giant, cowed.

Herrac turned to his three visitors.

"You were going to tell us the rest of what had to do with Giles in this matter of his death in France," he said.

Once again Jim saw that his two friends were waiting for him to speak first.

"Sir Giles and I," he told the table, "had been chosen by Sir John Chandos to execute a secret duty in France. With the help of some French informer, or informers, we were to learn where the noble Edward, our Crown Prince of England, was held prisoner by the French First Minister; and rescue him from that place, to reunite him with the expedition that was even then being sent overseas from England to bring him safely home."

He paused, rather hoping that either Brian or Dafydd would take up the tale. But Brian studiously avoided his eye and busied himself with drinking from his cup whereas Dafydd merely waited calmly, his eyes steady on Jim.

"In a word," went on Jim, "with Sir Brian and Dafydd's help, we did just that; and rejoined the English forces just as they met the French forces under the King of France, with which they were to do battle. Unfortunately, the King of France's Minister, from whom we rescued the Prince, was one Malvinne, a very well-known and powerful magician—much more able in magic than myself. Malvinne, after our rescue of the real Prince, had made with his magic a perfect duplicate of the young man, and brought that duplicate to the battle to be fought between the English and French forces. Using this duplicate, he was claiming that our young Royal Edward had abandoned his heritage; and thrown in his lot with King Jean and the French host—so that he would be fighting against his own countrymen."

"Somewhat of this we heard," frowned Herrac, "but I interrupt. Go on, m'Lord."

"So with the three of us you see here and Sir Giles as well to make four," said Jim, "in addition to our personal levy of men-at-arms from Sir Brian's estate and my own—"

From the corner of his eye, Jim caught sight of the grateful glance shot him by Brian, since Jim's way of phrasing the matter made it seem as if Brian's contribution had been the equal of Jim's.

"—And with these, acting independently," Jim continued, "it was decided."

"Sir James decided it, having the command in keeping," growled Brian.

"Well, well—in any case," Jim said, "there was a truce between the two armies until the following day. Our small group made plans to attack just as the truce ended. To attack, in fact, from behind the French lines, independently, King Jean of France and his personal bodyguard of some fifty to a hundred picked French knights in heavy armor. Now, with these were not only the magician Malvinne, but the false Prince he had made. This, to ensure that King Jean, Malvinne and the false Prince should be protected, no matter what else might happen between the French and English armies. If the French forces should seem about to lose the day, the bodyguard could protect those three in a withdrawal; so that there would be no danger of any of them being captured."

He paused. The men of the de Mer household were transfixed, from Herrac on down, their eyes unmoving on him. Giles was also staring at him, also almost as if hypnotized.

"So, aided by some small magic of my own—"

"He made us all *invisible,* Father!" broke in Giles excitedly. "We went through the baggage lines behind the French with no one suspecting at all and approached the rear of the last, or third line of the French, on the right flank of which the King and his force sat their horses in full arms and armor."

"Giles," said his father, but in a kinder tone than he had spoken to Hector, "allow our guest to tell the story as he sees fit."

"Yes, Father."

"Well," went on Jim, "to make a long story short, just before charging, we removed our invisibility; since it would not have been fair or chivalric in actual combat to continue it. In full sight, we charged the King's bodyguard from the rear. Our only advantage was that they had not expected anything from the quarter from which we had attacked; and also it took them a few moments to realize and get ready to resist our charge."

Christopher coughed. He had obviously been fighting the urge to do so for some minutes; and the cough came out in a strangled gasp. The rest of the family glared at him. He blushed brightly.

"Therefore," said Jim, "we hit them as they were only half-prepared to receive us; and with the aid of Dafydd, here, and several other greatly skilled bowmen he had gathered from the rest of the English forces, we were able to penetrate through the bodyguard and take the King, himself, prisoner. Whereupon he surrendered; and called upon his bodyguard to throw down their arms and submit. Which they did."

Jim paused. The strain of story telling was greater than he had thought. He paused to take a drink from his wine cup, and found it surprisingly refreshing.

"Where was Giles in all of this?" asked his father. "What part did he take in your charge?"

"Giles was not with us," answered Jim. "Earlier, to protect the true Prince Edward, I had taken both to the ruin of a small, stone chapel some small distance off. There was a short way in among the fallen blocks, though no exit from it. But it was only wide enough for one person to come down at a time. I left the Prince there—very much over his own protests, I should mention—and with him, I left Sir Giles, to bar the short passage to the Prince if any should attack. At that point, none of us expected that the Prince, to say nothing of Sir Giles, would even be found there, let alone threatened."

"This was before you charged and captured King Jean and his bodyguard?" queried Herrac.

"It was," said Sir Brian, "but a short time before—no longer than a man might give to his morning prayers."

"Thank you, Sir Brian. Go on, m'Lord, if you please," said Herrac.

"Once we had captured the King, the magician and the false Prince," said Jim, "our most earnest desire was to confront that false Prince with the real Edward. Therefore, I sent one of our men-at-arms to fetch both Sir Giles and the Prince. He returned only a matter of minutes later at full speed, with word that Sir Giles was under most fierce and cruel attack by a number of knights in armor, all bearing black marks painted across their visor. This was something that identified them as being the personal knights of Malvinne, the magician; who, with his magic, had divined the whereabouts of the real Prince; and dispatched his own knights to overwhelm Sir Giles, and capture, or kill, the real Prince Edward."

"How many of these were there, m'Lord?" asked Herrac, frowning.

"Our men-at-arms encountered some dozen and a half," answered Jim. "It is true, because of the narrowness of the passage, that the Knights of Malvinne could only come at Sir Giles one at a time. But the minute he had defeated one, another took his place; and they were picked knights of great strength and prowess."

"Then what?" queried Herrac, almost as eagerly as one of his sons might have done.

"I sent immediately to rescue Sir Giles and the Prince," said Jim, "and they returned with the Prince unharmed, but with your son suffering from nearly twenty wounds; and so weakened from loss of blood, that it was plain he could not live. You will want to ask me how many knights he encountered at that time, and how he dealt with them?"

He looked directly at Herrac and then at the sons and then back to Herrac again.

"It is what I want to know," said Herrac in a hard voice, that for the first time used something like the full volume of his bass tones.

"They counted eight knights fully dead, and four so badly wounded that they could not escape, and later died," answered Jim. "This was the price your son exacted for what he paid to protect the Royal Prince; and indeed, he protected him so well that no attacking knight got within sword's reach of him."

He had reached the climax of the story. But it was obvious that those listening to him were now captured by it and wanted to hear more.

"Our men brought Sir Giles as gently as possible to the place where we held the King and his now disarmed bodyguard. There was little we could do for your son. He had lost too much blood and was still losing it—nor was there any way to stanch the flow from most of the wounds. Nonetheless, what could be done, was done—"

"There was a lady, fair beyond any fairness you can imagine," broke in Giles, "who was most gentle with me and said many kind things to comfort me; not only about my situation, but about my size and my—er—nose. Would that I could return to France and find her again!"

It was a measure of the hold that Jim's story had taken of his audience, that Herrac did not rebuke Giles for speaking up this time. However, Jim turned to him.

"It's just as well that you never do, Giles," said Jim. "She's a Natural; which is something other than human, something fairylike. Her desire would be only to take you back to the bottom of the lake where she dwells, and keep you there forevermore. There is more for you to do in this world yet, Giles, I think, than spend forever being pampered on the bed of a lake in France."

"Fresh water?" murmured Herrac.

"Yes, Sir Herrac," said Jim, "fresh water."

"Then you are indeed fortunate, Giles. You hear?" said Herrac to his son. "Have you thanked the good Sir James?"

"I've—I've had no chance until now, Father," stammered Giles. "Indeed, my great thanks, James. Not only for opening my eyes now to the danger that lay with me in that beauteous lady; but putting me in position to win some honor on that day of which you speak."

"Well spoken, if a little tardily," growled Herrac. "Giles, you have brought honor to the family name."

Giles blushed.

"So, Hector!" said Sir Herrac, turning to the other son. "What do you think now, of the right of your brother to have a ballad written about him?"

"Indeed, Father—" stammered Hector. "I only wish that in my life I shall have the chance to prove myself half as worthy of such a ballad."

"Good!" growled Herrac. "Now, my Lord and guests, enough of Giles's story, welcome though it has been. Let us enjoy the rest of the evening and talk of other things. How was it on your trip here?"

"Well," said Brian, "it is a pleasure just to be abroad in springtime, at last after the winter just gone by. But perhaps you can enlighten us about a strange and perhaps unholy thing we encountered on the way to the castle, here. It was five knights in armor—"

A certain rigidity seemed to Jim suddenly take all the de Mers.

"—Apparently, with lances," went on Brian, unheeding, "but mounted upon steeds that we could not see. They came at us with all intent to bicker with us; but Dafydd ap Hywel, here, drove them off with arrows before they closed. And when we came to where one had fallen from his horse, there was nothing there but the armor, the lance and some clothes. All else, horse and the man within the armor, had vanished."

He stopped speaking; and now both he and Dafydd, as well as Jim, noticed the change in the faces of their hosts. Herrac's and Giles's features were set like granite outcroppings of mountain rock; and those of all the other sons had paled.

CHAPTER 4

The silence stayed for a long moment around the table, during which the eyes of Sir Herrac were hard upon all his three guests.

"It seems," he broke the silence at last, "that we must speak of one of our local troubles after all, the which I would have preferred not to intrude upon your visit."

He paused for a moment, then went on.

"I am happy to learn that your encounter with these enemies of man and all Gods was so successful," he said. "Because those whom you met were not ordinary opponents, but something other than Christian souls. They are called the Hollow Men; and we have suffered much from them. They are wholly evil, unlike even the Little Men. In fact, they are the ghosts of some of those who have died in this area we have come to call the Border, from the German sea to the Irish sea.

"There have been Hollow Men here from the time of the Romans," he went on, "who built the wall of which all men know, between England and Scotland, down to the present. Of these, those who, because of some evil in their lives, have been forbidden entrance into heaven or even hell, have become what we call the Hollow Men. Indeed, even those who worship the old gods like Odin are shut out of Valhalla; while others like them are shut out from their own pagan afterworld, no matter

what form it takes. In short, they are curst souls and will know
no rest until Judgment Day."

"Nor will we who have to endure them know any rest until
then," said Hector somberly.

This time his father did not rebuke his son, but merely shook
his head.

A common impulse seemed to go around the table, causing
them all there to fill their glasses or top them off, whichever
was needed, and drink deeply for a moment. They waited, but
Herrac said no more.

"What of the invisible horses, then?" asked Brian, once the
glasses had all been set back down on the table.

"They are possibly ghosts as well," said Herrac. "The Hollow
Men themselves have no form or body under ordinary conditions. However, if they can but fit themselves into clothing or
armor, they seem to become again the men they once were, with
the same strength and the same abilities. So discovers anyone
who has to fight one of them. Yet, if your blade should cut into
one, past the armor, it is the same as cutting empty air, for there
is nothing there beneath."

"Ah," said the voice of Dafydd, "that explains something."

Jim looked down the table at him.

"What's that, Dafydd?" he asked.

"Why, the behavior of the arrow once it had pierced the
steel of the breastplate of the one I struck, and from whom we
recovered arrow, armor and clothing," answered Dafydd. "The
arrow did not behave as if it had to penetrate flesh, muscle,
or even bone beneath the armor, but as if it had gone through
merely into an empty space."

He became thoughtful.

"There is a chance, there . . ." he said. "I must think on
it . . ."

"But if there was nothing there—and in that case how could
there be anything there to hurt?" asked Brian. "How was it we
found his armor and clothing on the ground, as if he had been
slain?"

"He had been slain—but only for forty-eight hours," answered
Herrac. "At the end of that time, any one of them who has
been killed comes back to life. Though, in this case, he
will have to find himself new clothes and armor before
he can be other than air. And he cannot begin even to
search for such clothes and armor until forty-eight hours

after he was struck down by your arrow, Master bow-man."

He paused to look directly at Dafydd, who nodded.

"That is the great curse of these Hollow Men," Herrac went on to the table at large. "We can slay them occasionally, we can drive them off, often, but their numbers are not depleted and they keep coming back. Moreover, over the years they have acquired a good store of armor and weapons, so that I doubt not but what the one you killed forty-eight hours from now, after he has found his way back to life, will shortly be able to turn himself once more into a dangerous opponent."

A silence fell on the table.

Jim was thinking deeply. There was a strong feeling in him that Herrac was holding something back—something worse about the Hollow Men than he had yet told them. An ugly thought came like a cold wind out of nowhere to Jim.

When Carolinus, friend and tutor in magic though he was, had first held a dream-conversation with Jim, when Jim had been in France the previous year, he had admitted that—without consulting Jim first—he had pushed Jim into a position of going into a contest with Malvinne, who was a AAA magician and infinitely Jim's superior, since Jim was only a D class magician. But Malvinne had sometime since fallen under the influence of the Dark Powers. Could something about these Hollow Men mean Carolinus had acted so, again?

Jim remembered now how opportunely Carolinus, appearing at Jim's castle apparently by chance, at the time when Angie had been strongly objecting to Jim making this trip, had taken Jim's side with arguments that had considerably weakened Angie's position.

At that time, Carolinus had pointed out that Jim's duties in this world could not be avoided, if he was to maintain his present reputation.

Jim had a sudden uneasy feeling that for his own reasons Carolinus might have pushed him into this particular situation deliberately. Though this was hard to believe. For one thing it had been determined, even before the dead body of Giles slid into the gray waters of the English Channel, that he, Brian and Dafydd should search out his family as soon as possible and tell them of Giles's end, as well as of the heroism it had involved.

On the other hand, there was that question of whether the Dark Powers actually had decided to concentrate on him, again.

It was beginning to stretch coincidence that he should first find himself in a contest with them in the matter of the Loathly Tower, upon first coming to this world with Angie. Then he should discover he was opposing them over Malvinne. Now he had landed in a place where there were unnatural beings who clearly were not on the side of good; and obviously were ripe to be used as pawns by the Dark Powers—even if they were not already so being used.

"Can you tell me some of the things they've done?" Jim asked Herrac.

"As many as you like," answered Herrac.

So, for the next hour, that is what he and Giles did, telling Jim of incident after incident while the levels of the wine in the pitchers sank and the pitchers were refilled again and again.

The attacks—or forays of the Hollow Men, since when they attacked in a force of fifty or more it could hardly be called simply an attack—apparently had two aims. Though their ranks included the souls of men going back through history, their primary aim seemed to be to get modern armor for all of them, and the best of the modern armor they could find. Secondarily, when alive, they apparently wanted food and wine, or the money with which to buy it; for there were those who would sell, even to them.

They always attacked against a lesser number, counting on their own numbers to overwhelm opposition.

In the beginning, perhaps this may have been partially because only a few of them were well armed and armored. But in the last couple of hundred years, it seemed to be because they did not fight well as a group; tending to be disorderly at all times and to lack any kind of unified command.

In fact, most of their attacks were with less than fifteen or twenty of their numbers, and aimed only at killing living people to get their weapons, armor, and whatever food, wine or wealth the victims were carrying.

Lately, however, their attacks had seemed better organized than the usual raids; and to have as an aim establishing control of a general area south of, and up into, the Cheviot Hills.

Also, eventually, when the wine had begun to show its effect visibly on the sons—though not on the father—the fact came out that, though no one could discover the source of it, the de Mers, like many of their neighbors, had recently been accused of acts that actually had been committed by the Hollow Men.

Enough of their neighbors had been so falsely accused that Herrac was beginning to think of seeing if he could not get a force together, after all, to attack the Hollow Men on their home ground. But at the present time, the number of such neighbors willing to join in was too small to penetrate deeply into that area of the Cheviot Hills held by the Hollow Men, where they might be encountered in numbers of hundreds, or even more.

At this point, Herrac abruptly introduced another subject.

"There is lately, also," he said, "strong new rumors of a Scottish invasion of this Northumberland; and possibly beyond, down into England's midlands."

"Say you so?" demanded Brian, interestedly leaning forward over the table.

"I do," answered Herrac. "Further, there is talk that the Hollow Men might use this opportunity of an invasion to rob and kill far and wide across the Border. Faced with the Scottish invaders, plus the Hollow Men—like ravens—ready to feed on a battlefield of corpses; such as our Castle de Mer, would stand little chance of not being overrun and all of us slain. For such as myself and Giles, this is the ordinary chance of life. But for my other sons, not yet knighted, and my only daughter—"

He glanced expressively at the sons seated beyond Giles.

"But England and Scotland are at peace right now, I thought," said Sir Brian.

Like Sir Herrac, he did not seem to be visibly affected by the large amount of wine he had drunk. About the only thing that showed in these two older knights was that they were speaking more openly about things than they had earlier.

"Yes," Herrac answered, "but all it takes is for one of the lairds who has a fair number of clansmen to set in motion what seems to be a cattle raid. They will end up picking up men on the far side of the border to swell their ranks before they come down upon us."

"Is it so?" said Dafydd.

"Indeed, Master Welshman," answered Herrac, "this tower has been our refuge too many times for me to count over its years; when attacked by a force great enough to burn and destroy our outbuildings, but not enough to reach us in the tower itself; and without the patience for a siege that might make us surrender—though they little know that in the worst case we need not surrender. The outer wall looks directly over the sea; and once in the sea—"

He stopped speaking abruptly. It had been accepted by this time that the three guests knew that the family had silkie blood; but it was one thing to have it known, and something else again to speak openly about it with those who were only recent friends.

In fact, with that sudden interruption of what he had been about to say, Herrac seemed to realize that he had said more than he had intended. Abruptly, he stood up from his bench at the table.

"If you will excuse me, gentles and Master bowman," he said, "these are things local; and need not concern you further. I must to bed; and—"

He looked down the table to his sons.

"—And these should be abed too. Come, Alan, Hector, William, Christopher, time is that you were asleep. Giles, because you are now a belted knight, and these are friends of yours, I leave you to stay with them as long as you wish."

But Giles rose to his feet also, stretching.

"If they will forgive me, Father," he said, "I think it were time I slept also. James, Brian, Dafydd, would you pardon me, if I should leave you now?"

"I've a better idea," said Jim, getting up in his turn. "I've no exact plans for tomorrow, but I've heard a lot tonight I'd like to sleep on."

Brian had gotten to his feet almost as quickly as Jim. Dafydd, however, still sat where he was. He looked at Sir Herrac.

"Would it be possible now," he asked, "for you to supply me with a candle to work by? There is a small thing that I would like to try making with one or more of my arrows."

For a fleeting moment, Sir Herrac looked uncomfortable.

"I am most deeply sorry, Master bowman," he answered, "but candles are one thing that Castle de Mer does not have. However, there is a cresset torch in your room, if your friends can sleep with it burning."

"For myself," said Brian, "I could sleep with the sun itself in my eyes, I believe now. I had not realized how welcome sleep would be, until I began to consider it. James?"

"I won't mind," said Jim.

But Dafydd looked at him shrewdly.

"It is in my mind," he said to Jim, "that you are being more polite than truthful, m'Lord. If our host will permit, I will stay here and work at this table, where the torches of the hall itself will give me light."

"Whatever you prefer," said Sir Herrac, quickly.

"Well—" Jim hesitated; but he too had drunk enough wine to be a little more outspoken than ordinarily, "yes, to tell you the truth, Dafydd, I'd rather not have anything but a low light in our sleeping room, if any. In fact, I was thinking of taking a torch there that would burn for perhaps no more than fifteen minutes, before leaving us to sleep in darkness."

"Let it be so then," said Sir Herrac. "To your sleeping quarters, my sons."

They all, except Dafydd, left the hall together, each of them stopping to pick up one of the already bound bundles of twigs that lay ready against the wall and light it from the nearest cresset. Giles took two, and led Jim and Brian to the room in which they had already deposited their goods. Once there, he handed the torch to Brian and hesitated for a moment in the doorway—

"I cannot tell you how much it means to me to see you again," he said.

Then, as if embarrassed by his own words, he ducked out of the door with his torch and disappeared down the hall. Brian put the torch he carried into the cresset on the wall. This moment, however, Dafydd suddenly appeared in the doorway.

"Forgive me, m'Lord—Brian," he said formally. "I had forgot that my shafts and tools were up here. I will be gone in a moment."

He crossed the room to the bags that had ridden behind his saddle; and carried all he had brought with him beyond what he had worn or carried. He picked up both his quiver and one small bag.

"I will return lightly and silently, I promise you," he said.

"No need to worry, Dafydd," said Brian, with a tremendous yawn. "I vow I could sleep through a taking of this castle, itself."

"No, indeed," said Jim, "you won't disturb us when you come in, Dafydd."

"I thank you both," said Dafydd, and vanished.

Brian sat down on the edge of the bed, finished pulling off his boots, and without any further preparation tumbled over and stretched out on the bed.

"It is a shame your magician's training forbids your lying soft as I am now," said Brian. "Well, well. Heigh—ho! Good night!"

"Good night," answered Jim.

He lay down on the mattress he had earlier unrolled on the stone floor and rolled himself up in it. The mattress was not very successful in softening the hard surface underneath; but from long use with it, Jim found it comfortable enough. He lay thinking over the evening's talk, while the torch burned itself down in the cresset, and finally expired from flames to glowing ends of smoldering wood, to absolute darkness.

Brian and Dafydd, Jim already suspected, were expecting to stay on more than the week, after all. It was simply not done to leave a friend and the friend's family just when they might be expecting an attack by overwhelming odds—

—Of course! How could he have been so stupid not to realize it until now? Understanding suddenly lit up Jim's mind. That was the "*bothering*" Herrac had been subtly inquiring of Giles, just before dinner.

There must be indeed something at work up here concerning not only the Dark Powers and the Hollow Men, but possibly a Scottish invasion of England as well. The de Mer Castle and family probably did face serious danger; and Herrac had been afraid one of his sons would blurt out a question or an assumption that these three champions of song and story would stay and help them deal with it. If Brian suspected this, Jim was on the spot. Brian—and Dafydd as well, for all his apparent mildness—liked to fight almost as much as they liked to eat. Not only that, but Brian's code of honor would never let him abandon the de Mers in such a situation and he would never understand it if Jim did—close friends as they were.

On the other hand Jim could just imagine how Angie would react if he did not appear on time, after all. Particularly if she heard about the situation up here.

Curiously, it was only with the coming of complete darkness that he found his mind working to some purpose.

He had contacted Carolinus once from France by willing himself to dream of the magician. At that time Carolinus had warned him that Malvinne also dreamed; and that this was a risky way for the two of them to be in contact, since Malvinne would know anything they said to each other.

Also, at that time what his dream had shown him was essentially a replay of the scene in which Carolinus had talked Aargh into following Jim to France, by telling the wolf that Jim was going to be in contest with a magician who had all the advantages over him.

Now, however, Jim could think of no reason why it should be dangerous for him to talk to Carolinus. Supposedly any other magician of Carolinus's rank, or just a little below, could listen in; and probably the same thing went for the Dark Powers themselves. Nonetheless, contact was important. He closed his eyes and tried to sleep while willing himself to dream of Carolinus.

Slumber came much faster than he had expected. In his dream he was walking up the front walk to Carolinus's little cottage.

But it was not daylight, as it had been when he had contacted Carolinus before. It was night. It occurred to him belatedly that, in fact, it was probably the same time of night there that it was where he was up in the de Mer Castle. Carolinus's little cottage was dark and silent.

Jim hesitated at the door. Waking people was not exactly the sort of thing he felt comfortable doing. On the other hand finding an opportunity—or even the capability—to dream about Carolinus in the daytime would be difficult. In addition to that, the question he had to ask was not only a question of some urgency; but it was a question that Carolinus had brought upon himself by his admission of last year. It was still with some hesitation that Jim raised his hand and knocked lightly at the cottage door.

There was no response.

He waited. The grass, the flowers, the little fountain that together surrounded the cottage, all were as they were in the daylight, but without color, like a photographic negative under the moon that was now shining above the surrounding trees. After waiting what seemed a very long time indeed, Jim grew a little annoyed.

He knocked again. Knocked hard, this time.

Again, for a long moment there was nothing. Then he could hear the sound of someone stirring around inside the cottage. A moment later the door was snatched open, and Carolinus, with a nightcap on and a long white nightgown, was staring out at him.

"Of course!" snapped Carolinus. "Who else could it be? Anybody else would have the decency not to wake me in the middle of the night."

"I think," said Jim, casting his memory back over the evening and the fact that they had in fact eaten right after sunset up at the de Mer Castle, "it's probably only about ten o'clock or a little after."

"Middle of the night I said; and middle of the night I meant!" snarled Carolinus.

He stuffed a corner of his mustache into his mouth and chewed on it—always a sure sign that he was thoroughly irritated. Then he removed the corner of the mustache from his mouth, spat out a few stray hairs and stood back from the doorway.

"Well, as long as you're here," he said ungraciously, "you might as well come in."

CHAPTER 5

Jim followed the magician inside, shutting the door behind himself. They stood in the center of the single room that was Carolinus's all-purpose establishment under one roof.

"Well?" demanded Carolinus angrily.

Jim was feeling some annoyance, on his own behalf. To begin with, he had come here with what he thought was a legitimate problem or at least a legitimate problem about a possible grievance; and Carolinus's customary crustiness was rubbing him the wrong way.

"At least you're not in that dragon body of yours," muttered Carolinus, "thrashing around and breaking up all my furniture."

Since Jim had never so much as brushed, let alone broken, any of Carolinus's furniture when he had been inside the house in his dragon body, this was a little unfair. Jim decided to ignore it, however, and push on to the main point of his being there.

"Carolinus," he said sternly, "have you sent me on some kind of mission against the forces of the Dark Powers again?"

"Sent you on a mission—?" Carolinus glared at him.

"Like you did last year, without my permission. When I found myself in France in a one-on-one duel with Malvinne; all of which turned out to be your doing," Jim said. "Have you or have you not sent me out to joust with the Dark Powers, again?"

"Interesting," said Carolinus, in an abruptly mild and thoughtful voice. "Let me see . . ."

His eyes became abstracted, and he stood for a number of seconds apparently lost in thought. Then his eyes focused once more, this time seriously, and came back on Jim.

"The answer is, James," he said, still mildly, "yes, you do seem to be involved with the Dark Powers, once more; and, no, it wasn't my idea you be so. It looks like either the Dark Powers themselves are actively starting to seek you out as an opponent again; or else Chance or History have some reason for pushing you into situations in which you and the Dark Powers, er—joust—as you put it."

"Well," said Jim, thoroughly out of temper by this time, "if that's the case, how do I reach Chance or History and let them know that I want no part of this?"

"Reach—" Carolinus stared at him. "Chance and History are natural forces, James! You can't talk to them the way you could talk to a human being. You can't even talk to them the way you could talk to the Dark Powers. The Dark Powers at least have some sentience. Chance and History are natural forces operating according to their own purposes. Even if you could reach them and talk to them, they wouldn't change for you, or move an inch from what they were going to do anyway."

"But you said one of them might have chosen me," said Jim. "Naturally I got the idea—"

"It's a different thing!" snapped Carolinus. He paused a moment. "How to explain? James, even you must have heard of King Arthur."

"Heard of him?" said Jim, annoyed. "I *studied* the Arthurian legend. He was either a myth or a series of myths which were originally thought to be Celtic, but which new evidence indicates may have migrated west with the Roman soldiery from as far east as the steppes of South Russia, from the myths of an ancient people there, the Sarmatians—"

"If you please!" Carolinus interrupted him.

Jim checked.

"Don't blither!" said Carolinus.

"I—" began Jim indignantly.

Carolinus held up a minatory finger.

"Nonsense, James," he said. "Never make statements you're not sure of. This century is a lot closer than your original one to the time when the actual King Arthur lived—and indeed was involved in many of the things that legend has him involved in, though not as quite such a heroic figure. He may not have been so bright with glory as young Prince Edward, whom we rescued from Malvinne—"

So, *we* rescued Edward from Malvinne, did we? thought Jim, a little bitterly. Carolinus had been home in England all the time—well, almost all the time. But Jim did not put these thoughts into words. He was more interested in getting information from Carolinus than in debating with him. The truth of the matter, which Carolinus knew as well as Jim did, was that Carolinus's only important connection with the rescue of Edward, the Crown Prince of England, had been putting Jim, Brian, Dafydd, Giles and Aargh to work on it.

In fact, the whole truth was all Carolinus had done (outside of secretly lending Jim magical credit) had been to point them in the direction of making that rescue and wait for them to do it. The equivalent of saying "sic 'em" to a dog.

"Still," Carolinus was going on, "Arthur was a potent figure in the hands of History and Chance—mainly of History. The point I'm making to you, my dear boy, is that there are people who find themselves at the point of a knife when food is to be scooped from the plate. Arthur was one. It may well be that because of your particular and rather peculiar background in originating on a future world, you are also at the point of such a knife. If so, there's nothing you, I, or anyone else can do about it. History and Chance may determine that you'll be locked into one conflict with the Dark Powers, after another. I hope that's not so. But on the other hand—it could be."

"Thank you," said Jim. "You're very cheering."

"Merely telling you the truth, my boy," said Carolinus. "Do you understand now?"

"No," said Jim.

"In that case," said Carolinus, "take my word for it. You've no other choice, anyway."

"Well, if that's how it is," said Jim, "and I'm destined to have battle after battle with the Dark Powers, shouldn't I be entitled to a little help? You're supposed to be my teacher. But outside of the first few moments, in which you taught me how to spell myself out of a dragon body and back into a human, and vice-versa, you've simply turned me loose to find my own way and solve my problems as best I can. Of course, you did lend me that magical credit."

"And you've been successful," said Carolinus, "even when I didn't help."

"With a lot of luck, yes," said Jim.

"Maybe luck goes along with not being helped," said Carolinus. "Remember, you come from a different place, you see things differently, and consequently you may perceive opportunities where somebody born and raised on this world, in this time, would not. Perhaps that's your luck."

"Nonetheless," said Jim stubbornly, "I think I could use some help from you. At least I could use some advice."

"Advice," said Carolinus, setting down the candle on an already overloaded table, so that it perched precariously on top of a pile of papers, which it could set on fire in an instant, on over-tipping. Not that any candle of Carolinus's would ever tip over, thought Jim. It wouldn't dare. "—is something I'm always glad to give you—if I have it to give. By all means ask me whatever you'd like to know."

"All right," said Jim, "how about the Hollow Men?"

"Oh," Carolinus made a dismissing gesture, "you mean those shades of rejected souls up along the old Roman wall that Emperor Hadrian had ordered built, roughly between what's now England and Scotland? They're essentially harmless."

"They haven't proved to be harmless," said Jim. "They've taken over an area south of and into the Cheviot Hills, which they keep for themselves; and they've raised trouble by preying on the neighbors and chance passers-by. We were almost the victim of some five of them on our way to Castle de Mer to tell them about Giles—oh, by the way, Giles is alive."

"I was aware of that," said Carolinus frostily, "also that he has regained his human form. Don't try to teach your grandmother to suck eggs. As far as the Hollow Men goes, officially they're still just a nuisance. Granted—a 'nuisance' in terms of this particular century and the conditions under which we live; which is a little more serious than a nuisance caused by the neighbor's dog on your front lawn, in the time you come from. But nonetheless, a nuisance."

"But what if the fact that they were a nuisance was deliberately put to use in some way by the Dark Powers, to further an attack by Scotland into England? An attack that might end up with Scotland holding at least part of Northumberland and being in a position to mount a second-front attack on the north of England, if King Jean succeeds in making a landing in the south and attacking England with French forces from there?"

"Hmmm," said Carolinus, pulling on his beard, "it's theoretically possible, I suppose. More than that, it could be a real possibility, given a number of other factors. But a French invasion—bah!"

"There's certainly a strong rumor of it—and of invasion from Scotland into Northumberland," said Jim, feeling no need to tell Carolinus such second-front plans had been an accepted historic fact to the historians of his world, "and the Hollow Men seem determined to make a real problem of themselves, by stirring up the countryside. Now, there may be something to be made of that, in terms of an attack from Scotland, and there may not."

"So far as that's concerned, James," said Carolinus, "you have me. I know nothing of military tactics and strategy. Also, I know very little about intrigue and politics. In any case, if this is the situation, what do you plan to do about it?"

"I don't know," said Jim, "but if Chance has me involved in that situation up there I'm in a pickle."

"Pickle? Pickle?" said Carolinus, irresistibly reminding Jim of a mechanical bird in a cuckoo clock. However, he did not feel it would be right to mention this, and besides there were more important things to talk about.

"Yes," he said, "you know what I'm talking about. Angie was very much against my making that trip up to Castle de Mer. You must remember that. You showed up in the middle of it and argued on my side of the case, which gave me whatever chance of winning I had."

"It's pleasant," observed Carolinus complacently, folding his hands over his small stomach, "to see you acknowledging my aid and usefulness."

"At any rate," said Jim, ignoring the other's words, "the agreement I had with Angie was that we would take, Brian and Dafydd and I, about ten days going up there. That's what we did. Then we would stay only a week, and take ten days to be back again. So that I wouldn't be gone any longer than a month. Now, if you're right and Chance is pitchforking me into some kind of situation up there, I may well be stuck there for more than a week. Do you suppose you could get in touch with Angie for me, and explain the situation to her? That I may be delayed a little while, but I'll be back as soon as I absolutely can?"

"I am hardly your messenger boy!" said Carolinus, his beard bristling in outrage.

"I was asking it as a favor," Jim said.

"A favor!" Carolinus snorted. Then the stiffness went out of his beard to a certain extent. "Well, I suppose I could pass the word along. Yes. Yes, I could do that. I see the situation . . . in fact—"

His eyes became abstract for a moment, a sure sign that his mind was seeing or doing things other than that which concerned his body at the moment.

"It may be I see it better than you. I've been concerned with getting a certain small thing taken care of—but that's," he said, becoming suddenly brisk and rubbing his hands together, "another situation entirely. Never mind that. I take it you haven't met the girl then, yet?"

"Girl?" echoed Jim. "What girl?"

"You'll find out when you meet her," said Carolinus, waving the question away. "The important thing is you want to know what you ought to do now. Hollow Men, a Scottish invasion, this silkie friend of yours . . . yes, you're definitely tied up in a moment of History that the Dark Powers are trying to exploit. Simply, what you should do is follow your nose. Go ahead and do about the matter whatever seems best to you."

"Just do what I want?" Jim asked.

"Exactly," answered Carolinus. "You've got to choose one side or another, Chance or History. Take History. Go along with it. You know why it's better not to go along with Chance, I imagine."

"It's—more risky, I suppose," said Jim, a little uncertainly.

"It's *sensible*!" snapped Carolinus. "Think about it for a minute. No one can be lucky all the time. Can they?"

"No," admitted Jim, "that's true enough."

"That means, whenever you try to work with Chance, sooner or later you're going to lose everything you've got. How could it be otherwise?"

The truth of this seemed so undeniable that Jim merely nodded.

"Well," said Carolinus briskly, "that takes care of that. You know what you're going to do. I need to get back to my sleep— if I can sleep after being aroused like this. The door's behind you. Open it, and out you go."

Jim turned, somewhat dazedly, his mind spinning with all sorts of possibilities. He opened the front door to Carolinus's cottage and stepped out through it. He turned back to see Carolinus in the doorway holding up the candle.

"Good night," he said.

"Good—" The last half of Carolinus's answer was cut off by the slam of the door.

CHAPTER 6

Jim found himself shaken rather violently by the shoulder. It baffled him completely; since a second before he had been standing on the walk outside of Carolinus's cottage with the door being shut in his face. Then he became more awake and discovered that it was Brian standing over him and shaking him.

"—And wake up!" Brian was saying. "Are you going to sleep the morning away? I've had breakfast already and Giles is down in the Great Hall starving to death, poor lad, because he won't eat without you. He thinks it's not mannerly—which of course it isn't, for one of our hosts. James! Wake up! Get up and come along down!"

"I'm—awake," growled Jim, barely able to keep his teeth from chattering with the energetic workout Brian was giving him. "Stop shaking my damn shoulder!"

Brian stopped.

"You're sure you're awake?" he asked.

"How else could I be?" muttered Jim, still in a growl. He yawned prodigiously and then unrolled himself from his mattress. Like the others, he had slept in his clothes with only his boots off. He fumbled for these now and began to draw them on.

"You're sure, now?" said Brian. "I've known many a man

fall right back to sleep, after sitting up and talking to you as sensibly as you please. Then you turn your back for a moment and he's snoring."

"I don't snore," said Jim.

"Certainly you do," said Brian.

"You snore," said Jim. "You're probably hearing yourself."

"No, no. I was wide awake at the time, just last night—or the night before. And I've heard you before that, James. You definitely snore—not loudly, I'll grant. Not like Giles, for example. That nose of his is a regular hunting horn for snores. But you do snore."

"I don't!" snarled Jim, and got to his feet.

It was all right for Brian. Brian was already up and had had his breakfast, which always made his first morning grumpiness over into his usual cheerful humor. But Jim had not eaten anything yet, was barely awake, and in fact his body—most of it—felt as if it were still asleep. He craved nothing so much as to crawl back into his bedding and drop off again. But clearly, Brian had effectively been sent with what was a polite summons for him; and it would be the worst sort of manners to ignore that.

He followed Brian down through three levels of the peel tower and out through the kitchen—it was most odd to always walk through a kitchen to come to a dining area—and saw Giles seated alone at the high table with the inevitable jug and wine cups in front of him. Giles jumped to his feet as Brian and Jim came in.

"James!" he cried, as full of morning joyfulness as Brian had seemed to be.

"Morning," growled Jim, sitting down at the table. He looked at all of the pitchers in front of him, hoping for one that held small beer, for both his mouth and throat were dry from sleep. But he found only wine. He poured a cup of that and swallowed it.

Actually, it went down fairly well.

Giles, meanwhile, must have been signaling the kitchen, because in almost the same instant he sat down his empty cup, platters were put before both of them full of boiled beef and heavy dark bread. He picked up a chunk of bread, thinking he had little appetite, but after chewing into it, then into some of the boiled beef, he began to realize more and more that he was literally hungry. Shortly, he was immersed in simply eating.

Brian sat silent, letting them get some food into them. Finally, Jim's plateful was reduced to a heap of bones, the bread was gone, and Jim had had several more cups of wine. He was surprised to find himself feeling very cheerful indeed. Also his mind was awake and beginning to work, remembering his dream conversation with Carolinus. He had six days left of the original schedule. He should use them profitably.

He raised his head and looked at Brian and Giles, both of them seated opposite him and drinking from their wine cups. Giles had eaten twice what Jim had, in little more than half the time.

"Well!" said Jim.

"Better, eh, James?" said Brian. "A man needs something in his stomach before he can expect to be polite toward the world."

Jim thought that Brian was exactly right; but at the same time he remembered how he had been shaken awake, and did not feel that he owed the other anything in the way of an explanation or an apology. In any case, he was awake now.

"I think you're right, Brian," he said. "Anyway, I'm fine, now. Ready for anything."

"Good!" burst out Giles. "Someone else came in this morning that I want you to meet. My sister."

He twisted his neck looking around the Great Hall.

"Where has that lass got to, now?" he said. He lifted his voice and shouted—and Jim discovered that he was almost as good as his brothers at making himself heard. "Liseth! *Liseth*! Where have you got to? Sir James is here now. *LISETH*!"

"I'm coming!" floated back in a feminine equivalent of the male de Mer voice, from somewhere beyond the kitchen and above them. It was perfectly amazing, thought Jim, how the people of this family could make themselves heard over noises and distances both horizontal and vertical where it might be thought that no human voice could reach.

"She's younger than any of us except Christopher," Giles said to Jim apologetically. "She has trouble sitting still for a moment. But she should be right here any second now. I told her I wanted her to meet you. Also, Father told her that she should meet you as soon as possible—should meet you and Dafydd and Brian, but she's already met Brian."

"I see," said Jim, letting his breakfast settle on his stomach. He braced himself for the coming meeting, wondering a little what a female version of the de Mer features, with their dramatic hooked noses, could look like.

"Here I am," sang a young woman's voice right behind him.

He started to turn, but by that time she had come around to stand beside the bench on which he sat, so he could see her simply by turning his head.

He stared at her. She was totally unlike what he had expected.

She was delicately boned, in contrast to her male relatives, so that she gave the impression of being almost a waif by comparison. The deep-set, silkie-dark eyes were there. And her hair was as flaxen a color as Giles's. Outside of that; everything was different.

After nearly two years in this world Jim had begun to pick up the reading of rank and duty from what individuals were wearing. In her case she wore a floor-length russet gown, with a high circular neck. Her hair was in two thick braids that dropped down behind it over her rather delicate-looking shoulder blades under the dress.

The gown, like the ones worn generally in that fourteenth-century period by other women he had seen, was fitted down as far as the waist, and then flared out to become voluminous. About the only sign about it that his now more experienced eye could pick up was the fact that the seat area of the gown was shiny, which indicated that she was probably a regular, if not an addicted, horsewoman.

The gown itself was of heavy wool, tightly knit. Clothes were bought and made in those days primarily to deal with the winter temperatures. You simply put up with being a little extra warm when summer came along. Moreover, in a castle like this, it was usually pretty icy inside, except at the very end of the summer; when the stone walls, floor and ceiling had had a chance to warm up.

Her feet were enclosed in shoes that were hardly more than slippers. They greatly resembled the Mary Jane shoes that were made for little girls in Jim's own twentieth century; and fastened with a single buckle and a button, which seemed to be made of bone.

The most remarkable thing about her, though, was the fairly wide leather belt that circled her slender waist, and had a number of keys dangling from it; as well as a number of other objects probably of household use, but which Jim at the moment could not identify. That belt could only mean that she was the chatelaine of the castle—in spite of her apparent youth she had been placed in the position of being hostess and, effectively, commanding officer over all the servants within the castle itself and its outbuildings, except the stable.

Jim was impressed. That type of responsibility and that type of control required a strength of character and a firmness that seemed too much for the frail-looking girl in front of him. But she would not be wearing a leather chatelaine's belt unless she could perform the duties that went along with it.

"Well now, Giles," she was saying, "are you going to ask me to sit down?"

"Oh—yes. Yes, of course," growled Giles, "though I was hoping you would have been here right from the moment James and Brian came down."

"You forget my duties nowadays," she answered, seating herself on the bench beside Jim and looking up at him. "Ever since Easter, I have been chatelaine by Father's command; and as long as I am within these castle walls, my duties leave me very little peace. There is always something in the kitchen, the wash house, or with the other servants generally, that calls for my attention and decision. That's why I'm so glad to get out on my mare and ride for a little while. But I'm here now— Sir James, I'm really so honored to make your acquaintance! I never dreamed of ever actually getting to meet someone who actually had slain an Ogre, almost like King Arthur. Indeed, there can be few folk who have."

"Oh, well . . ." said Jim.

It was a slightly awkward situation. Her comment called for some show of modesty; on the other hand even in Gorbash's dragon body it had been a murderous four- to five-hour fight, that had taken him to the very limits of his dragon strength. It would sound a little false to pretend it had been nothing important.

She put her hand lightly on his nearest forearm.

"I'm sorry," she said. "I didn't mean to bring up the subject if it was painful to you for any reason."

"It's not painful at all," answered Jim. "In fact, to be honest with you I'm rather proud of having done it. But there just isn't a great deal I can say about it—except that it was a hard fight."

"I'm sure it was," she said. "And you turned into a dragon

yourself right in that magician's castle to save your friends?"

"Well, yes. I did," answered Jim, "but come to think of it, that wasn't part of what we all told your father and brothers last night—"

"Oh, I asked Giles a lot of questions about you!" She smiled mischievously and her whole face lit up. "He even told me about this fairy who lived in the lake who fell in love with you and followed you for leagues and leagues right up to the battlefield between the French and English. That must have caused you some problems."

"Well," said Jim, "it wasn't so much her following me, it was a matter of getting away from her, once she had me underneath the lake. She had me convinced that the only reason I could go on breathing air was by staying where she had left me. But I was able to use a little magic of my own and get away. So it didn't amount to hardly anything after all."

"Just think of what it would have been like for your wife," said Liseth, "if you'd been trapped under that lake forever. To say nothing of your friends who needed you to rescue the Prince."

"So Giles told you about Angie?" Jim asked her.

"Oh, yes," she said, smiling again. "I asked him that too."

He had never really gotten over that business of being captured by the water Natural, Melusine, beautiful as she was. For one thing, Angie had never really believed that nothing had gone on between him and Melusine, while he was her prisoner on the bottom of the lake. But he had no intention of bringing that up now.

"As a matter of fact," he said, "Sir Brian, here, and Dafydd, undoubtedly would have managed to rescue the Prince even if I hadn't been able to rejoin them."

"I'm sure they would," she said. Her hand slipped from Jim's arm as she turned to Brian, seated on another bench on the far side of her but on the same side of the table. "And your wife must have worried about you too, Sir Brian," she said, "even though she'd be used to knowing a paladin like yourself could take care of himself."

"Paladin, nonsense!" said Brian, putting down the beef bone from Jim's plate, on which he had been absently gnawing; and washing what was in his mouth down with a quick swallow of wine first. "All the credit goes to James and Dafydd. As for a wife, I have none—yet, at least. I am promised to my lady love, the Lady Geronde Isabel de Chaney; but we are waiting for her father to return from the Holy Land, to ask his permission for the wedding. It has been no short wait—nearly four years now."

"What a shame," said Liseth. "But he should be coming home soon."

"If he is still alive," said Brian.

"That, too," she said a little somberly. "Here on the Border, we know the uncertainty of life, as well. We must plan for the years ahead, without ever being sure we will see them."

The momentary somberness passed like a cloud from the face of the sun and she turned back to Jim.

"Tell me, my Lord," she said, "how long do you think you'll be staying here at our poor Border castle?"

Before Jim could answer, they were joined by someone else, a tall, slim figure in archer's jerkin, carrying his bow, unstrung and cased, and his quiver, with the weather cover buckled down over it.

"And this is the last of my very good friends that I wanted you to meet," said Giles to Liseth as Dafydd reached the table, leaning his cased bow against it and putting his quiver on the table top. "This is Dafydd ap Hywel, the greatest of all archers in the world; he was with Brian at the Loathly Tower and with me in France!"

Liseth jumped to her feet, went quickly around the table to the other side where Dafydd stood, and curtsied to him.

"It is a marvelous pleasure to meet you, Master bowman," she said. "Pray, sit down."

"And it is likewise a pleasure to meet you, indeed," said Dafydd, still standing. "Will you also sit, and may I perhaps pour you some of this wine I see here?"

"Well—half a cup," said Liseth. "Thank you," she added as they both seated themselves. "Giles tells me that you are married also."

"To a very lovely lady, who was formerly known as Danielle o'the Wold," said Dafydd. "We have one son now six months old."

"Liseth," Giles interrupted them, "enough courtesy and of your duties as chatelaine. We must make some decisions here, at the table. Jim—what did you want to do today? I can take you fishing and there's some very large fish to be caught in the sea nearby here. It's good sport. Or we can go hunting, though we'll have to go probably some distance to find woods that have deer, or any game worthwhile—"

"None of that," interrupted Jim, suddenly making up his mind. He would indeed investigate what was at work here. If the Dark Powers were indeed being busy against him, it would be madness just to sit on his hands. "What I was thinking of doing, actually, was looking into the Hollow Men—"

"Excellent idea!" said Brian. "We'll find much more sport doing that than we will in fishing or hunting."

"Indeed I think it a very good idea also," spoke up Dafydd, who had just been served a plate of breakfast beef and bread. "I have been out this morning trying one of my arrows with some small changes in them; and I would look forward to an opportunity of trying it also on such targets, for which, as haps, I designed it."

"And I must go with you!" cried Giles. "You'll need a guide. I'll have to get Father's agreement, of course—"

"You must take me with you," interjected Liseth, almost softly but determinedly. "In fact you will need to, Giles, since I am the only one who may find out routes by which we may make our way to the Hollow Men."

Giles's head snapped around and he stared at her.

"Now, Liseth!" he said. "Father would never approve—"

"I think he would," said Liseth.

She was on her feet in the same instant in which she spoke.

"I'll go ask him now," she went on, and disappeared into the kitchen.

"It's true enough," said Giles gloomily. "She speaks to all the animals wild and tame, and knows more about the hills than all of us put together. And it's into the hills we must go in order to find the territory of the Hollow Men. Nor have I any great hope that Father will refuse to let her go. She has a way of getting what she wants from him.—Which reminds me, I was about to go and speak to Father, myself. As a knight and a grown man I don't need his permission; but this family survives by working together, like most Border families. He may not want me to be absent right now—though I doubt it. I'll be right back."

"Wait a minute," said Jim. "Just a second. I hadn't planned on taking anyone. In fact, I was thinking of going alone. What I want to do is creep up on one of their encampments without being seen so that I can watch them and maybe listen to what they say."

"Well, you'll not do it without me," said Brian. "What if you're discovered creeping up on them or listening to them? You'll need at least someone to ward your back if they come after you."

"Indeed, that is true," said Dafydd. "Besides, as I started to say, but had no time to, I am eager to try out a new sort of arrow I have just cut. It is designed particularly to go against the Hollow Men, if sobeit that the opportunity occurs to use it. That opportunity will be much improved if I go along with you in your seeking of them."

"And you can't seek them without a guide—either Liseth, or at least myself—to keep you from being lost in this area where you don't know your way," said Giles. "So that's settled. I'll be right back."

He was gone, in fact, less than a few moments. Liseth returned with him, a smile on her face that announced the fact that she had also been allowed to go along with them. It occurred to Jim fleetingly to wonder why nobody had asked his permission to accompany him this way. However, it would really do no harm to have the others with him if he was going into strange territory and possibly likely to encounter dangerous characters.

They took horses. Giles led them up and across some moorland and into an area of scattered trees and broken ground. This at last grew into a territory of miniature mountains and valleys, with streams rushing down the valleys.

Something about it struck a chord in Jim; but he could not think what it was until their horses carried them laboriously up over one crest and he looked down into a narrow little valley in which something almost too small to be called a river, but too large to be called a stream, made its way along through an accompanying narrow forest of bulrushes.

It was the bulrush—also known, Jim remembered idly from his botany, as the 'club brush'—that triggered the elusive bit of memory he was seeking. It was part of the poem by William Allingham, an early nineteenth-century poet. A poem called *The Fairies*, and one particular quatrain of it went:

> "*Up the airy mountain*
> *down the rushy glen,*
> *we daren't go ahunting*
> *for fear of little men . . .*"

Down below him was the rushy glen, and up where he was—
though he was probably no more than a couple of hundred feet
above the rushy glen—was the airy mountain.

He found himself wondering what else William Allingham
had written. Part of himself, he supposed, would always be
an academic. It was seldom that he was nostalgic for the
twentieth-century world he had left behind when he had come
here to save Angie from the Dark Powers. But this present
moment was one of them. If he was back home he could have
run down William Allingham in the University library and read
the rest of his poems. Had Allingham ever written anything to
match the poem about the little men?

> *"Wee folk, good folk,*
> *Marching all together,*
> *Blue jacket, red cap,*
> *And white owl's feather . . ."*

"Well, Liseth," Giles's voice interrupted his thoughts, "it's
up to you now. Where do we look from here?"

"Straight ahead," said Liseth happily. She was riding with all
the aplomb of someone who normally lived on horseback in that
form of saddle. She rode astride. The sidesaddle for women had
not yet been invented. Her voluminous skirts covered her legs
still, with propriety.

"I've seen three rabbits so far, and they all hopped off in the
same direction," she went on.

"What's that supposed to mean?" asked Giles.

"You'll see, Giles," she answered serenely.

She took the lead and led them on along the top of the crest
until they came to an incline splitting off from it that led them
down toward the valley below. It was by no means a track or
trail of any kind, merely a sort of slanting ledge that headed
downward, wide enough for one horse at a time. But she went
down there quite cheerfully, and the three fourteenth-century
men with her naturally followed without the slightest apparent hesitation, although it looked as if the ledge might pinch
out at any moment, or crumble beneath their horses' feet.
Jim, bringing up the rear, would have preferred not to try to
hide his own uncomfortableness with this sort of precarious
descent; but the casually indifferent attitudes of the rest stopped
him.

Eventually the ledge brought them to the floor of the valley itself. There was a certain amount of solid ground outside the area of the rushes; and from among the tall stems and the club heads of the rushes was the steady murmur of the stream itself.

"Are you sure you're going in the right direction?" Giles asked suspiciously of his sister.

"Absolutely," she said, not even bothering to turn and look at him. "Just around that bend in the valley up ahead."

They followed her and rode on, finally rounding the bend in the valley and—

There they were.

Jim's eyes opened as wide as they could. Right ahead of him he saw, in a group about fifty strong, not the Hollow Men at all; but the Little Men of Allingham's poem, just as the poem said, marching all together.

They were marching directly toward Jim. It was true their clothes were not exactly as Allingham had described. They wore armor of metal plates on leather.

Also, they carried a few things that the poem had not mentioned at all. To wit, short stabbing swords—almost Roman legionary-style weapons—at their belts; and all bore spears proportionate to their height; so that the spearheads clustered several feet above their regular ranks, some five across and ten deep.

The Little Men themselves looked to be around four feet in height and their spears probably did not exceed seven feet at best. But they were very stout and businesslike-looking spears, with glittering metal points.

Most of the Little Men wore bushy beards. But here and there among them Jim saw a clean-shaven face. With the beard missing, the typical face he saw was an almost heart-shaped one, coming down to a pointed chin, with bright blue eyes and a short, almost snub, nose. A nose that looked almost related to the delicate nose on Liseth, herself, so different it was from the hooked nose of Giles, and the slightly smaller one of Brian. Dafydd, of course, had the sort of impossibly narrow and straight nose that might be expected to go with the rest of his handsome face, and reflected the finer boning of his Welsh heritage, for all his height and width of shoulder.

Jim, himself, of course, had a perfectly ordinary nose, straight enough, but unremarkable otherwise; except for a slight crook in it that came from being broken in a volleyball game and the break never being surgically corrected.

But, just as they had seen the Little Men advancing on them, the Little Men had seen them advancing. At first sight, the spears of the two first ranks had swung forward and down pointing directly ahead, so that they were facing something not too different from a line of the ancient Greek hoplites in phalanx formation.

Then, evidently one of them either changed his mind or recognized Liseth, because there was a sharp command, and the spears swung up again. The whole marching group stopped abruptly, together, as neatly as a drill team. Led by Liseth, Jim and the others rode toward the front rank before them; and one of the Little Men in it, with a gray-flecked, gingery beard, stepped forward to meet her.

"Liseth de Mer!" said the Little Man—and his voice was surprisingly bass-toned and authoritative.

"All friends, Ardac, son of Lutel. My brother Giles, here, you know. Of these other three, all are close Companions of his, who saved his life when he was in France and killed, by bringing his body back for burial in the English Channel waters, from which he returned home. Just behind me—"

She turned her head to look at Jim. "Best dismount," she said.

"You were leading us to the Little Men all the time!" Giles hissed at his sister as they dismounted.

"Of course!" she whispered back. "Who more likely to know where Hollow Men are to be found?"

Jim and the others swung down from their horses. More on a level with the Little Men, Jim was able to appreciate what a sturdy bunch they were. They might be short but their bones were thick and their bodies were compact. They were standing now with the butts of their spears resting on the ground; but still they presented a capable-looking appearance as warriors. Liseth was continuing her words to Ardac, son of Lutel.

"—This is Sir James Eckert, a knight famous for slaying an Ogre at a place called the Loathly Tower—"

"We know of that Tower," said Ardac, son of Lutel, "but I had not heard of an Ogre-slaying there, particularly by a single fighter."

"—With Sir James is Sir Brian Neville-Smythe, who was

also with him at the Loathly Tower and slew a Worm by himself."

"Good fighters, they seem to be," said Ardac, "but you've yet given us no reason why they should be considered friends and allowed here; though I own that the fact that they have slain both an Ogre and a Worm puts them on our side of the Wall, so to speak. Who is the third?"

Dafydd came forward.

"I am Dafydd ap Hywel, look you," he said, "and if I mistake not, my blood is none too distant from yours, though we must go far back in time to see the connection."

"Ah?" said Ardac. "Where are you from?"

"He is," said Liseth, "a man of Wales. Though there are other reasons why you might find him a friend; he was also at the Loathly Tower and almost died in holding off with his arrows the harpies that dived on them from clouds barely overhead."

"That," said Ardac, "is something I would not have believed possible. Do you know this for a fact, Liseth?"

"All of Britain knows it for a fact," said Liseth. "I give you my word."

"And I, mine," put in Giles, "for what it is worth. I have seen this man and there is no better archer in the world."

"Do you say so?" said Ardac. "Where is his bow, then?"

"It is here," said Dafydd, stepping back to his saddle and laying his hands upon the cased bow which rode upright in its socket just behind his saddle.

"A bow—that?" said Ardac. "Rather a spear shaft. I've never seen nor heard of any bow half so large."

He jerked his head backward and to the two flanks of the formation behind him.

"Our archers carry bows less than half that size."

"It is not the size alone, to be sure," said Dafydd, "but the taper from the center to the ends. In that taper lies the secret of the longbow. I say this, who am a bowyer, or bow-maker, myself; as well as fletcher, or arrow-maker."

"If you are a maker of anything, you recommend yourself to us, cousin," said Ardac, "and I call you cousin, for I see and hear now clearly that you are indeed of the ancient blood. There was a time when our people owned much of north and west Britain and land beyond the water west of this island. But tell me this. It appears to me, now that we learn you're from Wales, that you bear some signs about you by token of which it would be that we might owe you ancient respect and obedience. Answer me if my eyes do not lie to me?"

"You speak of things from ancient days, which are now forgotten," answered Dafydd, "but in so far as you see what you think you see, you are correct."

"They are not forgotten by us, who are the People," said Ardac. He spoke sharply over his shoulder.

The front spears that had been leveled at the newcomers all this time returned to upright. For a second they lay in the hands of all the Little Men there, then suddenly shot skyward, held up at full arm's length, so that their bright points clustered suddenly in the sun like a silent shout of salute. Then Ardac spoke again and the spears came down.

"I thank you," said Dafydd simply.

"And now," said Ardac, "we would greatly wish to see you use this long bow of yours."

"Willingly," answered Dafydd, "if only we can come up with the targets for which they are intended—without which any demonstration would have little meaning—"

He broke off abruptly, for there had been a stir in the ranks of the Little Men; and they were now all looking off to one side. Jim, with Dafydd, Brian and Giles also looked off to the side, and saw approaching a wolf. For one wild moment Jim thought it was his old friend, Aargh, appearing here, as he had appeared in France the year before when he was needed.

But this wolf was smaller than Aargh, though not by much, and somewhat heavier of bone. He had appeared from among the rushes less than fifteen feet away, and was now approaching Liseth, head down, ears back, tail low and wagging.

For a moment, Jim felt a twinge of irritation. What was this about wolves that made them take so to human females? This wolf was not approaching Liseth with quite the complete appearance of surrender with which Aargh approached Dafydd's wife Danielle, whom he apparently prized above any other human. But close to it.

Liseth now, like Danielle, stepped forward and put her arms around the neck of the wolf, fondling him and scratching him amongst the fur of his neck ruff.

"I did not think to see you here, Liseth," said the wolf. His voice had the same harsh, unyielding quality that marked Aargh's.

CHAPTER 7

"I've brought some friends to meet our friends, Snorrl," said Liseth. "You see them there before you. The man closest to me is Sir James, Baron de Malencontri et Riveroak, and next to him in armor is Sir Brian Neville-Smythe. A little behind them, the tall man is Dafydd ap Hywel, a Master archer. Last of all in armor is my brother Giles, whom you have surely seen, even if he has never met you."

"I know Giles," said Snorrl. His yellow eyes roamed over the other three. "And you say these are friends. Do you trust them?"

"I trust them absolutely," Liseth said fondly. "They saved Giles's life."

"That is something," said Snorrl. "Very well, then, I will trust them also for your sake. They may listen."

"Why should we not listen, Sir wolf?" asked Jim curiously.

Snorrl's golden eyes focused on Jim.

"Because anyone unknown should not be trusted," answered Snorrl. "You ask a young and foolish question, Sir Knight!"

"Do not speak him so!" burst out Giles angrily. "He is not only our friend but a Mage!"

He turned on Jim.

"Show them, James!" he said.

Jim found himself, as often when that sort of challenge came up, in an awkward position. His best trick to date had been changing from his human body into a dragon one. But that meant taking off all his clothes and armor, or seeing them burst apart and reduced to near ruin—aside from the fact that he hardly felt like disrobing in front of Liseth, no matter how indifferent fourteenth-century attitudes might be on such things. Luckily, he lately had come up with a substitute. Accordingly, he took off his helmet and wrote a spell on the inside of his forehead.

MYHEAD→DRAGONHEAD

He felt nothing, as usual, but an increased weight on his shoulders; but the change had been, as usual, instantaneous. Certainly, the reaction about him was instantaneous.

No one changed expression. No one started or cried out. But a sudden absolute stillness took over both all the Little Men and Snorrl, as if he had made a spell to that effect instead.

He wrote the counter spell on his forehead.

DRAGONHEAD→MYHEAD

He could feel from the lessened weight on his shoulders, suddenly, that his ordinary head was back. He put his helmet back on. There was a sort of near-soundless sigh from the ranks of the Little Men, and Snorrl's sudden tension was gone.

"So, you are a magician," said Snorrl's voice. "As a magician you get respect from me, as from all beasts; since it has been known for many years that magicians are our friends rather than our enemies. I will not say I'm sorry, because the words I spoke were the words I thought. But I will give you credit from now on, Sir James, for your skill as a magician."

"To be honest," said Jim, "I'm a very low-class magician, as yet; and really don't rate the address of Mage. Which should actually be only for magicians of high skill and rank. But such magic as I have, I have; and you may believe me when I say not only I but my friends are friends to all of you. You can trust us as you might trust anyone you had known for a long time."

"Sir James," said the voice of Ardac, "we are a people who have some small magic of our own. But that is small magic, indeed; and we respect any of those who follow the hard road to higher learning in that art. Therefore you may count us your friends as if you had known us all your life. I speak for all?"

He turned to look at the rest of the Little Men. A murmur of agreement came from them.

"Thank you," said Jim. He turned back to Snorrl. "Can we hear this news of yours now, then?"

Snorrl turned to look at Ardac.

"I bring you word," he said. "It is of the Hollow Men; who, having only rare chances to eat, drink, or have to do with their own kind of females, have their main pleasures in killing and dancing—and the dancing is only a means by which they may start fights among themselves. There is a force of about a hundred of them again on the move; but this time in your direction here. They have penetrated into the upper valleys and will come upon you shortly, unless you turn aside."

"Into our valleys?" said Ardac. "They know this land is forbidden to them. They also know that we always go to meet them. Never have we turned aside from them, because we are of the old blood; and what is ours is ours, even if we die upon it. But, since all things are done by agreement of all, I will ask the rest."

He turned about to face the ranks of the Little Men behind him.

"What say you?" he asked. "Shall we stand aside and let the Hollow Men pass?"

There was a dead silence from the ranks.

"Shall we go forward and drive them from our valleys?"

There was no sound in response but once more every spear there shot upward to the full extent of the arm of the Little Man holding it, so that again a forest of the fiercely bright points stood together over their heads.

"Good," said Ardac; and the spears went down. He turned back to Snorrl.

"We thank you for your warning, Snorrl," he said. "Where might we meet them in an open space?"

"Above this stream and above the one that runs into it, you know the valley part that widens to a small meadow? There is firm ground there, vertical rock all around, and no place for them to go but back," said the wolf. "I will fight with you if you wish it."

"No, friend Snorrl," said Ardac. "You are of more value bringing us messages like this, than by risking yourself against these mad shades. It may be we shall lose some men to them. But we have the wherewithal to replace our numbers, and they do not. Nor will they gain any recruits from one of us, whose people once ruled."

"But I will join you, damme!" said Sir Brian. "I have yet to feel my sword strike home on one of them; and they had the effrontery to attack my Lord James, Dafydd and myself on our way to the Castle de Mer. Unless there is some reason why you will not have me, then, I'm with you."

"Sir Knight," said Ardac, "any who fight on our side are welcome, provided they do it with a full heart and for our common good, not just for some purpose of their own."

"I will fight under your orders," said Brian—then checked himself. He turned to Jim.

"Forgive me, m'Lord," he said. "I had forgotten that you command me."

Jim winced internally. Once more he was up against the fourteenth-century attitude that the person bearing the highest rank must be in command. Brian knew, better than anyone, how much more fitted he was to lead than Jim—since Jim had now been his pupil for two winters in the use of arms, and was not even beginning to be a match for his teacher. But the formalities must be observed. Of course, this meant that Jim must fight, too, though no one had asked him. Giles and Brian—particularly Brian—would be taking as much for granted. So, apparently, were Snorrl and the Little Men.

"I give you leave to fight as you wish, Sir Brian," said Jim. He turned to Dafydd and Giles. "The same thing applies to you, Sir Giles. As for Dafydd ap Hywel, it would be presumptuous of me to say him yea or nay."

"Why, then," said Dafydd's voice, "I will be very glad to fight. As I have said, I have a new form of arrow I wish to try out; and it is made for use on Hollow Men. This will be a most excellent chance to try it out."

"And I will fight with you," said Liseth, "except somebody will have to give me a shield and a sword."

"*You* will not fight under any circumstances!" said Giles. "Do you hear me, Liseth?"

"I hear you," said Liseth, "and since you are my brother and my elder and this a case of fighting, I suppose I must obey you. But it does not please me to do so!"

"Whether you like it or not is beside the point," said Giles, heatedly. "What would I tell Father, if I had to bring your dead body back to the castle? Would you wish me put in that position?"

"Well . . . no," said Liseth, her voice softening. "You are right, Giles. I must stand aside."

"You'll do more than that," said Giles. "You'll climb a cliff the minute we enter the valley where we're to meet the Hollow Men; and watch what chances from there. Snorrl can stay with you, if he will, and see you safely back to the castle if it should happen that none of us is able to escort you there when all is over."

"He speaks only truth, Liseth," said Snorrl. "No more than your father or brother would I care to lose you; and even if the Hollow Men come after us, I shall have no trouble losing them. Most of them, for some reason, are fearful of a wolf."

He clashed his jaws.

"I could say with good reason that it is because such as I are what we are; but it is more than that. Their fear of a wolf is something like the fear living humans have for ghosts like themselves."

"Then you, Snorrl, and you, Liseth, will move behind our schiltron," said Ardac. He turned to Jim. "By your leave, Sir James," he said, "we would prefer it if you four rode behind us, also."

"Of course. Whatever suits you best," said Jim.

"But—" Dafydd spoke up, looking at Ardac. "Travel back there, we will, if you wish. But I must come forward when we sight the Hollow Men, so that none of your people may be between me and my arrows when I shoot at them."

"Then come around our left side when the time is ready," said Ardac, "but, of your pleasure, return to the rear, before they and we actually come together."

"That I will," said Dafydd; and took a step backward, in token of agreement.

Snorrl, Jim and the rest moved around to the rear of the company; and they all began their march down the valley. The Little Men increased their pace. They were not trotting, but walking quite quickly, so that, even as short as their legs were, Jim and the rest had occasionally to trot their horses to keep up with them. It was curious, thought Jim, watching their disciplined movement ahead of him. Theoretically it should be almost slightly humorous, a bunch of small men like that, laden down with swords and spears and shields, moving swiftly up the valley floor like oversized toy soldiers.

But, somehow it was not. There was an air of purposefulness and professionalism about the Little Men that made them seem very dangerous indeed. Jim realized, with something like a start, that he would not care to be an opponent facing them right at this moment. They looked entirely too much as if they knew exactly what to do.

They reached the valley to which Snorrl had referred and found it still empty. Clearly, the Hollow Men had not reached it yet—which justified the speed at which they had traveled to get there.

Within general limits, it was very much like the other little valleys they traversed, which had been like a series of narrow openings in the rock, each connected by pinched ends, both above and below the stream that flowed through them.

This valley was something of an exception in that the stream with its surrounding bulrushes flowed down one side of the valley, right next to one of the rock walls; and behind the bulrushes, stretching to the farther wall, was a relatively flat meadow, tilting only slightly toward the streambed. Its surface sheltered by the cliff walls was already covered with grass, thick enough and tall enough here, in young, green spears, to lie down in a springy carpet underfoot.

At the far end of the valley, where the Hollow Men would be entering, the rock walls approached each other fairly closely. Still, there was space enough in the extended valley floor there for the Hollow Men to come through, possibly a dozen or more abreast.

Ardac took up his position at exactly the opposite end of the valley, where the rock wall came closer together and the front of the Hollow Men attacking them would necessarily be pinched between the valley walls and the boggy soil underneath the bulrushes of the stream, so that at most ten or a dozen of the enemy on horseback could attack at a time.

They waited.

Meanwhile, Liseth and Snorrl had left them, and were climbing the nearby wall of rock, which was not a difficult slope at all, but one that did require a certain amount of scrabbling on both hands and knees by Liseth. Shortly, however, they saw her with the wolf, outlined against the sky at the top of the wall to their left. She waved at them and Giles waved back.

"Will she wait to see what happens?" Jim asked Giles.

"You couldn't pull her away with ropes," answered Giles. "Not only that, but she'll want to tell Father of how things went down here. Moreover, of course, she hopes we'll win, and she'll be able to come back down and join us again."

It was perhaps twenty minutes before the Hollow Men put in their appearance. Their first numbers through the opening at the upper end of the valley checked on seeing the Little Men drawn up and waiting for them, but after a few minutes they came on again; and gradually their whole motley crew spilled out into the upper end of the valley.

Those in front were mounted upon the invisible horses; and seemed to be clothed in complete sets of armor. Those farther back appeared to have only bits and pieces of armor, but all were weaponed, with either sword, ax, mace, or long spear.

Once they were all into the valley, some hesitation appeared among them.

"What's holding them up now?" fumed Brian.

One of the Little Men in the last rank just ahead of them looked back over his shoulder.

"There are usually several would-be leaders among them in any group like this," he said. His voice was almost eerily like Ardac's; or maybe it was the particular timbre of the speech that must be common to all of them. "Usually like this, they pause while it's sorted out who is actually going to be in command. Ardac will take advantage of this."

"Dafydd ap Hywel!" called Ardac's voice in almost the same moment from the front of the formation.

Dafydd was already off his horse, had his bow uncased, strung and ready, as well as his quiver of arrows slung at his side ready for use. He stepped around the left edge of the formation of the Little Men, and went forward. Brian followed, as if the invitation had been a general one, and after a pause Giles followed also and Jim went with him.

Ardac looked around at them when they appeared with Dafydd, but said nothing. At the far end of the valley the Hollow Men were still milling around, obviously—according to what they had been told by the man in the rear rank—still in argument over who should lead or perhaps over which tactics should be used. Some eight Little Men with their short bows on their back had also shown up in front.

"It will be interesting," said one of them. "The Hollow Men are barely within a wounding bow shot. An arrow that strikes them will strike with hardly any force at all."

The voice of the small bowman was quite audible, but Dafydd paid as little attention as if he had been deaf. He had already extracted from his quiver an arrow that was identical in length with one of the clothyard shafts that were his war arrows.

But instead of the broadhead metal point that a war arrow would carry, the shaft of this one was fitted with an almost conical piece of metal that narrowed down from its thick end where it attached to the wood, and where it was no thicker than the shaft itself. It narrowed sharply, within no more than four or five inches, to what looked like a needle point.

Looking at it, Jim estimated that it had been a piece of mild steel, which had been painstakingly hammered and filed down into its present shape. An over-wrapping of bowstring covered the joint between wood and metal.

Dafydd fitted the shaft to his bow and drew it as usual to where the feathers on it were level with his ear.

He let it go.

The arrow rose no more than half a dozen feet in the air, and was traveling at about chest level on the leading mounted Hollow Men, when it reached their front ranks . . .

. . . And disappeared.

"He has missed," murmured the Little Man archer who had spoken before.

"Let us wait and see," said Dafydd.

A moment after that, one of the Hollow Men riding in the front rank fell from his horse, and the ranks parted as two more of his fellow horsemen, in line behind him, also fell. There was a swirl in the ranks drawing back, and it could be seen that the three bodies lay almost touching each other.

"In the name of the Night!" said the bowman who had spoken up twice now, in awed tones. "Can it be that he struck all three?"

"It looks like it," said Jim. "In fact, it looks to me as if the arrow passed through each one in turn."

There was a murmur of astonishment from the ranks of Little Men behind them. Beside Jim, Ardac shook his head.

"This passes understanding," said Ardac. He looked sideways and up at Jim. "—Unless his arrow had some magic virtue about it?"

"No," said Jim, "any virtue about that arrow was made by Dafydd ap Hywel himself."

He looked at Dafydd.

"Would it have something to do with that different point being on the shaft?" he asked.

"Indeed," said Dafydd, shading his eyes with his hand as he turned to look again at the front rank of the Hollow Men, which now seemed in some disorder, as if an argument was going on. "I own, I did not expect it to make such a successful appearance. But what it did, I made it in hope it would do."

"I don't understand," said Ardac.

Dafydd looked at him.

"It was what you, and perhaps some other said," answered Dafydd, "to the effect that while they are alive and within their outer casing, be it armor or clothes, they're possessed of the same solid body, though invisible, that they had while alive. But once that covering is pierced, there'd be nothing to oppose whatever pierced it, but the likeness of empty air. With that in mind, I made a point designed to go through armor and carry on, rather than one to slay only whoever is wearing the armor."

There was nothing wrong with Ardac's wits.

"You've met the Hollow Men before this?" he asked.

Dafydd looked at Jim, passing the question on to him.

"On our way up to the Castle de Mer," Jim said, "the three of us were set upon by five Hollow Men, all apparently mounted. Dafydd put arrows with the usual broadhead in four of them; and except for one who fell from his horse and left us only a bundle of clothing and armor, the rest disappeared in the mist. It was just at the end of day."

He gazed at the leader of the Little Men shrewdly.

"Why do you ask?" he said.

"Because they are acting a little strangely lately," said Ardac. He paused to glance once again toward the far end of the valley, where the argument was apparently still going on. "It is not impossible that five of them would set upon the three of you, particularly since you would appear to be strangers," said Ardac, "but for them to leave as they did is not their normal way. Unless all four were actually slain by Dafydd ap

Hywel's arrows, and it may well be likely that they were only wounded—"

"I doubt it," said Dafydd dryly. "The arrows went into the chests of the others at close to the same point as they entered the one who fell dead from his horse."

"Well," said Ardac, "in that case, being one against three, and up against a weapon such as they may not have seen before, any more than we have, they may well have decided to run. Otherwise, it is their way to come on. They do not fear death, since it is only a temporary thing for them. As long as one other Hollow Man is alive anywhere, those killed will ride again. But putting that aside, they have acted strangely in coming into our valleys this boldly. They know that we, of all people, will not back away, but rather attack at the sight of them. Also they know that we would die rather than yield an inch of our ground. This little piece of earth belongs to us still. Here are our wives and children; all that remains of our race. Any enemy shall reach them only over our bodies."

He pointed abruptly to the far end of the valley.

"Well," he said, "as I told you, they are ready to come on again. In spite of these arrows of yours that can slay three at once, and in spite of the fact that they face a full schiltron of ourselves. They cannot possibly hope to win against us. It is difficult to see why they would try such a move as this."

Jim had not stopped before to translate the word *schiltron* in his head. At first sight of the Little Men, and their spears, he had been reminded of the Greek phalanx. But there were other ranks of spearmen at other times. And *schiltron* was also the name for a spearmen's formation, as used by the Scottish armies against the English.

Particularly, by arming the first few ranks with extra-long spears, the Scots were able to oppose a hedge of steel points against the armed horsemen of the English. Their only vulnerability was to the archers that the English brought up from Wales and southern England. But, used by the Little Men here, the word *schiltron* seemed to imply more. It seemed to refer to a fixed fighting unit—rather like a Roman legion—and, in effect, the large rectangular shield which each Little Man carried and the short stabbing sword at his side was almost more Roman than Greek or medieval.

"Have you any more such arrows?" Ardac was asking Dafydd.

"No," Dafydd shook his head, "I made that one for trial only. I will make more now, sobeit I survive this day. But I have a quiver full of my broadhead arrows, and the closer they get, the more useful I can be with those. Also by that time your own archers will be at work. Let me try one more experiment."

Reaching into his quiver, he drew one of his broadhead arrows out, fitted it to his bow, and shot at the first rank of mounted warriors now advancing on them. This time the arrow flew low, so that it passed beneath the man—and immediately, he tumbled to the ground, not dead, but obviously unhorsed.

"At least I can put them afoot," said Dafydd. "Would you prefer that, or that I simply kill as many as I have arrows for?"

"Kill," said Ardac briefly. "Now, if you, Sir James and Sir Brian, with Sir Giles, will move out on the flank with our own archers, we will make ready to receive this charge of theirs."

Jim, Brian, Giles and Dafydd with the archers moved swiftly to obey. The first three ranks of the spearmen swung their spears down into position pointed forward, the first rank kneeling on one knee, the second resting their spears on the shoulders of those who knelt and the third rank resting their spears on the shoulders of the second. Nor had the move been made any too soon. The Hollow Men—at least those who seemed to be mounted—were coming on at a gallop; and the four with the archers were barely back in their original station, when that first rank was struck.

The Hollow Men were a good ten armed figures across in rank; and they came obviously prepared to die. At the last moment, their horses seemed to try to turn from the points; but they threw themselves from their saddles forward over what must be their horses' necks, deliberately landing among the spears and taking some of the sharp points through them, but beating others down with their weight and their flailing weapons.

They did little harm against the upward slanting wall of shields that opposed them, even overlapping each other in some cases; and very shortly were dead. However, there were others rushing in behind them, throwing the weight of their temporarily living bodies inside the armor also against the front ranks of the schiltron. Eventually they broke into its midst.

Jim, standing with Brian, Giles and Dafydd on a slope at the foot of the cliff, on the top of which Liseth and Snorrl stood watching, were at first able to observe, almost like spectators. Jim was interested to notice that the Little Men were evidently familiar with the Hollow Men's type of attack, and were prepared for it.

They let their formation be broken; but immediately regathered its members into small tight groups of what he could not help but think of as resembling anything so much as hedgehogs, all points facing outward, all shields up, and even in a position to be swung overhead against a blow from above. The Hollow Men were faced with the problem of breaking up what were essentially nuggets of ten to fifteen Little Men, bristling in all directions with spear points and almost completely able to cover themselves with their shields.

But now, suddenly, Jim found himself no longer a spectator. Behind the fully armored Hollow Men came those in partial armor—a sight that would have been ridiculous if it had not been so threatening. It looked like a cloud of armor broken down into its parts, from as much as would clothe the upper body of a knight to a single armored glove clutching a sword. These swarmed in on the Little Men—and now also on Jim, Brian, Giles and Dafydd alike.

The Little Men who were archers had thrown away their bows, drawn their short swords and run to join the nearest schiltron. Meanwhile, a swarm of armor parts surrounded Jim, Brian and Dafydd, who fought as closely together as they could, Jim, Giles and Brian protecting Dafydd amongst them with their own armored bodies. To Jim's surprise Dafydd had acquired a long, two-handed sword from some fallen Hollow Man; and was swinging this like a berserker at the pieces of armor that fought against them.

They beat back their cloud of attackers, but others came to replace them. Brian was shouting merrily as he fought, obviously having the time of his life. Giles had picked up the enthusiasm, for the two were calling back and forth, describing the kinds of armor they were knocking down, while killing the invisible men wearing them.

Even Jim found himself caught up—not so much as he had felt himself caught up in the life-or-death combat of his duel with Sir Hugh de Malencontri, the pawn of the Dark Powers and the knight whose castle Jim now owned; but as he had been caught up in a furious little combat he and Brian had been engaged in the previous spring, just outside the walls of

Brian's Castle Smythe, when that castle had been attacked by raiders from the nearby sea.

In fact, like all these hand-to-hand affairs, it turned at last for Jim into a blur in which one killed, or tried to kill, in order to stay alive; and the blur went on until, suddenly, all at once, there was no one in front of him left to kill.

He stopped, exhausted, leaning on his sword. Brian and Giles, equally breathless, were leaning beside him; and Dafydd—for a wonder, unwounded—was there also, but looking somewhat less winded.

Not only, Jim saw, was their own immediate area free, but the general battlefield seemed to have either been cleared of all attackers, or been left with nothing but Hollow Men who had been reduced to piles of clothing and armor.

As he got his wind back, he walked over to Ardac, who had sheathed his sword, laid down his shield and who greeted him wearily. Now Dafydd, with the other archers, had gone out to collect as many of his arrows as were salvageable.

"Well," said the Little Men's leader, taking off his helmet, "so ends that. But the attack was still strange."

"How so?" asked Jim. He was conscious of the fact that Brian, Giles and Dafydd had moved up behind him.

"Why, a few of them may have gotten away at the last minute, and we not noticed," said Ardac, "but they could have been no more than a handful. To all good purposes, we slew every one of them. That is not like them."

He took off his helmet, and ruffled his hair to let the air get to his scalp. The hair itself was plastered down by sweat, and, in contrast to his beard, black as jet. It made a strange combination with the beard and the bright blue points of his eyes.

"They don't usually fight to the last Hollow Man?" Jim asked.

Ardac shook his head.

"But I thought you told me that they didn't mind dying, because as long as there was one other Hollow Man alive, they'd be back and active in forty-eight hours."

"That much is true," said Ardac, scratching his head. "They are more willing to die than living men would be. But not to no purpose at all. Once it seems that they cannot kill sufficiently to make their own dying worth while, they usually withdraw. This time, they did not. That, coming on top of the fact that they had ventured into our territory, where we have taught them well not to, puzzles me."

He paused to run his fingers through his damp hair again to let the air get into it.

"Also," he went on, "they have hurt us more than they normally do, in their eagerness to throw themselves away in battle with us. We have six dead; and four more who will need careful tending to live. As I said in the beginning, we can replace our losses, but not if they come to this much, regularly. We will not stop fighting in any case, but if we lose more than we can replace, in the end we will die as a people. I do not like it. Whatever is afoot, I do not like it."

A distant piping sound came several times on their ears. Jim and Brian looked around themselves, puzzled, but Giles and Ardac looked up to the top of the cliff where Liseth stood with Snorrl. Belatedly, Jim and Brian looked up too. She was waving at them and making large swings of her arm against the sky.

"A fine climb, after this!" said Giles, disgustedly. "However, there'll be a reason or Liseth would not call us so."

He turned to look at Jim, Brian, and Dafydd—who was now back with them again.

"Will you join me in a saunter up the cliffside, gentlemen?" he said, wiping the sweat from his face with the hand not holding his helmet, which, like everyone else, he had taken off for coolness.

"If you think it necessary," said Brian; and Jim nodded. As usual, when the action really got going, Brian reverted to his natural role as leader.

It was a long climb and a hard climb to the cliff top. When they got there, it was only after they had sat down and struggled for a while to get their breath back before they were able to talk to Liseth. She now stood with a falcon on her riding glove, temporarily hooded with a scrap of cloth that looked to have been a light, flimsy scarf.

Winded as he was, Jim looked with interest at the falcon. His graduate training in the medieval area had brought him in touch with falconry, and he recognized the bird she was carrying as a peregrine falcon—a magnificent one. It was much more common for women to fly smaller merlins or hobbies. Or perhaps no more than the eyas—the smaller male of such long-winged falcons like the peregrine.

"You don't have to ask," she said. "I'll tell you. Father sent Greywings here up, knowing she would search and find me. Tied around one leg, she bore a piece of paper marked with a sword and a cloak. Some important visitor is at the castle now, or coming shortly; and we all should be back there as soon as possible."

She paused, sympathetically.

"So you'd best get started down the cliff to where our horses are," she said. "Lead mine; and Snorrl and I will meet you where the land levels out."

CHAPTER 8

"Why don't you just come back down the cliff with us?" grumbled Giles.

"I can't and carry Greywings." She reached out with her free hand and patted Giles apologetically on the arm. "If you want to take Snorrl back down with you—"

"Snorrl has no mind to go!" interrupted the wolf. "I'm up here to act as guard and guide to Liseth; and that's all I'll do."

"Oh, well," said Giles. He turned to the other three men. "It looks like there's not much choice in the matter."

So back down the cliff they went; the only consolation being, when they reached the bottom, that they could climb into the saddles of their horses and ride instead of walk back the way they had come. The Little Men had already vanished while they were going up the cliff and getting back down.

Not even the bodies of their dead were lying in the little open valley space; and, just as Jim had done instinctively, they seemed to have gathered up all items of apparel and armor that the slain Hollow Men had left on the ground behind them. The small stream, the bulrushes, the little stretch of firm ground was almost as if it had never been fought over.

So they rode back the way they came.

77

"No chance of our getting lost on the way back, is there?" Jim asked Giles.

Giles shook his head.

"No," he said. "I don't know this ground the way Liseth does, and nowhere near as well as the wolf does, who evidently goes everywhere and sees everything, but I know it well enough to find our way back. It'll be about a fifteen-minute walk of our horses to get back to where she and Snorrl are on level with us once more."

His estimate was remarkably correct. The only surprising thing to Jim came from the fact that he had imagined Liseth and Snorrl, following the tops of the cliffs, would find it slower going than they. But evidently he had been wrong. When they came at last to the level stretch of the ground Liseth and Snorrl were already there waiting for them.

Curiously, the falcon was no longer on the wrist of Liseth's heavy leather riding glove.

Giles had evidently remarked this also.

"What did you do with Greywings?" he demanded when they reached his sister. "Send her back to the castle? There's no one back there she can talk to, or who'd understand her if she does. They won't know whether she simply couldn't find us or . . . what."

Liseth shook her head.

"Greywings told me something, on our way back here," she said. "Ranging above the forest, high up—you know how peregrines are—"

Jim remembered from his reading that the peregrine was indeed a high-flying bird. Greywings could very probably have been cruising at two thousand feet or better, looking for them.

"—Greywings caught sight of a laidly Worm. There's never been any such creature around here. In fact, there've been nothing more than old stories about such; I sent her up to see if she could find it again and come back to tell me where it is."

They had been continuing to ride on together as Liseth had been talking. Jim suddenly drew back on the reins of his horse, bringing it to a stop; and the others automatically stopped with him.

"Wait," said Jim, in answer to their inquiring faces. "We'd better stay here, hadn't we? So she can find us again?"

Liseth gave a small, lilting laugh.

"Greywings can find us anywhere," she said. "Stop to think of it, m'Lord. She flies so high she can see miles in every direction; and if even a hare moves below her, she can swoop on it—although it's true that being a peregrine, and trained, she likes to take her prey in the air. Even if we reach the castle before she comes back looking for us, she'll follow us there and fly in through the open window to her regular perch."

"You're sure?" said Jim doubtfully as they started their horses up again.

"I? Yes, I'm very sure," said Liseth. "Your ordinary falconer may occasionally lose his bird to the wild. But Greywings and all the other birds and animals I know are like brothers and sisters to me. She'll come back to the castle if we've reached it before she does. I can talk to her then, if there's been no chance for it before."

"She's right, James," said Giles. "Because of that 'talking' there seems to be a special bond between her and them."

"All right, then," said Jim.

"We'd best trot," said Liseth, "now we're out of the rocks and it's safe to risk the horses' legs on open land."

They urged their horses to the faster gait, therefore, and headed for the castle.

It was a shorter distance going back than Jim would have guessed from the ride out. Possibly they had come back from a different angle and the distance itself this time was less. It was only a matter of about fifteen minutes before they were in the courtyard of the castle and dismounting. As he stepped out of his saddle onto the ground, Jim himself noticed Brian getting down. Brian staggered a bit as he got out of the saddle and kept his grip on the saddle horn. The face that Jim saw in side view was now white as a sheet.

Jim opened his mouth to ask Brian about himself; but Liseth was quicker, both in getting out of the saddle and in speaking. In fact, she was already up to Brian and putting her arm around him by the time she spoke.

"Sir Brian!" she said. "Have you been hurt? Were you wounded in the fight back there?"

"I have indeed, it seems, had some small touch," said Brian, in a thin voice, and collapsed on the ground.

"Help me!" cried Liseth, trying to lift Brian from the ground and failing, what with the man's weight and armor. "We must get him to bed and bleed him immediately!"

"No!" snapped Jim. "No bleeding. Carry him gently up to the room where we've been staying!" He was already taking a bundle from behind the saddle of his horse.

Giles and Dafydd had already reached Brian and picked him up. A second later they were being helped by the men from the stables who had been coming to take care of the horses. With four of them together supporting him, they carried Brian into the castle. Jim paused to turn to Liseth.

"Forgive me," he said, "but in this case I can make sure of healing him, more so than anyone else."

"Of course, with your magic!" she said. "But, m'Lord—hurry! I'm afraid his wound has been made worse by climbing that cliff and the ride back here!"

"That's what I'm afraid of, too!" said Jim grimly, and followed the others into the castle.

Up in the room that had been assigned to them, with Brian on the bed, they began to strip him of his armor and found that underneath it, his doublet was soaked heavy with blood.

"Lift him!" barked Jim. He had not intended to sound so autocratic; but his fear for Brian urged him on and, happily, all those around him took without question the fact that he should be giving commands.

Giles and Dafydd, with the help of a couple of the stablemen, lifted Brian clear of the bed, one man even supporting his head. Jim jerked the covers off the bed and literally threw them into the arms of Liseth.

"Take these to the kitchen and boil them; then dry them as soon as possible."

"At once, m'Lord!" said Liseth; and, with the bed clothes in her arms, literally ran out of the room.

Meanwhile, Jim was getting off his own armor to give himself freedom of movement. He turned to the bundle he had carried upstairs with him, unwrapped its outer cover of rough, canvaslike cloth, stiffened with wax, to reveal his own rain cloak. He spread this on the boards of the bed.

"Now, put him down on the cloak," Jim said. "That's right. Fine. Now we get the rest of his clothes off, and I want them taken to the kitchen too, to be boiled—no, wait!" he said, as Dafydd began to gather up the clothes that were being stripped from Brian's body. Brian would not thank him if some of his garments had shrunk to half size or looked as if they would never lose their wrinkles again. Cloth in the here and now was not the same thing as the wash-and-wear fabrics of his own world. "On second thought, hang them on something spread out in front of the kitchen fireplace, instead. Make sure all the fleas and lice are driven out of them."

He looked at Dafydd and Giles.

"Will one of you see to that?" he said.

"I will!" said Giles quickly. "I know which of the people in the kitchen can be trusted to watch the clothes as they hang, so that they don't scorch."

He picked up the last of Brian's clothes and followed his sister out of the room, also at a run. Jim found himself for once blessing the fact that errands to which you were ordered by anyone of superior rank, even if you were an Earl but the one who gave the order was a King, meant that you ran and did it, not merely walked to get it done. It was something that had grated on him when he at first had become acquainted with it in this world. But at the moment he appreciated its advantages.

Brian was now laid out naked upon the cloak. The cloak, Jim knew, had neither lice nor fleas in it and had been perfectly clean when it had been prepared for the journey under Angie's direction back at Castle Malencontri. Jim had kept it that way.

But lying on the cloak did not make the boards much softer. However, Brian was still unconscious and should not feel them.

There was no telling how much blood he had lost—except that it was a lot. Jim turned with an order for Dafydd; and then saw that by this time both Herrac and his two oldest sons were in the chamber.

"There is another thing yet to be done," he said to them. "If you, m'Lord Herrac, or someone at your direction can do it, I will appreciate it. I want someone to go to the kitchen and find me at least a dozen slices of moldy bread. It must not be rye, but any other kind of bread will be fine, provided it has on it a bluish-gray mold that looks rather fuzzy. It's the mold I want, not the bread, but bring the slices up to me in the cleanest cloth that the kitchen can give you. And I do mean cleanest!"

"Alan!" said Herrac, without even looking at his oldest son. Alan vanished through the door with the same speed that the other members of the family had shown.

Meanwhile, Jim had found and was examining the wound. Happily, in spite of Brian's heavy loss of blood, it did not look serious, provided infection could be avoided. Some sharp weapon had penetrated his armor and clothing and slid slantwise up his side, opening a long shallow slash from the bottom of his ribs, almost to his armpit. The wound was still bleeding, and Jim turned back to the contents of his bundle to take out a thick rectangle that seemed to be made of wax.

But the wax was only a covering. As he broke the bundle open, it showed a piece of cloth about two by three feet in diameter, thick and of soft, fleecy material. This Angie had given Jim to take along for his own use in case he should be wounded. Angie herself had seen it sterilized and dried under conditions that would not let it pick up infections and then sealed it herself in its wax covering, to keep it that way.

Jim folded the cloth into one long, thick strip. Gently, he pressed this strip against the wound, which was still bleeding, and held it close to Brian's body with one hand. He turned to Dafydd.

"Hold it there, firmly in place," he told the bowman; and Dafydd wordlessly obeyed.

With both hands once more free, Jim turned to the bundle again and took out several more cloths—these in long strips. With these he bound the pad Dafydd was holding on the wound, in place around Brian's torso. He fastened them tightly; and, although the cloth was soon soaked through with blood from the seepage of the wound, the bleeding did not seem to penetrate enough to cause Brian to lose more blood beyond the bandage.

Jim was not happy about using his only guaranteed clean piece of cloth before the wound had been washed out and the mold from the bread put on it. But the wound was still bleeding; and Jim's limited knowledge of first aid from his twentieth-century background did not suggest to him any pressure points on Brian's body that would stop bleeding on such a long, open slash.

He woke suddenly to the fact that the room was far from warm and Brian was lying there naked, in danger from the wound, and likely to be in danger from the cold that might give rise to an infection, that could in turn become pneumonia.

He felt up against a brick wall. He simply had no more clean cloths—and then his mind cleared and began to work properly.

Of course he had more clean cloths. Or at least, cloths that were more clean than anything the castle was likely to produce. He began stripping off his own clothes and piling them over Brian's unconscious body.

At last, down to his medieval drawers and shirt, he looked up from a Brian who was at last fairly well covered; to find that he was alone in the room with Herrac de Mer and Dafydd.

"I was not certain, m'Lord," said Herrac, "but I assumed that you would rather work your healing magic with as few watching as possible. Is there anything more that I or any of my people or family can do for you?"

"If there was some way of heating this room . . ." Jim found himself saying.

"But of course," answered Herrac. "A fire-pot can be brought in. Also we can fill and light the cresset on the wall, which will give you not only light but heat as well. Shall I order it done?"

"Yes," said Jim—and then suddenly thought of the problems of having smoke build up in the relatively small room. "Or perhaps, no. If we do that it'll soon be so smoky in here it will be difficult for me to work my—er—magic."

Herrac, who had already half turned toward the doorway, turned back again.

"It's true," he said, "that since this was our bridal chamber and bedroom, my dear wife and I—I had the windows glassed-in, hard and expensive as the glass was to come by. But because we had somewhat of the same problem, with the cresset burning and a fire-pot in the room on cold winter mornings, I had a vent made high in the wall to let the smoke out."

He walked over to the outer wall of the room, the one with the windows, and reached up to what Jim now recognized as a sort of small, iron door with a chain depending from it. He pulled this downward and the small door, obviously hinged at the bottom, swung out at an angle from that hinge at about forty-five degrees, leaving an opening through the tower wall to the air outside.

"But you won't want that opened until the fire-pot is here and the cresset alight, I would think," he said, looking at Jim.

"That's right, m'Lord," said Jim with a great sense of relief. "It was very wise and thoughtful of you to so arrange. Nothing could be better for a wounded man's chamber. Could you then order in the fire-pot and the cresset material so that it too may be set alight?"

Herrac nodded and, closing the little door, turned back to the room once more.

"Alan!" he said, hardly raising his voice, but which because of the family's vocal penetration, seemed to be capable of going right through the stone wall itself.

There was no answer. Herrac muttered something which was most likely a curse.

"Ho!" he shouted, raising his voice to its full formidable volume. "Whosoever is within hearing, come!"

He waited a moment, but there was no sound of an answer.

"I'll go order the servants myself," he said grimly. "Wait me. I'll be right back."

He disappeared through the doorway.

"My Lord," said Dafydd almost formally, "it is not for me to make suggestions to a Mage at work. But Brian's eyelids have fluttered twice now. He will be waking from his swoon shortly; and I was taught by my grandmother that one with great loss of blood should drink as much liquid as possible. Should I get some wine for Brian?"

"Not wine," said Jim hastily. "Water—no, not the local water, either. Small beer and plenty of it."

"It is in my mind," said Dafydd diffidently, "that Brian would prefer wine."

"He can prefer what the hell he likes!" Jim found himself snapping. "Small beer!"

"Yes, m'Lord," said Dafydd; and went.

Left alone with Brian, Jim saw his friend's eyelids flutter for what must be the third time. He hastily checked the tight-bound strip of cloth along the wound. It was still damp, but no more blood seemed to be coming through it. The next thing to do should probably be done as quickly as possible, even at the risk of starting up some of the bleeding again.

There were no germicides available in this fourteenth century any more than there had been in that of his own world—except for one that had been common knowledge going back to time immemorial.

This was that human urine both washed out a wound and seemed to have the effect of helping it heal without infection. Jim was just as glad to be alone for this process. Actually the ammonia and other elements in the urine were anti-bacterial.

But it was a good thing Brian was unconscious, Jim told himself. The ferocious burning of the urine on the open wound would have been hard to take.

He stripped off what lower body armor Brian still had on, and loosened the leather cord running through the points of his hose. Only then did he venture to go back and untie the knots holding the cloth strips binding the cloth on the wound tightly to Brian's chest. He lifted the cloth, loose at last, very gently, and was rewarded by seeing that while bleeding immediately started, it was not heavy bleeding at all. Once more, it was only a seepage of blood from all the surface of the wound.

Hastily he urinated in the wound itself; as concerned with washing it out as he was with protecting it. This additional assault caused the wound to bleed more heavily; and he hastily, with his hose now down around his ankles, replaced the folded cloth in the wound itself, and tightly retied the binding strips of cloth around Brian's body to hold it firm. Then he mopped up the excess liquid from the floor, using some extra bedding that had been supplied to the room.

Happily, once again the bandage stopped any flow of blood from beyond its own soaked fabric.

He barely had his hose back on and his points retied when Alan, Herrac's oldest son, reappeared with a shallow pan heaped with chunks of moldy bread. For the most part, Jim thought as he sorted through them, they seemed to be pieces off one or more loaves that people had started to eat and then left unfinished, for some reason or another. In spite of what he had said, there were some dark slices of rye bread among the other pieces. But most of it was apparently made from millet or something like that, because it was of a much lighter color.

More importantly, the mold was there. The mold that—if this world went on to have a twentieth century as Jim's world had—would eventually have the effective components of the mold separated out and labeled penicillin.

In this case, Jim had little choice but to use the mold just as it was. As he had described it to Herrac and Alan, it was a lightly tinged blue gray that sprouted rather fuzzily from the surface of the overage bread here and there in clumps.

Jim carefully scraped all the mold off onto a single large chunk of the bread that was relatively flat—as if someone had actually made an effort to cut a slice from the loaf and almost managed it.

Then, with the help of Alan this time, he once more loosened the straps, took the folded cloth from the wound and, with his fingers, spread the mold within the cut itself. Blood welled from the face of the wound at his touch, threatening to wash the mold back out. But he got most of it in, and the blood-soaked pad back in place, hastily enough so that he felt sure a fair amount of mold was still on the wound.

"M'Lord?" said Alan, almost timidly, when they were finished, looking across Brian's recumbent body at Jim. "If you don't need me any more, may I go now, then? Father is in a rage at having no one close when he needed them. He has threatened to hang some of the servants as a lesson to the others."

"He mustn't do that!" said Jim instinctively.

"He will not," said Alan. "At least, I think not. But it will do no harm if the rest of the family is there to help to take his anger out on; since he will not hang us, of course; and so he may return to his usual temper and the servants be safe."

"By all means," said Jim, "go—go as quickly as you can."

Alan ran out of the room.

There was a husky noise from Brian's throat, and Jim looked to see that the other had his eyes now wide open and was trying to say something, although this seemed a little difficult.

"Don't try to talk, Brian," Jim said. "Save your strength."

"What . . . hour is it?" almost whispered Brian, finally. "Is it time we were up and about? Have I overslept?"

"No such thing," answered Jim. "It's somewhere in the afternoon. Don't you remember? We fought alongside the Little Men against the Hollow Men. You were wounded—not badly at all. But you've lost a lot of blood. You'll have to be quiet for a few days."

Brian stared at him for what seemed a long time.

"Hollow Men?" he managed at last in that throaty whisper. "I . . . remember now . . ."

"Don't try to talk," said Jim. "Save your strength. You've got to rebuild it. I promise you, you'll be all right. I'll take care of you myself."

"Ahhhhh . . ." Brian's eyes closed again on what seemed a sigh of utter weariness. Looking at him, Jim made the guess that he was now asleep, rather than unconscious. In any case, there was nothing better that he could be doing than sleep, right now. Jim rearranged his hastily piled clothes on top of Brian to give him the maximum amount of warmth. That fire-pot and the materials to set the cresset afire inside it, should be along soon, he thought. Then the room would take on a more livable temperature.

He yawned abruptly in spite of himself. For the first time he realized that the mad rush that everything seemed to have been in, since Brian first collapsed in the courtyard, had left him feeling more than a little tired. He looked around longingly for something to sit on and found a bench.

He yawned again—and then stopped yawning abruptly, as something sharp pricked the nape of his neck.

His involuntary reaction to turn around and see what it was was stopped by a grating baritone voice with what sounded to him like a faint Scottish accent.

"Dinna move!" said the voice. "I ha' ye now, ye black wizard! Ye've done ye're last ill to folk like this poor lad on the bed here! It's the post and the fire for ye this time!"

CHAPTER 9

J im felt a sudden shock, as much at the misunderstanding as the danger. Evidently some sort of madman was behind him, with a weapon that was very sharp-pointed, indeed. He opened his mouth, but could not think of anything to say. Just at that moment, however, another voice intruded on the situation.

"And you are not to move a muscle either, Scotsman," said the voice of Dafydd, also now somewhere behind him. "That's a broadhead war arrow, a clothyard in length and right now drawn to its fullest in the bow I hold, the point of which you feel pricking your neck. Make one move toward m'Lord and that point will take out your spine and gullet together."

There was a moment of silence—baffled, Jim hoped, on the part of the unknown Scotsman who was holding the sharp-pointed something against the nape of Jim's neck. Then the accented voice spoke again.

"Y'may kill me," said the strange voice, "but you'll no' save your friend. A MacGreggor isna—"

The voice was suddenly interrupted by yet a third one, which Jim recognized as that of Liseth.

"Lachlan MacGreggor!" she said. "What are you doing to the Lord James? What's going on here—and why must Dafydd hold an arrow upon you like this? To keep you from doing some damage to this worthy gentleman?"

"Worthy gentleman he is not," said the MacGreggor voice. "He is a black wizard! And I'll rid the earth of him, as I'd rid the earth of any of his kind, no matter what yon cowardly bowman behind me may try to do."

"There are no wizards," protested Jim, taking his cue from something Carolinus had once said to him, "unless you want to count magicians who've gone wrong. I am a magician, true—"

"Enough of your clack!" the MacGreggor voice interrupted him. "Ye may miss the stake and the flames, but ye'll not miss the point of my sword—"

He was interrupted in his turn by the voice of Liseth.

Fourteenth-century humanity, Jim had discovered, were very uninhibited in what they might do, and even more uninhibited in their emotions. Their elaborate pattern of manners usually hid these things, but the ability to feel or do what was necessary was never far below the surface. Liseth gave further proof of this now.

Jim had noted that her voice had some of the qualities of her father and brothers, but he had not credited her with anything like the volume that the men had shown. He found out now he was wrong. Angie, his wife, he had noticed, had a very penetrating scream when she wanted to use it. He had to admit that Liseth's was even better.

"EEEEEEE!" screamed Liseth. "Father! Come quick!"

Her voice seemed not only capable of penetrating as many walls and floors as the peel tower possessed; but it had a high-pitched note that left Jim's ears ringing, so that he felt himself half-deaf for a moment.

When his ears cleared, he was conscious of voices far off, rapidly approaching, and among them were the tones of male de Mers—although he was unable to make out exactly the words they were using. Everybody stayed where they were for a few more moments and then suddenly the voice of Herrac exploded in the room.

"Lachlan MacGreggor! Put down that dirk!" he roared. "What? To draw naked steel in my house against one of my other guests—and you a MacGreggor! How can you explain this, Sirrah?"

Jim felt the point leave the back of his neck. He turned about and saw that besides Herrac and Liseth, there was Dafydd, still holding his drawn arrow tight against the neck of the kilted man who stood between him and Jim.

"I think you can put the arrow away, too, now, Dafydd," said Jim.

"Very well," said Dafydd, "but mark you, Scotsman! I can draw again faster than you can move a hand."

"And there'll be no aiming of war arrows by one of my guests against another of my guests!" thundered Herrac. "If my Lord James had not asked you to put it down, I would have so ordered you, myself!"

"Indeed," said Dafydd softly, "but an order has its value depending on he who speaks it."

Nonetheless, he had lowered his bow and released the strain on the bowstring. The kilted man swung about to face him.

"I'll know ye again!" he said. "How call ye yersel'?"

"I am Dafydd ap Hywel, a master bowman of Wales," said Dafydd, "and I am never hard to find."

"Have done, the both of you!" said Herrac. "Lachlan, what's this all about?"

"Why, I found this black wizard here, that you call the Lord something or other, working his will on this puir man on the bed, who is clearly either very sick from the wizard's own black doings; or badly hurt and in no case to resist them."

Jim's temper was finally beginning to kindle.

"I'm not a wizard, you idiot!" he said. "I'm a *magician*! Magicians are actual human beings who've studied magic for the good of their fellow men, as a doctor might study medicine. 'Wizards' are nothing but tales told to each other by people who know nothing and hope to scare each other!"

"That's done it!" shouted Lachlan. "I'll not stand by and hear my grandmother insulted!"

Jim stared at him.

"What's your grandmother got to do with all this?" he asked, honestly bewildered.

"It was she who told me about wizards and their ways!" said Lachlan. "You'll be saying that she lied?"

"Well, no," said Jim. "She may well have believed these stories she was telling. But—"

"Lachlan MacGreggor!" Liseth cut in. "You don't know who you're talking to, or what you're talking about. The man in front of you, who you think of as a wizard, is not only a *good* magician; but he, with the man on the bed and the bowman behind you, fought and slew the creatures of the Dark Powers, of which your Auld Hornie is doubtless one as well! It was a day-long battle they fought, against terrible odds in a place called the Loathly Tower in the fens of southern England; and songs have been sung about it ever since. I can only suppose you never heard any of them!"

"Why," answered Lachlan MacGregor in the mildest tone he had adopted so far, scratching his bristly and badly shaven chin, the stubble of which promised to be as red as his hair, if it had been let grow out in full beard, "I have indeed heard such a song, not once but more than once. You cannot mean that these are two of those who did that?"

"That's exactly what she means!" snapped a new voice, and Giles crowded forward between his sister and his father. "Not only that; but I was with the Lord James when he struggled with a true evil magician, in France! An evil magician with many times his powers; and not only worsted him, but saved my life, withal! I was with him some months and I can attest that there is no nobler, braver opponent of things evil than Sir James de Bois de Malencontri, who stands before you!"

"Say you so?" said Lachlan, narrowing his eyes at Jim.

"He does," boomed the voice of Herrac, "and so say all of us here. We summoned my daughter and him with his two friends back from hunting, to meet you. A fine greeting you have given him!"

"Ah, well," said Lachlan philosophically, "a man can not always be right. I shall forget what I thought before—and do you, Lord James, though ill it sticks in my throat to call an Englishman 'Lord'—forget and forgive me for any small error I may have fallen into."

A year before, when he and Angie had first arrived from the twentieth century of their own world, Jim would not have understood this speech as well as he did now. What he was hearing now, he knew, was the closest that a fourteenth-century individual like this could come to an outright apology—without abasing himself more than his pride would allow.

"It is already forgotten!" he said and stuck out his hand. "My hand on it!"

MacGregor took the hand; and outside of a small tendency to fall into a contest to see which of their grips were greater, which he began apparently unthinkingly and then broke off, sealed the bargain.

"Well," said Herrac, "all is well that ends well, then. But mark what I said about quarrels beneath my roof—particularly quarrels with naked weapons."

"My Lord," said Jim, "I, for one, will not only mark it but honor you for seeing that it is so."

"And I, too," said Lachlan hastily. "I learned my manners when under another man's roof as well as anyone in this land; and I own that I may have been a wee bit carried away by a natural mistake. Herrac, my old friend, this dirk of mine will not see the light again in your castle, unless you yourself give me permission to bring it forth!"

"Good," growled Herrac. "Now that that's settled, m'Lord James, is there anything else we can do for Sir Brian?"

"Nothing more right now," said Jim. "Just as soon as the fire-pot is here to warm the room and the cresset is lighted—"

"That should have been here already!" said Herrac, a note of anger back into his voice. He swung on Giles. "Giles, go see what's holding that up!"

He turned back to face Jim.

"Anything else, m'Lord?"

"I'd like somebody to stay with Brian," said Jim, "somebody to stay with him and call me if anything happens. If you'll find the people I'll tell them what they need to do. Oh, and we need that bedding back up on the bed here, just as soon as it has been boiled and dried."

"I believe it is almost dry now," said Herrac.

He turned to Liseth.

"Will you see to that, Liseth," he said, "and pick two stout fellows, or a pair of reliable women—or better, a pair of each— to keep a watch over Sir Brian here?"

He turned back to Jim, who was all but shivering in his medieval underwear.

"If you would deign to accept some clothing from one of my sons, or even some of mine," he said, "we would be most glad to make it available to you, m'Lord."

"Thank you, no," said Jim hastily. "As a matter of fact, I've got some spare hose and a cote-hardie in my luggage. I can put that on temporarily, until the bedding is back. I'll stay here until then."

"Very well," said Herrac. "I take it then, you would prefer that the rest of us leave you alone with Sir Brian. We will do so. Lachlan? Bowman?"

"If m'Lord agrees," said Dafydd, with a touch of stubbornness in his voice.

"By all means," said Jim, "go along with the rest, Dafydd. I'll see you all, shortly, and you too, Sir Lachlan—"

"If I happen to be a knight—as I am—" growled Lachlan, "you may ignore it. Such call-toys mean nothing to me."

This was news to Jim, who had understood that in the fourteenth century knights were as likely to be found in Scotland, as they were in England. However, he nodded.

"I will see you too then, Lachlan MacGreggor," he said.

They all went out, leaving Jim alone once more with Brian. He had not really noticed the coolness of the chamber until this moment, being caught up as he was with the emergency into which Brian had been plunged. But now, shuddering with the chill, he dug into his baggage; which was not extensive, since it was only what could ride easily behind his saddle on the way up here.

He found the extra hose and drew them on; then shook out the cote-hardie, which was very wrinkled from being rolled up in with the rest of his things, and put it on. The warmth from these garments was very grateful to him; but it was only a short time before Liseth returned with the fire-pot and the bedding, this time being carried by the two women and the two men who followed her.

Brian woke when the two men, with Jim's help, lifted him clear of the bed for long enough so that the bed could be made up. This Jim insisted on doing himself, reproaching himself silently with the fact that he should actually have gone down and gotten the bedding himself, to keep it from being contaminated by the hands of those who brought it up. Herrac was a good Lord of the Castle de Mer, as his century went, but no more than any other such were his servants models of cleanliness.

Jim could not complain, since his servants back at his own castle had their own limits as far as his pushing them into new, more sanitary ways. Angie had brought most of them to the point of washing their hands before handling food. But that had been stretching things about as far as would be accepted. The two men and women with Liseth were typical servants, therefore, as far as cleanliness of self and clothes went.

So, Jim kept his mouth shut about this, once the bed had been freshly made up and Brian had been put back into it and covered up. As far as he could tell in the process of handling the bedding and looking it over, it had not picked up any fresh vermin, at any rate; and the former ones would not have survived the boiling.

Once the bed was made and he had assisted the two men in lifting Brian back on to it, Jim turned to Liseth, having had time to think about the business of giving directions to those who would be watching Brian.

"Liseth," he said, "let me tell you what needs to be done here, and you can do a better job than I can of making it understandable to your people here. I want one man and one woman awake at all times. They are not on any account to drink from any pitchers or other utensils that Sir Brian uses. This is very important—"

—A mildly evil thought crossed his mind. He was about to take advantage of being reputed a magician, again.

"—If they do," said Jim, "they will be in danger of shriveling up like sun-dried toads."

He had the satisfaction of seeing the four servant faces blanch. His own experience with other such magical threats had made him sure in his belief that temptation would not overcome the fear of what he had just threatened them with.

"Also," he went on to Liseth, "they must keep the fire-pot and cresset going; and the chamber pot emptied and clean at all times. They must offer drink to Sir Brian whenever he is awake; and give him to drink whenever possible. Small beer only. We want to get a lot of fluid back into him to replace the blood he lost. Meanwhile, you and I will go down to the kitchen, find some calf's liver, chop it up fine and cook it over a stove until it becomes a soup. Can that be done, do you think?"

"Assuredly, m'Lord," said Liseth. "I can take care of it myself."

"Make sure that the people who take care of the cooking of the soup, and the pot they put it in to bring it up here, are both thoroughly scrubbed and clean, using soap."

"Soap?" queried Liseth.

"You're not familiar with soap?" said Jim. "It's a substance much used by us magicians."

He thought for a second.

"Very well," he said, "just have them scrub out the inside of the pot, then, until it shines, then fill it to the top with water and boil the water in it until it's been at a boil for the time it takes, reverently, to say at least ten *pater nosters*. Then they should take the pot off the fire, set it aside to cool until they can empty it out and fill it immediately with the liver soup. Bring that to the boil, then carry it up here; and we must try to get Brian to take as much of it as possible."

"Does Sir Brian like liver soup?" asked Liseth.

"Probably not," said Jim, "but he's to get it down, anyway. That, and as much small beer as he can manage. He is not, repeat not, to be given any wine; no matter how much he asks for it," he said. "Can you get that across to these four here?"

"Certainly, m'Lord," said Liseth demurely. She turned to the four servants. "If Sir Brian dies, it will be considered that you have killed him, through not taking proper care of him. Therefore you will follow the Mage's directions exactly, or else you shall all hang."

She turned back to Jim.

"I think that should take care of it," she said to him brightly. "Would you care to go back down with me to the hall now, Sir James?"

"Oh, yes," said Jim, "and they're to call me the minute anything unusual happens. Also, one of the women should feel his forehead from time to time to see if it is warmer than it should be."

"You heard that?" said Liseth to them. "What are you doing now, m'Lord?"

"Just putting back on a few more of my clothes," said Jim, wriggling his feet into his boots. Dressed, he went out with her into the hall and they headed down toward the Great Hall of the castle.

"Would you really hang them?" asked Jim, as they descended the circular, stone staircase, side by side. "After all, it won't be their fault if Brian should die—which I'm sure he won't. If anyone would be to blame it would be me."

"Why, what a question!" said Liseth, looking up at him with her soft, dark eyes. "We could hardly hang you, m'Lord. On the other hand, someone will have to be punished. And after all, that's one of the things servants are for. How does a man like you come to ask a question like that?"

"Oh, well," said Jim. He gave a broad wave of his hand, and left the answer more or less hanging in mid-air. To his great satisfaction, Liseth did not pursue it.

"Oh," she said, "Greywings is back, just as I said. I've talked to her; and yes, she found the laidly Worm again."

"Pardon me for asking," said Jim, "but what kind of Worm is a laidly Worm?"

"Oh," Liseth laughed, " 'laidly' is one of the Scottish words we use, too. It just means very ugly—something horrible to see. You understand?"

"Ah," said Jim, nodding, "go on, then. You were going to tell me that he found this Worm again?"

"*She* found him," corrected Liseth. "Yes, the Worm was sunning itself on the rock of a small cliff. Up somewhere probably in the Cheviot Woods."

"Somewhere up there, you say?" Jim asked. "Doesn't your Greywings know where she saw the Worm?"

"Oh, of course she does," answered Liseth, "but she doesn't think of places on the ground the way we do. I got out of her that it's only a short distance by wing from the castle here but that could mean anything from five to fifty miles, depending on how she flew there. In fact, it's more likely to be closer to fifty, if the Worm was actually deep in the Cheviot Woods, in Hollow Men territory."

"I wish we could find out exactly where," said Jim thoughtfully.

"I'll ask Snorrl the next time I see him," said Liseth. Snorrl had parted company from them before they had actually come in sight of the castle. It appeared he had no more love for buildings and their indoors than Aargh had displayed—Aargh being Jim's wolf friend down in his own home territory around le Bois de Malencontri.

"When will you see him next?" Jim asked.

"Oh, tomorrow, or in about a week—you can never tell with Snorrl, or with most of the animals or birds," said Liseth softly. "They aren't used to thinking of time and distance as we do."

"How about size?" said Jim. "How big was this Worm?"

"That was hard to find out from Greywings, too," said Liseth. "She started out by telling me that it was bigger than a hare. I knew it had to be a lot bigger than that, so I asked her if it was as big as a cow. She thought it over and said bigger. Finally I got her to say that it was at least as big as a wagon. I couldn't think of anything else for her to compare it to that would be any larger than a wagon."

"Did it have eyes on stalks?" Jim asked.

"Why, yes! How did you know?" answered Liseth. "She

did say that. Like a great snail, though otherwise like a large garden slug."

"It sounds uncomfortably like the Worm Brian fought at the Loathly Tower," Jim told her.

By this time they were at the foot of the stairs and entering the hall. They found Herrac with his sons and Lachlan MacGreggor and Dafydd at their usual high table. Jim and Liseth came up and, on Herrac's invitation, which was offered while they were still several paces away, they sat down on the bench of the side opposite Herrac himself.

"How is Sir Brian, then, m'Lord?" asked Herrac, pouring a cup full of wine in front of Jim. Liseth, he noticed, Herrac left to help herself—which she did.

"With luck, he'll be all right," said Jim. "As you know, it was mainly loss of blood. The wound's shallow but long, on his left ribs; and I've done for it what I can. Now, if he's taken care of, given plenty of liquids and if he'll just take as much as possible of a kind of soup I've suggested to Liseth be made for him, I think we should have him up and active before the end of the week. Even if he won't, by then, be up to doing much more than getting around by himself and joining us at meals and such, here in the castle."

"Oh!" said Liseth. "The matter had slipped my mind, m'Lord. I'll go get that soup started and be right back. With your permission, Father?"

"By all means. Go ahead! Go ahead!" said Herrac, waving her off toward the kitchen. She rose from the bench and disappeared.

"It's a shame he can't be with us at this moment," said Herrac, "when we have a serious situation to discuss."

Jim was aware for the first time of the soberness of the faces around the table. He took a large swallow of his wine, and then another, finally draining the cup. The rough, red wine tasted unusually good, and felt good inside him, once he had it down. He realized then that he probably had not only been thirsty, but under considerable tension working on Brian. He did not object as Herrac filled the cup again. Also, his mind was really not on the wine. He was busy trying to tie in this sudden visitor from Scotland with laidly Worms, Hollow Men, and the second-front possibility Herrac had mentioned and Carolinus had seemed to dismiss so airily.

Mages could be wrong.

CHAPTER 10

"I'll say aye to that," said Lachlan, filling his own glass moodily and then drinking from it. "Seeing as it's England that's to be invaded, and he's the only Englishman among us."

"Except for m'Lord de Bois de Malencontri," said Herrac. "He's English, also."

It almost came to the tip of Jim's tongue to assert that he was not English but American—or would have been under ordinary circumstances. But the problem of explaining what he would mean by that stopped him in time.

"Still," put in Dafydd, "there is something different about the fact that a Scotsman, a Welshman and a Northumbrian, even with one Englishman, should sit in council upon such a matter as this."

"Let us have done with oddities!" said Herrac sternly. "For that matter, Northumbria is become Northumberland; and nowadays we, also, are considered English. Moreover the matter concerns not merely Northumberland and England, but Scotland and Wales as well. If we are to be overrun by Frenchmen, we will soon discover we have exchanged King Log for King Stork. Have you not stopped to think that every Frenchman with the right to wear a sword will be looking for land of his own to make into an estate at the expense of whoever the former owner might be? That will include Wales—it most certainly will include England—and it may well threaten Scotland as well, once they are in power below the Border."

"Aye to that, too," grumbled Lachlan. "The gold that the French send is pretty enough; but no King spends gold for nothing but friendship; or an agreement so honored in the breach as the Auld Alliance, between his country and Scotland."

He looked directly into Jim's eyes.

"In a word, Sir James—which I will so call you, for the words come more kindly to my lips than those of 'm'Lord'—we are talking about an invasion of England from Scotland, backed with French gold, but made with Scottish lives and Scottish blood, that needs must be spilt before England can hope to be conquered—not that any hope of that there is."

"You're concerned about Scottish lives, then?" asked Jim. "How does it come a Scotsman like yourself would be here now, warning what may well be the enemy, of a planned attack by your own people?"

"Because Herrac has the right of it. We can all become prey to the French," said Lachlan. "Also I'm no friend of the MacDougall, who is the main force in inciting Scotland into this bloodbath with England. Not that I would mind a conquest of England that will work. But this one cannot and will not."

"And why won't it work?" asked Jim, suddenly keenly interested.

"Because the damned French won't show up when they're supposed to!" half shouted Lachlan, thumping the table with his fist. "They never have before, and they won't now! It's the men of the clans, France wants to pull its chestnuts out of the fire for it. Let Scotsmen conquer England; and then France will sail up, smiling; and let off its ships enough fresh armed men to slay and rout those very Scotsmen that have gained the land for them. How else can they gain by this?"

"You have yet to tell us, look you," said Dafydd, "what makes you so sure that they will do just this thing you say."

"Because the French have been always such!" said Lachlan. "They seek to buy Scotsmen to conquer England for them. It has always been their way; and it cannot be other than their way now. How would matters stand if Scots and French were faced with dividing England between them, somewhere down in the midlands? If ye wouldna have had a war between them for other reasons before that, ye'd have war between them then! Can ye think that anything else would happen?"

It was curious, thought Jim, how Lachlan's accent seemed to come and go. At moments he talked like the rest of them. At other moments he was hardly understandable.

"Knowing the English and French—I, for one, think not," said Herrac. "M'Lord James and Master bowman—and Sir Brian if he were here—I would say to you now that I am of the mind of Lachlan on this. Our Border has taught us that there will never be peace of any real sort between Scots and Englishmen. No more is there any Scot, or Englishman of the Border, who will willingly give up what he owns to a Frenchman. There is no doubt that what Lachlan brings us is the truth. What we are here to discuss is not whether it will or will not be, but how it will be; and how we may possibly blunt the spearpoint of its first movement southward."

"Do we know where the spearpoint is going to come from?" asked Jim. "And also what it'll consist of? If it's a full size army—"

"Would it were," said Herrac, with a sigh. "I fear me it is something much worse."

"Why? What's that?" asked Jim, surprised to see this powerful Border warrior, obviously one who had had a good deal of experience in the battles of his area, sound so defeated before any kind of conflict had begun.

"Why?" echoed Herrac. "Because it's not to be an army. It's to be our old enemy, whom you've met already. These who wounded Sir Brian, who lies upstairs."

"Who? Do you mean—?" said Jim, wanting to hear the name actually pronounced.

"The Hollow Men," said Herrac.

Bingo!

Right on the button, thought Jim—and the Dark Powers pulling strings on all of them.

"So!" he said aloud. "But I still don't see any great problem with it. At a guess how many Hollow Men are there—not more than a couple of thousand, say?"

"Probably not," said Herrac. "No one knows, of course. None living."

"Well, there you are," said Jim, feeling the effect of the wine making him a little more talkative than he would generally have been. "Any invasion force from Scotland that intended to make a serious attempt at England would need at least thirty thousand men, wouldn't it? Thirty thousand men on up. Maybe forty—

fifty thousand. Maybe even more—"

"How many men does it matter there are in the army of Scotsmen?" Lachlan interrupted roughly. "Whatever their number, England has that many fighting men and more. What matters is the advance force. The Hollow Men. What's to be done about even two thousand, if they canna be finally killed?"

"Well, they can be killed—" Jim was beginning.

"But temporarily only!" said Lachlan. "If they can come back to life in forty-eight hours, in forty-eight hours they can be back, killing mortal men who won't rise again! How do you think they've kept their land in the Cheviot Hills this long, and none been able to take it from them?"

"But—" began Jim argumentatively; and then suddenly realized he had nothing to argue with. What Lachlan had pointed out was at the very least an unmistakable problem. Still, he did not see how the fact of the Hollow Men, heading things up, guaranteed a bloody penetration deep into the land of England; without promising the highly unlikely, which would be an overwhelming Scottish victory. The Hollow Men were too few to guarantee a Scottish victory.

"De'il take ye, man!" said Lachlan. "Think! They canna lose—the Hollow Men cannot lose, I mean. As long as they leave one of their own back up in the Cheviot Hills—or better still, for safety, a small number of their own, then those that go can be killed as many times over as they want, and still return to enjoy what loot they may have picked up, plus whatever French money has been paid them!"

"But what good does loot and gold do them? Since they're dead and have no bodies?" asked Jim.

"They may be dead," said Lachlan, "but when they are alive they are as much in their bodies as you or I, and have the same appetites for food, drink, and women. This is the loathly part of them."

"Well, of course," agreed Jim. "Still . . ."

"While the Scots army will not win. Canna win! Sooner or later, a greater English force, with the help of such bowmen as our Welsh friend here—the same which has been the downfall of Scottish armies before this, for we have no strong archers of our own to match them—will surround and overwhelm the Scots."

He glared for a second at Dafydd, who did not change expression at all.

"All who do not escape will die. Most of the Hollow Men will die then, too; but a few may escape—particularly those carrying valuable loot, who will have left before the final battle. England will be able to throw all her strength at our Scottish forces, for I tell ye again—the French will not come!"

He paused and stared at them all for a second.

"The French will never land in time to help us. We will face England alone; and it is a country larger than ours, with more people, richer and stronger. Defend ourselves against it, we can; when they come to us, in our own mountains, and across our own lochs and rivers; but we canna go out against them and hope to win. I know this. Every good Scotsman knows it."

He gulped at his cup, then took a deep breath and went on more calmly.

"But the MacDougall will have it that the French will land. The English will panic and split their forces; and so we shall have easy victory before the French are much more than landed. After which we will be in a position to tell the French to go back from where they came. Which, according to him, they will be glad to do, since they merely came for the sake of the Auld Alliance, to give us aid!"

The last sentence ended on a sneer.

"What makes you so sure that the Hollow Men will be so successful leading the drive into England?" Jim asked. "True they're only dead for forty-eight hours once they're killed, but they can be killed; and surely, very soon enough, Englishmen will have them out of action to make them of little use to the Scottish host."

"Ye think so?" Lachlan refilled his glass, looking at Jim. "When the three of you met some for the first time outside the castle here, as Herrac has told me happened to you on your incoming, what was your first feeling when you saw them coming at you? Was it to fight—or to flee?"

Jim was caught in a cleft stick. Brian, and very probably even Dafydd with him may well have felt like running rather than fighting, when they first caught sight of the suits of armor on invisible horses galloping at them. He himself had been more intrigued than frightened. But once more to explain why something was so, he would have to venture into that quagmire he had avoided earlier. Explaining further how he did not really belong in this world; and how, on the much more advanced world he came from, people did not automatically think of magic and ghosts on seeing something they did not at first understand.

"The first reaction at first sight, is, of course, to run from such sights," he said. "Armor, clothing and weapons operating by themselves does seem to signal something not natural—"

"Ye admit it then!" said Lachlan. "Though you might have said so in shorter words. How do you think, then, the English are going to act, when they first see them, never having even heard of such before?"

"Neither had we," put in Dafydd, a little dryly. "And we went forward. Of course, not all may be as m'Lord, Sir Brian and I in this."

"But that's my point, man!" said Lachlan, swinging his gaze on him. "The Hollow Men will go far, because most will run from them at first sight. If they have enough of their invisible steeds, which are doubtless ghosts like themselves, it is not hard for a man on horseback to run down and kill men fleeing afoot before them. Not merely will the ordinary sort do this, an attack by the Hollow Men in full armor and on ghost-horses will be enough to throw into disorder any force that stands to oppose the Scots . . . at least at first."

He had to pause to catch his breath. He had almost been shouting.

"So, for some distance," he continued, "the Scots force will gain the advantage of any clash, and be able to get deep into England. Meanwhile rumor will have run before them, magnifying the Hollow Men, and making Englishmen even more fearful of them. In the end, true, there will be those who will close with them and discover they can be killed, at least temporarily. But by that time our Scotsmen will be so deep into England that they may be surrounded and cut off from returning. And as I say, the English can muster much larger forces—nor will they be slow at discovering that their archers, again like our friend here, are just the weapon needed to kill Hollow Men from a distance, in safety for themselves."

He stopped speaking. In the silence, Herrac spoke out.

"I hope you're convinced, gentlemen," he said, looking at Jim and Dafydd. "Whatever the outcome, it can't be good for the Scots, and the ground over which they pass as they go; for they will certainly loot, and bring fire and sword to anything on which these will act. The only way of avoiding the whole thing, including the promised landing of the French, would be to stop the Hollow Men ahead of time. And this, I confess, I've no thought how to do."

"You could round the Hollow Men up and kill them first," said Dafydd. "Was it not said, if my memory serves, that if all were killed at the same time, none could come back to life? The problem then, is merely to get them all together and surround them with a force from the Border—and I venture to promise that the Little Men would also help—and make sure that all are slain at one time."

Lachlan gave a short, derisive laugh.

"Lachlan," said Herrac to him, "your manners were never of the best, and they are not of the sort we would welcome now. Our two friends here at the table are doing their best to help us puzzle out this situation. Let us listen. They may not know an answer, but something they say may suggest one to us."

To Jim's surprise Lachlan's face suddenly lost the sullen expression it had worn almost since they appeared. He sat up straight, looked directly at Dafydd and Jim, and spoke to them.

"Forgive me," he said, without a trace of his accent. "It is true, as Herrac has said. I can be an ill-mannered kerle; and it comes to me that I have been so, just now. Will you forgive me, gentlemen?"

Jim and Dafydd both murmured quick agreement; Jim, meanwhile, puzzling over the word "kerle." He finally identified it as the Scottish form of the medieval English "carle"—a *"rude, bad-tempered lout."*

"Very well then," said Lachlan, "I thank you both for your courtesy. Now, I will listen."

He folded his arms and sat silent, waiting.

"Concerning this idea of getting them all together and killing them off all at once," said Herrac. "It is certainly an excellent answer to the situation—though I would have to point out that it is an answer that we have talked of here on the Border many times without coming to any definite plan. It is a little like the story about the mice who would bell the cat until one of them asked who would do it—and then there was a great silence, because the question was not answerable. We have men enough on the Border and more, all who hate the Hollow Men well enough to forget their individual feuds for long enough to rid the face of the earth of them. But again and again, the question remains. How can we ever know we've killed them all?"

"Has none been able to think of a way," said Dafydd, "to make certain that they were all together, in one spot at one time?"

"None," Herrac answered. He looked at the two of them. "Have either one of you any idea?"

"I know of none," said Dafydd, "but it is in my mind, and this I have believed all my life, that there is no question without an answer."

He turned to Jim.

"James?" he asked. "Can you not think of some way, natural—or perhaps magical—to make them be at one place at one time?"

Both Herrac and Lachlan fastened their own gazes on Jim with a new alertness, as they waited with Dafydd for Jim's answer. Jim looked back at them, thoughtfully and—internally—a little sadly. Once more he was encountering the universal and unbounded belief of fourteenth-century people in magic. The feeling that a magician could do anything, solve anything, by using means that were not ordinary.

"Offhand, I can no more think of a way than the rest of you," he told them. The alertness seemed to leak out of both Herrac and Lachlan; so that both men seemed to slump a little at the table.

"But," Jim went on, "if you'll let me think about it a bit, I can try to come up with an answer."

"Take all the time you wish," said Lachlan quickly. "We'll wait, and gladly. But I doubt that you've anything to tell us that's not been thought of and seen useless, before."

They fell into a silence at the table. Herrac refilled everyone's cup; and they all, except Jim, sat, drinking and staring either at the table top or at nothing.

This continued for some little time. Then Jim spoke.

"In situations like this," he said, "it sometimes happens that it's wise to know as much as can be known about the situation." He looked at Lachlan. "Will you tell me how you come to know about these plans, and as much as you know about the way things will be done—also who are the people involved in it?"

"Well," said Lachlan slowly and thoughtfully, "you see I've been at court myself—the Scot court, of course—these last ten months—" He coughed disparagingly, and took a sip from his wine cup before going on. "It was on business of my own, but also I was at the very court itself by favor of m'Lord Argyle, with whom I have some small connection."

He took his eyes from his glass and looked directly across the table at Jim.

"It was so I heard of it, this plan of an invasion," he said. "How it began—well, it was one of those whispers in the beginning, doubtless. Either a whisper at the French court by someone there, and word of it passed to those friends of France at our court, possibly the MacDougall himself. Then no doubt it was talked over and about by those same friends of France at our court; until, finally, the MacDougall—who has the ear of the King—began to speak of it to him."

"I see," said Jim, feeling some kind of acknowledgment was due from him.

Lachlan nodded.

"So the thing was talked up, and it grew in favor and gathered more people of the court behind it that were of the MacDougall's shape of mind. Until finally, plans began to be made."

He broke off and turned to Herrac.

"You met my Lord Argyle, yourself, Herrac," he said. "Would you consider him a wise head or not?"

"I would say he is," said Herrac.

"Well, my Lord Argyle saw no profit in this sort of a wild attempt upon England as France's pawn. Like myself and others, he knows how often the French have promised aid, and that aid that has only been coming in part. At any rate, he set me to the task of finding out the plans. How I went about that is my own affair, but I found that French money had been promised, that it was due at the court any day and that the MacDougall would be taking it down himself to bribe the Hollow Men to fight for the Scottish forces. He would give them part payment down only, ye understand. They are to have the rest after the expedition has been a success. But he and the gold will be leaving shortly for a meeting with the leaders of the Hollow Men, if they can be said to have leaders, which some doubt—"

Once more he looked at Jim.

"I was hoping that the men of the Border, or yourself, now that I find you here, could think of some way of turning his visit to the Hollow Men around so that they either refused to go or else can be brought to betray the reason for which they are bought. Ye see, I know when the MacDougall will be coming down, and roughly his route. It will be no trick to intercept him; and with enough men, we can do so and if nothing else, gain for ourselves the gold he is carrying."

"Lachlan," said Herrac sternly, "it's not just the gold you're thinking of, in this instance, is it? With the danger to Scotland and the Border and all the rest as an excuse to let you steal it?"

"I'm thinking of it all together!" said Lachlan, turning to him. "The point is that if he cannot pay the Hollow Men, they certainly will not perform for him. Ye see that clearly enough?"

"Indeed, it is obvious," murmured Dafydd.

"There, now!" said Lachlan, to Herrac and Jim. "The Welshman's mind goes right to the heart of it, as he aims the arrows from his bow!"

"It's a simple solution," said Herrac, "too simple. We here on the Border, and particularly those of us at the Castle de Mer, are well within reach of the hand of the King of Scots. He would soon get wind of the fact that we had a hand in stealing this French gold, and his armed men would be down upon us. I have no eagerness to have myself and my family hung from my own roof tree—or worse!"

"Well, now," said Lachlan, "the whole matter of the gold's a well-kept state secret. The King himself would not be quick to want it talked about, particularly if it were stolen—"

"What of the MacDougall?" Herrac interrupted him. "Aside from the King, the last thing I'd want would be MacDougalls swarming over the landscape and the castle because I'd slain or wounded their clan chief—or had a hand in the slaying or wounding. The results would be the same as if the King heard I had stolen the gold. No, Lachlan, simply stealing the gold is not by itself our easy and simple answer!"

"Well, then," said Lachlan, turning to Jim, "is there any way you could by magic cause the gold to turn to brass, or some such thing? The Hollow Men would be none too pleased if the MacDougall tried to bribe them with brass tokens."

"I don't know," answered Jim. A devilish thought stirred in him. "But if you want, I can find out."

Turning his head a little to one side, he spoke to empty air.

"Accounting Office?" he asked. "You have my rating as a magician on file. Can I turn gold into brass?"

"No!" replied a deep bass voice unexpectedly out of thin air about three feet above the ground where Jim was looking. "Even a AAA magician would have to have special reasons for making any such change. The balance of precious metals in the world is not to be disturbed, even by a minute amount."

For a moment after the voice of the Accounting Office had finished speaking both Lachlan and Herrac sat stunned. The voice of the Accounting Office was impressive enough by itself. Coming unexpectedly and out of nowhere right beside them in answer to Jim's question, was too much for men of the fourteenth century to take calmly. Only Dafydd, who had heard the Accounting Office respond to one of Jim's questions before, was not startled. He was, in fact, a little amused. He did not smile, but there was a glint of humor in the squint wrinkles of the sun-tanned skin around his eyes. The fact was, the other two seemed to be so robbed of speech that Jim became slightly alarmed, as the moment of their silence stretched out.

"Well," he said, to bring them out of it, "it seems that turning the gold into brass won't work either."

Herrac's eyes focused and Lachlan's eyes blinked, as he seemed almost to wake up. He shifted at once from astonishment into something like anger.

"Well," he said, "if ye canna turn gold into brass, what use are ye as a magician? What is it that ye can do?"

"That," Jim reproved him, "is what I've been busily thinking about. Let me think a little while longer."

"Weel, weel," said Lachlan, his accent suddenly very broad, "gang ye're ain gate, then. We'll wait on ye. We'll wait a whiles, at least."

Jim could not tell if Lachlan's reaction was one of disillusionment in discovering Jim was unable to turn gold into brass, or simply a weariness at what seemed the hopeless search for a solution. Jim drank a little of the wine from his cup and thought hard. The truth of the matter was, Dafydd was right. There ought to be no problem that did not offer some sort of solution. The only trouble here was that the sort of solution they needed had been looked for without success for a thousand or more years. In fact, even in his own century, there were still no lack of unanswered questions; and no way of knowing how long it would be before answers would be found.

Nonetheless . . . he thought hard.

"Tell me," he said to Lachlan, "you said you knew the route that this MacDougall would be taking, and about when he'd be going down it. Did I understand that you also know the number of fighting men he may have with him as a guard?"

"I do," answered Lachlan promptly. "He'll be starting his trip with several dozen. Either MacDougalls, or those who are friends of theirs. But, somewhere short of the Hollow Men's land in the Cheviot Hills, he will leave most behind and go on with only several; and even these will be left behind, at last some miles back from where he is actually to meet with the leaders of the Hollow Men."

"And at that time he will have the gold with him?" Jim asked.

"Of course!" said Lachlan. "Do you think those Hollow Men are going to believe him if the man merely talks about gold? It'll not be the whole down payment, ye understand. But it'll be enough to make them covetous of more to come. Also, it will be a load that he can carry easily by packhorse, alone, during the last short ways of his trip."

"Do you think it would be possible for us to set up an ambush for him at a point when he had left everyone else behind and he was by himself?" Jim asked.

"I see no reason why not," said Lachlan. He looked at Herrac. "My old friend here and his sons would be more than enough. In fact, if need be I could take him prisoner myself, though he has something of a reputation as a fighter with the English broadsword and shield."

"Have you thought of a plan, m'Lord?" asked Dafydd.

"No," Jim shook his head, "but I may be on the track of one."

They stared at him with new hope in their eyes.

CHAPTER 11

"Well, don't just sit there, man!" Lachlan exploded. "What's this plan of yours?"

"I'm afraid," said Jim, getting to his feet from the table, "I can't tell you right away. As you suggested earlier, Lachlan, it involves magic and I can only talk about that magic after I've made sure of it. So I'm going upstairs now to our room for a short while, while I do certain things magical—"

He broke off.

"I forgot," he said. "Brian is recovering from his wound in our regular bedchamber. I'll need a chamber all to myself, even if it's only a small one."

He looked at Herrac.

"Is there such a chamber?" he asked.

Instead of answering directly, Herrac turned his head over his shoulder and shouted for a servant.

"Ho!" his powerful voice rang out.

Within seconds there were three of the male servants at his elbow.

"Go fetch the Lady Liseth!" Herrac snapped. "I want her here immediately."

The male servants left at a run for the kitchen; and within another half-minute or so, Liseth showed up. This time, however, she was walking—if somewhat swiftly—since there was a difference between being summoned, and being sent on an errand; particularly if you were Chatelaine of the castle in which the summons occurred.

She reached the table.

"Yes, Father?"

"M'Lord, here, requires a chamber to himself in which to do some things magical," said Herrac. "Will you show him to such a chamber, and do whatever else he may require for these purposes? Thank you."

"Gladly, Father," said Liseth. She turned to look at Jim, standing on the other side of the table.

"If you'll come with me, m'Lord," she said, formally, and almost demurely.

"Thank you," said Jim, uncertain whether to address her as m'Lady in this instance—as he addressed Herrac m'Lord because of their respective positions as commanders of the castle—and compromising by not using any direct form of address or title toward her.

He went around the table and she led him back through the kitchen, upstairs in the peel tower to the floor just below the one which held the room in which Brian now lay. She was about to turn off down a corridor leading away from the stairs when Jim stopped her.

"If you'll forgive me," he said, "I'll have to go to the room that I shared with Sir Brian and Dafydd, to get my bedding. Could we go up there first?"

"Of course, m'Lord," said Liseth, and returned to the stairs to lead him up into the room.

Brian was still apparently sleeping there, and the pitchers were on a table that had been set up by his bed. The four servants gazed at Jim with scared eyes.

"He looks to be getting along all right," said Jim, to put them at their ease. "Has he drunk any of the small beer?"

"He has, and it please you, m'Lord," said the older of the two women, "if your lordship would glance into that pitcher next to him, he will see that it is now only about three-quarters full."

"Good," said Jim. "Keep urging it on him whenever he wakes."

A chorus of assent came from the servants. Jim found his rolled-up mattress that Angie had made, and tucked it under one arm.

"Now," he said to Liseth, "I'm all set. Lead me to the other room."

"This way, m'Lord," she directed.

They went back down the flight of stairs and along the corridor there and into a much smaller room. To Jim's surprise, it was furnished. There was a typical, very small medieval bed in a corner, also a rough straight chair of wood and a wardrobe taller than his head, of dark wood and with its two tall doors closed and bolted shut. The room itself was so small that he would barely have floor room on which to unroll his bedding. But what surprised him the most was a drinking cup with some yellow and white wildflowers in it, just before the narrow arrow-slit of a window.

Jim had never seen flowers in a medieval dwelling before— except in his own castle, where Angie brought them in to their bedroom. He stared at them; and then understanding awoke in him. He turned to Liseth.

"Liseth," he said, "is this your room?"

"It is, m'Lord," said Liseth. "I apologize for the smallness and meanness of it for someone like m'Lord; but all other possible rooms have not been cleaned for years, or are filled with such stored things, as—even removed—would leave an ill atmosphere for m'Lord."

"Well, I must say, I'm grateful," said Jim. "The room is not mean at all, m'Lady Chatelaine—even if it may perhaps be a little smaller than the one above. It will do excellently, since I have room to put my bedding on the floor. I was admiring your flowers, which add a very kind touch to the chamber."

"I am perhaps over-fond of them," said Liseth, "but when they and those like them bloom in the spring, I dislike to be separated from them, even for a night. So I bring some here and put them where a little sun will reach them. But they do not well, once they are picked and brought inside."

"Just as a suggestion," said Jim, "you might try putting a little water in the cup that holds them. Sometimes that helps flowers keep their freshness longer."

"Say you so?" said Liseth. "Now I think me of it, there has been something like that mentioned; but when I was very much younger and I had not paid attention. I will take your suggestion and add water to the cup—but not now, so as not to disturb you."

"That's good of you," said Jim. "Just a minute!"

Liseth had already turned to leave.

"I wonder if you could make sure that I'm not disturbed?" Jim said.

"No one will disturb you, m'Lord," said Liseth. "Not only are these upper floors for people whom no servant would trouble, but I doubt that any would have the hardiness to disturb a magician without orders before time to do so."

"One moment more," said Jim hurriedly, for once again she was turning to leave. "There are a few things I'd like to talk to you about for a moment. As you probably heard downstairs, I'm about to work some magic. It has to do with finding a way to solve the problem that Lachlan MacGreggor has brought. I don't know if you know about it—"

"Thank you, m'Lord," interrupted Liseth, "but I do know about it. All about it. Lachlan would hardly dare not tell me, even if my brothers or my father did not."

"I see," said Jim. "Well, we were seated at the table down there trying to come up with some answer to the situation; and I got the beginnings of an idea that might do it. It requires not only the magic, but certain information. I'll begin by going into a magic sleep. Once I wake up, I'd like, without delay, to find that wolf Snorrl again. I need him to tell me about locations in the Cheviot Hills, in the territory held by the Hollow Men. I understand he goes where he wills, including there, and knows every foot of the land for some distance in every direction."

"Yes. Yes, indeed he does," said Liseth. "I will try to locate him by sending Greywings out to look for him. Once Greywings finds him she will stoop on him and cry out at him. She cannot speak, and he may misinterpret what she means. But I'd think it most likely he would think that Greywings would not be coming to him in such a fashion unless I myself had some great need of him. Therefore, I think the chance is good that he will come to a meeting place near the castle that he and I both know well. If you and I can go there, and wait, once you have woken up—Have you any idea, m'Lord, about how long you want to sleep?"

"Not more than an hour. In fact," Jim went on, "half an hour should do it."

"In that case," said Liseth, "I'll send Greywings out right away. I'll be back here in fifteen minutes, and—being careful not to disturb you, with your permission—will look inside for a moment to see if you are awake. If you are, we can reach the meeting place I was talking about within very little time. Much less time than it will take Snorrl, unless he is very near to get there himself. This is important. For if he comes to the meeting place and finds me not, he may not wait for us. On the other hand, if he has been alerted by Greywings to the fact that I may be in some . . . difficulty, he will certainly not leave the vicinity of the castle. So when we leave the castle itself and go out to the meeting place, he will soon know of it and come to meet us there. So there is no danger of losing him completely, once Greywings has found him. There is only the very small doubt that he will not understand why Greywings is behaving as I shall tell her to."

"I think that's a very small chance indeed," said Jim, and meant it. "Very well. I'll expect you in fifteen minutes. If I'm still sleeping, would you mind waiting a while? Because I doubt that I'll sleep much longer—as I say, an hour at the utmost."

"Just as you say, m'Lord," answered Liseth, as she turned and went off.

Jim unrolled his mattress and laid it out on the available patch of floor. About to lie down on it, he looked again at the flowers by the window, and a strong feeling of nostalgia took him. The flowers reminded him of Angie; and all she had done to make their life together livable back here in fourteenth-century conditions. When Jim and Brian and Dafydd had won their fight against the creatures of the Dark Powers at the Loathly Tower, Brian finally hacking through to the Worm's vitals, Dafydd shooting down the harpies that burst suddenly upon them from the heavy bank of clouds only about a hundred feet over their head, while Jim—in a dragon's body—fought and killed the Ogre, single-handed.

He remembered Dafydd almost superhumanly deciding to live, after a harpy's bite which was invariably considered fatal, only because his present wife Danielle had finally said she loved him.

It had been then that Carolinus had told Jim that he had gained enough magic, in his balance with the Accounting Office, to take himself and Angie back to their own world and their own century.

Also, it had been then that Angie drew him aside, and told him that she wanted to do whatever he wanted to do, about staying or going. Jim, who had taken for granted that she would want to go back—although there were elements about this fourteenth-century world that strongly attracted him, medievalist and athlete in his own world as he was—had been completely floored by her attitude. Upon searching his conscience he had decided to stay, much to the joy of Sir Brian, Dafydd and the others and—just as she had said—with Angie's full agreement and support.

It had been after that, that they had taken over the castle of Sir Hugh de Bois de Malencontri and made it their own; since Sir Hugh, who had sold his services to the Dark Powers, had had to flee for his life. He had left England for the continent, unlikely to return.

The fourteenth century, Jim had found, was no bed of roses. In fact, it often seemed just the opposite—a bed of thorns. But Angie had done a miraculous job of making the castle livable for them and introducing to it some of the better elements of fourteenth-century existence, that had made all the difference to their dwelling in it. The flowers now reminded him of Angie; and he realized he could hardly wait until he saw her again.

But now it looked very much as if he would not be able to return at the time promised. Not only that, but he would be entering into contest with the Dark Powers with almost no magical powers of his own to help him.

The magic account balance that once would have taken him and Angie back to Earth—the Earth they had known—was now all but used. He had lived it up; staying here where he was and moving into Sir Hugh's former castle.

It was true that he had gained some of it back by his actions in France the year before, at the time of Giles's death and the rescue of the Crown Prince of England. But that gain had also been canceled out by the fact that he had necessarily violated one of the rules under which magicians operated. So he was still a magician with a D rating. Only if he ever got to be at least a AAA+ magician like Carolinus could he have hope of taking them back to their original home. It struck him now, not for the first time, that in spite of Angie's stout support, and hard work on behalf of both of them, he had given her a very hard row to hoe, in his decision to stay.

However, there was nothing to be done about that now, except to move forward as quickly as possible to get the current problem solved and the Dark Powers' present effort against him frustrated; by blunting their hopes of the Scottish invasion of England.

He lay down on the mattresslike piece of bedding that Angie had made for him, and which he had been careful to keep vermin free, then rolled himself in it. It had been designed so that he could do just this, so it not only cushioned him against the stone floor below him, but furnished him with insulation that would hold enough body warmth around him to let him sleep.

He closed his eyes and used a little bit of his magic. Mentally writing on a blackboard that was the inside of his forehead, he created the spell that would cause his astral body, in his sleep, to return to Carolinus's cottage near The Tinkling Water in the south of England.

SLEEPDREAM ME→CAROLINUS'S HOME

As always happened under these conditions, he fell asleep immediately; and found himself almost in the same breath standing outside the small peaked-roof cottage in the little clearing; with—now in daylight—impossibly green grass, and the tiny pool with its magically activated fountain spouting in its midst, so that its drops fell back to the surface of the pool with a tinkling sound that gave the place its name—The Tinkling Water.

CHAPTER 12

As usual at The Tinkling Water, the weather was delightful. The sky was blue, the tops of the tall trees surrounding barely stirred to a warm breeze; and it was exactly the same time of day which it had been in Castle de Mer just now, when he had fallen asleep. He walked up the gravel path to Carolinus's front door.

The gravel underfoot was neatly raked, though no one ever raked it. Magic, again. The last few times Jim had visited Carolinus this way, he had found the Master Magician in the bad humor that was almost standard behavior with him, except in emergencies. Jim had learned that he was gentle and kind enough underneath his irascibility; but because of the other's temper, when Jim reached the green front door, he knocked at it almost timidly.

"Not my day for groundhogs!" snapped Carolinus's voice angrily from within.

Jim knocked again, a more normal knock this time.

"It's me, Jim Eckert!" he called. Only Carolinus recognized him by his twentieth-century name. There was a moment's pause and then the door was snatched open from the inside and Carolinus's head stuck out.

"Yes, it is you," said Carolinus, in a voice that was anything but pleased. "What is it now?"

"This current problem concerning the Dark Powers," said Jim. "I need your advice. Could I come in—"

"No, no!" said Carolinus hastily. "Stay there. I'll come out."

He did so, and was closing the door behind him, when he paused and partially opened it again so that he could stick his head back inside.

"I'll be right back with you, my dear," he said, in a cooing voice that Jim had never heard him use before. "Just be patient a short while longer."

He brought his head back out, started to close the door, then changed his mind. He reopened it and stuck his head in once more.

"Have some Madeira, my dear," he crooned. "It'll help you relax. The bottle and glasses are on the table right by you there."

He took his head out and closed the door firmly, then turned to face Jim.

"Well?" he snapped. "You can see I'm busy!"

Only the fact that Jim was familiar with Carolinus's way of doing things caused him to take this without offense. It was just the way Carolinus was. He barked at everybody—including the Accounting Office voice, toward which Jim and everyone else was instinctively humble.

"Scotland's planning an invasion of England with French money," Jim said, using as few words as possible. "They plan to use the Hollow Men as an advance force—"

"Yes, yes. I know all about that, now," said Carolinus. "Get to the important matter. What's your problem?"

"Just that," said Jim hurriedly. "The Dark Powers have really set up a strong hand for themselves this time. The Hollow Men, if all goes well, ought to frighten and kill enough as they move south, so that the Scottish forces can move fairly freely behind them and get deep into England. Then at that point, the French are supposed to land an invasion fleet in the south of England. But the opinion of my Scottish expert is that the French have never kept their promises on matters like this before; and that means they won't do it now."

He paused to catch his breath. Then he continued.

"The result will be a mess, with a lot of people killed, both Scottish and English; and eventually, the Scottish army will be surrounded and destroyed by a much larger English force that has the advantage of being able to use archers like Dafydd ap

Hywell. You might want to stop and think about it; because if and when the French forces do come in, they'll probably come through here."

"I'd advise 'em not to!" said Carolinus, his beard bristling. Then his voice quieted and became more thoughtful. "But you're right, they'd devastate the rest of the neighborhood. All of them looking, as William the Conqueror and his army looked, for lands to take over, when *they* came ashore on September 27, the year of our Lord 1066. No reason anyone invading now should feel any different—except your Scots. They don't want land, they want loot."

"The Scots also want to protect their homes," Jim put in. "If English land is taken, there'll be attempts to take Welsh and Scottish lands too."

"True," said Carolinus. "Well, you're right. The Dark Powers do seem to have a strong hand this time. And you're baffled as to what to do about it, I take it?"

"Well, not completely baffled," said Jim carefully. "I have a plan of sorts, but it involves the use of magic. And you know my account is not the largest—"

"Now look here," interrupted Carolinus. "I can't, absolutely can't, give you any more credit from my own account. The Accounting Office cracked down on me last year, after I helped you out when you were rescuing—what's that lad's name, again?—Prince Edward."

"Oh, I wasn't thinking of borrowing any more credit from you—" said Jim.

"A good thing!" said Carolinus grimly. "The Accounting Office is quite right, you know. The amount of credit I shifted to your account—understand, this can be excusable under certain circumstances but not under those circumstances or in that amount—was just a drop in the bucket as far as the total credit of all magicians goes. Not enough to make any difference at all in the bottom line worth noticing. But, as they very rightly feel—and I don't blame them at all—if I'm allowed to do it for you, then magicians everywhere will be doing it for their apprentices, or even for other, poorer magicians; and the whole system of ratings built on the credit reserves of the individual will simply fall apart. Could lead to disintegration of the whole structure by which this present universe is kept in balance."

"As I said," repeated Jim, a little testily himself, for once, "I wasn't intending to borrow any more credit from you. What

I wanted was advice from you on whether the credit I had was enough to let me do what I wanted to do!"

"Oh?" said Carolinus. "Well, in that case—go ahead then. Go ahead!"

"What I want to do is tell you the plan and see what you think of it, first," said Jim. "The Scottish crown is sending one of its people with a down payment in gold for what the Hollow Men will be paid, if they agree to this business of leading the invasion into England. What I'd like to do is take that man's place; and that means magically making myself over to look like him. Now, do you think I can afford to do that?"

"That?" Carolinus frowned, but only slightly. "No, that shouldn't do any great damage to your account."

"Well, to tell you the truth, at this stage," said Jim, "I haven't thought much beyond that. My idea is to take the gold down to the Hollow Men myself, so as to meet their leaders; and get some notion of what their numbers are and what they can do. Eventually, I hope to surround them with a force of men of the Scottish-English Border, plus perhaps some help from the Little Men—"

"Ah, yes." Surprisingly, Carolinus smiled almost fondly. "The Little Men. They do go on, surviving century after century, don't they? Not bad people, really. You know originally they owned a great deal of land not only in the Scottish area, but down along the western coast in toward Wales and even over on the continent—"

"So they told me," said Jim. "Now, about what I was telling you. The idea behind all this would be to create an occasion that brings all the Hollow Men to one place; so that they can all be killed at once, and none of them ever come back to life again. If we can do that before the Scottish army is ready to go, then they won't have any Hollow Men to lead the way for them. You can imagine, the Scottish King is counting on the fear that the Hollow Men will create, penetrating down in England as bodiless, but fighting entities."

"Yes, mmmm," said Carolinus, thoughtfully combing his goatee with his fingers. "The clergy and the gentlemanly class may stand and fight for their own reasons; but the common Englishman may well run like a rabbit when he first sees a sword without a body coming at him."

"Exactly," said Jim. "So now, what do you think of the plan? You already said I had magic enough to make myself look like this courier from the Scottish court."

"Well," replied Carolinus, still thoughtful, "It's an ambitious plan. You're aware, of course—yes, I can see you are—that you'd have to kill every one of them off at the same time, so that none of them could rise again? Yes, yes. But, how do you ensure that you get them all killed off in this tidy fashion?"

"I'm not exactly sure," said Jim. "I've got some ideas. My hope is, if Herrac de Mer can raise the Border men in sufficient numbers and the Little Men will cooperate, all together we may be able to do it."

"And this is likely to involve more use of your magic?" asked Carolinus.

"I hadn't thought any would have been needed. Oh!" Jim interrupted himself. "Possibly, just the trick of having them wear sprigs of leafy branches in their caps to make them such that whoever looked at them would refuse to believe they were there—like I did in France. A practical equivalent of invisibility."

"A practical equivalent of invisibility, indeed!" said Carolinus. "But now you're talking about a new kettle of fish. The magic involved to make one of them practically invisible in this fashion is a bagatelle—"

"A bagatelle?" echoed Jim.

"A nothing," kindly explained Carolinus.

"Oh, I know what the word means—" began Jim.

"*If* you don't mind!" said Carolinus fiercely. "I was about to say—individually, a bagatelle. But I get the uneasy feeling you're thinking of making your whole army of Border men and Little Men invisible that way. That would add up."

"To more than my account could manage?" said Jim.

"Well, we can check with the Accounting Office if you like," said Carolinus, "but I've no doubt myself that it's well beyond what you're worth."

"How many people would my account bear—leaving a little magic left over for emergency purposes?" asked Jim.

"Well, for a short period of magic use," said Carolinus frowning, "and taking your magic used for a disguise, say—twenty men?"

"Umm," said Jim glumly.

"I know it's hard, my boy," said Carolinus, "but the road of magician was always a hard road. You just have to take the rough with the smooth; and if there's no smooth at all, then simply get used to the rough."

"Yes," said Jim.

"Well, if that's all you need to know," said Carolinus cheerfully, turning back toward the door of his house, "I'll be getting back inside. That poor little dryad in there will be thinking I've left her for good."

"What happened to her?" asked Jim.

"Oh, she had an unfortunate encounter with a water troll," said Carolinus, pausing and half turning back. "Now, they're both Naturals, you understand, but of different classes. As I explained to you once, only humans have any real use of magic. Naturals have only their own, built-in powers. But a water troll has something of an edge on a dryad generally as far as such powers are concerned; and under certain circumstances, this advantage can be really dangerous to the weaker party—like this particular little dryad. But, it's no worse than mending a wing of a butterfly. The main thing is to get her into a receptive state to let me do the mending. Essentially, it's as if I took out your appendix without anesthesia."

Jim gulped. Sir Brian might merely look nobly pale and pass out, while he was being cut open and a diseased appendix taken out of him; but he, Jim, would have to be strapped down on a table—and even then he knew very well he would scream to high heaven.

"Tut, tut," said Carolinus, "it's not as bad as it sounds. There are various ways of putting dryads and others into receptive states. And with dryads there's quite a selection. There's one that works very well. And with that, while it won't be anesthesia, she'll be happy enough so that it'll be tantamount to being anesthetized."

"Oh?" said Jim. "And what way is that?"

"Mind your own business!" snapped Carolinus. "I mean, you're going to have to wait until you've gone up a good two levels at least in rating as a magician, before such things can be revealed to you. Just take it on faith that I know the best thing to do; and I'll do it; even at some trouble to myself. And now, goodday!"

He turned about determinedly and headed toward the door.

"Wait!" Jim yelped.

"Now what?" snarled Carolinus, turning back to him, with his hand on the door knob.

"I didn't ask you about the Worm."

"What Worm?"

"There's a Worm up in the Cheviot Woods in Hollow Men territory," said Jim. "But I checked with the Accounting Office and the Dark Powers themselves don't seem to be around there. What does it mean—a Worm without the Dark Powers nearby?"

Carolinus frowned and his hand dropped from the door knob.

"A Worm, and no locus of the Dark Powers?" he asked.

"That's right—although I'm not quite sure what you mean by 'locus'," said Jim.

"A locus," said Carolinus pedantically, "is a place, or locality. A point on a line, say, having no dimensions but position—"

"I know the ordinary definition of a locus!" broke in Jim. It always irritated him when Carolinus seemed to forget that he had had an education of his own—a good one—back in the twentieth century of his own world. "What I don't understand is how you're using it here."

"I'm using it in the sense of a point of *concentration*," said Carolinus frostily. "The Dark Powers establish a locus—like the Loathly Tower, which you remember so well—and then having established it they set about it their special creatures to either foray out and do damage or to defend the point or place they've chosen."

"What's this Worm doing up in the Cheviot Woods, then, with no Dark Powers to foray for, or protect?" demanded Jim.

Carolinus stared at him. There was a long moment before he spoke.

"My boy," he said in an unusually reasonable voice, "I don't know. I just don't know. I've never heard of it before. I can't imagine why a Worm would be there. It isn't as if the Dark Powers could simply lose a Worm someplace. They create them once the locus is chosen, ordinarily; and they cease to be when the locus is eliminated. Beyond that, I don't know. Did you ask the Accounting Office?"

"No," said Jim. "You know the Accounting Office. I didn't think it would tell me."

A sudden thought struck him.

"Maybe the Accounting Office would tell you more than it would tell me?" he asked.

Carolinus shook his head.

"I know I speak to it rather sharply from time to time," he said, "and well I may, being one of the three most valuable accounts it controls. But it does me no special favors because of that. Whatever it might tell you would be the most it would tell any magician. You're lucky to have that much connection with it and get that much of an answer. But, Jim—"

He broke off suddenly and there was a note of deep concern in his voice.

"You must absolutely find out about that Worm, why it's there, and what its connection is with the situation, as soon as possible," he said. "I don't like the feel of it. I don't like it at all. For the Dark Powers to go outside their ordinary way of working—well, the whole thing worries me. Never mind this silly invasion matter. Concentrate on finding out why that Worm's there!"

"I will," said Jim. "In fact, I intended to—find out, that is. But since you take it that seriously I'll give it absolutely as much of my time as I can."

"Very well. Bless you, my boy," said Carolinus, turning back to the door and putting his hand on the knob. "Now I really must be going. I am indeed sorry, though, that I can't be more help to you. It's this out-of-this-world origin of yours that causes all the trouble. It's caused you to end up with enemies on a much higher level than any magician with a D rating would be likely to get entangled with. A master should always be helpful to his apprentice. But in this case my hands are tied."

"That's all right," said Jim. "I appreciate what you do for me, Carolinus."

"Thank you, my boy!" said Carolinus.

He turned to his front door, opened it and began to enter, his voice changing noticeably. "—And did you get tired of waiting? I'm sorry. But you have indeed drunk some of the Madeira. That's a good dryad—"

The door closed behind him.

Jim stood alone on the gravel driveway, the water of the fountain tinkling in his ears. He sighed. It was time for him to go, too—back to his own body in the de Mer Castle.

He closed his eyes, wrote the magical line that would send him there, on the blackboard inside his forehead. A second later he opened his eyes again to find himself rolled up in his mattress on the floor of Liseth's bedroom.

"You're awake!" said Liseth, herself looming over him. "And I barely got here too. Well, it was most gentle of you to wake up so promptly. I'm glad you did. Greywings has found Snorrl, and if we go right now, we can catch Snorrl while there's still some of the afternoon left. What do you hope he can tell you?"

"I need a place," said Jim grimly.

"I only mention it, because he may not want to tell you," said Liseth. "You know how he is."

CHAPTER 13

"Pardon me," said Jim, rolling over and over to unwind the mattress from around him. He got completely unwound and climbed to his feet, then squatted down again to roll the mattress up so that he could put it under his arm.

"You can leave that if you wish, m'Lord," said Liseth. "One of the servants will bring it around to your bedroom."

"Thanks," said Jim, "but if you'll forgive me I prefer to handle it myself and not have anyone else touch it. It's part of the magic I do."

"Oh!" said Liseth. "I should have remembered that. In that case, we should probably drop by the room where Sir Brian lies, so that you can leave the mattress with your other goods."

"Yes," said Jim, as they went out the door themselves into the corridor and headed toward the stairway to the floor above.

"As a matter of fact," he added, "I want to take another look at Brian before I go out, anyway. I should have been more instructive to the servants. They were to keep urging the small beer on him, one holding the weight of the pitcher to pour into his cup and even holding the cup while another of them supports his head as he drinks."

"I'll question them when we get there," said Liseth. "If they didn't understand this before, I'll make it clear to them."

"Thank you," said Jim, as they began to climb the stairs.

Liseth smiled at him.

"It is my pleasure, m'Lord," she said.

She had a face with cheeks that dimpled when she smiled so that she ended up looking twice as attractive as she did with a more sober expression. Jim felt a definite, physical stir of feeling toward her. Realizing what he was doing, he sternly pushed the feeling away from him.

"Thank you," he said again, this time rather woodenly; but Liseth did not seem to notice.

"Greywings found Snorrl less than half a mile from here," she went on. "By this time, if he hasn't reached our meeting place, he must be close on it. We'll go as soon as you've looked at Sir Brian."

"Good," said Jim.

"Good? Then why are you frowning?" asked Liseth, interested.

"I'm thinking of tomorrow," he said. "That packing I put on Brian's wound is going to have to come off and be replaced by another one. Have you boiled other cloths so that we have another long, soft one to replace the one on his wound now?"

"I have boiled a number of cloths of all shapes and kinds," said Liseth, "—or rather I made sure the servants did so. I also made them rinse and scrub off their hands as much as possible before handling the boiled cloths. Was that right?"

"It was," said Jim.

"I wish," said Liseth, as they reached the floor above and began their way down the corridor toward the room where Brian waited for them, "I could do more to help in this hap."

"Perhaps you can," said Jim, struck by a sudden thought. "May I look at your hands?"

Liseth offered her hands chest high for his inspection. She held them palms up.

"If you wouldn't mind turning them over, please, m'Lady," said Jim.

She turned them over. As he had feared, while the hands themselves were fairly clean, every fingernail had a rim of black under the end of it.

"I think you said you didn't have soap around here?" Jim asked.

"I am afraid so, m'Lord," said Liseth. "Indeed, I must confess that I'm not quite sure what this stuff is you call 'soap'."

"It's most usually made by boiling wood ashes and animal

fat together," said Jim, "and it makes cleaning things easier when you add it to the water in which something is going to be cleaned."

"Oh!" said Liseth. "You mean *soap*! I thought you meant something for magical use, with a same-sounding name. Why, yes, we make it every few months, in large vats. It is, as you say, good for cleaning. Also sometimes as medicine."

Jim felt a great sense of relief.

"Well, then," he said, "if you've got soap, there's no reason these servants up here can't thoroughly wash their hands and arms, using plenty of soap and making sure they clean under their fingernails."

"Under their fingernails?" said Liseth. "But anything that's safely under their fingernails isn't going to be touching Sir Brian or anything close to him."

"I'm afraid," said Jim, "that for a matter that involves healing by magic, it's necessary that there not even be any dirt under the fingernails. If you will forgive me for mentioning it, m'Lady, if you wish to help me with Sir Brian to the extent of actually handling him, I would appreciate your hands being as clean as if not cleaner than, those of the servants."

"Why, what a thought!" said Liseth sharply. They had just reached the room where Brian lay. "Of course, my hands will be cleaner than the servants'! They couldn't possibly get their hands as clean as mine! But you do mean I should wash until there is nothing to be seen under my fingernails at all?"

"And then wash some more," said Jim.

"By Saint Anne!" exclaimed Liseth, halting with an astonished expression. After a second, she followed Jim into the room.

Jim halted by the bed. Brian's eyes were open, and he was wide awake.

"How do you feel?" Jim asked.

Brian focused on him with a little difficulty.

"Why, well," he said. "A trifle tired at the moment; but give me a good night's sleep and I should be up and around by tomorrow—"

"Not tomorrow or the next day," said Jim. "You rest in that bed for a week. Have you been getting some of this small beer drunk?"

He peered into the pitchers as he spoke, and saw one of them was a little more than half empty.

"I have," husked Brian, "though I am a little surprised my host should think so little of me as not to provide me with wine. Would you—"

"It's not your host's doing," interrupted Jim. "I'm the one who insisted that you be given nothing but small beer."

"Wine—" began Brian; but Jim cut him short.

"Wine has too much alcohol in it for you right now," he said. "Your wound isn't dangerous, but you don't want to get a lot of alcohol into you."

"Alco——" Brian stumbled over the word.

"That's what's in wine that makes you drunk when you drink it," said Jim. "It's not good for you right now. Besides, you've lost a lot of blood, and we've got to replace that liquid in your body. Small beer will do a safe job of doing it. Small beer and as much as you can get down you."

"Why, there's no problem," whispered Brian. "If it is drunkenness you fear, you've forgotten that I hold my wine very well. I will therefore drink only my normal three or four bottles a day; and stop before I have got too much of this al—whatever it is—in me. And for the rest of the day, I will drink only small beer."

"It doesn't work that way, Brian," said Jim firmly. "Besides, we want to keep liquid in you, not take it out. And wine is a diuretic."

"Dia . . ." Brian stumbled. "These magic words! I don't understand, James—"

"It, er—" Jim glanced around to find Liseth close beside him, looking at him interestedly, and the eyes of the servants all upon him. There was no hope for it. The words "urinate" and "defecate" would mean nothing at all to these people. "Wine is what makes you piss."

"Does it!" said Liseth brightly. "Now that you mention it, I'm sure I've noticed the fact, myself. But surely, m'Lord, pissing is a perfectly ordinary and harmless thing to do. I hate to see the good Sir Brian, here, deprived of the wine that would give him strength and pleasure. Could you not relent and allow him maybe two bottles a day?"

"No!" said Jim.

Liseth and the servants and Brian, all good fourteenth-century characters, did not argue with him. He took his mattress over and laid it down with the rest of his belongings; then he came back to Brian's bedside.

"It was a shallow wound you took," he said. "We're going to have to change the bandages on it daily; and that may be a bit painful—"

Brian made a faint contemptuous sound.

"At any rate, if we take care of it you'll be up out of that bed in a week and riding in two weeks."

"Riding in two weeks!" Outrage lent strength to Brian's voice. "I shall be riding within two days, three days at the outside!"

"We'll see," said Jim. "Now I'll leave you with these servants and they have orders to offer you the small beer often. I want you to drink as much as you possibly can of it. Remember, Brian, I have put healing magic into this same small beer. You must do as I say!"

Brian subsided.

"Yes, James," he said in so small a voice he could hardly be heard at all.

"I'll be in to look at you frequently," said Jim. "Right now I have to go out with m'Lady Liseth here. But I'll see you in early evening and early tomorrow and so forth. As soon as you're really able to get up and move about, I'll give you permission. All right?"

"Nay," said Brian, "but I will do as you command."

Jim placed a hand under the bedclothes on Brian's good shoulder. "That's the way to be! Now, we'll all be back in to see you later."

He went out and Liseth automatically went with him.

In the corridor outside, and on their way down the stairway, Liseth bombarded him with questions having to do with wine and its effect on the human body. Her language, like that of all the other fourteenth-century men and women he had encountered here, was unabashedly frank; and he felt his ears getting red. He finally shut her up by taking refuge in his magician's aura of mysterious authority; and they continued to the front door, where Jim found she already had a couple of horses waiting.

A few moments later they were out of the courtyard and on a canter inland from the sea toward the hills and the trees beyond.

There were still a good two hours or more until sunset. It occurred to Jim that a lot had happened today. Then he remembered—he had become so used to fourteenth-century habits that he had forgotten—that this day, like all days in a time of candles (if you were lucky) and cressets (if you were less so) began at sunrise or a little before and ended a little after sunset.

Shortly thereafter, they passed into the relative shade of the newly budded trees, and the day seemed to have suddenly become at least an hour later. However, here the trees were not very close and they rode in and out of sunlight—for the sky was almost clear of clouds—until they came to a small clearing that to Jim's eyes looked absolutely empty.

"Is this where Snorrl was supposed to meet us?" asked Jim, as they pulled their horses to a halt.

"It's where I have met you," said the harsh voice of the wolf, and Jim looked down to see Snorrl lying on his side, perhaps a dozen feet off in the sparse, newly green groundcover of the open space. Jim would have sworn the wolf had not been there a second before.

Liseth got down from her horse and he followed her example. She dropped the reins of her horse on the ground and it stayed where it was—'ground-hitched,' in the cowboy language of Jim's former world. He dropped his horse's reins, and the action had the same effect on his steed.

This was somewhat unusual as far as horses of the fourteenth century went; but possibly had something to do, Jim thought, with Liseth's close rapport with all animals. Now, she led the way toward Snorrl, who immediately got to his feet and came forward to her; head down, ears back and tail wagging slowly after the fashion of wolves rather than dogs.

She squatted down—Jim had the feeling that she would have knelt for more convenience if the ground had not been damp from its spring condition—and scratched around his ears and under his chin.

"Did you need me?" Snorrl asked.

"Actually, it is m'Lord, the Mage, here, who had need of you," answered Liseth. Snorrl glanced over at Jim, but made no move to come up to him in the warm and friendly manner in which he had approached Liseth.

"What is it then, magician?" he asked. "Or Sir James, as I understand they call you."

"Sir James will be preferable," said Jim. "I wanted use of your knowledge of the Cheviot Hills. Particularly, of that area held by the Hollow Men, where no men dare go. I understand you go and come there, fairly freely."

"I do," said Snorrl. He snapped his jaws ringingly shut, then opened them again. "They are my woods, after all, and the Hollow Men only exist there because mortal humans like you cannot put an end to them. I have explained to you that the Hollow Men are not comfortable around me, whether I threaten them or not. They fear wolves as you mortals fear spirits."

"I, myself," said Jim, "do not fear spirits, Snorrl. I am prudently afraid, however, of evil—particularly of the Dark Powers. I assume you know of the Dark Powers?"

"Who doesn't?" growled Snorrl. "But they have no power and pose no threat to us who go on four legs. It is only you two-legged creatures with whom they dispute the Earth!"

"That seems to be the case," said Jim. "However, I've a question for you. In the territory of the Hollow Men, do you know of any place where they could all be gathered together, if necessary? A place from which they'd find it hard to escape?"

"There's more than one such place in the Cheviots," said Snorrl. There was a note of curiosity in his voice. "Why would you want them all gathered together; and how did you think it could be done, in any case?"

"That, Sir wolf," Jim answered, "I still have not decided upon. It is enough to know from you for the present that there are such places. I may ask you to show them to me, eventually."

"You would go in where the Hollow Men are?" said Snorrl, cocking his head at him. "Perhaps you tell the truth when you say you're not afraid of spirits."

"Of spirits, no," said Jim. "But I would take as much caution as the next man or woman against meeting a force of the Hollow Men, armed and ready for trouble. Aside from that, as I say, I may wish to see some of these places."

"All one to me!" said Snorrl, snapping at a fly that wandered by. "One Hollow Man or many. But Liseth, is it your wish that I take Sir James into the Cheviot Woods?"

"It is very much so," said Liseth, with a slight note of reproach in her voice. "What Sir James says to you, all of what he says to you, is with my approval and support."

Snorrl's ears, which had begun to rise, flattened back again. He turned to Jim.

"When do you want to go?" he asked. "Now?"

"No, not right now," said Jim. "For one thing, the day's light is almost gone and I would not have time to look them all over properly. Tomorrow, shortly after sunrise, might be a better time. But first, in any case—you said that there were more than one such place as I described. I would like to look at, say, the three of them which most closely fit my needs. Let me tell you more specifically what I would like."

"As you wish," said Snorrl.

"The ideal sort of place I have in mind," said Jim, "would hold all the Hollow Men—which I'm guessing at around two thousand in number. Possibly, because some of them would be only partially dressed, and therefore not in their full bodies, they could crowd into a smaller space than two thousand armed and armored men might. On the other hand, it would be safer to plan on as much space as could hold two thousand men easily, with a little open space left over."

"Go on," said Snorrl, as Jim paused, looking at the wolf to see if the other followed.

"—An open, preferably flat space, then," said Jim. "On at least one side of this—preferably on two, but not more sides— I would like there to be vertical cliffs, rock walls that are not easy for men in armor to climb. So that if the Hollow Men are attacked there from the two open sides, they will have no means of escape, but must stand and fight until the last one dies. These two open sides, then, should either slope down and away, so the forces that might attack the Hollow Men will be hidden; and preferably, in addition, be thickly wooded so the attackers can conceal themselves until they are close upon the gathering."

Snorrl's ears had come up and his head raised interestedly as Jim spoke.

"Sir James," he said, "it sounds greatly to me as if you actually plan such an attack."

"Put it," said Jim, "that I'm hoping for such an attack. The question I have for you is which three of these sites most closely fit those requirements—or are there none that do? Tell me, if you will, the advantages and disadvantages of those that you think do fit. Then tomorrow I'll go with you to look at each one in turn."

"I know three such you might consider," said Snorrl harshly. "Excellent traps for those two-legs-without-bodies. However, all three lie at some distance from here, and the closest is perhaps twenty miles, as you and those like you reckon distance. If you come tomorrow, I will wait for you by the first of them."

He turned to look at Liseth and speak to her.

"That grouse-killer of yours can find me from the air," he said to Liseth, "and then show Sir James the way there."

"It would be hardly easy for Greywings to first find you, then come back, then lead Jim to you," objected Liseth. "Cannot you meet Sir James here and lead him all the way to the first place yourself?"

"No, for two reasons," said Snorrl. "In the first place, why should I make a round trip of forty miles or more that I do not have to make? Secondly, by the time I'd met him here at sunrise and led him to the first place, enough of the day would be gone so that it would be a question whether we could look at both it and the two others before sunset. Then he would have his way to make back in the dark."

Snorrl grinned.

"I would not advise that," he said, "particularly since we will be in Hollow Men territory all the time."

He turned to Jim.

"Have you any better suggestion, Sir Knight?"

"As a matter of fact, I have," said Jim. "Wait at the first place as you said, and I, together with Greywings, will find you."

"Find me?" echoed Snorrl. "It would take you a week of days to find me, if not more."

"I don't think so," said Jim. "You've forgotten I'm a magician. I have my own ways of getting there with Greywings, and I think we can do it fairly quickly."

"Very well," said Snorrl. "I will wait for you at the first location until the sun is directly overhead. Then, if you've not come I'll be about my own business. I have no time to spend sunning myself all day for your purposes."

"It's settled, then," said Jim. He looked at the sky, which was showing definite streaks of red from the west. "We should be getting back to the castle, m'Lady. I hope this good weather holds for tomorrow too."

"It will," said Snorrl. He looked once more at Liseth. "If you need me, I'm always here, Liseth," he said.

"Do me one thing, Snorrl," said Liseth. "Take good care of Sir James. Please!"

Snorrl glanced at Jim.

"For your sake, Liseth," he said, "yes, he shall be safe as far as I can make him. I promise."

Almost as if he possessed magic of his own, Snorrl was suddenly gone. Liseth and Jim walked back to their horses, mounted them and headed back to the castle.

"Sir James," said Liseth, almost timidly, once they were headed homeward, "how do you plan to go with Greywings and find Snorrl as you said?"

"I have certain magic," Jim said. "If you forgive me, I'd rather not tell you about it, now."

He looked around at the already darkening woods. "Also, I'm never sure in conditions like this who might be listening."

"I take your meaning," said Liseth, "as far as your last words are concerned."

She shuddered.

So they returned to the castle together, in silence. Jim found himself feeling a little guilty at not being completely open with Liseth; but he reminded himself of how much he said to these people of another time was capable of misinterpretation and speculation.

There was no specific necessity for hiding the magical acts he had the ability to perform. But performing them might set off a train of thought or action on the part of those witnessing, which might prove to have consequences he could end up regretting having put in motion.

Accordingly, he joined the others for the evening meal, paid a couple of visits to Brian before bedtime; and found him asleep both times, but with a fair amount of the small beer drunk. Finally, Jim rolled himself up in his own mattress not far from Brian's bed, at a fairly early evening hour, since he looked forward to rising with or before daylight. He also left enough floor space for Dafydd, who was considerately yielding all the bed to Brian at the moment.

It was, indeed, before daylight when he woke. He had become enough of a fourteenth-century person to wake—most of the time—when he needed to. In this case, what he needed was to rise enough before sunrise to dress, eat and drink something, pack some more food and drink to take with him, and ride out from the castle.

He would have preferred to have left the castle on foot; but that would have attracted all kinds of attention. Knights did not go anywhere out of doors on foot when they could travel on horseback, any more than the cowboys of the western plains—those same who had trained their horses to stand "ground-hitched" if the reins were dropped to the ground—had walked when they could ride.

About half a mile from the castle, he got off and tethered his horse on a fairly long tether to a face of rock. It was only about twenty feet high, but vertical; and held a little niche into which the horse could back to face any predator that came at it. It was the most he could do for it; and it was for that reason that, with a somewhat guilty feeling, he had borrowed one of the de Mer horses from the stable; rather than riding out on his own war horse, who was too valuable to risk by leaving staked out all day like this.

He patted the horse on the neck by way of apology for leaving it alone like this and took the food and flask of drink he had packed. He carried these off until he was out of sight of the horse among the trees. Experience had taught him that horses did not take kindly to his turning into a dragon before their eyes.

A horse, quite clearly, did not bother to ask itself how a human could become a dragon. It concentrated merely on the most important fact—which was that there was suddenly now a dragon, complete with very large jaws and claws, in its immediate vicinity; and usually went wild with panic.

Once safely out of sight, he laid down his food and flask, then disrobed completely and rolled his clothing up, including his boots. After a moment's thought he added his sword, in its scabbard.

He tied clothes and food and weapons to his belt, looped the belt around his neck with the weight of the sword and scabbard behind, across his shoulders; fastening the belt, finally, with the tang of its buckle in the last hole. Then he wrote on the blackboard on the inside of his forehead:

ME→DRAGON

He felt, as usual, no perceptible sense of change, except that the package of weapons, food and drink seemed to move upward on his back as his neck became very much thicker.

Looking down at his former arms and legs, however, he saw that they had become the forelegs and the very strong hind legs of a dragon. And he could feel the weight of the wings on his shoulders, together with the tremendous muscles there that he needed for flying purposes. The bundle he had made up now seemed to be holding firmly between a couple of the row of triangular bones that ran along the outside of his spine.

He had slipped a note under the door of Liseth's room before leaving the castle, with clearly printed letters and simple words, telling her to give Greywings orders to show him the way to Snorrl; and explaining that he would be in the air in the form of a dragon.

He stretched his wings, feeling an actual pleasure in the latent power of those mighty wing muscles; and, with a leap, sprang into the air and began swiftly climbing upward.

It was dragon practice, even dragon instinct, he had discovered long since, to climb to at least a thousand or so feet, before starting to search for a thermal—in other words, an updraft of air from the surface below.

On such an updraft he could glide, making a circle with rigid out-swept wings, and without the effort of personally powering his heavy body through the air. Even with his great wings and massive wing muscles, straight flying was a tremendous task. He reached his height and searched the sky for Greywings. But there was no sight or sign of the falcon anywhere under that gradually brightening dome of pink whiteness that was the early day seen from this altitude.

It was difficult craning his neck to turn his head enough to see behind him, so he gave it up. The castle was dwindling in the distance back there. He had not found a thermal, and had instinctively gone into a glide which at a shallow angle was taking him back to the earth below. He pumped his wings again vigorously, climbing another five hundred feet or so, and thought he caught a glimpse of a speck in the sky that might be Greywings, before he went back into a glide again back toward the earth, still not having found the thermal he needed.

He was beginning to wonder a little bit at the difficulty at finding one of these updrafts. At dawn like this, with the sun hitting the night-cold ground, thermals should be beginning, at least; although such things as patches of woods and so forth might not yet have begun to set up a steady upward flow of warmed air from the reflected sunlight.

He had already lost what altitude he had recently gained and some more besides. Once more, a little angrily, he pumped his wings and climbed a good eight hundred feet in addition. Once more, he went into a shallow glide; and was just beginning to think that he had felt a thermal—though a small one, one too small to be of any use to a flier his size—when there was the harsh cry of a falcon in his ear and something dealt a stunning blow to the back of his head.

He shook his head, more out of habit than anything else. His dragon skull was quite thick enough not to be bothered much by a blow that in his human body possibly could have made him unconscious—as, clearly, the clawed knuckles of the falcon, both feet bunched together, had struck him at the end of a dive from the peregrine's obviously superior height.

Nor did he have to be Liseth to interpret what that angry shout of a falcon's had been. Roughly translated, it had meant, plainly enough:

"Stop this damn bobbing around and start flying in sensible fashion!"

It had occurred to him that if the falcon was to keep diving on him like that, however, he might have to do something about it. Possibly he might roll over on his back in mid-air, so as to catch the bird in his foreclaws, if not—lightly—in his jaws; to teach her that, she would just have to put up with the fact that dragons had different problems from falcons in moving through the air. But at that moment he finally found his thermal; and with relief went into a soaring circle, spiraling up a strong updraft away from the earth below.

He looked around for Greywings, half expecting another blow on the back of the head, and was abruptly relieved to see that the falcon was now circling on the same thermal at a hundred feet above him. Soaring was one thing they had in common. Even the peregrine could not fly steadily all the time, in spite of the fact of being able to dive on a prey at close to two hundred miles an hour.

As he watched, Greywings broke out of the thermal, headed west, with the rising sun behind them, found another thermal and began circling again. Jim followed. Clearly their search was now beginning; and they were beginning to work as a team.

He had needed to remind himself that Greywings, no more than himself, knew where Snorrl would be. But the falcon was headed into the heart of the Cheviot Hills, or rather just above the heart of the Cheviot Hills, and that was the direction where

Gordon R. Dickson

they were most likely to find Snorrl.

Jim looked over the terrain below with his own, dragon's, telescopic gaze. He could not see any place such as he had described to Snorrl within view, nor any sign of the wolf himself. He knew, however, that the falcon probably had much better vision than he did; and was that much more likely to spot the wolf first.

He simply concentrated on following.

CHAPTER 14

They spent a couple of hours soaring, from thermal to thermal, with short flights in between. The peregrine evidently liked to pick a post of observation above fifteen hundred feet; and Jim in his dragon body tried to take the same altitude, until he found that Greywings was uncomfortable unless she was at least a hundred or more feet above him.

He therefore made things easier for her by keeping his own altitude around the thousand-foot mark and letting her pick her own post above that. From her higher altitude, of course, she was able to observe more distance. Jim soared along underneath her, trying to remember what the advantages and limitations of sight were for a bird like her.

He assumed that she could not see in color, as his dragon's eyes could. The dragon's vision evidently was almost an exact duplicate of the human range, and saw colors pretty much the way human beings do. He knew it had been assumed that most animals saw only in black and white, and it had only been recently before he and Angie had left the world of their birth to come here inadvertently, that it had been discovered that wolves, and therefore possibly and presumably dogs, saw at least two other colors, one of them being red. He could not remember what the other color was.

He was disturbed at this point, by a memory about which he

was doubtful. It seemed to him that he remembered falcons, such as the peregrine—and for all he knew, all the class of hunting bird known as hawks, as separate from those known as falcons—also would miss seeing anything on the ground that stayed perfectly still—that their eyes were attracted by movement. If that was the case and Snorrl, waiting for them at the first of the possible locations that Jim was to look at, was lying down or not otherwise moving, Greywing's vision might pass right over him.

Jim, worried, began to concentrate more strongly on searching the ground below himself.

However, whether Snorrl had happened to move just as the falcon was looking at him, or whether Jim's memory was playing tricks on him, it was only about half an hour later that Greywings began to descend on a spiral, and Jim, following her down on his own updraft, saw they were approaching a place in the woods below that was evidently a little higher than the rest of the landscape around it.

It was backed by rocks, or cliffs rather, as he had specified, and the space seemed ample. But only one of the opened sides was treed; the other was a vertical cliff down to a stream for perhaps a hundred feet below.

This would not do. However, it was plain to Jim that if he turned up his nose immediately at the first spot Snorrl had found him, the wolf might become annoyed and refuse to show him any more. He therefore landed, which Greywings did not, only some fifty feet or so from where Snorrl was lying peacefully on his side.

Snorrl was instantly on his feet, standing sideways to Jim, his other flank facing the treed slope and poised, with one foot partially raised to take his body weight off it, with only the toe tip touching the ground.

It was almost the same pose Jim had seen in a photograph, that a psychologist and wolf authority friend of his had described as being in a "classical fight or flight stance"; in other words, the wolf had his body balanced ready to do either.

Jim hastily wrote the magical formula on the inside of his skull and reverted to his naked human form with the bundle and sword hanging down his back.

For a moment longer, Snorrl held his pose. Then circuitously and cautiously he approached Jim, still with his body balanced in such a position so that he could run at a moment's notice.

"It's all right, Snorrl!" called Jim. "It's just me, Sir James. I had to turn myself into a dragon in order to fly so I could cover the ground to get here along with Greywings."

He now noticed that Greywings had settled down on the branch of a nearby tree. But she too looked uneasy with the situation, and ready to take the air again in an instant.

Snorrl did not answer, although he circled a little closer. Jim, aware of the other's cautionary instincts, stood still and let Snorrl do the approaching. Finally, at last the wolf came up to him just barely to the point where by stretching his neck to its greatest extent he could sniff directly at the naked flesh of Jim's thigh. He did this, inhaling deeply for several sniffs, then apparently relaxed. He was still obviously out of humor.

"Never sneak up on a Northumbrian wolf that way!" he growled. "You could get yourself in trouble!"

Jim forbore to point out that if he had stayed in his dragon body it was more likely to be the Northumbrian wolf who would have gotten himself into trouble, if any physical dispute had evolved.

"I didn't sneak," he said. "I simply flew in, landed, quite openly, and changed back into my human form." He made an attempt to jolly Snorrl out of his bad mood. "You surely didn't think you'd be in any danger from a naked man?"

"You're not naked as long as that sword is hanging down your back," retorted Snorrl.

Jim was about to dispute this when it occurred to him that in a sense Snorrl was right. The phrase "naked man" in medieval times could refer to someone fully dressed, but wearing no weapons. It was at least one meaning for the words; and essentially Snorrl was simply working himself out of what had evidently been a rather serious fright on seeing a dragon land almost beside him.

"So you're a dragon?" said Snorrl, now, almost as if he had read Jim's thoughts.

"I'm not a dragon," said Jim. "I'm an ordinary human being. I'm Sir James. But I'm also a magician and I can change into a dragon. Haven't you ever seen a dragon before?"

"There aren't any around up here that I know of," said Snorrl, "and I'd know if there were. It gets a little cold for them in winter time; and I understand they don't like cold, though they can take it if they have to. It's those big thick bodies. They must give off heat like a cow if they're in any closed-in place like a small cave. But, as I say, there don't seem to be any around here—though I knew what you were, right enough."

"Then you should have also known that dragons don't go around hunting wolves," said Jim. "They eat cattle and other herbivores like that; they don't prey on other predators."

"I don't know what you mean by all those long words," said Snorrl. "But a Northumbrian wolf takes no chances. A wolf who takes chances is a dead wolf, sooner or later."

He broke off.

"Anyway," he went on, "you're here. This is the first of the places I was telling you about. Does it suit your purpose?"

Jim felt that he was obligated to make some show of looking the place over. Accordingly, he stopped just long enough to put on his hose and gambeson and sling the sword about his belt. Then he patrolled the perimeter of the space, looking up at the cliffs, which were undeniably unclimbable, at the woods, which were certainly thick enough for people to hide in, and finally over the cliff edge at the nearly sheer fall to the stream below. Finally, he came back to Snorrl, who had been waiting for him at the spot where they had been speaking before.

"It's almost exactly what I want," Jim said. "But you see, I want the Hollow Men fenced in against cliffs with no escape and to be able to surround all open sides by whoever we can bring to attack them. That means I need all sides to slope away and be thickly treed. This cliff here—a Hollow Man who took off his armor to become invisible might be able to get down it somehow, and escape. Our whole plan is to have a situation where none of them escape. So they'll all be killed off at once and none of them ever rise again."

"I wish you luck," said Snorrl harshly. "The cliff won't do, is that it?"

"The place is a possibility," said Jim diplomatically, "but I'd like to look at your other two spots first and see if one of them isn't more suitable."

"Very well," said Snorrl, turning away from him. "All one to me."

He trotted off into the trees.

Jim hastily got back out of his clothes, bundled them up and fastened them to the sword belt, put everything back around his neck and changed back into a dragon. The minute he did so Greywings took off in a sudden explosion of flight and started upward herself, as if the change had alarmed her. Jim leaped into the air and followed.

However, from this point on, he did not so much follow Greywings as let Greywings follow him. He was able to find Snorrl moving among the trees in the woods and simply stay above, moving from thermal to thermal as they went slightly westward and downhill until Snorrl brought Jim at last to the second site, where Jim landed and turned himself back into a human.

After dressing—because even with the warming of the day, the air was chill in early spring—Jim explored this second place. It was almost perfect. Its dimensions were slightly greater than those of the first one he had seen—there was no doubt about there being room here for two thousand standing men even in armor, and even allowing for a few on horseback. The cliffs were unclimbable, rising up from the ground on two sides; and scaling down into boulders and rubble at their ends. There was no cliff falling from any side.

Instead the slightly raised, slightly green open space was surrounded by woods. It even had a stone ledge at the foot of the cliffs rising from it, that could act as a stage or platform from which the Scottish messenger and the leaders of the Hollow Men could speak to the rest of them. The only difficulties were that there was a stream coming in a sort of near waterfall down one face of the cliff, and this formed something of a small pool at the bottom before spilling out in a small creek that flowed across the open space and into the trees. The difficulty with that creek was that the ground for several yards on either side of it was boggy, and would make for bad fighting ground when the time came. It would be easy to slip and fall in the damp surface underfoot.

The other objection to the area was that the trees immediately surrounding it were rather more sparse than they had been at the first place. Obviously, any attacking force would have to wait farther back in them, to be hidden from those gathered in the open space, particularly in daylight.

"Well?" asked Snorrl, after Jim had made his circuit.

"It's very close to being exactly what I ´want," said Jim, allowing the enthusiasm to sound in his voice, though he doubted whether Snorrl paid much attention to the intonations of the human speaking to him. "I could use some more trees so that it would be more thickly grown, right up to the edge here; and I could do without that stream running across it; but outside of those things, it's fine."

"Do you want to look at any more, then?" asked Snorrl.

"Yes. You said you had one more, didn't you?" answered Jim.

"That's right," said Snorrl, "and it's only a little distance off. You could walk it."

"Thanks. I'll fly," said Jim. He took up his clothes-bundle, fixed it in carrying position, and turned back into a dragon. Then he sprang into the air. Snorrl had already disappeared into the trees, but Jim located him without difficulty. Jim was also pleased to see, proceeding along with them and almost a speck in the sky, so high up she was, Greywings in attendance.

Snorrl had been right about the other location being close. It must have been less than a mile. Jim sat down in his dragon body with a thump, in the middle of what was almost a perfect circle of level earth that would be thick with groundcover in another month, but already had a few sparse ends of greenery poking out of the dark earth.

Looking around himself, he was amazed. This place was so ideal that it might have been constructed solely for his purposes.

He changed back into his human body, dressed and went to look it over. The cliffs were there with no stream and circling not merely perhaps half the open area but more like two-thirds of it. On the open sides the trees marched up small slopes right to the open ground; and they were close and thick.

He made the tour of the area feeling more pleased every minute.

"You like this one," Snorrl announced.

Now how had the wolf known? Jim asked himself. That a creature who was essentially indifferent to such obvious things as the intonation of his voice should be so perceptive was magic of another fashion.

He stared at Snorrl; but refrained from asking directly how the other had sensed his reaction. When he got back to his own castle and had a chance to talk to Aargh, he would tell Aargh what the situation had been like and perhaps Aargh would tell him how Snorrl had known. Or, knowing Aargh, perhaps not.

"I don't know how it could be better," said Jim. "The forest is thick about it, there's no stream dividing it with soft ground on either side. In fact there's nothing wrong with it at all. Except—"

It had suddenly struck him that the circle of open ground was far too small a space into which to crowd two thousand human bodies; let alone allowing for an equal number to attack them. He was almost ready to laugh at the irony of it. It was like the case of Cinderella's step-sisters in the fairy story, who could not cram their large feet into Cinderella's glass slipper, try as they might. He was faced with the same problem.

"It's too small, I'm afraid," he said to Snorrl. "There isn't room enough for all the Hollow Men here, let alone space for us to move in and kill them."

"I didn't think you'd be easy to please," growled Snorrl. "I was right. What do you expect me to do, go hunting for some more places for you to look at?"

"These were the best three, I thought you said?" Jim asked.

"That's right," said Snorrl.

"Then it's settled," said Jim. "We'll use the second place, the one you just showed me with the stream and the rather thin woods next to it. I should have known that no place would be just what I wanted."

"I could have told you that," said Snorrl. "It's a failing among you people that go on two legs, with rare exceptions like that of Liseth. Nothing really ever satisfies you."

"No," said Jim, "I am satisfied. I like and want the second place."

"Well enough," said Snorrl. He sat down for a moment to scratch with vigor with his left rear leg high on his left side, then got to his feet again and shook out his fur.

"Maybe you'll tell me now," he said. "How do you plan all this? What's to happen?"

"A good deal," said Jim. "A great deal, even before we start. First we have to capture a man who's coming from Scotland. Would you like to be a part of all this?"

Snorrl looked at him both cautiously and curiously.

"Why should I stir myself for your sake?" he said.

"Because you'd enjoy it," said Jim, who had not known Aargh for almost two years and fought alongside that over-sized English wolf without learning something about wolvish nature.

"Ah, that," Snorrl answered after a moment of silence. "Perhaps, if it was something I'd like to do."

"It all depends," said Jim. "Tell me something. We humans smell, don't we?"

"All creatures smell," said Snorrl, "humans often a bit more than others. They even have some interesting smells, though they don't seem to appreciate those particular smells much themselves. The smell of rotting flesh never seemed to please any human I know."

"Well, yes," said Jim, rather wishing he was back in his dragon body, which had never seemed to notice or object to rotting flesh when finishing off the carcass of a cow found dead in a field. Dragons, he had discovered to his surprise at a time when he had been one, could be scavengers like vultures, when it came to certain types of foods like meat.

"All right, then," he said, "humans smell. Do Hollow Men smell?"

"Of course they do!" snapped Snorrl. "In fact that may be one reason they're afraid of me, since I know that they're there even when they haven't got clothes on."

"And I take it," said Jim, "that, like humans, they all smell differently."

"So I can tell one from the other?" said Snorrl. "Certainly. You don't look alike, do you? Neither do they, nor would they, if you could see them. So they don't smell alike, either."

"Good!" said Jim. "Then you're just what we're going to need. You see, we plan to intercept this man coming from Scotland with gold for the Hollow Men, so that the Hollow Men will lead an attack into English territory."

"Gold! Silver!" said Snorrl. "What two-legs can see in those cold pieces of stone I don't know."

"It's somewhat hard to explain," said Jim. "Anyway, the point is he'll be coming and he'll have gold. So, we plan to capture him. Then I'll take his place and go down there. There, I'll hand out gold to at least some of the Hollow Men. Eventually I'll hand out gold to each one of them. What we want to do is make sure that no Hollow Man comes up twice to get paid. If you're by my side, you'll be able to tell me if someone coming up is someone who's been up there before. Won't you?"

"I don't see why not," said Snorrl. "If nothing else they'll have handled the gold by that time and I can tell they've been up before that way."

Jim looked at him in surprise.

"Gold doesn't smell," he said.

"No," Snorrl grinned evilly, "but gold that's been handled by smelly people-hands does. You'll have handled it in passing it to them, then they'll have handled it, so some of your smell will be on them."

"You mean you can smell something that faint with your nose?" said Jim, astonished.

"I can if it's fresh," said Snorrl. "Give it three hours and I won't be able to tell what's what. But if you've handled gold and then they handled it, a little of your scent will have picked up—that I can smell for perhaps the next hour or so—up close, of course. Besides, I'll probably recognize the smell of most of them and remember the ones who've been up before."

"Fine," said Jim, "you can lie there beside me as I hand it out and look at them. You'll like that, won't you?"

"They'll walk around me as much as they can," said Snorrl, his yellow eyes gleaming, "but I'll know. Yes, I'll like it."

"Would you like it a little more if I use my magic to make you about double your size in appearance?"

Snorrl looked sharply at him.

"You can do that?"

"I can," said Jim.

Snorrl opened his jaws in what Jim had learned, from watching Aargh, was a wolf-equivalent of a laugh; although it was entirely silent.

"Then there's no doubt about it!" said Snorrl. "You can count on me being beside you, then—and anywhere else you need me."

CHAPTER 15

B ack at the castle, Jim went in search of Liseth, mindful of the fact that enough time had gone by so that they would have to change that first bandage on Brian's wound.

He found her at last, however, with her sleeves rolled up in the kitchen; supervising what looked suspiciously like a normally unheard-of general washing. She insisted on feeding him first before rebandaging Brian, pointing out that it was now full noon.

"Noon, already?" he said. "Why, it seems I just left here an hour or so ago and it was dawn then."

"Yes," said Liseth, "and don't think I'll quickly forget the fact that you didn't take me with you. I know I would've been a help."

"You would, indeed," said Jim, as soothingly as possible. "However, there was a certain matter of magic concerning myself and Snorrl which needed to be discussed privily between us. You'll learn of it eventually. I have to beg your forgiveness for not letting you know about it now."

"Oh, well," said Liseth. She rolled down her sleeves and turned away from the huge vat of water in which what looked like about a half-ton of assorted clothes and other laundry were floating, "if it's that, of course . . . but I shall remember that you promised to tell me. You must tell me first, before anyone else, if you wish to make up for leaving me behind!"

"I can only promise," said Jim, in his most courtly manner, "to do my best to tell you first."

"Well, a gentleman's—nonetheless, I shall expect it," said Liseth. "You say you need my help now to change the bandage on Sir Brian?"

"Yes, indeed," said Jim. "Particularly I want you to make sure that the cloths we use are absolutely boiled clean, and that they have been handled by clean hands only."

"I had them carried after boiling only by the four who attended Sir Brian, and that only after they had satisfied me that they had used water and soap to make their hands as clean as if they had just been born. They put the cloths to dry on a screen before the fire over there. Shall we take them up with us?"

"I'm afraid I'd better wash my hands first before handling them," said Jim.

"I can carry them," said Liseth. "Would m'Lord care to examine my hands?"

She held them up for his inspection, first palms up and then turned over. They were indeed clean, and there was no hint of dirt under the nails.

"Never have I seen hands—" began Jim, frantically searching his mind for a compliment, and finding one just in time that would be in terms of this world, "since I first took up the practice of magic, that were so clean!"

"Oh, well," said Liseth lightly, but there were suddenly small pink spots on the skin above her cheek bones, "I'm my father's and mother's daughter, after all. I should do all things properly. Do you want to go up, then?"

"Why yes," said Jim, "and then I can eat lunch afterwards, after all."

"Oh! M'Lord, I forgot!" said Liseth. "Certainly not. Sir Brian is not in such dire straits that he cannot wait for you to break your fast, since I suspect you've eaten nothing so far today. Sit you down at the high table and it will be brought to you."

She whisked off to the kitchen; and Jim let her go, seeing no real benefit in mentioning he had eaten before leaving. He sat down at the high table, discovering he did have an appetite, anyway, after all. In the process of examining the three locations with Snorrl he had forgotten all about the food and drink he had carried with him.

He decided he must find someplace to either hide the package or get rid of it. Possibly the easiest thing sometime this afternoon would be to eat the bread and meat he had brought and empty the bottle—not necessarily down his throat, however, since wine was too plentiful in his diet in any case.

The food arrived. The same bread but different meat, and, of course, more wine. Jim polished off the food, but drank as sparingly as possible of the wine.

Still, he found when he was ready to get up from the table he had drunk quite a bit more than he would have done a year ago, on a lunch occasion like this.

It might be, he thought, that he was becoming used to it. If so, it was not surprising. The water was not safe to drink; and he really sympathized with Sir Brian drinking the small beer. Small beer would keep you from dying of thirst, but that was about the best you could say for it.

It not only was flavored differently in every place you came to, with every kind of condiment from rosemary to onions; but it was always a thin, flat, bitter brew with little to recommend it except that it was almost certainly safer than the local water.

At the same time he found himself worried somewhat by the thought of what the steady and fairly heavy intake of wine might do to his liver over a matter of years. Particularly if he ended up staying here for a lifetime, as it looked like he and Angie very well might.

The normal way of summoning people around the castle was simply to shout. It did not seem to Jim that it was polite for him to shout for Liseth, the way one of her brothers or her father might do. He compromised.

"Ho!" he shouted.

A servant appeared. One who conspicuously had not yet washed his hands, nor apparently changed his clothes in several years.

"M'Lord?" he asked, bowing slightly.

"Tell m'Lady Liseth that I've finished eating," said Jim.

"At once, m'Lord," said the man and went off at a run toward the kitchen.

A moment later, Liseth put in an appearance with an untidy bundle of clean cloths in her arms. Jim was about to offer to help her fold them up neatly so as to make an easier package to carry, then glanced at his own hands and thought better of it.

"Shall we go, then, Sir James?" said Liseth. The fact that she addressed him by his knightly title rather than his rank indicated she now felt like a full partner in the upcoming operation. A recognition on her part that from now they were going to be co-workers.

"Absolutely," said Jim.

They took to the stairs; and, after a four-story climb and a walk down the corridor, reached the room where Brian lay. He was awake when they got there, and being given some of the small beer to drink by all four of his attendants. In fact, what Sir Brian was doing was drinking and at the same time swearing at them roundly—Jim suspected because the clumsy way they were holding him was putting pressure on his wound. But, being who and what he was, the knight was finding other excuses to complain.

"Damme! Don't hold me like that!" He was roaring at the man holding him up from the bed and the other man supporting his head. "And you don't have to hold my head as if you were going to twist it off, either! I can hold my own head up. All the lump-fisted, pig-brained—"

He broke off on seeing Jim and Liseth enter.

"Ah, m'Lord, m'Lady," he said in a voice so entirely welcoming and different that the change was almost comic, "a good morning to you. See for yourself, James, I'm probably half-healed already!"

"That's what I intend to do, with m'Lady Liseth's help," said Jim.

"Put me down, you stupid cattle!" snapped Brian reverting to his earlier manner and addressing the four servants. "Can't you see m'Lord is here to examine me? Make room there! Stand back!"

The four gently lowered him to the bed and scurried away to the far walls.

He turned to Jim and Liseth again.

"Well, James," he said, throwing his arms wide on the bed, "examine me!"

"In a moment," said Jim. "I must wash my hands first." Liseth had already turned to the servants and apparently done nothing but glare at them, but they were already producing a basin, some water and some soap.

"It's part of the magic, you understand," Jim explained to Brian as he pushed up his sleeves and prepared to immerse his hands in the bowl of water that was being held for him.

"Oh!" said Brian. Then he frowned, doubtfully. "James, I never remember seeing Carolinus wash his hands."

"And I should think not!" said Jim, with as much indignation as he could manage. "An honored, esteemed, AAA+ magician like Carolinus wash his hands in front of any non-magician? Unthinkable!"

"Of course," said Brian humbly. "Forgive me, James. I didn't realize."

"Of course not," Jim said, in a kindly voice. He looked suspiciously at the water in the basin in front of him. "Has this water been boiled?"

"Oh, yes, m'Lord," said one of the women servants, who was not holding the basin and therefore could give a sort of a bob which was neither a curtsy nor anything else, but passed for an acknowledgment of the situation. "Only yesterday."

"Yesterday!" said Jim, now summoning as much anger into his voice as he could. "Yesterday won't do any good! I want some boiled fresh."

"Lucy Jardine!" snapped Liseth at one of the women. "Down with you to the kitchen this instant and bring up a bowl of water fresh from one of the vats that are boiling right now and have had nothing—no clothes or anything else—in it!"

"Yes, m'Lady," said Lucy Jardine, and ran out.

"It ill becomes me," said Sir Brian after a moment to Jim and Liseth, "not to offer you the hospitality of something to drink. But I fear me this magic small beer might not be quite to your taste exactly—"

"Why, it would be excellent," cooed Liseth. Then she looked uncertainly at Jim. "That is, if Sir James—"

"I'm afraid not," said Jim sternly. "Recall the special duty we're engaged in here, m'Lady. It would be for the best if neither of us had anything to drink, small beer or anything else."

"Ah! Well, there you are," said Liseth to Sir Brian. "I'm sorry, Sir Brian."

"Not at all, m'Lady," said Brian. "It is I who am regretful to be such a sorry host."

They continued exchanging deprecatory compliments for a number of minutes. At one time this would have astonished Jim. But he had learned it was the small talk of polite society under conditions like this. After a while, Lucy Jardine returned with the basin, the water in it steaming visibly and her face contorted by pain.

"Set the basin down!" said Jim hastily. "Lucy Jardine, if you ever have to fetch such a basin of water for me again, take a couple of cloths—clean ones, that is—and use them to hold the basin in bringing it up."

"Thank you, m'Lord," said Lucy, wringing her hands behind her after putting the basin on the table. "But m'Lady did specify that the basin should be filled directly from water that was freshly boiling. Luckily there was a vat of such in the kitchen."

"Well, remember what I told you in the future," said Jim. "Come here, let me look at your fingers where you held it."

Very shyly, she came up to him and displayed hands that had been at least partially washed, and therefore did a better job of showing the fact that she had acquired some blisters on the fingers that had pressed against the metal of the basin.

"Go down again to the kitchen," said Jim, "and have someone down there rub grease thickly on those fingers and then wrap them each gently with a strip of dried, freshly boiled cloth, if there's any left. Also send somebody up here to take your place with Sir Brian."

"If it please m'Lord," said Lucy, "I can come back myself and do all that I should. These small things on my fingers are nothing."

Evidently, Jim decided, Sir Brian's stiff upper lip had its counterpart among the servants as well.

"Very well," he said, "come back yourself, but have the fingers taken care of as I told you. Go now."

She went. Once she had left the room, he cautiously tested the water that was in the basin. It was still hot but down to a level of heat where he could safely put his hands in it. He took the cake of soft, and very greasy, soap that one of the men servants was holding out to him, smeared it all over his hands and cautiously immersed them in the water. After washing his hands vigorously, he turned to Liseth and took one of the clean cloths he suddenly realized she was still holding. The weight of what she had carried was not great, but it was an awkward bundle.

He dried his hands on the cloth, and laid it down on Sir Brian's bed.

"You can put the other cloths here, m'Lady," he said.

She unloaded her arms with a perceptible air of relief.

Jim turned to the two men servants.

"Now, the two of you," he said, "would you slide the bed and Sir Brian on it out more toward the center of the room so that m'Lady and I can get on opposite sides of it?"

They obeyed.

Moving around to the far side of the bed, once the servants had gone back against the wall, Jim faced Liseth on the other side.

"Now, m'Lady," he said, "let me show you how we will fold these cloths."

The cloths were of all sorts of different material, but largely of woven wool. They had, of course, shrunk in the boiling water. However, Liseth had evidently anticipated this; and started out with much larger pieces of cloth than they might have needed otherwise. What was left, Jim with Liseth folded into either squares or long strips, the long strips to be those that would act as a bandage directly on Brian's wound. Jim reserved two of the thinnest, hardest cloths—which must have been, he thought, linen. He unfolded these and arranged them so as to wrap around the other cloths and keep them fairly germ-free; so that they would not need to be freshly boiled before the next bandage change.

He was not at all sure that this would keep the under-cloths clean enough for covering an open wound. But then, everything he was doing here was by guess and by gosh; plus a few little snatches and bits of first aid he remembered from his own time and world.

Ah, well, he thought to himself, after all, they could only do the best they could. It would, in fact, have been the best he could have done for himself; if—as was more than likely— one of these days he ended up in Brian's position and without Angie around to help.

Brian and the four servants watched them interestedly. When all the cloths were folded and taken care of one way or another, Jim lifted the bedclothes off Brian's upper body and exposed the long strip of cloth that covered his wound.

"I'm afraid the bandage will be stuck to the wound; and it's going to be rather painful when I pull if off," he said to Brian.

"My dear James," said Brian, "what of it?"

"Well, nothing," said Jim. "I just thought I'd mention it."

"Pull away," said Brian, with a wave of his hand.

Jim accordingly did. The bandage was indeed, glued hard to the wound by dried blood. Outside of a small twitch at the corner of Brian's mouth, the other gave no sign that there was any discomfort at all in having the cloth yanked loose from the slash in his side. As soon as they removed it, the wound began to bleed again. Somewhere, Jim had been told that this was a good sign; and that the wound should be let bleed for a little while to help clear itself of any possible matter or infection that had gotten into it since the first bandage was put on.

Accordingly, he waited a few moments, mopping up the excess fresh blood from the edge of the wound. The strip of cloth they had taken off was an ugly sight with jellied red and black blood striping it all the way down, where the cloth had rested against the wound.

Jim could not help feeling a little queasy, looking at the open, bleeding wound and the strip of cloth. The flesh was flushed slightly around the wound. But looking closely at it, Jim did not think that it had become infected.

Looking up, however, he found no echo of his feelings in the faces around him. Brian was looking almost proudly at the blood on the bandage, Liseth was examining it with bright-eyed interest, and the servants were crowding forward to look at both wound and bandage themselves.

Jim passed the bandage to Liseth, who immediately handed it off to the nearest servant, who happened to be one of the two men.

"You've been watching closely," Jim said to Liseth, in as authoritative a voice as he could manage. "This is the proper magic treatment for all such wounds, and you may have to do what we're doing here now for Sir Brian if I have to leave the castle for some days."

"You're leaving, James?" asked Brian interestedly. "Not for a few days yet, I hope. I will be up and about in that time, and we can go together."

"I'm sorry, Brian," said Jim, "but I'm going on a secret mission; and it will be best to leave you behind to help take care of matters here, if necessary."

"Damn it now!" said Brian. "Am I all that necessary, with the whole de Mer family here?"

"I will be taking some of the de Mer family at least, along with me," said Jim. "Particularly Sir Herrac, if he is willing to go. That will leave you as the only experienced knight with age and authority on hand."

"True," said Sir Brian. But he was obviously downcast.

"You've said nothing about this to me—this leaving," said Liseth across the bed, looking fixedly at Jim.

"It is not just the proper time and opportunity," said Jim, looking meaningfully at the servants—not without a feeling of guilt, since he knew that they were merely an excuse in this case. But the trick worked, both with Brian and with Liseth.

"Ah. Of course," said Liseth. "And that is why you will be wanting me to take care of Brian while you're absent?"

"Yes m'Lady," said Jim, "if you will be so good."

"It will be my duty, of course!" said Liseth. Whether by accident or design, she managed to move just then so as to jangle the keys at her belt. "So that's why you have me here with you now, not so much to aid you in what you're doing, as to learn how such things are done. But you have not taught me the spells to magic the small beer."

"That's something else I haven't had time to do. But I will, before I leave," said Jim, making a mental note to make up some kind of odd arrangement of words that would give the impression of putting a spell on the beer.

"As well as other magic elements," said Liseth, driving the point home.

"Much of the magic is in the handling," said Jim. "As it is in the use of soap and water this way. But I promise you, you shall be fully informed before I leave. Now, we must get a new bandage on that wound."

He chose one of the long strips that were laid out on the linen he had spread on the bed, having Liseth take the other end.

"Now," he said to her, "either one of us can do this alone, using both hands, but it is more effective and the chances of getting the bandage on straight are better if you put your end down and I put mine down at the same time. Ready?"

"Ready, m'Lord," said Liseth, frowning fiercely at the end of the cloth in her hands. She held it poised above the end of the slash that was closest to her.

"Good. Now I'm going to count one, two, three, and then say 'down'," said Jim. "Ready? One, two, three—down!"

They put the bandage on the wound, and then Jim showed Liseth how it should be tied down with cloth strips around

Brian's chest. When it was all done he put the covers back over Brian's naked chest.

"Now, we'll bundle all the boiled strips up in these other pieces of cloth I've spread out, then tie them up tightly, you and I," Jim said to Liseth. "Then we'll put the bundles at the back of the table here, if we can make space for it—no, we can't make space. Well, we'll put it at the foot of the bed. Be careful, Brian, not to kick it off onto the floor."

"Of course I won't," said Brian.

"It's of utmost importance that those cloths inside there are not touched by anyone else but me or Liseth and—that they eventually touch no one else but you," said Jim.

"I understand," said Liseth. She turned to the servants. "Do all of you understand?"

There was a chorus of voices assuring her that they did.

"Now, m'Lady, we must be getting back downstairs," said Jim.

"Could you not stay a while and talk?" asked Brian, so wistfully that Jim almost gave in.

"I'd like to, Brian," he said, "and if there's time before I leave, we'll have some long talks. But for the present it's important that I gather Dafydd and all the men of the de Mer household here with me in the Great Hall for a discussion of sorts."

He put one hand apologetically on Brian's good shoulder, and Brian covered it for a moment with his own hand.

"I will be patient, James," said Brian, "I promise you."

This meek and trusting assurance threatened for a second to break Jim's composure; but he kept his face as stern as he could and simply nodded.

"I know you will," he said. He took his hand away and turned to Liseth. "Shall we go then, m'Lady?"

"If m'Lord wishes," said Liseth.

They went out. On the way down the stairs, Liseth bubbled over with questions, that Jim did his best to either satisfy or parry. The first and most important was whether she was to be included in the conference down in the Great Hall.

Jim had no real reason to keep her away from it, although he found himself worrying about what kind of suggestions and intrusions she might make into the conversation. Perhaps, he thought, he could slip a hint to her father to keep her quiet during the important parts. If her brothers could be called curious, it had to be admitted that Liseth outdid all of them together two times over, in curiosity. She wanted to know the why and wherefore of everything.

To get her mind off that, Jim went into the business of the care of Brian while he was gone. He explained that cloths should be boiled fresh every day and be ready in case anything had happened to those left over from the day before. In fact, to be completely safe, freshly boiled and dried cloths should be used every day, provided it was she herself who carried them upstairs. He managed to convey, without exactly saying so, that her carrying them upstairs somehow helped to infuse the cloths with the healing magic. Liseth took this as a compliment.

In all things, Liseth expressed herself as being not only able, but willing to take care of everything exactly as he said. Then she brought the conversation back to the business of the gathering.

"My father and my brothers, with Lachlan, are out around our own land, right now," she said. "I don't believe any of them have left the vicinity of the castle, however. Shall I send servants to call them in?"

"If you'd be so kind," said Jim. "Tell them I consider it most urgent that we talk together as soon as possible; and that right away would not be too soon. Particularly this should be impressed on your father."

"That is easily answered," said Liseth. "I will ride after my father myself. I know where he will be found. As for your friend the bowman, he is actually in the castle, or just outside somewhere, working away with those special arrows that he's been making against the Hollow Men; like those that had such success against them yesterday, when we were with the Little Men."

"That reminds me," said Jim. "I have to talk to the Little Men, too, as soon as possible—after I've talked to your father and brothers, of course."

"Say you so?" said Liseth. "Then we will need Snorrl again. I can send Greywings after him, but he will be out of humor if he has to travel a long distance to get back here, after just being with you."

"I will apologize to him when I see him, then," said Jim.

"I would advise you do not," said Liseth seriously. "Snorrl is not like we people. An apology means nothing to him. He does

not apologize himself or understand it from others, except as a
sign of weakness."

"Thanks for telling me," said Jim.

He should have known that, he told himself. He should have
learned it from Aargh. In what other, possibly important ways
might he be misjudging Snorrl?

CHAPTER 16

"I believe," Jim was saying three hours later, when they were finally all assembled about the high table, and the afternoon was drawing to its close, "I've got a plan to deal with the envoy from Scotland with the gold and the Hollow Men both. Particularly, a way to perhaps get rid of the Hollow Men forever."

He paused and licked his lips. He had sat at that table waiting for these others as they trickled in one by one, beginning with Dafydd, and ending with Herrac himself, who—surprisingly enough—took longer to arrive than his sons. As a result, Jim had been killing time, faced with continual servings of food and wine. He had managed to avoid most of the food but had drunk more wine than he would have liked at a time when he wished to be clear-voiced and persuasive.

However, it now appeared that his initial statement to the rest of them had been bombshell enough in its own right to make up for any blurring in his voice while he uttered it.

"Did I understand you to say, m'Lord," said Sir Herrac, his voice overriding and instantly silencing the clamor that had been set up by his sons all suddenly speaking at once, "that you thought you had a way to rid us forever of the Hollow Men?"

"I believe we have that chance," said Jim. "It'll require a force of fighting men from the Border area; and the assistance of some others—whom I plan to go find tomorrow with the wolf Snorrl, if he also can be found by that time to lead me to them."

"Then let us hear it, in God's name!" said Sir Herrac, with more emotion in his voice than Jim had heard there since his mention of his dead wife.

"Yes, m'Lord!" echoed Liseth, her eyes shining. She had been accepted as one of the party at the table, along with Dafydd and Lachlan MacGreggor, whom Jim had also needed there, and whom he had forgotten to mention to her in his first talk of the conference he wished to have.

"That will do, daughter!" said Sir Herrac to her. "Remember you are here on the condition that you listen but do not speak, at least without asking my permission first."

"Yes, Father," Liseth dutifully repeated the litany that seemed to come almost immediately to the lips of all the de Mer children in their father's presence.

"Now, m'Lord James," said Sir Herrac, turning once more to Jim, "I believe you may have been about to answer me."

"Yes, indeed," said Jim. "The plan is essentially simple. With Snorrl I've been able to find a place from which the Hollow Men, once all gathered together, can't easily escape if attacked in a certain fashion. I'm going to try to make each one of them pick up his gold personally—to make sure they'll all be there."

"It will take a large force," said Herrac, "to kill them all, though. I know not how many friends I can bring to our help."

"I thought of that," said Jim. "I suggest that the schiltrons of the Little Men, who fight on foot, with spears, charge the Hollow Men first when they are unprepared, then open lanes through their ranks for the Borderers when the Hollow Men begin to turn and fight."

"The Little Men!" exploded Herrac; and all his sons, as well as Lachlan, began speaking at once.

Herrac quieted them down.

"Go on, Sir James," he said grimly. "The Little Men, you said."

"Yes," answered Jim. "I'd like to see them included in this. Not only because they are hereditary enemies of the Hollow Men, going back even before the time of the present families of folk like you on the Border. But because they may have certain abilities and advantages that we lack; to make sure that when we finish every Hollow Man there will be slain. This, of course, so that none of them can return to life again; and you'll all be free of them, at last."

Herrac rubbed his massive chin thoughtfully with an equally massive forefinger.

"Not all Borderers completely trust and like the Little Men," he said, "though—to be truthful—I know of none who hold any particular feud with them or grudge against them. It is only that there are stories . . . As to the Little Men's attitude toward we people, I have no idea what that would be. You will have to make sure of that for yourself. But assuming that something like this can be done, and done successfully, what was your plan for getting all the Hollow Men—mark me, *all* the Hollow Men— into this place where they might be trapped and killed?"

"That too," said Jim, "is essentially simple, although it will make use of some rather unusual methods; and, to be truthful, some magic on my part."

He turned to Lachlan MacGreggor.

"I believe you said something about this envoy being close to the Scottish King?" he said.

"I didna say *something* about it," said Lachlan, "I said it. Otherwise it couldna be. For one thing, the sum of gold the man will be carrying. It'll be the complete first part of the bribe for all the Hollow Men; and that's a weighty sum for the King to entrust to anyone but one of his closest lap-dogs. So the MacDougall, who will be the envoy, will undoubtedly come himself, as I told ye earlier, mounted and with a small guard of men; and pack horses with the gold loaded on them."

"You know him by sight," said Jim, "this MacDougall?"

"Know him? Och, man, how could I not? I've seen him often enough at court and elsewhere," answered Lachlan. "There's some that think him a braw callant, but he's a wee man in my estimation and over-Frenchified for my taste. What's my knowing how he looks to do with this?"

"I plan to take his place," answered Jim.

Lachlan stared at him, and then let out a hoot of laughter.

"I've no mind to insult you," he said, once he was through laughing. "But you're a little over-large and heavy in the shoulders and upper body to pass for the MacDougall, and nothing in your face that's like his. And even if you were his twin brother, you haven't his airs and fancy manners."

"I know that," said Jim, "but believe me, these are all things that possibly can be remedied by magic."

At the mention of this potent word, everyone around the table sobered, including Lachlan. There was a moment of satisfying silence.

"I believe," said Jim, breaking it and speaking to Lachlan, "you had a plan for intercepting this MacDougall and the gold in any case. A plan you wished to suggest to Sir Herrac, here."

"Aye," said Lachlan, moving a little uneasily on his bench and staring down into his wine cup. He raised his eyes to Jim. "But that was something different, in that it had nothing to do with this talk of magic."

"I assure you," said Jim solemnly, "*hic!*"

The wine that he had been absent-minded enough to drink so much of while waiting for the rest to appear apparently had tripped him up after all.

"You'll not be drunken so early in the afternoon?" asked Lachlan, eyeing him shrewdly.

"No—*hic!*" said Jim, stumbling over another hiccup. "This is part of a curse put on me by another magician many years ago, that I've never completely overcome. It'll pass. Simply ignore it."

"Indeed," said Dafydd, coming to his rescue, "and I have heard of a man who died of the hiccups, with no magic to combat them."

"Exactly," said Jim. He continued, hiccupping every so often but determinedly ignoring it. "Luckily, it only happens at rare intervals. At any rate, as I was saying, you had a plan to capture MacDougall and the gold, Lachlan?"

"Aye," said Lachlan again, having become suddenly very cautious and very pronounced in his Scottish accent, "but I'm no' that sure it will run in harness with what you've in mind."

"I'll have to ask you to let me be the judge of that," said Jim stiffly.

He had learned the hard way over the past year that, when in doubt with fourteenth-century people, it was sometimes wise to assert whatever authority you had. "I'm the only one who controls magic at this table," he went on, "and knows how it would work with whatever you had planned. So, let us hear your plan in detail."

"Well," said Lachlan, putting the accent aside, "it's simple enough. I know his route, and when he was due to leave, which would have been a day and a half ago. The place I had in mind to ambush him and his men was a place where the road he will be following passes between two steep slopes well covered with trees. He'll have no more than half a dozen men with him. More would draw attention. He should reach this spot about afternoon tomorrow."

He paused to empty his wine cup and refill it.

"We have enough fighting men at this table," he said, "though I would Sir Brian was able to join us, for he's a man that I would believe no stranger to the clash of steel—to take care of his escort. The MacDougall is no great body with any weapon, except that English broadsword and shield, nor of any great courage, in my opinion. If we cut down his men, before he knows what's happened, he'll have no heart but to surrender—himself and all with him."

He paused thoughtfully for a moment.

"Also," he added, "there's an advantage in taking the man and his gold with just those of us who are here, so that the fewer who know about it the better."

There was a further moment of thoughtful silence on the part of all there.

"There are my five sons," said Herrac, breaking it, finally. "As well as m'Lord James—yourself, Lachlan—and the bowman. Perhaps you are right that we are in numbers to take care of them. But I would not lose one of my family, do you understand, for all the gold that this man could be carrying!"

"You will not," said Lachlan energetically. "I give you my word on't! The men with him will be men used to fighting, true; but we shall take them at such a disadvantage that they will be out of their saddles before they know what's happened. Old friend Herrac, if you would feel safer by taking some of the other fighting men you may have around the castle here, I will not say nay. Not I, any more than you, would wish to see even one of your family badly hurt or slain."

"No," said Herrac slowly, looking up and down the table at the eager faces of his sons. "But we cannot leave the castle without a commander. Giles, you must be the one to stay."

"Father!" exclaimed Giles. "And I the one knight only, among your sons?"

"For that very reason, that I leave you in charge," said Herrac. "With Sir Brian wounded and abed—"

"Forgive me, Father," said Giles, daringly interrupting his parent for the first time that Jim had heard any of his children do so, "but I believe Sir Brian would rise to any trouble, if it should appear. In fact, I spoke to him about when he might be up and about. And he spoke of tomorrow or even the next day. This I know is too soon. But I think if the castle were attacked and he needed to take command, he would do so, wounded or not."

There was a long moment of silence.

"That," said Herrac finally, "I can believe. From what I see of the man—if needed, he would be on his feet and sword in hand, if he bled to death for it."

He sighed.

"All right, Giles," he said, "I give you permission to go with us. After all, any neighbors we have who might essay a move against us should be with us, instead, at the battle with the Hollow Men."

"Thank you, Father," said Giles strongly.

"Actually," said the voice of Liseth unexpectedly, "I could also be useful, if only—"

"Liseth," said her father, turning to her. "Under no conditions do you go. That is understood?"

"Yes, Father," said Liseth, literally between her teeth. "If it is your command."

"It is," said Herrac. "Also, think you a minute. Who else would take care of Sir Brian if you were to go?"

She bit her lower lip.

"There is no one else," she said quietly, "that's true, Father."

"How long—*hic*—" Jim asked Lachlan, "will it take us to get to this place where we might ambush the MacDougall?"

"Less than a six-hour ride," said Lachlan. "We can leave early in the morning. Then we can be in position by afternoon. Even if he is early and comes that afternoon instead of the morning of the next day, we will be ready for him."

"Well, then," said Jim, looking around at the rest of them for once without the urge to hiccup, "I take it it's settled, we leave early in the morning."

"It is settled, as far as I and my family are concerned," said Herrac. "Since Lachlan has already declared himself for it, there is only the bowman—"

"I will be with you, of course," Dafydd's soft voice cut in on Herrac's.

"Then I counsel we eat and drink now, and to bed early," said Herrac. "We will be rising before daylight, because there will be some getting ready before we leave in the morning. Even though time, according to Lachlan, is on our side."

"Good—*hic*—" Jim stood up rather hurriedly and stepped backward over the bench he was sitting on to free himself from the table. "In that case I might beg m'Lady to find me once more an extra chamber where I can make my own preparations. They involve magic that may keep me busy for some time. M'Lady, let it not be your room that you give up to me this time. Surely, servants can be found to clean and make ready another chamber?"

"It can be done, and will," said Liseth, rising herself. "Come with me."

"As soon as that is settled, return to eat!" Herrac's strong voice followed them. "M'Lord, you are the most important of us all to this expedition. I would see you fed, given to drink, and released early."

"I'll be right back," promised Jim. He followed Liseth into the kitchen, where she recruited a number of the servants; and they all trooped upstairs onto the same floor where Liseth's own room was. Liseth led them to a room that was filled with old odds and ends of furniture for the most part, as well as other clutter, very dusty and dirty. With amazing assurance and expertise she put all the servants with her to work at clearing the room and thoroughly cleaning it.

"You may go back down to the dinner table, if you wish now, m'Lord," she said, once this was done, turning to Jim. "I will stay a little longer to see that the servants are getting all things done here. There will be a bed, a chamber pot, a cup and a jug of wine and a small table and chair here when you return; if you give them two hours in which to get all prepared."

"Thanks," said Jim. "I'll get back downstairs, then."

He hurried down the curving stone steps that followed the inner side of the wall of the peel tower, finding that his hiccups had vanished along the way. Consequently, he was able to reenter the Great Hall and sit down to dinner with the rest, without that annoying and involuntary interruption from time to time. But he was very cautious about drinking any more wine. When Lachlan pressed him to refill his cup, he once more invoked the name of magic as an excuse to avoid it.

"Too much wine," he said portentously, "can badly alter the spell."

Lachlan, as well as the rest, seemed suitably impressed by this. Jim made himself as good a dinner as he felt able to eat; and when Liseth returned to join them at the table, he asked that a pitcher of small beer be added to the pitcher of wine that was to be set in his bedroom.

As soon as possible he returned back upstairs, to find the dirty and cluttered room completely changed. It was now completely clean—by fourteenth-century standards. The cresset in its wall was alight, and there was more fuel for it piled against the wall beneath it. The bed, the table, the chair, the wine and beer were all as Liseth had promised.

He had thought it wiser to accept the bed, without making a point of not needing it. But now that he was up here without Liseth, he got his rolled-up mattress to put on the floor of his own new chamber. The truth of the matter was, what he wanted was simply a good night's sleep. He closed the door with some assurance that no one, not even Liseth or Herrac, would enter without knocking first. Then he unrolled his mattress on the floor, rolled himself up in it; and was asleep before the cresset had burned out.

It was one of those nights that seemed to pass in a mere wink of both eyes for a second. He went almost immediately asleep, and was awakened, almost immediately it seemed, by a knocking at his door.

"One moment!" he called back.

He unrolled himself and rerolled his mattress, got to his feet, poured some of the small beer into his cup and swallowed, shuddering at the taste of it. It was, however, wet, and welcome just at the moment. Rubbing the last of the sleep off his eyes, he went to the door and opened it. Liseth was outside. He let her in.

"My father is already waking my brothers, m'Lord," she said. "I took it upon myself to rouse you. If I can be of any help in your making ready—"

"That's good of you," said Jim. His mind was too fuzzy at the moment to come up with more than those few words. Meanwhile she had stepped by him, and in the first pale, pre-dawn light filtering through his window, looked curiously at the bed.

"You did not sleep at all, m'Lord?" she asked as Jim went back and picked up his mattress, tucking it under his arm.

"I had certain duties," said Jim, as meaningfully as he could while still not fully awake. "I'm sure m'Lady understands."

"Oh, yes!" answered Liseth. Jim checked suddenly, aware of a sensation inside him that he had been too numb with sleep to appreciate until now. He turned to Liseth, who had also stopped and was looking at him curiously.

"Would you leave me in this room by myself for a few minutes more? It will only be a moment. Let no one else enter."

"No one shall so much as approach its doorway, m'Lord!" said Liseth fiercely. "You can trust me."

"Oh, I do!" said Jim. She went out, closing the door behind her.

Left alone, he hastily began to unlace from their points the leather cord that held up his hose, and approached his chamber pot. It had been a long night and he had not woken once. He urinated in the chamber pot with a great sense of relief, then hastily redid his points and went back out and hastily up to Liseth.

"I did not mean to be so long," he said.

"Long?" said Liseth. "But it was only a moment, as you said."

"Ah," said Jim, fully awake now, "under conditions of magic, time is sometimes different. You have heard of those stolen by the fairies, or Naturals, who thought they were gone only days and returned to find that years had gone by?"

"Oh yes," said Liseth again, "my nurse used to tell me all those old tales. I particularly remember the tale of Cinderella and her slipper—and how the Prince she married made her wicked step-mother and step-sisters dance in red-hot boots at their wedding. I laughed and laughed!"

"Er—yes," said Jim.

They went on down, to the foot of the stairs; and out through the Great Hall and into the stables. These, unlike the kitchens, were in an outbuilding at a small distance from the tower, in the courtyard.

It was only when they stepped into the furious scene of activity that was the stable, that Jim remembered he had left his weapons, his armor and most of the things he would need for at least an overnight trip still up in Sir Brian's room. He was searching his mind for some way of making a further excuse to go back up and get them, when he noticed them in a pile by the stable door of his war horse, Gorp.

"Why," he said, "my weapons and armor and all other things needed have been brought down from Sir Brian's room!"

"I was so bold as to have the servants bring them down for you," said Liseth. "Did I do wrong, m'Lord?"

"No, no!" said Jim. "You did exactly what was right. You picked out just the right things, just what I'd need. I'm indebted to you."

"Indebted to me?" echoed Liseth, frowning. "Surely not, m'Lord. These are only those things that belong to you. Nothing of mine or of the Castle de Mer has been added to them."

"Ah," said Jim, "pardon my ill choice of words, m'Lady. We magicians sometimes speak a little differently from ordinary people. I should have said I'm obliged to you."

He saw at this moment a groom come out of the stall that held Gorp, leading the horse, which was already saddled and with Jim's lance upright in its socket to the right front of his saddle.

"I will assist you in donning your armor, m'Lord, if you wish," said Liseth.

Looking at her, for the first time, it struck Jim that the expression on her face was definitely very demure. For the first time he realized that he might have become attractive to her, as he had found himself to be—even in his dragon body—to Danielle o'the Wold. In both cases it had been the same thing. It had been the aura of magic about him. Danielle had fantasized that he was an enchanted Prince. Or, at least, that was what Danielle seemed to be doing, unless she had simply been using Jim to make Dafydd, her future husband at that time, jealous.

Magic and everything to do with it in this world seemed to have the same sort of attraction for its inhabitants as lotteries had in the world Jim had grown up in and left. In both cases there was the dream of marvels, wonders and riches to be gained by even being close to someone with magic. No doubt, as with lotteries, the chances of gaining any of these things that magic promised were one in a million; nonetheless it was exciting even to be in the vicinity of such a possibility.

Hastily, Jim began to get into the armor, pausing only to eat from the bread and meat and drink from the wine that was being handed around to them. Liseth helped him put the armor on. It did not slow him down any to see that Herrac and his five sons were already armored, packed and on horseback, and Lachlan was almost armored and ready—in spite of being still somewhat drunk from the night before; and scowling at Jim and Liseth, for no apparent reason.

CHAPTER 17

T hey made, Jim had to admit, as they rode northward with the rising sun of morning to their right, a pretty effective-looking band. He had read once, in an excellent book on the Scottish Border, how most Borderers could put an armed force out of bed in the middle of the night and into the saddle, ready for the hot pursuit of raiders who had driven off their cattle, within something like twenty minutes or so.

He, himself, was riding in the lead of the little troop, which went two by two where it could on the trail they followed, and single file where the way was narrow. Beside him was Sir Herrac, who bulked enormous in his armor, on a large, heavy-headed war horse which seemed well able to carry its rider, plus its own armor of hanging mail.

Jim had not sought out this position; but had found it made available to him, so obviously that he had no choice but to take it up.

The truth of the matter was, he thought to himself, that he was once more in the grasp of that almost ridiculous fourteenth-century method of assuming that those of highest rank should naturally lead—officially, at least, in any time and at any place. Particularly when the proceeding was toward possible battle.

Right behind him rode Lachlan and Sir Giles, both of whom he knew had more right to be up front here than himself. For that matter, Dafydd also should have been riding ahead of him—but it was unthinkable, of course, that a bowman should lead belted knights, under any circumstances.

The trouble was, that in this upcoming ambush of theirs, they, all of them—even including an old, experienced warrior like Herrac, who knew these woods—would still expect him, Jim, to command the fight on their side. And all because he'd been idiot enough when he first landed on this world to claim that he was a baron, thinking it would be a help.

That claim had got him into more trouble since than all the help it could possibly have afforded him.

He rode along with his face apparently serene, but his mind whirling inside. What he knew about ambushes you could put in a thimble and still not see with a microscope. Particularly, ambushes involving fourteenth-century weapons and fighters.

Damn it, he thought to himself, he should have had time before they set out to contact Snorrl again and alert him about the ambush. Also time, above all, to meet with the Little Men once more and somehow get them committed to join in the final battle against the Hollow Men. It was typical of the people riding with him that they did almost all things wrong end to.

Even Herrac, here, was setting out to kidnap an envoy and a chest of gold belonging to the King of Scotland, without even having bothered to check with his fellow Borderers, to see if they would help in the battle that was planned to result from the kidnapping.

Jim wished very much that he could talk to Lachlan MacGreggor and find out from that individual what kind of plans the Scotsman had originally had for the ambush. But there was no polite way to fall back from riding at Herrac's side, at this moment. He would just have to be patient until they stopped for some kind of a break, or finally reached the place that was to be their destination.

It turned out to be waiting until they reached their destination. There were no breaks along the way that allowed him any chance at an extended conversation with Lachlan. In the end, Jim was forced to hold himself in until they had reached the spot on the trail which Lachlan had picked for the ambush.

They were a little off the trail. Not so much in a clearing, as in a spot where the pines around them were not growing too thickly. Yet there was room to unsaddle the horses, and sit down together; to help themselves to some of the bread, meat and wine Herrac had had brought along on a baggage horse.

"Well, you've seen the place now," said Lachlan, once they had eaten and were comfortably into their wine. "It's a bonny spot, is it not?"

Jim had to admit it was.

The trail they had been following—his companions spoke of it as a road; but since nothing had been done to make it into a road, Jim thought of it as a trail—was simply a track worn into the earth. A wagon might have gotten down it; but it would have had to have been a very thin wagon. In fact, the trail, as Jim persisted in thinking of it, was really fit only for a couple of horsemen riding abreast as they had been.

For some distance before they had reached their present position and ahead of them as far as Jim could see, the land through which the trail ran was fairly level. However, from where they were now, for some seventy-five to a hundred yards before and about the same distance behind them, the ground sloped upward on either side away from the trail. Both sides were thickly treed; as had been most of the landscape through which they had passed just recently.

The angle of either slope was not remarkable. On this side, they were no more than twenty yards from the trail, and the ground they stood on could be no more than three or four feet higher than the trail itself. It was thickly covered with pine needles, however, which made even the hoof-strikes of the horses almost soundless; and on foot a man could move noiselessly, indeed.

They had not lit a fire, first because the day was warm enough not to require it, and secondly because they did not want to advertise their presence. Moreover, the sun was now at noon overhead, and its heat was enough to make Jim, at least, uncomfortable inside his gambeson and armor. His companions—just as Brian and Dafydd had seemed indifferent to the chill on their way up to the Castle de Mer—now seemed indifferent also to the warmth of the day.

Temperatures, apparently, from a fourteenth-century point of view, were something over which you had no control; so, when there was no way of alleviating them either with clothes or walls, you simply ignored them. As the Greeks of classical times were said to have done with headaches.

"There's no sign of anyone approaching, down the road," said Herrac. "Therefore, I think they will not come for a while at least. In fact, I would think that they might well be several hours from us yet. If we have not seen them by the time the sun is westering, I would assume that we will also not see them until tomorrow. What is your counsel on that, Lachlan?"

"You're right enough," said Lachlan. "They'll cease their travel as the day darkens and chills; and set up camp for the night. The MacDougall was ever a man who liked his comfort. He'll want a fire going and food and wine at his elbow, well before sunset."

"As I thought," said Herrac. "Therefore, we have time to become settled about our plans. What're your commands, m'Lord?"

There it was, thought Jim fatalistically. He was in charge whether he liked it or not. Perhaps the others would have wisdom enough to give him reasons why what he told them to do was not practical. He hoped so. A thought occurred to him.

There was one thing he was allowed, as leader. It was that, in typical leadership fashion, he could call for the opinions of those who would be fighting with him. Normally, this would mean sampling the opinions only of those who were sub-leaders. But since they were too small in numbers to really have more than one leader, everybody could be invited to have his say.

"I must know something more about the situation, before I decide specifically what we should do," said Jim. "Lachlan, perhaps you'll tell me what you had in mind?"

"Why, I'd have told you, anyhow," said Lachlan, who was sitting beside him. They were in a rough circle seated cross-legged on the pine needles. "They'll be riding two and two, down the road, with the MacDougall in the lead, with—it might be—a sumpter horse behind him; and then, it might be, the six or eight armed men he'll have with him, mounted, with one or two horses carrying the gold in their midst. At a signal, we charge on foot down upon them—"

He turned to Herrac.

"You'll have seen me do this in wee fights we've been in together before," he said to Herrac. "It's a matter of ducking under the bellies of the horses, ripping those bellies up with our daggers—and out with us, the other side. The horses will rear, and most of their riders will go off them. Those that hit the ground will be fairly easy for the killing. The MacDougall himself is likely to do little, if once his men are taken down. But one of us should go ahead to bar the road before him, lest he take off at a gallop with the sumpter horse and maybe the horses carrying the gold as well, and we, unhorsed, are left behind."

"Well—" began Jim, but he was interrupted by Herrac.

"Are you suggesting," said Herrac; and, although his voice was not raised more than a little, it seemed to roll ominously forth under the shadow of the pines, "that we others also descend from our horses to attack on *foot*?"

"We'll do a deal better that way," said Lachlan.

"I had thought you knew better what knighthood implied!" said Herrac. "When I took my vows to be belted knight, it was not to leave lance and horse behind me and fight on foot like any common man-at-arms! Nor was it to duck under a horse's belly and slice open his guts like any naked Heilandman! When I fight, I fight as a man and a knight should, on horseback, shield to shield and sword to sword, if there is not room for lance-work. And so shall fight my sons."

"And so say I also, Father!" cried Giles.

"Ah, you're become as foolish as the English theirselves!" cried Lachlan in disgust. "And you call yourselves Northumbrians!"

There seemed to be the nucleus of a fair-sized quarrel threatening to break out between two of the most important members of the expedition. Jim hastily spoke up to deflect the controversy.

"I make it a point," he said, "not to ignore any experienced man's words. It may, indeed, turn out that we will fight in several different ways. And if Lachlan's way is the most effective for him, certainly he, at least, should fight that way—"

He looked around the circle of faces.

"Meanwhile," he asked, "what is the opinion of the others here?"

"There's one here whose opinion is made up for him already," said Herrac. "Lachlan, you warrant this MacDougall is harmless?"

"If y'mean by that he'll nae fight if his men are slain," said Lachlan, suddenly back into his accent, "there's nae doot to it. If y'mean a knife in the ribs when ye're not looking, why then, he's up to it. Have no fear."

Herrac turned to look at his youngest son.

"Christopher," he said, "you will be the one to sit your horse and bar MacDougall's way. Understand, you sit, only. You make no attempt to close with him!"

Christopher did not smile. Lachlan also turned to him.

"Christopher," he said, "big as you are, for all your youth, in armor and with lance leveled ye'll hold the MacDougall as well as an army."

The sixteen-year-old son of Herrac had the appearance of someone who would like to look sour, but dared not with his father's eye upon him.

"Yes, sir," he said wearily. "It's understood, Father."

"Mind you just sit your horse, though!" said Lachlan. "For if ye make a move toward him, he may well feel he has no choice but to fight for his life. Then, my lad, you may find yourself facing a man of some experience, weight and skill. I'd not give you a chance, then. But sit your horse, tall as ye are, not moving, lance leveled and visor down—and he'll never doubt but what ye're one of the paladins of Arthur's Round Table, brought back to life to face him."

Christopher allowed a slight smile to creep onto his otherwise unhappy face.

"Well," said Herrac, "it seems that Lachlan here will only fight on foot; and I and my sons will only fight a horseback. How does this affect what plans you had in mind, m'Lord?"

Jim decided to run a little test.

"You mean to tell me," he said sternly to Herrac, "if I commanded you to fight on foot, you and your sons would not do so?"

"Sir James," said Herrac, looking directly back at him—and there was a world of meaning in the difference that he used Jim's knightly title rather than addressing him as m'Lord, "I am a knight, and have my knightly honor to consider; and the honor of my sons rides with me. We will not fight on foot."

Well, thought Jim, that was that. He had grown experienced in having the door of medieval custom slammed in his face. It was plain Herrac meant exactly what he said. That meant he would stand behind it with his life.

"It ill beseems it," the soft but carrying voice of Dafydd broke the silence, which was beginning to threaten to be awkward, "for an archer to speak up in such a company of gentles. But I feel I would be wrong not to point out that, hidden by the trees and at such close range as is possible here, I could almost offer to empty all six or eight saddles without any of the rest of you stirring hand or foot."

This statement gave rise to a new silence. Jim saw that it would be necessary for him to actually take command, or else the whole expedition would disintegrate.

"Very well," he said hastily. "These, then, are my orders. Lachlan, you will go in as you described, dagger in hand, beneath the bellies of two of the horses and out the other side. But I direct you to attack, not one of the horses belonging to one of the riders, but the one or two that seem to be carrying the gold. If you cut their girths and even half their gold is dumped in the road, those we fight will be less likely to try to abandon it. Meanwhile—"

He turned to Herrac.

"You, Sir Herrac and your sons," he said, "will attack on horseback, as you wish, directly at the riders. But with Christopher barring the way, there are only five of you, and myself, and I gather it's likely there will be at least six of them. I have no doubt that you consider yourselves more than equal to those six, by yourselves. Nonetheless, I am more concerned with winning the day, than with how little force we win it."

He paused to take a long breath.

"Therefore, you, Dafydd," he went on, "will take up post in the woods; and before anyone else moves you will clear as many saddles as you can with your arrows. Sir Herrac, you and your sons will ride the moment Dafydd's arrows have been discharged. Lachlan, you will move at the same time, counting on the turmoil of the assault by the others to distract attention from the horses carrying the gold. Are all things understood?"

He was careful not to ask if his commands were agreeable to the others, but to take it for granted that they would be. In fact, this worked to perfection. No voices were raised against what he had said. Instead both Lachlan and Sir Herrac nodded. Dafydd merely smiled.

"Well now!" said Lachlan cheerfully, reaching for the wine skin. "It only remains for us to wait their arrival. For my part, I consider that gold as good as in our hands."

He began pouring wine into everybody's cups.

But, as it turned out, Herrac was a true prophet. MacDougall and his train did not pass until about mid-morning of the next day.

What caught the eyes of those in ambush, first, the next day as they waited just inside the screen of the first trees beside the trail, was a flash of gold coming toward them farther up it, and still out in level territory. But the flash was not of the gold with which the Hollow Men would be paid; but of gold facings on the surcoat over the armor of the lead rider in the procession.

That flash of gold, and the arms beneath it—which Lachlan immediately identified as the MacDougall arms—not even counting the pennant flying from the upright staff beside the sur-coated man's saddle, announced that their quarry approached.

They stood where they were, hidden by the trees, watching until the MacDougall's group was only some thirty or forty yards from the beginning of the area where the ground swelled on either side. Then Jim turned to the others.

"Christopher," he said to the youngest de Mer, "you had better move up the trail at least a dozen yards, and stay out of sight until after the attack. At the moment of the attack, and only then, move out to bar the trail ahead."

He turned to Herrac and Sir Giles.

"Sir Herrac, Sir Giles," he said, "you and your fellow riders should pick a position well toward the rear, since you will need room to build up speed for your charge, though that will be dif-ficult in an area treed this quickly. I leave it up to you to choose less distance and a clear route to the trail, or more distance and the need to weave around trees in making your approach.

"Lachlan," he said to the Scotsman beside him, who had already stripped down to his kilt, and looked of a mind to get rid of that too, including sword, shield and all else but his naked poignard, to be carried by the hand of his naked right arm against the enemy.

Lachlan glanced up at him.

"Lachlan," he said, "you should be closest to the trail of all, since you are less likely to be seen than armored men on horse-back. You can hide quite well behind a tree, even if part of you is showing, and you must have a short dash to the trail in order to be sure you strike the part where the gold-carrying horse or horses are, whether they are in the midst of the guards, or not."

"Well, now . . ." Lachlan said with unusual slowness.

"If you will forgive me, Sir James," said Herrac, "Lachlan being as he is, and I knowing him as well as I do, I believe it would be best if, instead of being closest to the trail, he is furthest from it."

"Aye!" said Lachlan hastily. "Aye, have no fear that I can reach the train in time and at the right spot. But I must wait further back."

"Oh?" said Jim, puzzled. But, since neither Lachlan nor Herrac offered any further explanation of this he sensed that there was a reason which it was either uncomfortable or impolite to give at this moment; so he wisely went along with it.

"Very well, Lachlan," he said, "pick your own spot. I trust you to do as you say. In that case though, since I was going to stay close to the trail with you, I will instead join you two, Sir Herrac and Sir Giles, if so please you."

"We will be honored, m'Lord," said Giles, so quickly that his father did not even have a chance to answer.

"Honored, indeed," growled Herrac, casting a reproving glance at Giles for taking the initiative in answering.

Those approaching drew closer. Jim, sitting his horse with the de Mers among the trees, was suddenly aware, from some distance behind him, of a faint sound. He could not really believe what he was hearing, so he listened closely. In a moment he heard it again; and the sound was unmistakable.

It was a hiccup.

He looked at Herrac, but that Border knight's massive face was stony and his eyes all on the trail. He gave no sign that he had heard anything himself.

He did not really need to answer, thought Jim to himself, abruptly. What he had heard was a hiccup and it was even farther back than this, and the only person who could be making that sound was Lachlan.

Apparently, something about being on the verge of getting into a fight caused Lachlan to break out in hiccups. That it was a sign of fear, Jim discounted without seriously considering the possibility. Lachlan was simply not the type to be afraid in a moment such as this. What it probably was, was a reaction to the excitement and tension of waiting. Nonetheless, it was interesting.

It was particularly interesting, because when he himself had had the hiccups back at the castle, from too much wine, and Lachlan had come in, Lachlan had expressed surprise, saying that Jim could hardly be drunken this early in the afternoon. It occurred to him now that possibly Lachlan thought that he had found someone else with the same disability; and that Jim might have just come into possession of some particularly exciting news.

In any case, there was little chance of the riders, who were now entering the section between the two slopes, hearing the hiccups. Even if they did, it was too odd a sound in too unlikely a place for them to either notice or be alarmed by it.

The MacDougall came on. He was a resplendent and handsome sight, sitting with ramrod back on a beautifully caparisoned, if also armored, horse. He was perhaps three horse-lengths in front of a man who seemed to be a groom, riding a small, very hairy horse with broad hooves and leading a much better-looking horse loaded with luggage. A horse-length or so behind the groom rode, two by two, the riders in half armor. There were, in fact, eight of them. Obviously they were the guards of the gold, which—as Lachlan had predicted—was in two ornate chests, one each side of a pack horse between the front four mounted guards and the back four.

Jim gave no signal, trusting to Dafydd to know when was the best time to shoot. Therefore it was that, ready as he thought himself, he was taken by surprise when suddenly the last four men, riding behind the chests on the horses, fell from their saddles; or leaned forward unnaturally against the necks of their mounts, with the shafts of arrows protruding from their backs.

Then, everything happened at once.

There was a wild yell from behind him, and a perfectly naked Lachlan ran past to his left, toward the road, leaving behind himself Herrac and his sons, who were just now getting their horses into movement.

Then the horses were in movement and things degenerated into the kind of blur that every armed fight that Jim had been in so far had fallen into.

His own horse, Gorp, blundered into a tree, so that he fell behind the de Mers. A moment or so later when he reached the trail, Herrac was in the process of almost literally hammering one of the guards into extinction, with his superior size and strength; and Giles was hotly asserting his superiority over the other man-at-arms.

Things at first glance looked well, but just then Jim noticed that one of the three other sons was already down; and, of the two who were left, both were being driven backward by the guards who had opposed them, for all the young men's size and strength.

It was simply a case of experience. Jim had no doubt that a father like Herrac would make sure his sons all practiced daily with their weapons, particularly in mock battle with each other.

But all the preparation in the world did not teach you half as much as actually getting into your first fight. Jim had found that out himself, the hard way.

Brian had continued to tell him that he was no more than at best a mediocre fighter, with fourteenth-century weapons. His lance-work was unmentionable, and he was no more than passable, at best, with any of the other arms. However, the one weapon he had given Jim some credit for being able to use effectively was the combination of broadsword and shield.

After a difficult time, Jim had finally learned the trick of tilting his shield to make an opponent's sword-slash glance off it. This, combined with a certain natural talent for the type of sword-work in which a broadsword is used more like a club than anything else, had finally brought Brian to the point of telling him that in an emergency these were the weapons he should use.

Though to be sure, events could change that choice, as they had in his legal duel with Sir Hugh de Bois de Malencontri, the former owner of Jim's castle. Then, Jim had won that fight with a long, two-handed sword; but only by taking advantage of the fact that Sir Hugh was somewhat overweight and that he, Jim, had unusual spring and strength in his legs.

Lachlan had successfully cut the girths of both the horses carrying the chests, so that both chests lay on the ground; and was dancing, naked and poignard in hand, around MacDougall's groom, who had produced a short-handed battle ax from somewhere among his clothing.

But the next to the youngest son of Herrac's was near to being beaten from his saddle by his opponent, and was in dire need of help; which his brother was not free to give to him— nor indeed was Herrac nor Giles.

The excitement of the moment came to a sudden boil in Jim. With a blood-curdling whoop, he stuck his spurs into Gorp and charged on the horse into the attack, to the rescue of the endangered son.

CHAPTER 18

Jim cannoned into the man-at-arms who was driving back William de Mer, at the same time getting in a blow with his sword hard enough to send the man-at-arms halfway out of his saddle. The collision came with both his own weight and that of Gorp—who was not only a good-sized horse; but, furthermore, outraged. Jim had never stuck spurs into him before. Wanting to get back at somebody—anybody—he screamed and struck out at the smaller horse of the man-at-arms with his front hooves, almost as if he had been a properly trained war horse.

Jim had no time to appreciate this, however, since he was busy fighting with the man-at-arms himself. The other regained his saddle; but, so unexpectedly caught by a second opponent, and particularly by one who was standing up on his stirrups and hitting down at him from a slightly larger horse, found himself suddenly on the defensive.

He switched his attention completely from William, who drifted off, clinging to his horse; while his former opponent did his best to turn matters into a duel directly between Jim and himself.

If Jim had not been so carried away—it struck him later that some of Lachlan's enthusiasm might have gotten through to him, because there was something oddly terrifying about a naked, armed man charging a line of armored enemies—he might not have done so well. As it was, however, Jim simply proceeded to overpower the man-at-arms, hammering him out of the saddle, Herrac-style.

Suddenly, the small battlefield was still. Horses and men alike were standing, or sitting panting, or lying on the ground. And nobody stirred until Herrac leaped from his saddle like a twenty-year-old and ran to the son who had been knocked out of his saddle.

"Alan!" he cried on a note of anguish. He fell to his knees beside the young man and lifted the limp head onto his knee. "Alan—"

His thick fingers tremblingly began to unlace the binding of Alan's helmet. He got it off at last to show the young man's face, paper-white, and his eyes closed.

Jim felt a sudden, ugly emptiness. Alan was the oldest son. To Herrac, the death of his first-born son would be unusually severe; unconsciously as well as consciously these many years, he had been planning for and training Alan to succeed him as master of the castle and its lands.

Jim got down from his horse, pushed his way past Lachlan and the other sons and knelt on the other side of Alan. He held his hands over the slackly open mouth and smiled across at Herrac, who was holding Alan's head and rocking back and forth like a tower of doom about to fall on anything nearby.

"He's breathing," said Jim.

Herrac burst into tears.

Once upon a time the sight of such a man crying would have been shocking to Jim; but he had found out long since that both men and women of the fourteenth century cried as easily as children. And certainly Herrac had reason to do so, on hearing that his son still lived.

"Help me!" said Jim to the sons. "Help me get his armor off him—gently. I'll see what I can do."

Hearing that a magician promised to use his efforts toward Alan brought the other sons, even including Sir Giles, out of the fascinated trance with which they had been staring at their brother. They clustered around Alan and gently began to get his armor off.

Jim carefully searched Alan's body with his hands, looking for any sign of a wound, but found none. He took the other's lax wrist and felt for a pulse. It was there, and regular but slow.

He frowned, but quickly erased the frown at the flash of sudden fear in Herrac's eyes.

"Alan seems perfectly unhurt," said Jim. "The only danger could possibly be concussion . . ."

He lifted his head and looked at the two nearest brothers, those who had been next to Alan when they charged the men-at-arms.

"Did either of you see what happened to Alan? When was he hit by the man-at-arms he rode against?"

"The man-at-arms hit him once," said Hector, one of the two spoken to. "It did not look like a hard blow to me, Sir James, but Alan fell immediately out of his saddle."

"Hmm . . ." said Jim.

His fingers explored the skull beneath the unruly hair of Alan's head, now springing back into shape since the helmet had been removed that had squashed it flat temporarily.

"It could be a concussion," he said again. The other thought that was in his mind was that there might be something about Alan himself that had caused him to go into a faint on being hit. But since this took him into an area of medicine about which he knew nothing at all, and besides could only frighten the de Mer family without offering any comfort or reassurance, he said nothing about it.

"Bring me some water or wine," Jim said.

It was brought. Jim made a few passes over it with one hand, while muttering under his breath, for the general purpose of cheering his audience with the thought that something magical in addition to the ordinary moistening of skin was at work here. Then he took one of the wadded cloths that he carried in a very unfourteenth-century pocket Angie had sewn on the inside of his shirt, dipped it in the wine—it would be wine, after all, that they brought, of course, he thought—and carefully bathed Alan's face.

For a moment nothing happened; then as the damp cloth continued to moisten the wan features, Alan's eyes flickered and opened.

"What—what is it?" he muttered confusedly. "Father—I mean—Sir, where am I?"

"On your back on the ground, laddie," said Lachlan loudly, "after being knocked out by one of the MacDougall's men. Y'recollect that now?"

"Yes . . . yes . . . I remember." Alan's eyes looked around him, and fastened on his father. Herrac darted forth a hand and caught the nearest hand of his eldest son.

"Alan!" he said. "You're all right!"

"Why, yes, Father," said Alan. "I never felt better in my life. Forgive me for lying down like this to talk to you—"

He sat up and suddenly clutched at his head with both hands.

"What is it!" cried Herrac.

"A headache, Father . . ." said Alan between his teeth. "A headache I did not expect, that is all."

Jim took hold of the young man's shoulders and pushed them gently back to the ground.

"Lie still for a while longer," he said. "Someone fetch me a jacket or something from one of those dead men or prisoners of ours." He was a little surprised even as he spoke to hear the callousness of his own voice. But a couple of years here had changed him. "Then bring me any other coverings you can find, so that we can keep Alan warm for a little while while he lies still. We'll wait and see if that headache doesn't get better."

"It's nothing, Sir James," said Alan on the ground. "I'm ashamed to have mentioned it. Let me up—"

"Stay where you are!" said Herrac. "Whatever Sir James says, do!"

"Yes, Father," said Alan, lying back against the roll of unidentifiable cloth that had been placed under his head by one of his brothers.

These others were now busily undressing both the dead men and the groom, who was not dead but had one arm hanging limply; and his ax was stuck in a tree about ten feet from the road, as if it had been thrown there by a practiced hand— undoubtedly Lachlan's.

"Sir Herrac," said Jim, getting to his feet, "perhaps you'd be good enough to stay with Alan for the moment, while the rest of us look into other things that need to be done here? Lachlan, I think we should talk to this MacDougall."

"Aye. That we should!" said Lachlan, with what Jim could only interpret as a very evil grin. Lachlan was testing the point of his poignard with his other hand.

"I said 'talk' only!" said Jim. "Come along with me. You too, Giles."

Leaving Sir Herrac with Alan and his other sons, Jim walked forward to the MacDougall, who was still sitting his horse and facing forward toward a motionless, gleaming, iron figure that was young Christopher. The sixteen-year-old had kept his word. He looked to have not moved a muscle; and to Jim, now on foot as they moved toward him to reach MacDougall, Herrac's youngest son did indeed make a dangerous-looking sight, blocking the trail with leveled lance.

They reached the man in the golden surcoat. He turned his head to look down at the two of them.

"Well now, Ewen," said Lachlan, in a tone of satisfaction before Jim could get a word in edgewise. "It looks like you'll be paying us a visit!"

"Sir," said Jim, "whatever your rank—"

"He's called one of these new-fangled Viscounts," Lachlan put in.

"M'Lord MacDougall," said Jim, "I am Sir James Eckert, Baron de Bois de Malencontri. You are my prisoner. Step down from that horse."

"And most quickly, Ewen," said Lachlan, testing the point of his poignard again. "Ah, but I'd much recommend that you do so with speed."

MacDougall swung down from his horse, however, in leisurely fashion. Standing, he made less of an impressive figure, since he was a good four inches shorter than Jim, and at least two inches shorter than Lachlan. But his thin face with the high cheek bones was heavily marked with contempt.

"There are footpads on every road these days, it seems," he murmured and his hand slid in under his surcoat. The point of Lachlan's poignard was immediately at his throat; and his hand stopped.

"It was a kerchief only I was reaching for," said MacDougall softly, slowly pulling out a wispy piece of cloth that would seem more likely to be carried by a woman. A faint scent of perfume wafted from it. "There seems a damned smell around here, for some reason."

"Go on like that," said Lachlan dangerously, "and you'll have no nose to smell with. Did you pay no attention to the name of the man who holds you prisoner? It's Sir James Eckert— the Dragon Knight."

Jim was completely unprepared for the result these words produced. MacDougall's composure fell apart.

"The—Dragon Knight?" stammered MacDougall. "The . . . the sorcerer?"

"MAGICIAN!" exploded Jim, suddenly unreasonably angry. "The next man that uses the word 'sorcerer' to me is going to wish he hadn't!"

"Yes, yes, Sir James!" said MacDougall in a trembling voice. His face had gone as white as Alan's had been when his helmet had been taken off. "Of course, m'Lord Magician. I am your prisoner, of course. What is your will?"

Jim thought quickly. He glanced back at the knot of de Mers still clustered around the fallen Alan. The MacDougall could not have got a close enough look at Herrac and his sons to know who they were, and the less he knew the better, if he was going to go on living. Jim turned back to Lachlan.

"Lachlan," he said, "would you take m'Lord the Viscount here into your special care? We will be leaving this place as soon as all is ready. I don't see even the groom on his feet. Is he or any of the men-at-arms still alive but too hurt to travel?"

"Nae more!" said Lachlan, with that fierce grin again. "I cut all their throats. With any luck it'll be thought a band of thieving cattle lifters robbed and slew in this place, when the bodies are found."

Jim suppressed a shudder. It was the kind of butchery that was completely at odds with his twentieth-century nature; but it was the way things were done here. Any prisoners who were valuable, in terms of ransom or otherwise, you brought along. Any who had no particular worth were simply slain, since you had no provision for keeping them; and could not trust them if you did.

"Very well, then," said Jim, again. "Keep m'Lord with you. I'll go forward and get the knight we've had standing guard upon him until now. Keep your prisoner well away from the rest of us. You understand?"

He had referred to Christopher as a "knight" deliberately, to make MacDougall feel better about letting himself be held here. But it did not seem to cheer the other up visibly.

"Was I born in the last hour?" said Lachlan disdainfully. "Weel, I understand!"

"Good, then," said Jim, and left Lachlan and the MacDougall behind him while he walked forward to where Christopher sat his horse. Christopher did not move as Jim came directly up to him. Jim paused and laid a hand on the iron knee of the youth.

"You did well, Christopher," he said in a low voice.

"I didn't stir, Sir," boomed Christopher inside his helmet. "Just as Father said."

"Keep your voice down," said Jim, still keeping his own tones low. "There's no reason why our prisoner in the golden surcoat behind us should know who any of us are besides Lachlan and myself. You're free of your duty now. Ride on back and join your father and your brothers around Alan. Tell him to send another one of you in armor, and with his visor down, to let me know when Alan's ready to ride."

He thought of something just in time.

"I mean *really* ready to ride, not just braving it out. His headache had better have much lessened, before he even tries to get onto his feet; and at any sign of dizziness he should lie down again. Then he's to ride at a walk; and others of you stay with him until he gets back to the castle. Then he's to be helped immediately to bed, and stay there. Those are my orders as a magician. Can you tell your father that, word for word?"

"Word for word, Sir," said Christopher, in a lowered voice.

Jim had no cause to doubt him. In this period when written messages were almost unknown, except in Latin, as penned by members of the religious establishment, most messages were verbal ones, which the messenger was trusted to carry and deliver without variation to the one who was ultimately supposed to hear it. It was necessary; and consequently most people could do it. Jim had little doubt that Christopher would be word-perfect, as he said, in repeating Jim's message to Herrac.

"Very well, then," said Jim. "Further, tell your father that Lachlan and I, with our prisoner, will either follow or precede you by enough distance so there's no reason for the MacDougall to guess who you are. There's no point in bringing trouble upon Castle de Mer. In fact, Lachlan and I may well not return there; but camp out with the prisoner at least for one night and possibly more. We'll get in touch with Sir Herrac when the time comes. Meanwhile, he should see about whether his Borderers will gather and join forces with the Little Men, should I be able to get the Little Men to come into a fight on our side with all of the Hollow Men."

"That, too, m'Lord," said Christopher. "I will most faithfully tell him."

"Good," said Jim. "Now circle around through the trees and back to your father, and I'll walk back to get my horse. Then I and the MacDougall will remount our horses. Lachlan can get his clothes back on and also remount. Then I'll decide what the three of us will do."

It was a good half-hour or more before Alan was actually able to be helped on his horse and ride. Meanwhile, Herrac's other sons had converted two of the horses of the dead men-at-arms into beasts of burden for the chests of gold the packhorses had been carrying; before they had run off after Lachlan had ducked beneath them and cut their girths.

Also, meanwhile, Lachlan himself had gone back in the woods, regained his clothing and weapons and mounted to rejoin Jim with MacDougall; who had apparently been too afraid of Jim all this time to attempt to make any kind of conversation.

Jim was just as glad not to be talked to for a few minutes. He was busily thinking of what should be done next. He must first get away on his own and he must contact the wolf Snorrl. Also Liseth—no one else but Liseth could lead him to the Little Men—so that he could ask their help in fighting with the Borderers in the final battle with the Hollow Men.

He suspected that Lachlan would not take too cheerfully to the idea of mounting guard on the prisoner alone, while Jim was gone for several days. Lachlan was much too likely to slip his poignard between the other's ribs and save himself any further bother with the man they had captured.

These were not easy questions to answer. Lachlan would take orders only to a degree; in no sense with the obedience of Herrac's sons—and even Herrac, himself.

About one thing Jim was determined. They would not go back to the castle. He would have to think of how to break the news of this to Lachlan. Luckily, he had a little time before that would become necessary. They would have to follow Herrac and his sons for some distance back toward the castle before parting ways with them, in any case. When they at last did so, it would be time enough to let the Scotsman know that they were not going all the way. Lachlan could well not be pleased at the prospect of probably spending several days in the woods with their prisoner.

But for now, he, Lachlan, with MacDougall, back on their horses, merely moved off into the woods to let Herrac and his sons ride back past them down the track that Jim still thought of as a trail, then followed. This, they did.

Lachlan, Jim assumed, would be in agreement with the idea of keeping MacDougall in ignorance of who besides Jim and himself had slain MacDougall's guard and taken the gold with which he had been sent to bribe the Hollow Men. Consequently Lachlan said nothing as they watched the de Mer family go by them and get a good distance ahead of them, more than far enough for them to be unrecognizable in their armor to MacDougall.

Then, he, Jim and MacDougall began to follow. It had been a ride of another six hours coming out to the spot where they had waylaid the golden-surcoated clan chief. It took even longer going back, since Alan was obeying orders and riding at a slow walk, which meant the rest were doing the same.

Consequently, it was getting on to late afternoon by the time they reached the point where Jim began to feel that they should part company with Herrac and his sons; and the trees, which now stood less thickly around the trail, were throwing long shadows at a slant toward the still invisible seashore against which Castle de Mer was built. Jim had still not worked out anything that he thought would be a foolproof argument with Lachlan. But he had to break the news, anyway, so he simply dived into it.

"Lachlan," he said, "I think we'll tie our prisoner to a tree, after taking him off his horse; so that we can be sure that he won't get loose in under ten—or fifteen—minutes anyway. Then you and I are going to step off a little ways and talk."

Lachlan smiled his evil smile, looked at the MacDougall and winked. The wink was obviously intended to promise all sorts of unwelcome things to be done upon the body of MacDougall with the edged weapons at Lachlan's disposal. But for all Jim could see, the unvoiced threat bounced off their prisoner without doing anything more than stirring his attention for a second.

So far, MacDougall had not said a word. He continued silent as they turned off the track and found a tree about a foot in diameter, and all of them got off their horses.

Lachlan, himself, took on the job of tying MacDougall's hands behind him around the trunk of the tree. It was obvious to Jim, although MacDougall did not allow the wince to show in his face, that Lachlan was pulling the leather thongs of the bindings cruelly tight. But Jim said nothing; and MacDougall neither spoke nor showed by his expression that anything at all uncomfortable was being done to him.

"Weel, now," said Lachlan, standing back and regarding his handiwork. "That should keep you for a while, Ewen."

"You know," drawled the MacDougall, "you used to be able to speak quite passable English. What would have caused you to have lost the ability, I wonder?"

"Och!" said Lachlan. "Ye're mistaken. This is the way I talk all the time. Because I'm a Scotsman, all the way through. While you, y'rself, are half-French and half-English inside."

MacDougall ignored this; and Jim led Lachlan off in among the trees until they were well out of hearing, but their prisoner was still in sight. They had led all three horses along with them; so that even if MacDougall got loose, they could run him down.

"Well, now," said Lachlan, with no trace of a Scots accent in his voice at all, "what is it you've got in mind?"

"I'll tell you," said Jim. "I think this is as close as we should get to the Castle de Mer. You, and I and our prisoner back there."

"As close?" echoed Lachlan, staring at him. "Now why would you say that?"

"Well," said Jim, "we don't want him recognizing the Castle de Mer and identifying Sir Herrac and his family, do we?"

"Not if we can help it!" said Lachlan. "But if that's the only problem, we can cut his throat right now and have it done with. I thought you'd some reason in mind for bringing him along this distance, anyway."

"I have," said Jim. "Remember? I was going to use magic to make myself look like him."

"Well, then, what's keeping you from it?" exploded Lachlan. "Make yourself look like him, then; and have it done with!"

"I'm afraid it can't be done just that fast," said Jim. He began to feel a little uneasy. He had a good two inches of height on Lachlan, if it came to an argument and a fight, and possibly ten or fifteen pounds heavier. But he was not at all sure that he was any physical match for the other. Lachlan's shoulders were almost unnaturally broad; and his skill with the weapons hung about him would undoubtedly be something Jim himself could never match. This was a situation to be won by diplomacy.

"You have to understand," said Jim, "it's not enough for me to look like the man, merely. I also must sound and act like him; with the same sort of movements and gestures, and ways of standing and sitting and walking—just in case some of the Hollow Men may have met with him before and know what he's like."

"Now, if you move and talk a little different from him than they remember, what of that?" demanded Lachlan. "If you look like the man, you are the man. Why should they question any further than that?"

"I think you underestimate the Hollow Men, Lachlan," said Jim.

"I do not!" snapped Lachlan.

"Permit me," said Jim. "No offense. It's just that, being a magician, I understand some things that ordinary people don't. These Hollow Men are not ordinary people, themselves. Effectively, they're ghosts. The possibility of the body of a man they know being taken over by someone else might not occur to you, as long as he looked exactly the same. But it could well occur to one of them. There's only a single way around it I can see. I'll have to stay with him a day, perhaps, and study him."

"Perhaps, yes," said Lachlan—and then brightened up. "And perhaps, no. Come to think of it, I can tell you how the man walks and talks and sits. Haven't I seen him a matter of years now at the court and other such gatherings? All you need to know you can learn from me. There's no need for Ewen, himself, at all."

"I'm sorry," said Jim firmly, "but there is. I'm very glad to hear you can tell me all this; and it may make all the difference, your being able to do so. But I must also watch him with my own eyes for a little while. That means we stay out in the woods with him. Now, what I wanted to ask you was—do you know of some kind of shelter near here where we could put up for a day or so?"

Lachlan looked at the ground for a long moment, without answering. Then he raised his eyes to meet Jim's.

"Yes," he said. "I'd have no wits at all if I wasn't ready to admit you've some right on your side. Very well, we'll spend our day or so in the woods; and I do know a place for it. It's a bit of a distance and a bit of a climb, but I know of a sheiling that has a hut on it. A hut that will at least keep the rain off us; and let us build a fire to warm ourselves without having the wind blow all its warmth away. Let's go back, untie Ewen and all remount."

They did so. It took them more than an hour to reach their destination. By this time, the sun was almost on the horizon, and the last half-hour of that had been considerably more than what Jim considered a bit of a climb; considering they had to dismount and almost pull the horses up after them for short stretches.

But when they came at last to the up-land pasture—because that, Jim had learned, was what a sheiling was—there were no cattle on it yet. Also, a small hut did indeed stand back in a little hollow against the face of the slanting meadow, itself, so that the hill protected it from the wind on three sides.

"Well, now," said Lachlan, cheerfully rubbing his hands together as they started across the meadow toward the hut. "Now we'll see what's what."

CHAPTER 19

The hut, when they got inside it, proved to be a rude shelter indeed.

It was no more than a door, four walls and a roof; with a smoke hole in the ceiling above a firepit in the earthen floor beneath.

It was filthy, and it stank—things Jim had gotten used to in dwellings on this world a great deal grander than this— including some castles he had been in. However, some months without an occupant had lessened the stink, which was a combination of human body odors, raw cattle hides, and half a dozen other nameless smells. And the filth was dirt only. Jim considered them lucky. The place could have had far more repellent substances about its floor than that.

They tied their horses to stakes set in the clay wall of the hut for that purpose, and carried the gear inside. Lachlan's first step was to use a good length of rope to hobble the feet of Ewen MacDougall.

The MacDougall clan chief had been silent through most of the trip. He seemed to have lost his immediate first terror at learning that it was Jim who had made him prisoner. But he was obviously still cautious; and further, plainly intended to give away nothing. He answered only when a direct question was addressed to him, as a demand.

They got a fire going in the firepit, and luckily there was enough of a breeze above them so that most of its smoke was drawn out the smoke hole. With eyes watering only slightly, they settled themselves as close to the fire as possible and began to make a meal out of the meat and bread they had along with them. At Jim's order, they shared it with MacDougall; although Lachlan protested that this was a waste of good provender.

However, with the food down, Jim began to make an effort to talk to MacDougall.

"M'Lord Viscount," he said, blinking against the smoke of the fire, at Ewen MacDougall who was also blinking, "a little discussion between us will help us both. Now I know why you were headed as you were; and why you were carrying the gold you had with you. I know all about your plans. As it happens, they won't work. They'll end in ashes, like a house that's caught fire. But how much you're hurt by them will depend on how much you're willing to talk with me and work with me."

He waited, but MacDougall said nothing.

"Well?" demanded Jim. "Do you intend to talk openly with me, or not?"

"Och, ye're wasting time on the man!" said Lachlan disgustedly. "He hasn't the wit to understand what ye tell him. He still thinks it's a mighty thing he's doing; and his honor won't permit him to say a word."

"That can't be so," said Jim, keeping his tone as conciliatory as possible as he watched MacDougall.

"Wait and see!" said Lachlan. He opened the door of the hut and stamped outside, apparently indifferent to the fact that the moon was not even up and there was little to do outside there except take care of bodily necessities. Of course, thought Jim, the latter reason may have been why he had left them.

Jim went on trying to talk to MacDougall. But he did not answer. He was obviously very frightened of Jim, deep down; but he still would not cooperate. Meanwhile, Lachlan had come back in and Jim turned his attention to him.

"Lachlan," he said, "there's something I need to speak to you about out of this man's hearing. Could you make sure that he doesn't get into any trouble if the two of us leave him alone?"

"That I can," said Lachlan. He proceeded to use everything including the saddle girths from MacDougall's horse's saddle to tie the other to the frame of a bed that was little more than a wooden tray on the ground with some dried grass inside to soften it.

"Now," said Lachlan, standing back. "He'll do for a few minutes. But I'd not give him much more than a few before we come back, slippery callant that he is."

"Good," said Jim, and led the way outside, closing the door behind them.

By now, the moon had begun to show itself above the trees higher on the hill above the pasture. It shed very little light, being only approaching full, but it was better than the starlight only that had been available before. Jim led a few steps away from the hut and then turned toward the shadowy form and features of Lachlan, who had halted facing him.

"How am I to get him to talk?" Jim asked. "I have to study him—how he talks, how he walks, how he waves his hands. A dozen things. But the way he is now, I'm not going to learn anything."

"I could have told y'that!" said Lachlan disgustedly. "Ye'll never see such things in him up here on this sheiling. What ye must do is see him in something like the court setting he's used to; and there's no such thing near here like that, except Castle de Mer. Moreover, to see him as he normally struts and talks, he'll have to be let loose in most of the castle rooms, with only guards on the outer door to keep him from leaving the building."

"But that will involve the de Mers!" said Jim. "The very thing I don't want to do!"

"Ye've no choice," said Lachlan. "If ye want what ye say ye want, that's the only way to get it. Let him play the honored prisoner and you'll see all the ways of acting the man is capable of, including his flattery of Liseth, who will be the only gentlewoman within sight and hearing of him."

Jim stood silent, himself. But he could see no other way out.

"I could have told ye this from the start, if I'd understood what ye'd thought ye'd might be able to get out of him up here," said Lachlan. "He'll never show it here. For one thing, a wee cattle hut like this is no setting for him. Also, there's none of the type of gentles he's used to showing off to, unless he gets to the de Mers'. He'll have to go there, and he'll have to know he's there. We can solve that easily enough afterwards, with one thrust of a dagger."

Jim winced in the darkness. That was not the type of solution he was hoping to come up with.

"I still don't—" he was beginning.

"Be sensible, man!" said Lachlan exasperatedly. "It's a popinjay ye have in there, and popinjays only dance on the proper perch. It's not their nature to do anything else. Is there no way ye can understand that?"

Jim had encountered this sort of situation before. He had constantly to remind himself that he did not really know these people. Even after almost two years he did not know all about how they acted; or even a great deal about why they chose to act, when they did. In a case like this, he would simply have to trust Lachlan; and hope that somehow he could come up with a solution that would leave the MacDougall alive and still keep the de Mers from retribution at the hands of the King of Scotland.

"Very well," he said, "we'll go on down to the castle tomorrow, then."

"Now ye're talking some sense," said Lachlan. Turning away from him, the Scot went back into the hut. Jim followed.

MacDougall had made no attempt to get out of his bindings—which seemed to earn him Lachlan's contempt, instead of approval.

"He was always a poor play-toy of a man," Lachlan said to Jim. "He was afraid that we'd come in and find him half loose and maybe one of us would be annoyed enough at that to cut his throat right now. Well, we should get some sleep. But for all that he made no move while we were outside talking, it's best we take turns sleeping. Would ye care to go first on the bed, or shall I?"

"You first," Jim said. For one thing, he had no intention of lying down on that possibly verminous box of meadow-straw. For another, his mind was still churning, trying to come up with ideas to make his wild plans work. He had a general idea of what he wanted to do; from impersonating the MacDougall to arranging things so that all the Hollow Men had to be in that spot that Snorrl had found for him. But the details were something else again; and these hovered in a limbo full of question marks.

So he sat by the fire—or at least at a distance from it, where its smoke and heat were endurable, while Lachlan tumbled into the box of hay and was asleep within seconds.

Twice during the night Jim was given the chance to sleep while Lachlan stood watch. He rolled himself in his cloak, giving Lachlan the usual excuse that magician's requirements kept him from using anything like a bed, and twice he sat up watching a motionless, and occasionally sleeping, MacDougall; but when morning came he had still not come up with one useful idea beyond those he had had the night before.

As soon as the sun rose, they ate what was left of their food, cut the bonds of MacDougall and let him hobble around for a while until the effect of his cut-off circulation was restored, at least to the point of letting him get on a horse and ride.

They reached Castle de Mer just about noon, were welcomed by the whole family and immediately set down at the High Table with food and drink; including, at both Herrac's order and Jim's request, Ewen MacDougall.

In spite of the wine and the good food, and the relatively comfortable benches, after being tied hand and foot on an earth floor all night, it still took MacDougall the better part of an hour to thaw out and start acting as he might ordinarily have acted, if visiting in someone else's castle.

He began to talk with the de Mers, and in particular with Liseth, whom he evidently took to be possibly younger and much less intelligent and experienced than she was. In fact, he preened himself to her to such an extent that her brothers began to develop the beginnings of a dangerous scowl upon their faces. It was only Jim's giving an appealing look to Herrac, who was wise enough to understand what was going on, and Herrac's voiced order to his sons, that prevented trouble.

"Remember at all times, my children," he said, letting his large voice roll forth when there was a point of the conversation at which it was appropriate to do so, "that though m'Lord MacDougall here may be our prisoner, he is also a gentleman and a guest in this castle, and we must always show all courtesy to him. I know you will do this."

The sons understood—the implied command in Herrac's last line, if not the reasons for his ordering them to act as he had said.

Shortly after Herrac said this, Jim himself took advantage of the fact that he had more than enough food and drink to do him for the moment, and announced that he needed to talk to Liseth about Brian and look at his friend, and perhaps Sir Herrac would excuse them both from the table now.

Herrac was instantly obliging; and Liseth rose from her bench with alacrity. They went off, followed by MacDougall's disappointed eyes—fastened on Liseth, of course, rather than Jim.

"I do indeed want to know about Brian," said Jim, as they began their ascent of the winding staircase toward the invalid's room. "But I also want to make other plans with you. But to Brian, first. How has he been since I left? Also, were you able to change bandages every day; and how did the wound look each time you did?"

"We changed the bandages each morning, as you demonstrated, m'Lord," said Liseth. "The wound seems to be mending apace—indeed, with almost miraculous speed, thanks no doubt to your magic, Sir James. It hardly bleeds now, when the bandage is pulled loose—which is a marvel, considering it has only been a couple of days. There is no sign of the redness in the skin around it that you warned me to look for, either. Moreover, Sir Brian himself has become more lively; and more demanding of wine and something more than the soup we have been feeding him. In fact, I leave you to deal with his demands in that direction when we get upstairs."

"Thanks for warning me," said Jim grimly. Brian would indeed be starting to get restless, no matter what kind of shape his wound was in.

"I'll answer him on that matter, and perhaps even relent a little bit to allow him some wine, meat and bread," said Jim. "But I want to look at his wound first before I yield in any way to him on other things."

"We have discovered some young onions, already up and growing in a sheltered spot of the castle wall," commented Liseth, as they continued on up. "We might include those with whatever extra food you allow Sir Brian, as a special treat. They will be the first of the spring vegetables."

When she said this, Jim's own mouth began to water; and he felt a tremendous admiration for Liseth's calm proposal of this. Not only she, but whoever had discovered the onions, and everyone who had heard of them, must have shown an iron discipline in not leaping upon the first vegetables they had a chance to taste since the last of the winterstored root vegetables had been used up.

One of the things that had never occurred to him as a twentieth-century person, was how, in the middle ages, you missed vegetables—fresh vegetables, at least—for nearly nine months of the year. Then, when you did finally get to a vegetable, particularly one you liked, often its season was all too short.

He imagined that Liseth, and everyone else, had been giving a great deal of attention to the castle's vegetable gardens for some time. The servants who first discovered these onions might have been kept from immediately grubbing them up and eating them by the fear of what might happen to them if they did. Particularly if word got back to those two who were Lord and Lady of the castle.

But it would have taken real self-denial on Liseth's part— and she surely must have been the first one to hear about the onions—to suggest they be given only to Sir Brian. On the other hand, he reflected, honor had long since laid its iron hand upon her as strongly as upon the male members of the household.

Naturally the only wounded man in the castle should have first offering of the new vegetables. On the other hand, it would have been all too easy to invent some excuse for not giving them to him—possibly the argument that they might not be good for him just at the present moment.

"Hah!" shouted a fully awake Sir Brian, as Jim and Liseth came in through the door of his room. "You are returned, James! Come, let me kiss you!"

Jim endured this with the best possible composure. Brian, close friend that he was, still had about as much body odor as any other of the fourteenth-century individuals Jim came up against, and lying in the same bed for several days had not improved it. Nor his unshaven face.

"Now!" said Brian, releasing him. "Tell me all that has occurred."

Jim proceeded to do so, as he turned back the covers and began to uncover the wound. The bandage came loose with very little difficulty; and once the wound was uncovered, it only seeped blood in a few places. There was no sign of inflammation around the edges of the wound.

Jim was secretly astounded. It was true that the original slash, though long, had been hardly more than skin deep. But it was through skin that wrinkled with every movement, and for anything like this to heal this much in just a few days was literally unbelievable, particularly under the germ-laden conditions of the environment.

The wild thought crossed his mind that perhaps on this world people simply healed faster. But Liseth had been surprised also.

A more sensible—but still very farfetched—explanation came to him. Here, as it had been in his own fourteenth century, the only adults you saw were survivors. Probably for every grown person you saw there were four to five infants, children and teen-agers who had not survived to the age of twenty.

He knew that inheritance and accustomation could arm people to deal with exposure to germs and viruses that others could not stand. Back in his own castle, the local people could, with no trouble—though they much preferred at least small beer—drink the water from the castle well. The only time Jim had tried it he had trouble believing, even in remembrance, how sick he had gotten. Angie was always careful to boil any water that she and Jim were likely to encounter, not only in drinking but in cooking.

However, right here and now it was Brian's recovery that was the matter under consideration; and the patient clearly was aware of it.

"Well, what say you, James?" demanded Brian ebulliently. "I am practically healed, am I not? There is no reason why I cannot get up and join everyone else in the castle. If you like, I will not attempt to ride for a day or two; but it is really not necessary. I could take to the saddle right now if I had to."

"I've no doubt," said Jim, abandoning the story of what had been gone through to get the MacDougall, "that you could get up and ride if both arms and half of each leg was cut off. But that doesn't mean I'm going to let you. I need you whole, in no more than a couple of weeks; and that means I don't want you running into trouble, from the chafing of clothes against your hurt, or anything else—let alone riding a horse before I think you're ready to do."

"Come now, James—" Brian began.

"No, I mean it, Brian!" said Jim, interrupting him. "I will need you desperately in two weeks—or less, even! I will need you if you can only accompany me to advise. On my word as a gentleman and my status as a magician, I swear to you that you must do as I say for a little longer!"

Brian sagged back limply on the bed.

"James," he said pitifully, "you cannot know what it is like to lie here, hour after hour with these servants—" He interrupted himself to turn and apologize to Liseth. "Forgive me, m'Lady, no offense is meant to those under your command. It is simply that I must be up and around, or I will burst!"

Jim realized suddenly that the knight meant it; and against his better judgment, his will to resist crumbled.

"I'll tell you what, Brian," he said. "If you'll stay as you are, with a fresh dressing on your wound, moving as little as possible on the bed until dinner time, then we will come and carry you—"

"I need no carrying!" exclaimed Sir Brian.

"*Carry you*, I said." Jim raised his voice grimly. "—Let me finish—down the stairs to join the rest of us for dinner. Then, after dinner, perhaps you could move around a little bit. But with someone on either side of you; in case you find yourself weaker than you expect."

"I?" cried Sir Brian. "Weak? After a few hours in bed? That could not, will not and never will happen!"

"Nevertheless, those are the conditions," said Jim. "Do you agree to them?"

He held his breath. If Brian pushed any more, he might give in some more; and he was sure that in that case Brian would do himself more damage than could be easily repaired in time.

"Very well, James," said Sir Brian, "but I vow I had rather be put to the torture than spend even another afternoon in this bed, with these servitors!"

"Good!" said Jim, on a great exhalation of breath.

"Now, about some decent wine for me to drink—" Brian began.

"Yes, yes, we'll let you have some wine," said Jim. "But only a little, because you'll undoubtedly drink more with dinner and you'll have to watch yourself there and take only a little then, too. Do you understand?"

"Praise the Lord and Saint Stephen!" said Sir Brian. "Send one of these cattle for the wine right away, for I vow that I may perish of thirst before they get back, as fast as they run."

"You!" said Liseth, pointing at one of the servants. "A pitcher—"

"Half a pitcher," quickly interrupted Jim.

"Half a pitcher for Sir Brian!" said Liseth.

The man she had pointed at ran out.

Jim and Liseth stayed long enough to see Brian take his first deeply appreciative swallow of the wine brought by the servant.

Then Jim made excuses for both of them and they started back down the stairs again.

"Now," said Jim, when they were alone on the stairs, "as far as what you must do here at the castle and I must do outside it in the next two days, listen to me closely. Because all our futures depend on it."

"Yes, m'Lord!" said Liseth enthusiastically.

Looking down into her bright, young face and brown eyes, it occurred to Jim for the first time that this was the other side of the coin from Brian fretting at being confined to his bed. Very possibly, Jim's appearance with Brian and Dafydd at the castle—and particularly his own activities—were a welcome spice to the ordinary life of the de Mer family.

Perhaps, even, this was particularly so to Liseth, who in spite of her general maturity was young enough to become happily excited, if given half the chance.

"I need your help with this prisoner—er, this Ewen MacDougall," said Jim.

"Yes, m'Lord."

"I can't remember. Were you with us or not when I explained that my plan was to try to take the place of him, using magic to disguise myself to look like him? So that I can then go to the Hollow Men and get them to assemble all in one place, so that both Borderers and the Little Men can destroy them once and for all—utterly?"

"Oh, I know all about it, m'Lord," said Liseth. "What service can I perform for you, as far as the MacDougall is concerned?"

"Just this," said Jim. "The magic I use will be enough to make me look exactly like him. But I'm also going to need to learn to act like him. So what I have to do is observe him in his various moods, and particularly when he is together with other people. Now, he's attracted to you—"

"Do you think so?" asked Liseth innocently.

"Why, of course he is," said Jim. "Not only your beauty and your youth, but your wisdom and ability to command a castle like this as chatelaine has to have impressed him well beyond the ordinary, already."

"You really do think so?" said Liseth.

"Yes, I know so," said Jim. "Now, what I want you to do is to draw him out. He'll try to seek your favor, anyway. Please cause him to work as hard as possible at it. Stretch out the process of having him attempt to—"

He could not think of a good medieval equivalent for the twentieth-century phrase "make a pass at you," so he ran down rather weakly.

"I think I understand," said Liseth. "You wish me to draw the gentleman out, to make him seek my favor, and so show himself in all his ways."

"That's it!" said Jim. "You've got it exactly. I'm hoping the man will spread his feathers like a peacock, to win your attention and your liking. That way I can observe him doing it; and later on we'll have the double advantage that once I have changed myself into a likeness of him, I can try acting *as* him in front of you; and you can tell me what I'm doing right or what I'm doing wrong. All you have to do is entice him—"

"*SIR!*"

CHAPTER 20

J im stared. Liseth had changed completely.

She had drawn herself up stiffly; and her face was white and imperious. Her voice rang with some of the unbelievable penetration of the de Mer voices in general. Jim winced, half expecting her tones to carry all through the peel tower; so that in a second or two he would see a couple of the brothers above him on the stairs and another pair at the foot of them, all coming at him at the same time.

The as yet unknighted de Mer sons might not show themselves as very capable against worthy warriors like the experienced men-at-arms MacDougall had taken with him. But Jim was no worthy warrior, himself—as Brian had bluntly told him, more than once. Besides, the thought of encountering four opponents, who probably totaled well over seven hundred pounds on the hoof, was something no reasonable man would go out of his way to look for.

Of course, many knights like Sir Brian were not particularly reasonable. But Jim was.

"Liseth!" he said, involuntarily making a hushing gesture with his hand toward her. "What—"

"*Sir!*" She had not softened a bit from her appearance of a few seconds before. "Am I to understand you right? You want me to draw out this man, only? Nothing more?"

"Of course, nothing more!" said Jim. "No other idea ever crossed my mind—"

"Because, Sir!" said Liseth. "I'll have you to understand that I have my honor! And the honor of my family! I am a virgin and unwed! I cannot think that a gentleman would suggest—"

"But I didn't suggest!" protested Jim. "As I started to say, what you seem to be talking about never crossed my mind. I'm only thinking of you drawing him out in public. Unless it's in a room full of people, you can ignore him completely. Stay away from him absolutely! No, I only want to see his airs and graces demonstrated in public so I can learn them!"

Liseth reverted to her pleasant self so quickly that Jim could hardly believe she was the same person who had been sounding those ringing "Sirs!" in his ears a second or two before.

"Forgive me, if I misunderstood," she said, lowering her eyes. "I am still young, and a weak, simple maiden, alas. It is not always easy for me to understand the whys and mysterious talk of Mages like yourself, let alone men old enough to be my father."

Jim really did wince inside this time. He was absolutely positive that he was no more than eight years or so older than Liseth, at the outside, and probably less. But it would not be sensible to go into that matter right now. The main thing was, she was back in an agreeable temper.

"Not at all, not at all," he said soothingly. "You're incomparably wise for your years. I assume it's because of your excellent heritage; and the responsibility you've undoubtedly taken on in this castle, where there've been no other women of your rank all these years. It's because I know you can control men that I propose such a thing as this to you. You will allow Ewen MacDougall only so much nearness as you wish. I was sure that you could handle this by yourself."

"I will not say I cannot," said Liseth. "Part of what you say may be true. I *have* been alone in this castle and I *have* learned something of how to handle men. Very well, then, I will do as you ask—and, anent this matter of knowing how to handle men. I pray that you will let me go about this in my own manner, and trust me; no matter how I act toward m'Lord MacDougall. Believe always that I am concentrating only on your wishes. It may seem to you that I am not doing as you had expected; but in that case, be patient. You will find I've only taken the surest route to the ends you desire."

"Absolutely. I trust you. I'll be quite content with you doing everything your own way," said Jim, wishing he could wipe his brow, which now felt cool in the updraft of air through the open tower down which their stairs was descending.

He hurried to change the subject.

"On other matters," he said.

"Yes, m'Lord?"

"The next day or so, I must get in touch with Snorrl once more," said Jim, "so that he can show me the way to some of the Little Men. I can't waste any time suggesting to them that they come in on our side to fight the Hollow Men. By the by, do you know if your father has sent any word of our intentions to his friends along the Border?"

"I believe he has," said Liseth. "In fact, I know he has. But you must seek any answers on that from him."

"I will, indeed. Thank you," said Jim. "So, now, if you will send out Greywings at the first opportunity to hunt for the wolf—"

"I already did so, the minute you appeared at the castle," Liseth said. "You see, I knew you would need Snorrl. She should locate him sometime today; and Snorrl will not expect to meet anyone until tomorrow's morn. We will both go forth to meet him then, fairly early. If I rise before you, m'Lord, I will knock upon the door of your chamber. Do you the same for me, if you should rise very early."

"I don't know where your chamber is," said Jim.

"Oh, that's right," said Liseth. "Well—yes you do. You had to use it one time to make some magic."

"Oh!" Jim was embarrassed. "Of course. Yes, I will knock on your chamber door if I'm up early."

Privately, he decided he would do nothing of the sort. The chance of his actions being misunderstood, if not by Liseth then by others of the de Mer clan, was not worth the risk.

He had forgotten, until Liseth fired up a little earlier, that these men and women of gentle rank really held honor as a valuable, if not a vital, thing. He had no doubt that Brian and Giles, for example, would die for theirs if they thought that was necessary. He had very little doubt that Herrac, and the kind of daughter and sons he had raised, would have the same sort of reaction.

A man or woman's "*word*"—meaning "*word of honor*"—was literally a type of currency. Dishonorable people of rank, or those of very high rank, might sometimes disregard it. But if it became known that they had, any but those of high rank risked being stripped of any belief in what they said; and would probably encounter nothing but contempt from then on, from others whose honor had never been stained.

"Well, then," said Jim cheerfully, "if you can help me get Snorrl to take me to the Little Men tomorrow, and we find them the first day, and I spend a day talking, and then either by Snorrl or one of them get guided back close enough to the castle to reach it by myself, then we're all set."

He paused, a little out of breath from stringing so many "ands" together.

Quite suddenly, he remembered something.

"I understand from Lachlan," he said, "that MacDougall was due to meet with some representatives of the Hollow Men in something like five days. It'll probably take me a week or so after that just to set up a gathering of all of them. Which is probably just as well, because representatives of the Little Men will have to meet with representative Borderers headed by your father, before that; and I may have to be present at the Borderer meeting, to—er, make myself useful in any way I can. I'll talk to your father about that. Do you know where he is now?"

"I believe he is still in the Great Hall with the others," said Liseth. "If you wish, I can go ahead and speak to him and draw him off to the side where you can speak privily."

"Would you?" asked Jim. "I'd appreciate it."

They had reached the bottom of the stairs by now.

"Wait here," she said, and darted off toward the kitchens and the Great Hall beyond.

Jim waited, shifting from one foot to another as he stood at the foot of the stairs, and thinking about Little Men, Snorrl, Borderers, Hollow Men and the possible dangers inherent in having the whole de Mer clan think he had acted in any way improperly toward their daughter/sister. An early spring fly buzzed by, having undoubtedly come in one of the open windows of the castle—since none of the windows were glazed except the one in the bedroom where Brian now lay—and buzzed off again, possibly in search of the kitchen. If so, it had headed in the right direction.

Eventually the overpowering figure of Herrac appeared in the doorway through which Liseth had earlier vanished.

"M'Lord," he said, "forgive me for not drawing you aside before, but I thought it best to give an appearance of complete normality for a short while in front of the MacDougall. If you will follow me now, I will take you to a chamber where we can talk."

He led Jim through the doorway and off to one side, down through a narrow passageway against the curve of the white stone wall of the peel tower, lighted only by the daylight now coming through the arrow slits along the wall to their right. Eventually the arrow slits vanished and the passage moved between solid walls on either side, lit only by a couple of arrow slits at its far end.

Luckily it was not a long passage, and before they reached the end of it, Herrac had turned into a room which opened out again on the outer wall and had enough arrow slits to light it with some effectiveness—aided of course by the still-strong afternoon daylight.

It contained no bed, but a number of benches with backs— that being a better description of them to Jim's mind than to call them chairs—and also a table with storage areas built in underneath its top, so that it was not that far distant from deserving the name of "desk." Herrac dropped into one of the chairs beside the desk and waved Jim to another.

"I have sent for some wine to be brought us. Shall I simply tell you what has happened and what I've learned since you left us last?" he said. They were the first words he had spoken since he had met Jim at the foot of the stairs. "Or have you something more urgent to speak to me about?"

"Only one thing," said Jim, feeling that spreading the word himself would be a form of self-protection. "I've asked the Lady Liseth to help me in drawing our prisoner to show off his courtly airs and habits; so that when I change myself to look like him, with magic, I can also display the same movements and behaviors. The Lady Liseth understands, of course, that this is simply a matter of her public behavior with MacDougall. I am not asking her anything beyond the bounds of good manners, or anything that would be in any way distasteful to her."

"Of course," rumbled Herrac, "I agree. You are a gentleman, as well as being a magician, and I would not conceive of your suggesting anything improper to my daughter. Tell me, has she agreed to this?"

"She has," said Jim, "just now, as we were leaving the room where Sir Brian lies. —By the by, I have given him permission to come down to dinner. But, on the matter of Liseth and MacDougall. I assumed her agreement would be subject to a chance to tell you about it, and make sure that you also agreed."

"As a matter of fact," said Herrac, "she drew me aside from the table in the Great Hall just a moment since, told me about it, and did seek my agreement. But I could hardly doubt that any daughter of mine would be anything but polite to a visitor in my home."

He paused.

"Besides," he said, "you may have noticed yourself, that she does not take kindly to nay-saying, even by me, her father."

Since Jim had seen none of the de Mer children do anything but agree utterly and immediately with Herrac, this was somewhat of a surprise to him. But he hid it.

"It is odd," went on Herrac, more to himself, "but the boys were always more biddable. My dear Margaret always had more success than I in guiding Liseth."

He paused. His eyes were looking past Jim at something that was not in the room. Jim, who had been about to speak in the momentary silence, closed his mouth again.

"She was so young to die, my Margaret," said Herrac, in a strangely muted tone of voice, "—to die so suddenly, without warning. It was in the middle of the night and we were in bed together, asleep. And I woke, for even in my sleep I felt the first pain that hit her; as a man, fighting while pressed close against his sword-companion, feels the shock of the blow his companion takes, through the other's body into his. So, I woke.

" 'What is it?' I asked her.

" 'Hold me!' she said—oh, in such a stricken voice—and I put my arms around her and held her to me, as I would have held her against bear or lion, or Satan himself. And she clung to me . . ."

The man's voice had risen; and he seemed to swell as if he threatened to fill the room. His eyes now blazed at whatever he saw past Jim; and Jim himself was suddenly as tense as Dafydd's strung bow.

"Then the second great pain came." Herrac was not even talking to Jim now, but to himself—only very much out loud.

"And this one I felt as she did, a pain beyond speaking that went right through me as it went through her.

" '*Margaret*!' I cried.

"But she was gone. And I held in my arms . . ."

Tears were now rolling down Herrac's face, and his voice choked for a moment, so that he could not go on. But he seemed to grow even larger, so that everything in the room, including Jim himself, seemed to shrink. For now, his eyes were the eyes of a madman.

"I was at the funeral," he went on, "but I saw only Margaret and heard nothing. But for some months—"

He spoke suddenly between clenched teeth.

"—no man dared cross my path. For fear I would see, or think to see in him, some slight—present or past—against her; and I would kill him!"

Herrac's great fist crashed upon the top of the table, so fiercely that Jim started and winced at the same time. For it did not seem that living flesh and bone could take that blow against the thick wood of the tabletop.

"—*Kill! Kill!* For want of killing the thing—the death—the thief in the night—that had taken my Margaret from me. If I could have found It, I would have killed It, I would have cut and crushed and slain It like a roach under my foot . . ."

Suddenly he slid out of his chair, dropping to his knees, and started to pray with bowed head.

"Lord God, you have taken her to you. Hold her safe until my coming, when she will want for safety no more. And forgive her any sins that unknowingly she committed—for surely she could have committed none, knowingly. And teach me patience and strength that I may endure in this world until I have accomplished all the things she would have wanted— to see all my sons safely into manhood, my daughter safe, and all things right, so that I am no more needed here. . . ."

His voice trailed off into silence.

"Amen," he said.

Slowly, he got back up into his chair and stared around at Jim and the room for a moment, as if he was seeing them for the first time.

Finally, his eyes focused on Jim.

"Not even the servants would come near, for those months," he said, in more normal tones. "Only my children brought me food and drink, and led me to my bed, nights—Liseth first

among them, for all Alan was eldest. And in time, I came to
live with what had happened—though sometimes, as now, it
returns to my mind, unawares; and the wildness comes back
on me."

His eyes were now completely sane again.

"Forgive me, Sir James," he said, "but there are indeed
moments when I remember; and then I cannot help myself.
Tell me, you have a wife, do you not?"

"Yes," said Jim.

"Then you know what it is to love, in a way even the minstrels do not know?"

"Yes," said Jim, even more softly, his thoughts for the moment
many miles distant.

Herrac passed a hand over his face, wiping away the last
traces of his tears.

"But we came here to talk of important matters," he said, in
his usual voice. "I know all that my daughter could tell me,
as well as what you proposed. Yes, I have sent messengers to
certain of the other Borderers, as you wished."

Jim cleared his throat.

"I'm very pleased Liseth told you, herself," he said, "so we
can get right to work. Perhaps you'd tell me how our plans were
received by the other Borderers. Including, if you had a chance
to do so, about this business of meeting the Hollow Men for a
final battle that will end them, and joining with the Little Men
to fight."

"I have sounded out a good number of my neighbors,"
answered Herrac. "You must understand that, while we have
our small disputes, the one with the other, from time to time,
in general we are quite able to join together against a menace
like the Hollow Men. I heard from none who were not strongly
in agreement with fighting them, if they could all be cornered
in one place. On the subject of joining forces with the Little
Men, however, I was faced with one question—you will forgive
me—to which I had no strong answer. Why, indeed, do we need
the Little Men? I was asked by many. I had to send them what
answer I could. Which was that you, as a magician, consider it
of vital importance that the Little Men be present; but you had
not told me why, so that I assumed it was something magical
and not to be said to us ordinary mortals."

Recalling at this point that Herrac and his children were all
silkies, for a second the term "us ordinary mortals" struck Jim

a little oddly. However, he ignored it, and went ahead with his answer.

"Actually, m'Lord," he said, "you were giving exactly the correct answer. There are reasons magical which cannot be told. They're vital to our making sure that all the Hollow Men are killed, so that none rise to trouble either you or the Little Men any more—"

"Where is that wine I called for?" interposed Herrac unexpectedly, glaring at the door.

He turned back to Jim.

"Forgive me, m'Lord," he said. "I am listening; please go on."

"Well," said Jim, "I was just going to remark that whatever the reasons, the Borderers must have the Little Men there. I mention this because when I get to speak with the Little Men again tomorrow—I expect much the same question from them. They will want to know why they need any help but their own in this final battle with the Hollow Men. I can only tell them, as you have told these others—and if you like I will tell it to your fellow Borderers myself—that it is absolutely necessary that both Borderers and Little Men be engaged together in this final battle. Aside from those reasons which must remain hidden, there's the fact that, while you and your neighbors have suffered from them for some hundreds of years, the Little Men have suffered from them much longer than that, and have a right to be in at the end. As a fighting man, you must see that for yourself, and I would trust that the other Borderers you talked to, also being fighting men, would also see it."

"Certainly what you have to say are strong reasons," said Herrac, rubbing his large but close-shaven chin thoughtfully, as was his habit.

"But you see, m'Lord," he went on, "what it boils down to is that the Borderers are being asked to go to a place as yet not named, and fight a battle alongside those about whom they have always been wary. All this, simply on your word alone that the place is right, and the results will be as you say. As I may have said, all I talked to were in favor of the idea of eradicating the Hollow Men. All were a little doubtful about whether they wanted to join in on what little they knew about it so far."

"If you, yourself, joined with me in meeting the Little Men and heard their answers," said Jim, "do you think they'd be reassured? Then you could tell them as much as I've told you.

Would they be more certain, then, that I could get the Hollow Men to that place? I assume they'd take your word for the fact we captured the gold MacDougall was carrying with him; and that they wouldn't doubt that the Scottish King is planning an invasion of England through Northumberland."

"Both things would make a great difference," said Herrac. "If I tell them of these things, do you have time to get to the Hollow Men and also meet with the Borderers, themselves?"

"I think we'll make time, somehow," said Jim. "I say we, because I indeed planned to ask you, and Liseth, to go with me when I meet with the Little Men."

"I shall willingly go anywhere with you that will serve to bring this matter to a good end," said Herrac. "I feel—"

There was a knock on the door of the room. It opened without an invitation to enter; and a somewhat sweaty servant came in hastily, carrying a slab of wood bearing two pitchers and two cups. He came to the desk and set them down on its top.

"And where have you been all this time, sirrah?" thundered Herrac at the man.

The servant seemed to shrink by at least a third of his height.

"M'Lord . . ." he stammered, "the tray on which I usually bring pitchers and cups like this was not to be found. It took some extra time to find this piece of wood to serve in its place."

"Well you brought it now! Out with you!" snapped Herrac; and the servant vanished quickly, closing the door softly behind him.

Herrac poured two cups from one of the pitchers, both of which turned out to be full of wine.

"Where was I?" he asked himself. "Oh, yes, I'm willing to do anything that will aid in this endeavor. Certainly I can see the usefulness of the two of us together, meeting with the Borderers. Perhaps we should take Lachlan as well."

"I've no objection to that," said Jim, picking up his wine glass and sipping from it as Herrac poured half of his down his throat.

"As for the business of my going with you to meet the Little Men—I have no objection to that either," said Herrac. "But will they stand, when they see me coming? I'm not known along the Border as a particular friend of the Little Men—though not probably as a known enemy, either."

"They're not all that fearful," said Jim; and then he realized he had let a slightly ironic note creep into his voice, so he hastened to add, "particularly when we'll be approaching them in their numbers. We will also have Liseth and Snorrl to vouch for us. Now, I have made arrangements with your daughter to summon the wolf Snorrl, who should be here tomorrow morning. If he is, we should go right away to see what arrangements we can make with the Little Men."

Herrac frowned.

"Talk to the Little Men, before you speak to the Borderers?" he asked.

"It would take you several days to arrange a meeting for me with the other Borderers, wouldn't it?" Jim asked.

"That is true," said Herrac. "Still—"

"If you'll forgive me," said Jim. "I believe that bringing the Little Men to agreement to this may be the more difficult task, since they're a different sort of people from us. Also, there's this matter of time. If we can get to the Little Men tomorrow, we'll have saved some days. And time looks to be rather short; for a number of reasons, but mainly because the Hollow Men were expecting the Scottish envoy in a few days, now. Also, they'll want him to meet with some of their representatives, first, before a meeting can be arranged with all of them together. Then, it'll take time to gather them all together in the place we want."

"Very well," said Herrac, yielding. He drained his cup. "Let it be as you say. The end is worth the means."

He pushed his cup from him and stood up.

"Now," he said, "let us both return to the Great Hall. Liseth will already have this MacDougall casting interested eyes in her direction. And I, as well as you, wish to observe his actions."

There was a note in Herrac's voice that boded ill for the MacDougall if he should cross the line of ordinary social courtesy where Liseth was concerned. Jim thought that Liseth had really had no need to worry on many counts—the least of these being Jim's utter lack of desire for her to do more than put the MacDougall in play—as it were.

CHAPTER 21

As Jim and Herrac approached the Great Hall, noises from it began to be heard above the sounds of the kitchen. Most unusual noises. Jim heard the plunking of some stringed instrument, along with a great deal of thumping and an occasional sound rather like a war-whoop.

Jim looked at his companion for an explanation. Herrac looked back at him a little sourly.

"My sons are dancing," he said. "Apparently MacDougall has put them up to this; and I wouldn't doubt but what Lachlan has had a hand in it, also, that wild Scot!"

They stepped into the Great Hall, and up onto the platform that held the high table. Only three people were seated at the table right now. One was Liseth, looking reserved as a maiden carved from ice, near one end of the table. Across from her sat Dafydd; and farther down the table on the same side as Liseth, MacDougall lounged, his face in an expression that nicely blended a mild curiosity and disdain. Somewhat the same look with which a person might watch performing fleas.

Down on the main floor alongside the lower table that stretched away toward the front entrance, in an open space, Christopher had produced a lute, and was now playing a tune on it while Lachlan was dancing.

Jim stared at him in a certain amount of amazement. He had seen Scottish dancers before, at fairs and festivals and special occasions. But by and large they had been young girls. Even in their case, he had marveled. They had seemed to float in the air, weightless above their pointed toes that just touched the ground; doing complicated things with their legs, meanwhile, and with one hand on a hip while the other was held up over their head.

Lachlan was doing the same thing. He had taken off his shoes; and in spite of the sounds of the impact of his weight against the wooden floorboards of the hall, he too—for all his size and muscle—seemed to be floating as he did the same sort of dancing. In a semicircle around these two were the other sons, one or the other occasionally twitching as if he would like to step out and dance himself.

Herrac sat down in his customary place at the center of the table, which put him closer to the MacDougall than to Liseth, and watched what was going on with a resigned air.

After a moment, Lachlan stopped and motioned forward one of the sons, who immediately began, himself, to dance, while Christopher went on playing. To Jim the dancer did not seem to be doing badly; but his brothers hooted with laughter. His face got red, but he went right on dancing, occasionally giving vent to the same sort of war-whoop that they had heard on the way in, and which had evidently been emanating from Lachlan.

Jim looked again at Liseth and MacDougall, as he took a seat between Herrac and Dafydd. MacDougall was just now sidling down the bench along his side of the table to Liseth. He spoke to her in a low voice. Only the fact that Jim was seated near her allowed him to catch what he said.

"If I could persuade your excellent young brother to play us a more sedate and courtly type of dance," MacDougall said in her ear, "would my Lady deign to tread a measure or two with me?"

Liseth did not turn her head.

"I've already informed m'Lord," she said in a voice that dripped distaste, "that I am not interested in speaking or having anything else to do with him, beyond what is my duty as chatelaine of this castle."

MacDougall gave a deep sigh and slid backward along the bench—but, Jim noticed, nowhere near as far away from her as he had been a moment before.

Since the Scottish envoy seemed to be doing nothing that Jim would have to notice, memorize, and in time imitate, Jim decided that he might possibly get another duty out of the way. He leaned over to Dafydd, and whispered in the bowman's ear, so quietly that no one else at the table could have heard.

"Dafydd," he said, "could you step out with me for a moment? I need to talk to you."

Dafydd nodded silently; and as silently got up from the table. He and Jim went back through the kitchen and out behind it, into the empty corridor leading to the chamber where Herrac and Jim had talked.

Once he knew they were well away from all other ears, Jim stopped and turned to face the other.

"What caused all this dancing?" he asked curiously, before diving into the subject he had to discuss with Dafydd.

"M'Lord MacDougall," answered Dafydd; and it was impossible to tell from the cool tone of the bowman's answer whether he approved or disapproved of what he was talking about, "asked if by chance there was a lute or other such instrument around the castle. He offered to sing a few songs if this was so. It seems that Christopher, the youngest—"

"Oh, yes," said Jim. "I know Christopher."

"Christopher had such a lute," went on Dafydd. "Not only that, but he could play it himself. Yet he brought it, tuned it, and m'Lord MacDougall sang us several songs, mostly through his nose, in such a strange manner that we could not make out half the words. Love songs, I think he said they were; and indeed, they were most mournful, which I take the loving of such as he to be."

"I see," said Jim.

"Then, after he had sung several songs, he invited one of the others to take the instrument and sing, but only Christopher could play the instrument; and he would not sing. Whereupon, Lachlan leaped up and said he might not be able to sing; but he could dance if Christopher would play for him. Christopher said he could. Then you came in a little after."

"I see," said Jim. "Well, that explains that. I was just interested to know what was going on. At any rate, that isn't the reason I asked you to step out here and talk with me, Dafydd. There's a far more serious matter."

"Indeed, James?" said Dafydd.

"Yes," Jim answered. "You know my plans for concentrating the Hollow Men in one place; and then attacking them with both the Borderers and the Little Men. Also, I plan, as you know, to pass myself off as MacDougall."

He paused. Dafydd nodded.

"Well," went on Jim, "it all needs to be done on a very tight schedule; and I can't afford to get held up at any one stage of setting up the battle. For example, what I've got planned for tomorrow has to go forward without any kind of a hitch; so that I've time to do the other things."

"If it be not done tomorrow," said Dafydd, "then it can be done another day, surely. If you will forgive me, James, I have noticed this in you many times before. You are over-concerned with time, and the possible lack of it. It is much better not to worry about such things, see you. If what we look for tomorrow comes not to pass, then something else will. We only have this one lifetime and it will wend its way as it chooses."

Jim had a sudden feeling of empty helplessness. Once again, he was up against a difference between fourteenth-century thinking and the twentieth-century thinking with which he had grown up. So many things beyond their control could interfere with the plans of people in that medieval time that they had come to consider it merely a fortunate chance if they happened to get where they intended, at the time they had originally expected to get there. In fact, as a result of these uncertainties, they simply, usually, did not expect to get something accomplished at any particular time at all. They would get where they were going when they got there.

"You're probably right, Dafydd," he said, "but I do very much want to see the Hollow Men destroyed and I want the Little Men and the Borderers to fight side by side for once and discover each other—as they will—which I think will be a good thing. Don't you think so, too?"

"Indeed it will, if it is to be," said Dafydd.

"You see, that's the point," said Jim. "It may be; and I see a chance of making more sure that it will be, if no time is lost in doing various things by way of preparation. Tomorrow, Snorrl the wolf should be here to lead us once more to the Little Men. Liseth is going out with me in the morning to meet him. I'm taking Herrac along as well, to speak to the Little Men in the name of the Borderers, if Snorrl agrees to take us all; which I now believe he will. Liseth has told me that he has never refused her anything before. I'd like you to come, too."

"I will always be glad to go anywhere you wish, if sobeit I am free to do so; and certainly I am now," said Dafydd. "But why would you be wanting me along with you tomorrow?"

"Why"—Jim found himself a little unsure as to how to phrase it—"you seemed to make a particular impression on the Little Men, the last time we met them. I was thinking that having you there on our side would serve to prove that what was planned was a good thing. Now, of course, if you don't want to seem to be agreeing with that for some reason, I'll understand."

"But I do agree, man," said Dafydd, with almost a little edge to his voice. "How can you think otherwise? For not only have I said that I think your ends are good ends; but we are Companions since the time of the Loathly Tower and before, and will be Companions therefore, as long as our lives last. Will we not?"

"Oh. Certainly!" said Jim. "It's just that I didn't want to impose on your friendship—"

"Between us, James," said Dafydd gently, "there can be no talk of imposing, see you. I would that you not use that word to me again in making a request of me."

"Certainly. Gladly!" said Jim, feeling as if he had blundered horribly, and at the same time not quite sure what he had done wrong. "It's just that I had to ask you and—damn it, Dafydd, I'm doing the best I can with everybody in this matter. And it's all mixed up. For one thing, we have to be careful to keep it secret from Brian that this is going forward; otherwise he'll insist on being with us."

"He will be with us in any case," said Dafydd, "or after us— if he discovers we are gone after we have already left. He will need to be told he cannot go before we leave, if that is what you wish."

"I plan to tell him before we leave," said Jim. "I'll explain that I do plan to take him along, on horseback, to the battle, if he's able to come with us by that time. I've never seen anything like the way he's healing. He may be so well by that time that not taking him will be ridiculous."

"Indeed, I think that is how it will likely be," said Dafydd. "Very well. Shall I find you in the morning, or will you find me?"

"You're better at waking up early than I am," said Jim. "Particularly, you're better at waking up at a certain time than

I am. Would you come and wake me up as soon as the sky begins to brighten? And then we will wait in my room until Liseth comes for us or—"

A sudden thought struck him.

"Perhaps we should go and wake Herrac first and then come back to the room."

"That will be very well," said Dafydd. Abruptly he smiled warmly at Jim. "Look not so glum, m'Lord. Things will go well tomorrow; and if they do not, it shall be no fault of ours. What more can men ask?"

"Perhaps you're right," said Jim.

"Indeed I am," said Dafydd. "Now, what is your will? Do we stay here, go someplace else, or return to the hall?"

Jim roused himself to current necessities.

"We go back to the hall," he said. "I've got to watch that damn MacDougall until he does some things that I can imitate once I've made myself over to look like him."

He led off, and Dafydd went with him.

"To be sure, you are now beginning to swear somewhat in the English style," said Dafydd. "And I must say, m'Lord, it appears well in you. Frequent oaths, such as Sir Brian uses, have their use in getting rid of the noxious humors within a man. And, concerned as you are for many things, you have no lack of such humors to get rid of."

"You don't swear much," said Jim, casting a sideways glance at him as they once more reentered the hall.

"Ah," said Dafydd, "but that is because I am a man of Wales; and, like the Little Men and as you mentioned about them, we Welshmen, too, have different needs and different ways."

They found their places back at the high table, and were welcomed there by Herrac, who had been sitting gloomily by himself and drinking; since there was nothing else to do. He passed them both cups and filled them. Down on the floor, one of the other brothers was now dancing—or trying to dance—with instructions and orders from Lachlan, who clearly had no high opinion of any of these boys when it came to getting up on their toes and moving as he, Lachlan, had.

Jim sat and watched Ewen MacDougall. But Liseth was still being an ice-maiden, which puzzled Jim seriously. This was not exactly the reaction he had asked of her. Happily, in time he remembered Angie his wife, occasionally saying pretty much the same sort of thing Liseth had when the de Mer chatelaine had warned him to trust her, even if she seemed to be acting in a way that he did not expect. Clearly, what she was doing now, she evidently thought would bring the MacDougall to heel earlier.

And, in fact, thought Jim, watching them, to a certain extent it seemed to be working. As the afternoon wore on, MacDougall became more and more a suitor. And, gradually, Jim saw Liseth apparently seeming to thaw under this concentrated pressure.

In the end, she finally agreed to tread a single measure with him, of a more courtly dance. It turned out Christopher knew only one tune that would suit itself to that sort of dance. But he played this; and MacDougall decorously led Liseth at arm's length through the paces of the dance, explaining the moves as he made them. Whether she really needed this instruction, Jim could not make up his mind. But she followed MacDougall's directions docilely enough.

However, once the dance was over she returned to being an ice-maiden, at her end of the bench; and continued that attitude through dinner and up to the point where she left for bed.

Jim followed shortly thereafter. The time he had set for getting up in the morning was early, even though he had adjusted to fourteenth-century standards to a certain extent. He knew, particularly after the amount of wine that he could not avoid drinking without giving offense to his hosts if he stayed, he would feel like death warmed over when Dafydd finally came to wake him up in the cold pre-dawn.

CHAPTER 22

No one in the group had a hangover the following morning, as Snorrl conducted them through the rugged country that led into Little Men territory. Of course, thought Jim, Lachlan was not one of them this time. Jim and Herrac were in full armor, including lances; Dafydd rode behind them all with his long bow slung over one shoulder and a quiver full of arrows on his hip. Liseth rode on the other side of her father from Jim; or if the way became too narrow, she dropped a little behind. Snorrl, of course, ranged ahead.

They were all fully armed. Liseth even had a broadsword in its sheath, attached to a belt hidden, like the broadsword itself, in the folds of her outer dress and under her cloak.

It was unheard of for a gentlewoman to wear a sword. But Jim felt sure that she would not be wearing it without her father's knowledge and approval; and if he agreed to her carrying the weapon, then undoubtedly she had learned to use it.

In addition, she would also undoubtedly have a dagger hidden somewhere else about her. It was not only Scots like Lachlan who carried the *skean du*—or *"black knife"*—in their stockings. This last was a short but broad-bladed dagger narrowing rapidly to a needle point; a weapon that could be very effective at close quarters, as well as being invisible until needed in the ordinary course of events.

The thought of Liseth and a possible *skean du* in her stocking or boot reminded Jim of a new problem that had cropped up.

Last night at dinner, Brian had joined them, as he had been promised, helped down the stairs, much against his protests, by Liseth on one side and Jim on the other. In spite of the knight's objections, Jim noticed that the other had a tendency to lean fairly heavily on him from time to time; and guessed that if nothing else the several days in bed had had the effect of making him a little unsteady on his feet. The amount of blood in his body should by now have pretty well replenished itself. It was simply a matter of the slash itself healing safely; and it was still showing a remarkable ability to mend fast.

So, they had negotiated the stairs on the way down with no trouble, and Brian had been welcomed by all—including a rather distant and lordly welcome from Ewen MacDougall.

Whether it was the tone of this welcome, or a natural antipathy of some sort, MacDougall and Brian seemed to be automatically at swordpoints from the beginning. MacDougall talked deliberately about court doings and Brian had let him talk. Until he mentioned tournaments.

At that point, Brian had chimed in with a few reminiscences of his own about tournaments, mentioning rather casually that he had been fortunate enough to win this tournament and that tournament; that he had been honored with the chance once to cross lances with Sir Walter Manny, and on another occasion with Sir John Chandos. He wound up by asking MacDougall very casually if he had ever had the fortune to break a lance with those same two well-renowned gentlemen and soldiers, or others of equal fame.

He had obviously found the chink in MacDougall's social armor. The Scot Viscount had indeed been engaged in tournaments, though nowhere near as many as Brian—who, in fact, had been eking out the living of his very poor estate by his winnings in them. The winner of an encounter normally gained the horse, armor and weapons of his opponent, unless the opponent chose to ransom them back from him; and this source of income was about all his broken-down Castle Smythe had to keep it going.

Not merely that; but since MacDougall's tournaments had been all in Scotland, he could not name knights of such international reputation as Manny and Chandos, as opponents. As a result, for the first time since he entered Castle de Mer, he was being made to look less of the completely experienced courtier than he had been presenting himself.

Brian had kept a perfectly straight face while he was doing all this. MacDougall had given no sign that he was aware of being belittled. Also, no one else at the table, even Liseth, seemed to take any particular note of the fact that MacDougall was being put down by Brian. But everyone was, of course, aware of what was going on.

The end result, however, from Jim's standpoint, was unfortunate. That type of exchange between two medieval knights could lead eventually only to armed conflict between them. Jim hated leaving them behind, with no other company but Lachlan and Herrac's sons. Lachlan seemed as likely to encourage a quarrel as prevent it; and none of Herrac's sons had the age and authority to prevent open trouble between two such men of rank and reputation, if matters should get out of hand between Brian and MacDougall.

Jim worried. Brian was still in no case to get into a fight with another man who was in good health. Such an encounter could not only mean Brian losing face, but possibly being badly hurt, if not killed. Even if the encounter was disguised as a competition. The wound on Brian's side was not yet healed enough to endure the activities of a body in battle.

However, there was no help for it. Jim told himself he would simply have to wait until he got back; and meanwhile there was nothing he could do about it. However, telling himself this did not make the worry disappear from his mind. For Dafydd, he thought, undoubtedly it would have. But for Jim, the worry was there and it stuck.

In fact, it kept him company until they went over a little lip of land between some of the same sort of sharply vertical cliffs that he and the others had climbed, following their fight with the Little Men against the Hollow Men.

Abruptly, then, they found themselves moving down a slope into a very pleasant little valley that stretched for some distance, widening as it went, with something at the far end of it that could be buildings, and possibly tilled land. However, not fifty yards in front of them was one of the "schiltrons" of the Little Men—drawn up in ranks with spears leveled. Jim could still not help himself thinking of them as phalanxes—but he made a mental note to use the other word, here.

Standing a few paces before the front rank of the schiltron was the Little Man whose bushy face Jim recognized as being that of Ardac, Son of Lutel. The same leader he had met at the time of their mutual fight with the Hollow Men. Ardac kept his eyes on Jim, more or less ignoring the others as Snorrl led them all up to him.

"Magician," Ardac said, as Jim and the others halted before him, "you are not unwelcome, you and your friends. But you come here more frequently than we like strangers to visit our land."

"It's a matter of absolute necessity that brings me," said Jim. "I believe we've got a chance at a great accomplishment to discuss with you. One you'll find most welcome, as we find it welcome."

He reined his horse a little to one side so that Ardac had a full view of the other humans with him.

"Do you know everyone here?" Jim went on. "You remember Dafydd ap Hywel, who fought with us—"

"We remember Dafydd ap Hywel for more reasons than that," said Ardac. "But continue."

"You know Snorrl, of course. You know Liseth; and surely you also know Herrac—Sir Herrac de Mer, father of Liseth de Mer."

"We know them all," said Ardac. His eyes lingered for a second meeting with Herrac's and then came back to Jim. "We still have not heard why you come into our land again."

"I've just said," answered Jim. "We've a prospect which I think you'd want to discuss with us and your other leaders, whoever they may be. May we go to them, or dismount and wait here for them? Or in some ways set up a meeting where we can talk and explain what we have in mind?"

"We shall see," said Ardac. He turned around, stepped back and spoke to one of the soldiers in the front rank. The soldier, still carrying his spear and shield, left the rank at a run, circling the schiltron and going back, still running, toward the shapes in the distance that might be houses.

"There will be a wait," said Ardac. "You may dismount and make yourself comfortable on the ground here if you wish. We also will wait."

He turned to the ranks behind him and shouted a single word. Jim was not quite able to make out whether it was the way it was uttered that kept him from understanding it, or if it was in a language he did not know.

The soldiers of the schiltron laid down their shields and swords and sat down themselves, cross-legged, still in their ranks. Dafydd and Liseth, Jim noted, were already dismounting. Herrac and he followed suit. They also sat. Ardac had already seated himself, only half a dozen feet in front of Jim.

"Word has come to us," Ardac said, "that one of your number who fought with us against the Hollow Men was wounded. How is his health now?"

"He's healing—very fast," said Jim. "It was a bothersome rather than a dangerous wound, after all. Something sharp cut a long slash along his ribs on one side."

"I am pleased to hear it," said Ardac. "Of our wounded, one died and the rest are recovering."

"I'm very pleased to hear that, too," said Jim. He was doing his best to bring a less formal and more friendly atmosphere into being between him and this leader of the Little Men. "I was impressed by the way you all fought in that encounter with the Hollow Men. I think no one else could have done as well."

There was the beginning of a sound from the throat of Herrac, beside Jim, the sound cut off before it had more than a chance to get started. Ardac's eyes swung to the huge knight, and for the first time a faint smile parted his bewhiskered lips.

"You would say that men of your own kind would have done as well or better, Sir Herrac de Mer," he said to Herrac. "I will not argue the point with you. This is a matter of opinion. Let us each keep to his own. Does that suit you?"

"It suits, Ardac, Son of Lutel," said Herrac. His voice was as neutral in tone as Ardac's had been. Abruptly, he smiled slightly also. Ardac reached out a hand.

Wordlessly, Herrac reached out his own long arm and took the small fist in his larger one for a moment. Then they let go.

"If your reason be good, Sir Herrac," said Ardac, "you are welcome on our land, even if you come alone."

"I thank you, Ardac," said Sir Herrac. "That is courteous of you."

"We do not deal in courtesy here," said Ardac. "We have friends or enemies. I have just named you as one of our friends. That is all. Neither courtesy nor anything else is involved."

"I understand," said Herrac, nodding his head slowly, in such entirely reasonable a tone that Jim could almost see Ardac's stiffness thawing slightly before his eyes.

Snorrl had flopped down on the ground when the rest of them sat. He lay now on his side, had closed his eyes and was apparently deeply asleep. They waited. No one said anything, and the sun was warm. Jim felt an urge to drowse off himself; and only brought himself back to full alertness by reminding himself of the seriousness of the situation.

Ardac had called them friends. Nonetheless, the schiltron in front of them barred their way any farther into the valley as well as the stone face of a mountain might. They were accepted onto the land, but not into the homes of the Little Men, very obviously.

After what seemed a long time, but was probably only about half an hour, Jim saw a movement in the farther reaches of the valley. Movement which approached them, and finally resolved itself to four teams of eight armed Little Men, each team carrying by poles on their shoulders a sedan chair in which sat another Little Man, obviously much older, white of beard and dressed in white robes.

Still, with these loads, the bearers ran—although they seemed to either keep in step so well, or otherwise match their footfalls so that their running hardly jolted their burdens. Just how it was done, Jim was not able to figure out; even when the four older Little Men had been brought right up to the front of the schiltron and their sedan chairs put down on the ground by the bearers.

Things still did not look too promising, Jim thought. His general impression of all four of the older men was that they were all glaring at him and the others; rather than merely looking them over. After a long moment the white-bearded Little Man on the right lifted his hand. He and the others reentered their sedan chairs. The carriers picked these up again; and carried them around to the side and back of the schiltron until they were about forty yards off. Far enough so that they could obviously talk amongst themselves without being overheard by the visitors.

Ardac went with them and once the sedan chairs were set down again, a consultation was evidently held between Ardac and the white-beards.

After a little longer, Ardac came back to Jim and the rest.

"Now," he said to Jim, "we will listen to you."

Jim took a deep breath.

"We have a plan," he said, "by which the Borderers and the Little Men working together can catch the Hollow Men all in one place for once and slay them all, so that not one is left to raise the others back to whatever sort of life it is they have."

"We know of your plans," said Ardac.

Jim looked narrowly at him.

"How do you know?" he asked.

"Because I told them to him," broke in the harsh voice of Snorrl. He was still lying lazily extended on the ground but with the upper eye visibly open. "What little I did not know I learned from listening to you when you slew all of that party on the road from Scotland except the one you took prisoner. There was also what I heard when you, Lachlan MacGreggor and the prisoner, were in a small hut on a sheiling."

Jim swung to face Ardac.

"If you knew all about this before we got here," said Jim, "why meet us this way and bring your—"

He could not think of a proper word to indicate a rank he did not know. He merely gestured toward the men with the white beards—

"—out to meet us?"

"We do not know everything," Ardac said. "What we do not know and what we want to know, is why you should want us involved in this matter together with your tall people. We know more about this land and its people than anyone else. We know there are more than enough Borderers to win such a battle by themselves. Just as there are more of us than are needed to kill off all the Hollow Men in the place you have picked."

He paused.

"You frown a little," he said. Jim immediately straightened his face up. He had not realized that he had been frowning.

"You have only seen me and this schiltron," Ardac went on, "so you have no evidence that there are others beside myself, particularly since you have now seen me twice and no other schiltron-leader. But there are many schiltrons and many leaders. I am here this second time to meet you only because I was the one who had met you before. Now, why do you want to mix Little Men and Borderers together to make a force to destroy the Hollow Men, when it is not necessary?"

"I think," said Jim, slowly, "that it's very important that both Little Men and Borderers be involved in this as partners. For one thing, both they and you have suffered from the Hollow Men. But for another, there may come an even more important time some time in the future, when it will be necessary for all of you, and all of the Borderers, to join forces against some common enemy. If you fight together this time, then you will be able to point back to it when, in the future, you have little choice but to fight side by side."

Jim stopped talking. Ardac said nothing, but stood, apparently thinking. He made no attempt to take Jim's words back to the white-bearded Little Men waiting off in the distance.

"I'm not asking you to become close to them!" said Jim earnestly. "I'm not asking them to necessarily get close to you. I'm simply asking you both to fight on the same side for once; so that you know that it can be done—both you and they. I've no way of proving this to you—that it's important. You take my word for it or you don't."

"You're right," said Ardac suddenly and unexpectedly. "Your word is all we have."

He turned about without a further sound and went off to the white-bearded Little Men; and stood talking to them for some time.

Jim stood watching them from the distance. He felt a little irritated that these white-bearded leaders would not come forward and talk with him directly, but must relay what they had to say through Ardac. But at that moment, he heard a soft murmur in his right ear, low-pitched enough so that no one else there could hear it, which was the voice of Dafydd.

"They are not what you think, Sir James," murmured Dafydd, "those with the white beards. They are not rulers, they are only older Little Men of wisdom with whom Ardac consults. On the basis of that consultation, he avails himself of their wisdom, and so makes his own decision—which the Little Men as a whole will afterwards follow."

"The Little Men as a whole?" muttered Jim, but carefully, without turning his head to show that he was talking to Dafydd. "But he said he was only a leader of a schiltron among many leaders of schiltrons. I got the impression that they were all equal, those schiltron-leaders."

"Indeed, they are so," said Dafydd, "but as I say, they are not like—"

There was a slight pause, so slight as to be almost a catch of Dafydd's voice. "—us. They are different, and have their own different way of handling matters, see you. If Ardac decides to fight with the Borderers as you wish, then all the other schiltron-leaders will be ready to fight with him. Just so, he would follow if another schiltron-leader made a decision. He and the others who lead groups of Little Men like this are the real leaders of the people. Though, in truth they are people that have no leaders in the sense we think and say the word. But over many centuries they have come to think much alike, and they trust each other to a greater extent than—"

Again the little hesitation in Dafydd's voice. "—we do."

"I see," murmured Jim.

He had just gotten the words out of his mouth, when Ardac turned away once more from the white-bearded elders and came back to him.

"We will fight with you against the Hollow Men, I think," he said, "provided all is in order. There is one question left to resolve. Who commands this battle where Little Men are concerned?"

"I—I'm not sure," said Jim. "I mean, it hasn't really been settled yet. Possibly I myself will be known as the commander, but wise and experienced soldiers like yourself and Herrac among the Borderers will certainly have a great deal to say about what is done—"

"Then we cannot do it!" said Ardac.

"Can't do it? Why not?" demanded Jim.

"Because the Little Men must only be led by one of their own blood," said the Little Man. "Perhaps I and some other leaders of schiltrons will be invited to your councils, but we will not be a part of them. We could only be a part of them if one of us were one of the chief leaders."

"But this is an impossible demand," said Jim. "There is no way—"

He stopped. He had been about to say there was no way the Borderers would accept a Little Man as a major leader amongst them.

"It must be so," said Ardac. "The Little Men have always fought as a unit. If we are to fight side by side with the Borderers, we and they must be a unit. That means one of us must be amongst the leaders; and considered as one of them, by the Borderers."

"You mean," Jim said, finally understanding, "whoever commands the Little Men must be trusted by the Borderers as much as they trust each other?"

"That is so," said Ardac.

"As I say," said Jim, "it's impossible. We have Little Men

and we have humans. There are no others."

Herrac, Liseth and all the others had drawn close about him as he was speaking. Desperately, he wished that Herrac or one of the others would speak up, and help him resolve this difficulty. But at the same time he knew that they could not. The only possibility was to insist on the necessity for the two sides joining in the battle. He opened his mouth to do this, but another voice beat him to it.

"Perhaps," said a soft voice behind him, "the Little Men would accept me as their leader among the Borderer leaders of the battle?"

It was the voice of Dafydd. Jim stood silent. He had completely forgotten that the Little Men had saluted Dafydd when they were there. Even at that, he had trouble believing now that the salute meant they would accept him as one of their own.

Ardac had stood silent a moment. Then without a word he turned and walked away once more to the white-bearded men.

"Now what?" said Jim, frustrated, speaking the words as much to himself as to anyone else. Ardac's reaction had convinced him there was almost no hope that the Little Men would accept Dafydd. But even if they did, how would the bowman be received by the knights among the Borderers? They would hardly agree easily to the admitting of a commoner to their councils of war.

Ardac was coming back.

"Magician," he said, stopping in front of Jim, "we accept Dafydd ap Hywel as our leader among and with the Ordinary Men. But only on the condition that he bear his proper title. *Prince of the Sea-washed Mountains!*"

"Prince!" said Jim and Herrac, together. They and Liseth turned to look at Dafydd, who had gotten to his feet, taken his bow off his shoulder and was leaning on it, frowning.

"My forefathers put aside that title long since," said Dafydd slowly. "I know not if I have the right in their name to take it up again."

"It is either that, or you fight alone, Sir Magician," said Ardac.

A long silence held them.

Finally, Dafydd sighed and took his weight off the bow. He stood tall, straightening his shoulders.

"For the purposes of this battle, and for the time of this battle only," he said, "I take and accept the title which is mine by inheritance, *Prince of the Sea-washed Mountains*. After that, I ask that all not only cease to use that title toward me, but forget as well as they can that I have ever borne it. This is my demand!"

"I agree," said Jim, without hesitation. He looked at Herrac. Herrac was still staring, half frowning at the bowman. He got to his feet and Jim followed.

"This is no play-title," he said, "then?"

"Indeed it is not!" said Dafydd, rising himself.

He had lifted his gaze and he looked Herrac directly in the face. Herrac was still somewhat taller than Dafydd, but for a moment they seemed of equal height.

"When we leave this place I am Prince of the Sea-washed Mountains, and I remain Prince of the Sea-washed Mountains only until the battle is over. This must be agreed upon and accepted by all. The Little Men agree?"

He looked at Ardac.

"We do," said Ardac.

"And I agree," said Jim. He looked again at Herrac. "What of yourself and the other Borderers?"

"I cannot promise the other Borderers until I have spoken to them, and heard agreement from them," said Herrac. "But I will agree for myself and for the sake of what we fight here."

He turned to Dafydd.

"—And for what I've seen of you and heard of you myself, noble Sir."

"You need not use a title unless it is absolutely necessary," said Dafydd. "Bear in mind, Sir Herrac, that though the title remains and the rank remains, we are as men, one to one, as we have been and as we will be again in the future. So we are now."

He extended his hand—a gesture no bowman would normally make to a knight. Herrac reached and took it. They held for a moment, and let go.

"It is settled, then," said Ardac. "When shall we meet to discuss the plan of battle?"

"Give me a week and a half. A week and a half to two weeks," said Jim. "There are things that must be done first. However, it would help if we were in touch meanwhile."

"There will be one of us within a short distance of your

Castle de Mer at all times during the coming two weeks," said Ardac. "If you send the falcon Greywings, it will come to us. Like your daughter, Sir Herrac, we speak to the birds, as well as to other beasts."

"And they speak truth," interposed Snorrl's uncompromising voice. "That is why we, the free people of the wild, have been friends with them these many centuries."

They looked at Snorrl as if by silent consent; and saw him on his feet, stretching and yawning hugely, as if he had just woken up from his nap.

"Therefore, now it is time for me to lead you back to those closed walls you call a castle," said the wolf.

CHAPTER 23

"Prince of the Sea-washed Mountains," said Herrac, more or less to himself, but aloud so that his companions heard. "Prince of the Sea-washed Mountains . . ."

"Are you having a problem with the title?" asked Jim.

"It fits the tongue a bit awkwardly," Herrac said, looking both at Dafydd and then at him. "But most, it is a title that sounds like something out of an old story. I am wondering if the other Borderers will take it seriously—particularly when they see Dafydd, who is most obviously a bowman, even if we dressed him up in court clothes borrowed from our visitor MacDougall."

"We'll leave him as he is," said Jim. "You can say to your Borderers he's a Prince in disguise, and you will tell his title to them under a seal of secrecy, since it should not be known that he is in this part of the country."

"Yes," said Herrac, "I had assumed I should do as much. But still . . . that title. Your Borderer is not used to fanciful titles, or ones that come strangely to the tongue."

"Perhaps, now," said Dafydd, "I can solve your problem for you. *Prince of the Sea-washed Mountains* is how my original title would be said if you speak it in the language we talk nowadays. Originally the name was—"

He uttered a string of liquid syllables that made no sense at all to Jim, and which was obviously nothing that the rest of them could say.

"Do you suppose that you would rather the saying of that?" asked Dafydd, smiling.

All of the rest of them, even Liseth, tried. But obviously what their tongues produced was not what Dafydd had said.

"Sir James came the closest of all of you," said Dafydd. "Perhaps you might use what he says in addressing me."

"What was it you said?" Herrac demanded, turning in his saddle to face Jim. "Would you say it again, Sir James?"

"*Merlion*," said Jim. He was aware himself that a couple of syllables were missing, and that there was none of the musicality in his version of the word he had just spoken that Dafydd had sounded in his. But it was something he could say—and possibly the others, if they needed to.

"*Merlion*," echoed Herrac. "Well, it is better than Prince of the Sea-washed Mountains; or will be, in talking to my fellow Borderers."

He brightened up suddenly.

"In fact, with your permission, noble Sir," he said, looking at Dafydd, "we can improve upon it for the purpose of a Borderer's ear. Would you object if we use for you the name '*Merrrlon*'?"

He had extended the "*r*" in the word, to give it a Scottishlike roll or burr.

"It will sound, then," he went on, "more like to the normal sounds they are used to."

"I care not what you call me," said Dafydd, smiling. "Between us all I am still Dafydd ap Hywel, master of the bow. Let me be Prince Merlon, then—though I cannot say the '*r*' as you do, Sir Herrac—to all other people. It makes no difference. It is a title that is here for a moment and will be gone again shortly."

"Good!" said Herrac; and they all rode happily on to the castle.

Back there, Jim was relieved to find that open trouble had not broken out between Brian and MacDougall. But Brian, having had a taste of being up on his feet, was determined to stay there. Though, mindful of Jim's emphasis on the fact that he curtail his wine drinking, he had now had what he considered his quota for the day and was working his way through some small beer.

He was seated at the high table with MacDougall when

they arrived. He and MacDougall had evidently seen a certain amount of reason in avoiding open conflict; they were talking to each other with a fair amount of agreeableness. Jim drew Herrac, with Dafydd, off to one side; where they could speak privately for a second without being overheard.

"I think I would like to meet with the Borderers as soon as possible," said Jim. "Whether they should also meet Dafydd at this time, I leave up to you to decide, Sir Herrac."

"Our meeting with them is easily managed," said Herrac. "In fact, I have appointed one for this evening, here in the castle. But it will not be any open gathering. They are to come quietly and we will meet apart from the Great Hall and they will leave after we have talked. And—"

He glanced at Dafydd. "—my apologies to you, Prince Merlon; but I think now is not the time for you to meet with these Borderers. No, let me resay that. I cannot see the good of it, but if Sir James does, then I will agree. Sir James, himself, as a knight of repute and honor as well as a magician, will be accepted by them without question. But I think it is best we tell them about you first, before we introduce you, or any of the Little Men who are going to join us for the final making of plans."

"Any plan will be welcomed by me," said Dafydd. "I will be here, about the castle, if needed. If I may go by what Sir James has said, it will be a week or two before we attempt to trap the Hollow Men, in any case. Is that not so?"

"Yes," said Jim, "it's so. I suggest we tell them about you tonight, only if it seems a good time to, and then call you in if the news suits them. After my meeting with the other Borderers tonight I'm going to have to leave again—this time for several days. Because now's close to the time I impersonate MacDougall and meet with the leaders of the Hollow Men. Tomorrow I'll have to leave with a horse carrying the gold; and, come to think of it, perhaps it would not be a bad idea if you went with me, Dafydd, rather than my borrowing some men-at-arms from Sir Herrac to act as guards. The fewer of us to meet them, the less suspicious the Hollow Men we meet are going to be."

"Indeed, that too is welcome to me," said Dafydd.

That ended their talk, and they rejoined those at the high table. The socializing went on through the afternoon and through dinner. Once the actual eating was over, Brian began to show signs of tiredness; and with only a little protest, allowed both Jim and Liseth to help him back up to his room. They went up the stairs with him, and Jim had a chance to speak to him, away from the Great Hall.

"Will you be able to get along with the MacDougall while I'm gone?" Jim asked.

"If he behaves himself," said Brian, "I'll push no quarrel. Only if he attempts to push, will I answer the man in any way necessary."

"Now don't be foolish, Brian," said Jim. "Your wound won't let you get into armor and have it out with this man as you would, in the ordinary way. Besides, he's a prisoner, and shouldn't be getting into fights anyway."

"It's up to him, then," said Brian. Jim noticed that he had not promised anything. "Between you and me, I think he'll not seek for trouble. He has had time to take my measure; and I do not believe he would stand against me for more than a few minutes, either with lance on horseback, or on foot with any other weapon. I think he is aware of that fact, also."

"No doubt that's true, Brian," Jim said, as they turned down the corridor toward his bedroom. Brian wobbled a little on the turn and grinned weakly.

"That small beer," he said, "it goes right to a man's head."

"It's not the small beer," said Jim, "it's the wine you took today; and the fact you're still not a well man. Remember MacDougall knows that; and may think to take advantage of it. For my sake—for all our sakes, Brian—do your part to stay out of any open battle with him."

"So," said Brian on a long sigh as they entered his bedroom and headed toward his bed. He let himself gingerly down into it, then relaxed with another deep sigh. "I will do my best, James. You know I always do my best."

He closed his eyes and was asleep before they could leave the room. They went back downstairs to the high table, although Jim had privately decided that he would be disappearing himself shortly if he was going to get a good night's sleep before leaving early in the morning to find the Hollow Men. He had already asked Dafydd to wake him; and the bowman was an infallible alarm clock, as long as time was expressed in the common terms of the medieval period—"daybreak" . . . "nightfall" . . . "moonrise" . . . etc. and the churchly hours of worship.

However, before Jim and Liseth reached the hall, they were intercepted by Herrac at the foot of the stairs and Herrac led Jim off by himself to another room in the tower.

For such a simple-looking fortification, the peel tower managed to have a regular rabbit warren of rooms of various sizes. Herrac took him to one which he had not even guessed existed. It was a good-sized room, enough to hold twenty or thirty people; although the number he saw around the long table set up there now, under the burning cressets—for this room had no outside walls, merely air holes in the ceiling to let the cresset smoke out, hopefully to the outside—were only eight individuals.

Herrac led him up to the two empty spaces left at the head of the table, and introduced him to the others.

"Gentlemen," he said, "this is the Baron Sir James Eckert de Bois de Malencontri."

"I'm honored to meet all of you," said Jim.

The men at the table either merely nodded or made noncommittal noises. The table itself was set with food and drink, and all of those there were clearly busy helping themselves to both.

As Jim took his seat with Herrac beside him, he had a chance to look them over. All wore swords, indicating this was not just a neighborly visit. Beyond this one common note, they were a burly bunch; no two dressed the same. Some wore kilts, others trews—which were sort of like the kind of pants that used to be called plus-fours, ending at the knee—but like the kilts in that they all showed a particular tartan.

A few were dressed simply as any English knight might have been, out of armor; in hose and some kind of upper jacket of various cut, over interior clothing. All wore hats, no two of them alike. This, too, was something Jim had learned about the fourteenth-century period. It was the period of hats. He had guessed that there must be some hundreds at least of different hat styles, for it seemed that every man he met wore a different kind.

But Herrac had already begun to introduce the men around the table to him.

"The gentleman immediately to your left, m'Lord," said Herrac, "is Sir John the Graeme, who can put over two hundred men into the saddle if he is agreeable to joining us. Just beyond him is Sir William of Berwick, who brings one hundred and twenty horsemen to our aid, if sobeit we fight together. Just beyond him . . ."

Jim's head very quickly began to swim with the names of the other Border leaders he was meeting. Most of them seemed to have place names, but there was a good-sized minority who were introduced by clan names, instead.

Searching his memory, Jim remembered that just because someone like Sir John the Graeme had the name and wore the Graeme kilt, did not mean that he was in any way a speaker for that clan as a whole—except for whatever small part of it might be personally attached to him.

In fact, many of the men who might ride behind Sir John Graeme might do it under a multitude of different names, for the Border was a stew of people from many different clans. Scotts, Elliots, Kerrs . . . but the introductions were over now, and all the rest of those at the table had stopped their eating and drinking and were sitting staring at him.

"Ballads speak of you as a magician, Sir James," said John the Graeme, as the first to break the silence.

So much for the Borderers accepting him without question, as Herrac had said.

Also, Jim noticed that Sir John Graeme had not addressed him as m'Lord; and he guessed from this that the fact that he was taken to be of the English nobility did not necessarily recommend him to the men before him. The Border, he had always heard, thought of itself as a world apart; and certainly such Northumbrians as he had met so far had not forgotten that once their area was a kingdom of its own under the name of Northumbria.

"That's right, Sir John," said Jim. "I am not the highest-ranked of magicians but I am a qualified one."

"Perhaps," said Sir John—he came down hard on the word with a touch of local accent so that it came out "*pairhaps*"— "you wouldn't mind showing us some proof of the magic you can do?"

"Sir John!" said Herrac. "My son Sir Giles has been with him and seen him work as a magician. Sir Giles is not with us at the moment, but he is in the castle and I can have him here within minutes. Do you wish to question my son's word?"

"Och, Sir Giles's word! Certainly not," said Sir John. "It's just that in sic a situation, that is not so much the usual thing and to which we will be committing good men who may be hurt or slain, it's natural to wonder about a man who says he's a magician."

"It is hardly something *said*—" The tone of Herrac's voice was beginning to deepen ominously. Jim stood up and put a hand on Herrac's shoulder.

"Sir John," he said, looking directly at the Graeme, "I will be perfectly glad to give you an example." He thought of his low account with the Accounting Office, and mentally crossed his fingers that the other would not take him up on what he was about to say. "If you will show me that you are a skilled swordsman, as a knight must be, by standing up right now and striking a blow with your weapon at the knight next to you."

Reflexes on the Border were not slow. The knight next to Sir John Graeme—Jim had forgotten his name—was on his feet in a moment.

"Now, now," said Sir John soothingly to the standing man, "calm yourself, Wullie." Sir John had been careful not to stand up himself. He looked now back at Jim.

"You make a worthy point, Sir James," he said, still soothingly. "You have not seen me in battle and I have not seen you at your magic; and neither is a thing lightly demonstrated. You are quite right, and I crave your pardon. We should take each other on trust; and on the word of our good host and his worthy son, Sir Giles."

He turned to the knight who had stood up beside him.

"Seat yourself once more, Wullie," he said soothingly. "You know I've no desire to draw sword upon you, or you upon me."

Sir William of Berwick sat back down at the table.

"Well now, Sir John," said Herrac grimly, "if you've fully satisfied yourself about everyone concerned with the situation—"

"To be sure—to be sure." Sir John waved a hand almost as large as Herrac's. "Let us continue. Perhaps Sir James will be good enough to tell us his plans."

Jim was still on his feet. He debated sitting down again, then decided against it.

"I assume you've already heard them from Sir Herrac," he said. "Nonetheless, you can hear them from me now, if you want. I intend to gather the Hollow Men at a certain place, which can be told to you. I will know the time of their gathering; and once they are all in position there we will move in

close around them, under the screen of trees that surrounds part
of this area—the rest being fenced in by unclimbable cliffs."

He paused to see how they were taking this. They were all
closely attentive, but noncommittal.

"I will have gathered them together under the pretense of
paying them to spearhead an expedition by the King of Scotland
into the north of England," he said. "Not so much for what
damage they can do; as for the fear they can spread among the
English by the fact they are ghosts. I will tell you my feeling
about how forces should be arranged, once we are there. At
any rate, you will see me, because I will be upon a ledge of
rock a little higher than the floor of this place where they are
met, handing out to them, one by one, the gold."

He paused again. They still listened, but showed no com-
mitment.

He went on.

"The gold, in short, will be the bait that will make sure we
have all of them together. I will have made the rule that no
Hollow Man will be paid unless he shows up; and the evidence
over the centuries has been that none of them trust each other
enough to have another of their own kind collect for them.
When I give a certain signal you will all move in. Remember,
the aim is to make sure that every one of them is dead. So that
none still lives to give those killed the ability to rise again."

"It may well be a bloody cockpit, this place you talk of," said
another knight down the table, whose name Jim had forgotten
already and completely.

"It could hardly be otherwise," said Jim. "The only reason
to support it being so is the need of doing away with the
Hollow Men once and for all. Over the centuries the families
of all of you have paid many times over in goods, money and
family, compared to what we will be spending in that spot at
that time."

"That is true," said Sir John Graeme, thoughtfully staring
at his hands, closed together before him on the table, "but if
the figure of two thousand Hollow Men that Sir Herrac has
given us—"

"Have any of the rest of you better guesses?" Jim asked.

There was silence around the table.

"As I say, this figure of two thousand Hollow Men," Sir John
went on as if nothing had been said by Jim, "means that we
must commit most of the strength of those who are here, and

possibly that of a few others as well, to be sure that it is a battle to the death—a battle to the death of all the Hollow Men."

"Exactly," said Jim. "That is why I have talked to the Little Men and got their agreement to fight with us."

All the knights around the table made sudden movements. None of them showed extreme startlement, but Jim read shock in every one of them.

"I did not tell them that," said Herrac, in a low voice to Jim, but one which the rest of the people at the table could hear.

"Have any of you a good reason why you should not fight alongside the Little Men in this matter?" Jim asked boldly. "They've suffered also, and for more centuries than you have, from the Hollow Men. They've fought them valiantly, holding their borders against attempts by the Hollow Men to move in on them. They have a right to be there at the final killing. Not only that, but being as they are, with their particular weapons and their way of fighting, they will help bring the battle to a speedy conclusion."

"They are not mortal or Christian," said Sir John Graeme, looking up at Jim. "They are not of us. How do we know that they aren't Satan's children—or even secretly in league with the Hollow Men in this? It would not be the first time an ally had betrayed righteous men to their enemies."

"I can assure you that they are not and what you fear will not happen there," said Jim.

"Forgive me if I seem again to doubt you," said John Graeme, who seemed more and more to be the speaker for the group, "but your assurance is a thin rod upon which to lean if we are to commit all our strength to this battle."

"I can give you some reassurance on that," said Jim. "For the Little Men refused to follow but a leader of their choice. And it seems that they will accept one among us only. A man who is here at the castle in the disguise of an ordinary bowman, but who bears a high rank which both Herrac and I privily know.

"For certain reasons the Little Men are willing to accept him as their leader. But him, only, if they fight by your side. The one I speak of is just without this chamber right now. If you like I can bring him in."

They all looked startled—including Herrac, who did a good job of seeming to turn an astonished and inquiring face to Jim.

"Forgive me, friend Herrac," said Jim, possibly a little more emphatically than was necessary, "for not mentioning this to you sooner. He will come in, of course, only with your permission and the approval of those here. But I asked him to stand close, so that he might be available if necessary. Perhaps that necessary moment has come?"

He had turned his head back to face all the others around the table as he said this. There was a long silence; and then one of them nodded, then another nodded. Finally the wave of agreement ran completely around the table; ending, as Jim had more than half expected, with a nod from John Graeme.

Jim looked at Herrac, got a nod from him, and rose to step to the door and open it.

"Noble Sir," he said, "would you deign to step in here, if it so please you?"

Out of the corner of his eye he could see every man there straighten up in his chair. "Noble Sir" were words that were used only to royalty.

All there could not help but recognize it as such.

Dafydd came through the door. He was not carrying either his bow or his quiver; but it was as Herrac had said earlier—he could not have been mistaken for anything but a bowman, no matter how he had been dressed. There was a general set of body signals in the way he moved and the way he stood, that certified to the fact that this was a man who used the bow. As Jim shut the door behind him, he advanced to the end of the table and stood behind Herrac looking at them all—looking down at them all.

Jim came back past him and, standing behind his own bench, turned toward Dafydd. "For special reasons," he said, "may I ask your Highness to introduce yourself to this company—since no one else can introduce you properly?"

"Willingly," answered Dafydd. "Gentlemen, I am the Prince of—"

—And once again he pronounced that string of liquid syllables that neither Jim nor anyone else had been able to properly imitate.

"Sir Herrac?" asked Jim. "Since he is known among us by the name in the disguise he now adopts to preserve his privacy, would you speak that other name? It may come more readily to the tongues of these gentlemen, as it did to us."

"He is the Prince of Merlon," said Herrac, pronouncing the name "Merrrlon" as he had suggested.

There were silent stares from everyone around the table—
and a long silence.

"Pardon me, noble Sir," said one of the men at the far end
of the table, at last, clearly taking no chances that he might
be committing a social error by not using this newcomer's
proper title, "but are you not Welsh? Something about your
voice seems to say you are Welsh."

"Indeed," said Dafydd, smiling—and for the moment, standing as he was, he did appear unmistakably regal as he looked
down at all of them. "And since I'm in the disguise of a Welsh
bowman, how else should I sound?"

Jim turned to Herrac.

"With your permission, Sir Herrac," he said. "And with
that of your Highness"—he looked back at Dafydd—"I will
give these gentlemen some explanation of how you happen to
be here."

"Let it be so," said Dafydd.

Jim turned back to the people at the table.

"Where are your manners, gentlemen?" he said. "None of
you has risen; and his Highness is still on his own feet."

Herrac pushed back his bench and rose to his feet. Around
the table, the others also rose hastily.

"Sit. By all means sit," said Dafydd, with a wave of his
hands. "And if someone will be good enough to bring me a
seat, I will join you."

Slowly, those around the table reseated themselves. Jim
offered his own bench to Dafydd, who took it, managing in
his own inimitable manner to appear to lounge—and lounge
in princely fashion, at that—while the others were essentially
forced by their benches and the table to sit stiffly upright. It
was true that all of them had been bred to the saddle and to
seating themselves in this manner. Nonetheless, there were none
there who could have lounged with the cool indifference that
Dafydd displayed. It outdid MacDougall's earlier performance
by a country mile.

"With the permission of your Highness," Jim said to Dafydd,
seating himself, "I will explain how you happen to be here at
this time, when you are so badly needed."

"Continue," answered Dafydd, with another wave of his
hand.

"Gentlemen," said Jim, addressing the table at large, "the
Prince Merlion has heard of our problem with the Hollow

Men; and—since his people once had a like problem—comes specifically for the purpose of aiding us in our task. I need not ask gentlemen like yourselves to keep his true rank and name secret. I believe he will solve the problem of all of us, as to fighting alongside the Little Men. The Little Men have already recognized his identity and his rank at first sight (for they have long memories, as all know); and they have also already welcomed and accepted him as their leader among us in this endeavor, if sobeit takes place."

Several of the knights began to speak at once. Then all fell silent except the single one at the end of the table who had spoken about the Little Men not being mortal before.

"With your pardon, noble Sir," said this individual, "but where is the kingdom that you come from?"

Jim spoke up quickly, to insert himself into the gap.

"It is indeed close to Wales," he said, "which is why his Highness adopted the disguise of a Welsh bowman." He was scrambling to come up with an explanation on the spur of the moment. "However, the kingdom in which his Highness is Prince was a very old kingdom, that has since sunk below the waves. In spite of this, his people magically continue to live, underwater, and none in this island knows of them. Am I right, your Highness?"

"You are," said Dafydd, unruffled.

"A wall of magic bars their kingdom off from the land as we know it, so that it seems nothing but sea where they live," said Jim.

He went on.

"But," he added, "I, being a magician, was able to pass through that wall and move underwater to where he and his people live. I entreated his help, and he was good enough to come. He was reassured; since I asked him to come to this castle of Sir Herrac's, a knight of whom he knew."

It was Herrac who looked startled now. Jim cast a meaningful glance at him. All there were perfectly aware that Herrac was a silkie; and therefore able to travel in the waves and below them, and presumably also to visit such a kingdom as Jim described.

"His Highness's people had known the Little Men well, many more hundreds of years ago than the families of any of you have lived in this area. They were close friends at a time when his Highness's country was above water. That was why they recognized His Highness at once; and accepted him as their leader if they were to fight together with you—which I may tell you, they were not eager to do otherwise."

Jim stopped to let this point sink in.

"In fact, they had flatly refused, at first, until he had consented to be leader to them," he went on. "He will bring some of them with him to our council table before the actual battle; but it is he who will have the overall command. You see, he knows, as you do not, that the Little Men are indeed mortal. Only, they are in some small ways, magicians as I am, myself; for only humans may make and use magic. All Naturals and other creatures owned and created by the Dark Powers are given powers suited to their purpose, but do not control them, any more than a falcon controls his ability to see closely the surface of the ground below him from great heights."

There was a long silence after Jim had finished speaking. Then Sir John Graeme turned to speak directly to Dafydd.

"Noble Sir," he said, "it will be an honor to fight beside you in this small matter."

CHAPTER 24

Jim and Dafydd, with their horses and a pack horse carrying the chest with gold, were making their way through the Cheviot Hills, with Snorrl as a rather wraithlike guide, flitting into visibility before them to signal the way for a moment, and then disappearing again.

Jim was puzzling over the fact that a problem that completely sweeps you up into it at the time, once solved, becomes nothing at all; and you are immediately swept up and enclosed by another problem. He had seen the Borderers' agreement to fight with the Little Men as the big hump to get over. But, with Sir John's acceptance of Dafydd as Prince Merlion and Dafydd's leadership of the Little Men, the rest of what possible opposition there might have been, among the group gathered in the de Mer castle by Herrac, crumbled.

An agreement had quickly been reached to meet together at a certain point in the Cheviot Hills that all knew, on a certain date that Jim would announce. It would be between one and two weeks away from the present. Also, they would meet again on the evening before the battle.

The morning following, they would gather with their men in the woods at a place to be appointed, not too close to where the Hollow Men would be meeting to collect the gold.

Once all the Borderers had arrived, they would move together as a group, coming up gradually to surround the area where Jim (acting as the Scottish envoy) would have insisted that the Hollow Men gather to get their pay in advance.

Now that it was all over, it seemed to Jim that there had been no real problem at all to getting the cooperation of the Borderers. He knew this was not so but it *felt* so. In any case, what was deeply worrying him now was exactly how he should deal with the leaders of the Hollow Men when he at last came face-to-face—an unlikely word to use, but he could not think of any other—with them.

"We're not far from the place of those leaders of the Hollow Men you wanted to talk to," said Snorrl, unexpectedly appearing by Jim's left stirrup and trotting alongside. "They've been there several days already; and you'll find it no sweet place to the nose of such a two-legged one as yourself."

"It can hardly be very bad, if they are but ghosts," spoke up Dafydd, riding beside Jim on his other side.

"They're not being ghosts right now, Master bowman," said Snorrl. "They are in every way as human as yourself, except they cannot be seen except when they are dressed. And being like the rest of you, they make the sort of messes that you humans always make. Although these may be a little worse, since they have no respect for anything, each other, or even themselves."

He opened his jaws once more in the silent wolf laugh.

"Only me—that is the one thing they respect."

"Why is that?" asked Dafydd curiously. He had not been in earshot when Snorrl had first mentioned this to Jim.

"I know not—neither do I care," said Snorrl. "I only enjoy to see them fear me as men fear devils!"

"Well, in any case," said Jim, "we'll just have to put up with the smells."

"That you will," said Snorrl. He closed his jaws. "I take it you will not be wanting me in my magicked form at this meeting?"

"No," said Jim, "not until the final gathering. I think the full effect of you will be greater if they don't know you're going to be there."

Snorrl laughed again.

"It may well be you're right," the wolf said.

He lifted his nose suddenly in the air as he went along.

"They have set a sentinel," he said, "to warn them of your

approach. He's in the low branches of a tree up ahead. Go a little further, and he'll see you. I'll leave you now and meet you again after you've left the camp. Only remember to come back in this direction; though I will be watching and find you, in any case."

With that, abruptly, with that magiclike behavior of wolves, he was gone.

With word that a sentinel would soon be looking at him, Jim decided he could delay using his small magic account no longer. He had been dressed in those clothes of MacDougall's which would fit him and rode MacDougall's horse. Unfortunately— the other being much smaller—Jim wore his own clothes and armor. But he had been careful to put on the MacDougall's resplendent surcoat over it—and that should be enough to identify him to the Hollow Men leaders.

He wrote on the imagined blackboard on the inside of his forehead:

ME, APPEAR LIKE→EWEN MACDOUGALL

He felt suddenly loose inside his clothes and armor. He had completely forgotten how literal spells could be. He now had not only the face of MacDougall, but the smaller body of the other man, after all.

Happily, the stiffness of his armor hid most of this. In particular, his breastplate held the surcoat out as impressively as before. Jim sighed. No wonder the magicians' Accounting Office would rate him no higher than a Class D magician, even when he was apprenticed to one of this world's only three AAA+ rated ones. He would probably never, thought Jim glumly, be anything but a Class D.

He pushed the thought from him as he and Dafydd, with their pack horses, continued to approach the camp of the Hollow Men's leaders.

They saw no signs of a sentinel or anyone else; but they smelled the camp before they got to it and when they stepped inside, all the clothing and armor in sight was not lying on the ground but up in the air, molding human shapes.

Jim rode without pausing into the clearing, Dafydd beside him and the laden horses following.

"I had hardly believed the wolf when he said they ate and drank, when playing at being alive," murmured Dafydd in his ear. "But plainly he was only truthful."

So, even his fourteenth-century nose had remarked the powerful stench of the camp. It smelled like a compound of human waste and decaying food. At least, Jim hoped that it was decaying food, and not the decaying corpse of some unfortunate, present-day mortal who had had the misfortune to cross their path.

But he could see no signs of a corpse. The clothed and partly clothed Hollow Men were a clump in the center of the clearing. He rode directly to them without saying a word, and pulled up his horse perhaps six feet from them.

Some of the clothed or semiclothed figures either in iron or cloth immediately moved around him to approach the chest-carrying horse behind him.

"Leave that load alone!" snapped Jim. "If you simply rob me now, no more will follow!"

A stream of profanity and obscenity came from the closed visor of a fully armored figure in the front of the cluster of Hollow Men, ordering those who had gone forward to come back. They did so, more slowly than Jim would have liked.

"So you're the MacDougall," said the suit of armor. "For myself, I am Lord Eshan. We seem to be Lords, both of us, do we not?"

"One might say so," answered Jim, as indifferently as he could. He made use of one of the gestures of the MacDougall, which was to pull forth a kerchief from his sword belt, and wave it gently back and forth under his nose. "Hell of a stench here!"

"You'll like us as you find us, MacDougall," said the suit of armor. "Now, you and your man get down off your horses and we'll talk."

The armor turned to half face those behind and around him.

"That means the rest of you can listen, but you don't talk. I do the talking!" he said to the articles of clothing and armor clustered there. "Now back off and bring us some wine and three cups!"

Jim and Dafydd dismounted and sat down cross-legged, facing the suit of armor, which had taken a seat on the ground cross-legged before them. A shirt, but nothing else—in fact more of a nightshirt than a shirt—wafted up to him with the empty left sleeve end some inches behind a wine skin, which still had horse fur on the outside and was crudely sewn; and three cups that clustered in mid-air with their handles together, a few inches in front of the equally empty right sleeve.

The invisible hands at the end of the sleeves put the cups on the ground before Jim, Dafydd and the armored figure, and poured them full from the wine skin, which was then restoppered and laid handy to the right gauntlet of the armored figure. The armored Hollow Man raised his cup to his visor, opened it and tilted it backward. When he sat it down again it was empty, and he refilled it. He made no effort to refill either Jim's or Dafydd's cup.

Meanwhile, both Jim and Dafydd had lifted their cups to their lips. As it approached Jim's mouth, the wine within it seemed to smell to Jim with the same odor as the rest of the camp. As for the cup itself, it was old and dirty.

However, it occurred to Jim that men many years dead could hardly be carrying infectious diseases around with them, though decaying food or drink could be. So, with an effort he put the cup to his lips and tilted it, but did not allow the wine within to touch his upper lip or enter his mouth. He sat the cup down again and as he did so he saw Dafydd also setting down his own cup, the wine in it apparently untouched.

Jim fluffed the handkerchief under his nose.

"You've already heard from someone else, I take it," he said disdainfully to the figure in armor, "of what the King of Scotland requires from you. Now, I have come directly from him, as a special messenger. Our concern is, of course, that both sides keep their bargain—yours—"

He paused disdainfully for a second.

"And, of course, ours. Consequently, the payment will be made in parts. Once you have performed your share of the work by foraying into England and throwing the English into as much panic as possible, the Scottish army will eventually catch up with you; and then your duty may be considered to be over. This was our understanding of the agreement. Is it yours?"

"By Mithras, but it is!" said the Hollow Man in iron. "Now open up that chest you've got strapped to the horse's back there."

"One moment more." Jim held up his hand. "You agree very readily; but you've not heard all I have to say. The final payment will be forthcoming once the Scottish army catches up with you. That is agreeable to you?"

"It is. Now, let's see the color of your gold!"

"A moment more," said Jim.

Dafydd stood up beside him on his feet and stretched with his arms over his head. Putting his arms down, he let the strung bow slip off his shoulder, and catching it in his hands, almost absent-mindedly pushed the bowstring up so that it was strung.

He did this as if not even noticing what he was doing. But he kept the strung bow in his left hand and his right hand hooked by a thumb to his belt just above his open quiver of arrows.

"This man of mine," said Jim, "is a bowman I borrowed from the castle of a knight nearby. He's not a bad fellow; but he must play with his bow and arrows all the time. Would you believe it? He could draw and put an arrow through you before anyone around here could move. And at this distance, would you believe it also, these damned English longbows send an arrow right through armor as if it was merely cloth?"

"You're threatening me?" snarled the armored figure.

"I? Threaten you? Of course not," said Jim. "Just making polite conversation, don't you know, as we Lords together are like to do, even if the lower orders have less manners."

"I think it's time to see the gold," said Lord Eshan.

But there was not quite the certainty to his demand that there had been before. His visor was facing toward Dafydd, who had taken an arrow from his quiver to examine it and now was rubbing its notch up and down on the string of his bow.

He went on.

"You may not be able to see them; but there are over twenty of us here. One bowman, whoever he is, can't put an arrow in each one of us before we cut you to pieces!"

"Of course not! No, no," said Jim. "Even if we thought of such a thing, the only one Dafydd would be interested in putting an arrow through would be you."

"You don't frighten me," snarled the armored figure. "Kill me, and in forty-eight hours I'll be alive again!"

"But in the meantime, someone else may have taken the leadership of you Hollow Men," said Jim, lazily gazing about the camping area. "Might not that be so?"

"No, it's not so!" snarled the armored figure. But still, to Jim's ear, complete conviction was lacking. After a moment the other went on again. "All right, have your say of whatever else there is to be said. Then we get to business."

"Well," said Jim, almost dubiously, "perhaps, after all, we

should start by opening the chest now."

The Hollow Men behind their leader did not wait for permission from him. They made a rush on the pack horse; and Jim heard the chest thump to the ground, with a jingling noise inside it, as if the rope holding it to the horse had been cut.

"Why, damme," Jim said, "there was no need to cut the ropes. We'll need that chest later on again, to bring the rest of the gold."

"It's nearly empty!" a shout went up behind Jim. "Eshan, there's only a handful of coins in the bottom! There's not even enough here for us, let alone for the others!"

"What's that you say?" Eshan lumbered to his feet, and Jim also got quickly to his.

"You better get some answers quick, Eshan!" shouted the same voice. "You're the one talked everyone into this. Here, we get no more coin than we'd pick up from any handful of travelers!"

"By the bones of St. Peter," said Jim languidly, "but you do jump to conclusions, you Hollow Men. There were those who thought you were completely untrustworthy; and that we were fools to trust you. Nonetheless, our King decided to do so. I have much more to say. You'd best listen to it."

"All right, all of you back here behind me," said Eshan. "We want the gold, don't we? All right then, we've got to listen then, don't we? Back with you, all of you. We'll hear what he has to say; and then if the answers don't suit we'll know what to do!"

"And just in case one of you may linger behind, with nothing on to betray his presence behind us," said Jim, flicking his kerchief at a fly which landed for a moment on one of his knees, "you should be advised that there is another one of us who is out in the woods now watching everything that's going on here. If someone of your band should try to creep up unseen on Dafydd, here, from behind, or myself, he would warn us immediately."

Another stream of invective came from the armored figure.

"—You lie!" he wound up. "We know these woods. We saw you coming before you knew you were close to us. There was only the two of you at any time."

"But you're quite wrong, you know," said Jim. He raised his voice, "isn't he wrong? My friend, you are out there, watching aren't you?"

"I am," came back a harsh voice that was so close that it seemed almost to be in the clearing with them.

There was a moving together of the group behind the armored figure, and a muttering among them.

" . . . That was the voice of a wolf," Jim heard one of them saying in low, uneasy tones.

"You've got a wolf out there?" demanded Eshan.

"By all the Apostles," said Jim, calmly but also foppishly, "but you do ask questions! Now, to this business of how you are to get the rest of the gold. You're ready to hear that now?"

"What do you think I've been after, ever since you sat down?" demanded Eshan. "Yes, that's what we want to hear. And quickly!"

"As to quickly," said Jim in the same tone, once more sniffing delicately at his handkerchief, "I am even more eager than you to have this conversation over and be away from this unbearable stink. Well, then, it's very simple. I have selected a place which is drawn on a map that I give you now—"

He passed over a piece of white cloth, with a rough map, drawn with charcoal, of the place he had selected within the Cheviot Hills; and laid it on the ground before Eshan.

"Since you know these woods so well, I'm sure you'll have no trouble finding it," he said, "and when you do reach it you'll know you've found the correct place by the fact that there will be a flag there, an ordinary stick with a piece of white cloth tied to it. You follow me?"

He looked at Eshan.

"Yes, yes!" said Eshan. "Get on with it."

"Very well," said Jim. "You will also recognize it by how it looks. It is backed on a couple of sides by cliffs and there is a sort of ledge on which you, m'Lord Eshan, and I, can supervise the handing out of gold to each one of the Hollow Men. Because, you see, we do not really trust you. We feel that each Hollow Man will have to be paid individually, by himself."

He paused again, to give his words emphasis. Eshan said nothing. Jim went on.

"So you and I and Dafydd here, and perhaps one or two others, will stand on this ledge with the gold, and the individual Hollow Men may each come up, in turn. As each comes, he will be given his first payment of one-quarter of the gold due him. The second payment of three-quarters, as I said, is to come once the Scottish army has caught up with you deep in English territory, and if you have done properly. You are agreeable to these terms?"

"Yes, damn you! Go on!" said Eshan.

"You should meet us where this map shows, then, every Hollow Man who wishes to be part of this gold-gaining expedition, ten days from now. I will attempt to be there by no later than mid-morning; but I may be as late as noon. But everyone who is a Hollow Man and wishes to be a part of this foray must already be there. If any come after I have arrived, they will not be accepted and not paid."

"May your grave be defiled by donkeys!" snarled Eshan. "These last terms won't do for us! Only us, the leaders, will collect the gold and hand it out. We don't trust you, either."

Jim shrugged and made as if to get up.

"Well, then," he said, "there's no more to be said—"

"Sit down again!" said Eshan. "Yes, I said sit down! Maybe we could do it your way. Maybe your way is best. All the lads will want to be sure that they each get their fair share; and this is the way to let them make sure they do. Maybe it's a good plan. All right. Ten days from now in this place you've mentioned. Don't worry. But be sure you bring enough gold. Because every Hollow Man is in this!"

Pulling the dagger from its scabbard on the sword belt on his side opposite where his sword hung, he pushed its point into the spot Jim had marked on the piece of paper. He turned his head to look back over his shoulder at those behind him.

"Any objections?" he said, in a dangerous voice.

None of those behind him said anything.

He turned back to present his closed visor to Jim.

"It's settled, then. Ten days. But we better find the flag, and you better bring the gold as you say, and no tricks!"

"Oh, tricks," said Jim disdainfully, tucking his kerchief into his sword belt as he stood up. "We leave such child's play up to you."

He turned and walked back to the horses where he looked down at the chest, on the ground with its top flung back, but no gold of any kind within it.

"This chest will need to be put back on the horse," he said, looking back at Eshan. "Either that, or we will have no way to bring you the gold when the time comes, and consequently it will not be brought."

"Fix it!" growled Eshan. Half a dozen of the partially clad Hollow Men apparently moved forward, and went to work. Within a few moments the chest was once more trussed up.

"Excellent!" said Jim, mounting, as Dafydd reshouldered his bow, requivered his arrow and mounted beside him, picking up the lead rope of the pack horse. "Now, as evidence of our deep trust and faith in you, here is a payment for you, the leaders— since leaders should always receive more than followers."

Jim reached in behind and under his saddle and pulled out a roll of cloth that seemed very heavy. He threw it toward the Hollow Men. It made an arc of maybe eight feet in the air and hit the earth with a solid clinking sound.

The Hollow Men made a rush upon it like hounds on a chunk of thrown meat. Jim and Dafydd turned their horses; and, leading the pack horse with the empty chest upon it, they rode back into the shadow of the woods.

Jim changed hastily back to himself.

They had not gone more than enough distance to be well out of sight and sound of the clearing than Snorrl appeared, trotting at the left of Jim's horse.

"Back to that place you call a castle?" asked the wolf.

"Yes," said Jim. The matter with the Hollow Men had gone off well, but, strangely, he found himself touched by a sense of foreboding for which there seemed to be no reason.

"Back to the castle by the most direct route and losing as little time as possible."

They had been four hours finding the Hollow Men and some three and a half hours in returning. This, plus the time spent at the camp itself, had brought them well past noon. So that when they reached the castle, they found out that the process of preparation for battle was already underway.

Forges were alight, spears were being repointed, swords were being resharpened, armor was being checked and occasionally hammered where a dent had gone too deeply into it. Needless to say all these activities were taking place in wooden outbuildings around the courtyard. Except in the cressets, fire-pots and the stonewalled kitchen at the base of the peel tower, fire was not to be tolerated near the castle and its contents. Always it had been the greatest enemy of the medieval home, whether humble hut or castle.

Brian, of course, was also outside, supervising the refurbishing of his own armor, while seated on a stool near one of the forges. He caught sight of Jim and Dafydd as they came through the gate.

"James! Dafydd!" he cried, pushing himself to his feet. He started toward them, but stumbled slightly.

"Stay there!" shouted Jim. "We'll come to you."

He rode his horse over to Brian and dismounted there, as did Dafydd, just behind him. Grooms came to lead their horses away and Brian clutched Jim and Dafydd, each of them in turn, in a bear hug.

"Does it not do your heart good, James," he shouted, "to see so much fair activity going forward toward a good end? When is the bicker to be, James?"

"Ten days from now," said Jim.

"Ten days? I shall be whole as a wormless apple and fit as a buck in spring, by that time!" said Brian. "Ah, but it is glad tidings you bring me, James!"

Privately, Jim thought that even at the unusual rate at which Brian had been healing, he would be in no shape to be part of the battle with the Hollow Men when the time came. How to keep him out of it was a problem that would somehow have to be resolved in Jim's mind between now and when they rode out to the meeting with their allies and their enemies.

"And the Hollow Men?" cried Brian—he suddenly realized what he was doing and lowered his voice almost to a whisper directed at Jim's nearer ear. "Did they take the bait?"

"They did," answered Jim, in an equally low voice. Not because he was afraid that the Hollow Men might be listening; but that the many other ears around them might pick up the information; and later speak of it where the word could be picked up and carried back to the Hollow Men, themselves, through those with which the leaders spent their own first installment of gold.

"Ah! Then let us inside, and drink a cup!" said Brian exuberantly, flinging an arm around either one of them and starting toward the Great Hall.

They went along with him, his arms still on their shoulders; and, if he leaned a little heavily on them from moment to moment, neither Jim nor Dafydd mentioned it.

The high table in the hall had no one sitting at it. As Jim sat down with Dafydd and Brian, he turned to Brian and asked him about MacDougall.

"Where is he, with all this going on?" Jim asked.

"Up on the roof of the tower, or looking at the country from the battlements—with Liseth," said Brian.

The last two words were said with a peculiar emphasis and Brian emphasized it with a brief wink on the side of his face that only Jim could see. Jim opened his mouth to ask about this, but Brian had already turned and was shouting to the servants for wine. There were cups on the table but all the pitchers were empty.

Jim's sense of foreboding came back again, more strongly. He had not told Brian of his plan with Liseth to draw out the MacDougall, so Jim could study how to act like him; and he could think of no other reason why Brian should find something secret and amusing in the fact that Liseth was with the MacDougall, when the last time Jim saw the two of them together, Liseth was seeming to barely endure the presence of the Scottish Lord.

But the opportunity, if he had had one to ask, was already gone; and evidently from the way Brian had conveyed the news, he had not planned to discuss the matter in front of Dafydd. Again, why this should be so, Jim did not understand.

He wondered if the uneasiness was beginning to cause him to find meanings that were not there, in things that otherwise would be perfectly ordinary. It could be so. But something inside him refused to believe that explanation.

It was only later, when their table had been joined by two of the de Mer sons and these were deep in the process of questioning Dafydd about fights he had been in, that Jim felt his sleeve plucked by Brian and, turning to look, saw the other beckoning him to slip away from the table.

CHAPTER 25

Jim followed Brian with uneasiness. There was no particular definite reason for this; but the feeling of foreboding he had felt on leaving the camp of the leaders of the Hollow Men had never quite left him, and now Brian's unusual action reinforced it.

Brian led him off through a doorway into the corridor that had led to the room where he had met with the leaders of the Borderers earlier. But they did not go as far as that particular room. Instead, Brian stopped and waited for him in the corridor itself, as soon as they were about a dozen or so feet from the doorway and well out of earshot of what was being said at the high table—and therefore, Jim thought, undoubtedly out of earshot of anyone who might overhear them.

"James," said Brian in a hollow voice as Jim came up to him, "I am undone!"

The word "undone," which in the twentieth-century world from which Jim came would only have meant that Brian had somewhere about himself become unbuttoned or unzipped, here had a particular portentous ring—and, Jim had learned, a rather portentous meaning.

Here it meant that the person's plans, whatever they were, had all gone astray and he saw nothing but disaster staring him in the face. Certainly, besides saying this, Brian also looked it.

His face had become almost tragic in its unhappiness.

"Brian!" said Jim, sincerely touched. "What's wrong?"

Brian put a hand on Jim's arm.

"James," he said, "I am in love."

"Why, yes," said Jim, slightly at sea as far as his understanding was concerned, "and the Lady Geronde Isabel de Chaney is well someone that anyone could be in love with. Why should that trouble you?"

"But it is not her I love—any more," said Brian.

"Who is it, then?" asked Jim. A sudden terrible suspicion struck him. "Not—"

"Yes," answered Brian, without waiting for him to complete the question, "that angel on earth. Liseth de Mer."

"Brian," said Jim. "You're not serious!"

"On my soul be it," said Brian, placing his hand on his chest over the place where he imagined his heart to be—actually he was rather far to the left.

Jim was caught wordless for a moment. He had never encountered Brian Neville-Smythe in this particular state. In fact he had never had anything much to do with medieval men who spoke of love seriously at all. There was a certain amount of playing with the word under courtly conditions, or by the minstrels, but the general attitude of those around him had always been that no one, except a few rare people like Herrac, took it seriously. But here was Brian, looking almost ready to swoon with emotion.

"But—" almost stammered Jim, unable to think of anything else to say, "you are pledged to the Lady de Chaney."

Brian dropped his gaze to the floor.

"Alas," he said.

"Alas?" said Jim. "Brian, I've known you for about two years, now. You're my best friend, and we've been together under all kinds of conditions; but you never gave me any impression but that you were deeply in love with Geronde Isabel de Chaney."

Brian heaved a deep sigh.

"Indeed," he said, "I believed so. Had I not come to this place, I might still be believing so. For she is a fair lady, that lady whose favor I've been carrying all these months and years since her father left for the Holy Land on crusade. But, she is no more than a candlelight to a star when compared to Liseth de Mer."

Jim was beginning to sort out his thoughts.

"When did you fall in love with Liseth?" he asked.

"The first time I saw her," answered Brian.

"But you're only telling me about it now?" asked Jim. "Why?"

Once more Brian looked down at the floor.

"I did not admit it to myself," he said, raising his eyes to Jim, "until I saw her treating kindly that popinjay from the Scottish court. Oh, I know it is naught but play-acting—she herself has told me so, when I at last ventured to speak to her of my love. But all the same . . ."

"What did she say when you spoke to her of your love?" asked Jim.

"She laughed," said Brian tragically. "Laughed."

"She was probably trying to give you a polite way out of it, by pretending to make a joke of it," said Jim, rather heartlessly.

"I have no doubt that that was her intention," said Brian, "for with all the other virtues she is the soul of kindness and gentleness. Moreover, she knew that I knew my love for her was fated never to be returned."

"You knew that?" said Jim. "And yet you spoke to her?"

"I had to," said Brian. "I would have burst, else! Or I would have run wild and passed my sword through that MacDougall, even though I later learned he was no true rival."

"Well . . ." Jim hesitated. "Why were you so sure your love was fated not to be returned?"

"How could it be otherwise?" said Brian. "She comes of an honorable family and is honorable herself. As I myself am honorable. And as you have mentioned, I am pledged to the Lady Geronde Isabel de Chaney. Pledged upon my word of honor. My life must be that I go back and someday marry her—but I will do so now knowing that I have left behind me the only one I could ever truly love—Liseth."

There was a moment of silence. Jim was busily trying to think of the proper thing to say. Brian evidently felt no need for words.

"Men have on occasion not married the ladies they were pledged to," said Jim.

"Not honorable men!" said Brian, drawing himself up. "No! I am chained by my own word. As I am a gentleman and a Christian, my word shall never be broken!"

"Well," said Jim, "what of the feelings of the Lady de Chaney if she learns that you have this love for Liseth?"

"Oh, she will learn of it," said Brian, "for I am duty bound to tell her of it."

"Brian!" said Jim, closing his eyes and clutching at his temples—a theatrical gesture he thought that he would never in his life perform naturally. Now, much to his own surprise, he found that he not only did it almost automatically, but that it gave him a moment of temporary relief. At all costs, he was telling himself, he must talk Brian out of this nonsense.

"Have you thought how unhappy the Lady de Chaney will be, if she is told that you are marrying her out of a sense of duty, instead of true affection?" he asked.

"It will make her unhappy, true," said Brian, "but in honor, how can I do less? Just as in honor I can do nothing less than wed her and never see Liseth again."

"Now look here, Brian—" began Jim, and then broke off as he realized he hadn't quite formulated what he wanted to say.

"Yes, James?" asked Brian, looking up at him.

"Think, Brian," said Jim, in the most reasonable tone he could manage. "What color hair has the Lady Liseth?"

"Blonde. Surely you have noticed that yourself," said Brian, looking at him a little surprised.

"I had. I just wanted to make sure you had," said Jim. "Now tell me what color is the hair of the Lady Geronde Isabel de Chaney?"

"Why blonde, also," said Brian. "Why these questions, James?"

"In a moment—" said Jim. "Answer me first, is the Lady de Chaney short or tall—as ladies go?"

"Short," said Brian. "But—"

"And the Lady Liseth de Mer—short or tall?"

"Short, also," said Brian. "Really, James, I don't understand the purpose of these questions."

"You'll understand in a moment," said Jim grimly. "Now, isn't it true that you have gone for several years loving Geronde Isabel de Chaney but being unable to marry her because her father, who is her guardian and the only man who can give permission, has gone off to the Holy Land and not been heard from since?"

"But I told you that, myself, many times," said Brian. "Of course, James, it is true."

"Very well. Now think a moment," said Jim. "Promise me you'll think over seriously what I am about to say to you."

"I will, James," said Brian. "Whatever you tell me, as my best friend and wisest counselor, can only be for my greatest good. I will think it over with all the power within me."

"Several years back you fell in love with the Lady Geronde Isabel de Chaney, who is beautiful, short and has blonde hair. For nearly four years now you and she have been unable to marry as you both greatly desire. Now, up here in this castle, you encounter another young lady who is short, blonde, and whom you undoubtedly find beautiful. Is all this true?"

"Every word of it is true," said Brian solemnly. His tone changed. "But I'm damned if I know what you're trying to tell me!"

"Just this," said Jim. "And this is what I want you to think over most seriously, both before you answer me and in the days to come. Is it possible that you, attracted as you are to women who are short, blonde and beautiful, fell in love with one who is a neighbor of yours; but was kept, to your own great unhappiness, from wedding her. Now, four years after you have waited and waited for marriage with this lady you love, you suddenly encounter another lady, short, blonde and beautiful, but free to marry. Is it possible, Sir Brian Neville-Smythe, that in some sort of desperation you have transferred your unavailable hopes for love from the Lady de Chaney to the Lady Liseth de Mer because she is available?"

Sir Brian looked at him hard for a long moment.

"Very well, James," he said fiercely, "I will think on that—now!"

He stood, accordingly, staring at Jim and saying nothing. The moments went by. Jim began to feel more and more uncomfortable but still Brian said nothing.

Finally, Brian's lips parted and he spoke.

"No, James," he said, "I have thought it over most seriously. The facts of the matter are that I was never in love with the Lady Isabel de Chaney in any deep sense. It was merely a passing fancy of the last three years—that and her being close where I could see her frequently. It is Liseth de Mer that I love with a great, true and pure love."

"Brian—" began Jim, exasperated; but Brian broke in on him.

"So, James," he went on as if Jim had not spoken, "what do I do?"

Jim heaved a deep sigh.

"Brian," he said, "I don't know. That is—I've no advice for you now. Give me until this business with the Hollow Men is over, will you? And I'll think about it. Meanwhile, you will not tell anyone else about this? And you will not lose your head and do any damage to Ewen MacDougall, meanwhile?"

"I promise, James," said Brian, "on my word. Save that he force a quarrel upon me, I will not even look askance at him, whether he is with Liseth or not."

"Good," said Jim. "Let's go back to the high table."

They did so. In the interval in which they had been away, Liseth and MacDougall had evidently come down from leaning on the battlements, or whatever else they had been doing, and were seated at the far end of the high table, talking in such low voices, that they could not easily be overheard.

Not that there was much danger, because the two de Mer sons, in this case Christopher and Alan, were both still asking questions of Dafydd, and when either of them spoke, they drowned out any other conversation that might be heard at the table. Jim sat down with Brian on Dafydd's side of the table, at the opposite end from MacDougall and Liseth.

True to his word, Brian did not even look at the couple, but concentrated his attention on the conversation between the two de Mers and Dafydd, and eventually began to join it with reminiscences of his own.

Jim sat, immersed in his own troubles. He had a busy time ahead of him, in which he would be involved both with the Little Men and the Borderers, in getting them to work together. From what he could see at this end of the table, Liseth at the other end seemed to be enjoying MacDougall's company quite well. In fact, almost too well.

It would be a royal kettle of fish if Liseth actually did fall in love with the courtly MacDougall. Even worse, if she told this to Brian; and as a result Brian actually did push the MacDougall to the point where the other challenged him, and they fought. Jim had really no doubt about Brian's ability to dispatch the other man—if Brian had just been completely well.

Since he had been sixteen, Brian had been making a living for his impoverished lands and castle by the one thing permitted to someone of his class—fighting. On top of that, he had the natural attributes of a fighter. His reflexes were as quick as Jim's; and Jim's, on the volleyball court, had been one of his two strengths—the other being his powerful leg muscles that allowed him to jump higher than most for the ball.

Also, the training Brian had gone through in growing up, and everything he had done since, had built onto a fairly ordinary-sized frame of bone some of the hardest muscle Jim had ever felt. Moreover, to top it all off, MacDougall was, if anything, smaller than Brian—and possibly weighed less. It would be doubtful indeed, if in the kind of slugging contest that sword fights between knights actually became, Brian did not cut the MacDougall to pieces, skillful though the Scotsman might be in certain ways or with certain weapons.

At this moment Herrac came in, and Jim started up from the table, to intercept the older knight and draw him aside just as Brian had drawn Jim, himself, aside. He wanted to discuss with the Lord of Castle de Mer all that had gone on with the Hollow Men.

They ended up talking in that same room where they had talked before. The one that Jim had come to think of as Herrac's "study." Certainly, it was a room private to the ruler of this particular castle. Herrac listened to all that Jim had to say, in silence. Not moving, or showing any particular expression. However, when Jim was done he sighed.

"Ten days," said Herrac, "is short enough time to make ready. It is even shorter if we are to make certain that the Borderers and the Little Men fight together. They may both have agreed to do so—but that is a far cry from their actually so doing, once blood is up and battle is joined. For one thing, how do we place them, one with another in line of battle?"

He hesitated.

"The Little Men fight as spearmen on foot," he said, "after the manner of the lowland Scots. While your Borderer feels best on horseback. But there is no room in those trees to get up any speed or unity for a charge on horseback."

"No," said Jim, "I think a charge on horseback can be managed. Look here."

He drew from his most unfourteenth-century pocket a duplicate of the map he had given the leader of the Hollow Men. Only this map concentrated on the actual open space between the woods and the cliffs.

"Look," said Jim again, spreading the cloth map on the table before Herrac. "What I'm going to propose is that the Little Men make the first attack. The Hollow Men will not at first make the connection between the Little Men and the fact that I might have betrayed them, or that they are in a deliberate trap."

He paused to let Herrac absorb this idea. Herrac nodded thoughtfully.

"In the time it takes them to realize that they are under attack," Jim went on, "the Little Men should have driven them back some distance from the edge of the wood on most sides. Then, once the Hollow Men become adjusted to the situation and begin fighting back, the schiltrons should open up spaces between them and let the Borderers through, on foot or on horseback as they prefer."

He paused again.

"Go on," said Herrac.

"This should result in a situation in which the Borderers on horseback are fighting those of the Hollow Men who come to the meeting place mounted on their own invisible horses," Jim said, "and the Little Men should be dealing with those on foot. Together, Borderers and Little Men should finally form a ring that keeps closing in on the Hollow Men; until, toward the last, the Borderers should slip back and allow the schiltrons of the Little Men to close together and drive the last of the Hollow Men against the cliff and make sure of their death. What do you think of it as a plan?"

"Why, only one thing," said Herrac. "It will be hard to draw off any Borderer once he has been committed to the battle, but you have them withdrawing so that the schiltrons can close together."

"I think they will have their hands full with those Hollow Men who escape being caught in the closing ring and either try to escape or make it out into the open area of the clearing. The Borderers should make a second ring to take care of these, so that none escape."

He stopped speaking and waited. Herrac pondered the map, tracing with his finger in the air above portions of it here and there.

"It may work—but I know of nothing that is sure in war plans," he said at last. "So that this of yours may as well be ours as anything else."

He raised his eyes from the map to look directly at Jim.

"You realize," he said, "the Borderers will expect as their pay for being in the battle the right to take the gold that you have brought to give to the Hollow Men. Will the Little Men be wanting this also?"

"I asked Dafydd about that on our ride back just now from seeing the Hollow Men," said Jim. "Dafydd says he doesn't believe the Little Men have any use for gold. They want only to clear enemies from their land—the enemies who are the Hollow Men—so that their wives and children will be out of danger and they can all live in peace. Their attitude toward gold is different from that of ours."

"God knows, it is a fair thing to hear," said Herrac, with another sigh, "that any people at all do not go mad at the prospect of gaining gold. You had best make sure of this. But if it is so, then a large danger between the two forces will no longer be there."

"I intend to," said Jim. "Tomorrow I'll go see the Little Men again, to tell them of the time—ten days from tomorrow, with a council the night before the attack. Meanwhile, will you go to the Borderers, and get them to recruit as many men as they think they need?"

"I will do so," said Herrac.

"Good," said Jim. "Also, as soon as I'm back from the Little Men, I'll go with you to talk to the Borderers myself, taking Dafydd along to speak for them as much as possible. It may well be that they'll believe what he tells them, where they wouldn't believe the same thing from a Little Man. The only thing is, one or more of the Little Men may want to come with Dafydd to that meeting, to make sure that they've got their own people listening to how the Borderers react."

"I know not how the Borderers will accept Little Men being at their councils," said Herrac.

"You have to convince them that they have to let some of them in. The leaders, at least," said Jim. "Also, speaking of leaders, I feel it most important you be the leader of the Borderers in this."

Herrac hesitated.

"I have avoided being such, though I know many would like me to lead," he said thoughtfully. "But a leader makes enemies whether he intends it or not; and I wanted to start no arguments or feuds that my sons would have to deal with after I was gone. I have always let Sir John the Graeme do the leading."

"This time," said Jim, "it has to be you. You remember my meeting with Sir John the Graeme. He'll be determined to go his own way, if only to show that he's not being pushed into anything by me. You, on the other hand, understanding the necessity of the thing, will do as we've privily agreed between us you should."

"Well . . ." Herrac hesitated once more. "Very well. I will offer to be the leader. But enough must decide to follow me; and it must not anger Sir John too much. For he is powerful on the Border locally, and I do not wish my sons to have him for an enemy. Also, if he pulled out of the endeavor, some others would go with him—and we need all those we can get."

"He struck me as a wise man," said Jim. "One who wouldn't hesitate to use strength and force to get what he wants; but one who also knows when to bend with the prevailing wind. I think if there seems to be a general attitude that wants you as leader, he won't make any real effort to oppose you."

"You read him well," said Herrac with a little smile, looking at Jim. "One would think you had been on the Border all your life."

"As you know, I haven't," said Jim. "But from what I've seen, men are pretty much the same everywhere, when it comes to leading or following. In the end most followers want to follow the leader they trust the most; and I believe that the Borderers have a greater trust in you than in anyone else."

"It may be so," said Herrac. "We'll hope so. I may take this map to show the Borderers?"

"I would be pleased to have you do so," said Jim. "It was with that idea in mind that I drew it."

They went back to the high table in the Great Hall. It was getting close to dinner time; and Herrac took his customary center position at the high table. Jim sat down beside him. Since they had left, Lachlan and the other de Mer sons had joined the group. The table was lively with talk; and soon Herrac himself was drawn into it.

Jim said nothing. He was no longer watching Liseth, or MacDougall, or even Brian. His mind was full of how he would go about dealing with the Little Men tomorrow and what he would say to them.

CHAPTER 26

J im found even more trouble in dealing with the Little Men
the next day than he had expected.

"—How many of these Borderers are there at this meeting
you want us to join them in?" asked Ardac, son of Lutel, when
they were met at the valley entrance again. Jim and Dafydd had
found their way to them, once more with Snorrl's help, and it
was shortly before noon.

"There were eight at the first meeting. They expect more for
this. At a guess the figure could go as high as eighteen instead
of eight," said Jim.

"In that case," said Ardac, "we take eighteen of our schiltron
leaders to meet with them."

Jim had expected that they would want representation; but
not on this scale.

"That's not a wise thing to do," he said. "Three or four of
you, maybe. Possibly even five. But not more than that if you
really are willing to join them in this battle to exterminate the
Hollow Men."

"And why shouldn't we have as many of us there as there
are of them?" demanded Ardac. "We will be providing half the
fighting men, at least; and if I know the Borderers, probably
more than half. As I said to you, I think, at some earlier time,
we could handle this matter by ourselves."

"But not as surely," argued Jim, "let alone the fact that if you do it alone, nothing will have been accomplished to draw your people and the Borderers closer together. And as a magician, I think I told you I see the time coming when the two of you must fight side by side in larger wars."

"So!" said Ardac. He half turned to look at the five white-bearded Little Men, this time standing more than five feet behind him. He turned back to Jim.

"They hunt us down on sight like animals. They circulate a thousand evil stories about us. They blame us for many things, for which, like the stories, we are not responsible and which are untrue. But we must go to a meeting under-represented while they do not?"

"Sir James is only telling you the way of the minds of these men," put in Dafydd, standing beside Jim.

"Are we not men too?" blazed Ardac. "We have preyed on no others, through thousands of years. Always they have preyed on us. Rome crushed us with an iron heel. The Northmen, the Scotti, the Picti, all came to find and attack us, to take our lands and anything else we had. We did no more than fight them off."

He paused for a second, then went on in a calmer voice.

"Until we saw that there would be no peace until they were driven further back than their own borders; and so we spread out down as far as . . ."

He pronounced a name sounding very much like Dafydd's name of "Kingdom of the Sea-washed Mountains," in the same tongue as Dafydd had named himself. It was eerie to Jim to hear it coming so easily from the lips of the bearded Little Man, when he and Herrac and everyone else had struggled to say it with no success.

" . . . There we found a people—your people!"

He looked at Dafydd.

"A people who did not attack us, a people who treated us like other men, which is what we are—forbye we have a little magic picked up over the centuries to aid us to stay alive. Yet are we MEN! And these were the only ones who welcomed us as like them. So we lived in harmony with them until their land sank under the sea. But by that time we were drawing back under new invasions, this time by the Normans so that we shrank up here into this territory, this heartland, where we will die before we give another yard. But mark what I just said—we are men! Men! Just as the Borderers are men. This, they must understand!"

"Indeed, I believe they will come to it," said Dafydd softly, "but slowly, mark you, for it is the way of mankind—your people and mine, included—not to change their minds on large matters suddenly, but only slowly over a period of time as the truth begins to soak through to them.

"If you like," he went on, "Sir James or I will ask it as a special favor, that you come yourself with no more than three or four others. Bear in mind, you will have me there to speak for you, and they recognize me as being far above them in rank. Have no fear that you will be under-represented."

"We must talk of this!" said Ardac. He whirled about to the five white-beards; and together they went off to a distance, large enough so that they could not be overheard. They talked for some time. Meanwhile, Jim and Dafydd stood in the full glare of the mounting sunlight and the day warmed to where Jim, at least, was uncomfortable in his clothing and his armor.

Finally, Ardac came back, with the five old ones moving up also, just behind him.

"We place it upon your honor"—and once more he uttered the name that neither Jim nor anyone else not a Little Man or Dafydd had been able to speak—"to hold good on your promise that we will not be under-represented there if I only come, and three or four others with me. But I warn you, we will take no scornful remarks, no allusions to us as being any less than men. Promise me also that you will warn your Borderers will be made aware of this in advance, before we all speak."

"I promise," said Dafydd, "by the honor of my name—" Once more the liquid syllables. He turned to Jim. "Sir James?"

"You have my promise also," said Jim. "On my honor be it—the Borderers will respect you or I myself will declare the meeting closed."

"And will they listen to you when you say that?" asked Ardac.

"They'll listen," Jim said. For a moment he felt a sudden flush of heat and anger inside him. "I am a man of magic. I can close any such meeting, whether those there like it or not!"

There was a pause.

"Then," said Ardac, "we are in your hands. I will be there on the appointed evening, with at least three other leaders of our schiltrons. The plan of battle of which you have told me will suit us. If it is changed, then perhaps we do not fight together after all—unless the change suggested is one we find even more agreeable. On your honors be it, Sir James Eckert, and—"

A final time, he used Dafydd's ancient title and name.

On the way back to the castle, Jim rode silent for some time. He was foreseeing great difficulty with the Borderers. Finally, it was Dafydd who broke the silence.

"Will you try to understand them, James?" Dafydd said, as their horses paced side by side.

Jim was touched. It was seldom the bowman addressed him without prefacing his name with a "Sir." Then Jim remembered that for the moment Dafydd could be speaking from the standpoint of the Prince of the unpronounceable name, which gave him every right to address Jim as an equal, or even subordinate. Nonetheless, the feeling of being touched remained. He had no need to ask who Dafydd had meant by "them."

"Believe me, Dafydd, I will," he said. "I do understand the Little Men's viewpoint; at least as far as someone who's not one of them can. I can't pretend to know it as they know it, because I've never had to live as they've had to live, all these generations."

He looked at Dafydd, hoping the other would believe him.

"But certainly they've the right to any form of representation they like. They've more than earned that over the centuries. Only, unfortunately, we're face-to-face not with what's right, but with what'll work. I tell you, Dafydd, I can't explain it, but I'm positive that the Little Men and the Borderers are eventually going to have to work hand-in-hand, come to be friends and—maybe even become one people, someday; so that perhaps there may not be any more Little Men; but just occasionally a Borderer, shorter than he might otherwise be."

"You may be right, James—I don't know," said Dafydd. "I've no real connection myself, now, with that kingdom sunk beneath the waves that they speak of. Those of us who chose the land lost touch with our people below long since. But we still feel a living bond with them; and I still feel a living bond with the Little Men. In the end, if they are to survive—if their blood is to survive in the veins of people to live after us, they must, like all of us, become acknowledged as one of the race of men, and indistinguishable from those around them."

Jim and Dafydd rode on together, after that, in silence. It was all very well, thought Jim, for him and Dafydd to philosophize on the future of the Little Men. But, as he had just said, what they dealt with were the realities of the here and now; and the fact that the Borderers would not take easily to the idea of giving the Little Men anything like an equal say in the battle.

Somehow, the Borderers must be brought to allow this. Desperately, Jim wished that he had the unlimited magic account that he had once taken for granted he had, during the former year in France, when he had used magic whenever he felt like it.

He was having to do all this, now, with nothing but the advantage his twentieth-century knowledge of things gave him—that and his own native wits. He could also do, he thought wryly, with a slight improvement in the native-wit department. Because, right now, he did not see exactly how he would bring the other Borderers around. But he must try.

His fears turned out to be only too justified the following evening after they had returned to Castle de Mer, and ridden off to another nearby castle built around a peel tower, where a further meeting of the Borderers was being held. This time there were some twenty-four of them in the room. Evidently the word had spread and more of those who could join in had put in an appearance.

There were so many, in fact, that only about twelve could be accommodated at the heavy, oak-topped rectangular table at which there were benches. The rest had to stand around the sides and toward the back of the hall where they met. Herrac, Jim and Dafydd were given benches—Dafydd only reluctantly, and that on the basis of his supposedly high rank as the Prince of a far country. Aware of the reluctance, Dafydd said that he would rather stand, and graciously offered his bench to Sir John the Graeme, who took it with polite, but rather cold, thanks.

Dafydd remained standing, behind Jim and Herrac. His bow was still over his shoulder and his quiver at his side. He had not taken them off because none of the others around him had taken off their swords; in spite of the polite rule that when visiting a neighbor the sword was removed, even if other weapons were carried about the person. As at the earlier meeting, it seemed to be generally conceded that this was a council of war, rather than a neighborly visit.

The meeting started out with a number of introductions of Jim and Dafydd to those who had not been there before. By this time, Jim had forgotten all but the names of a few of those he had met, but the ones he did remember, like William of Berwick, a round-faced, round-bodied man in his forties, under thinning gray hair, stuck firmly in his mind.

That part of the business over, Herrac spoke—and there was an almost instant silence as he began to explain that since their first meeting, Jim had seen and made arrangements both with the Hollow Men and with the Little Men; and they should all appreciate this effort for which he had been uniquely equipped, being magician as well as knight. He then turned the speaker's position over to Jim so that Jim could tell them about both meetings.

Jim stood up, to make sure that everyone in the room could not only hear but see him, and again told them first the plan, which was to entice all the Hollow Men to this one particular spot where they could be trapped, under the guise of paying them the first installment of Scottish money; then described how his encounter had gone with Eshan, the leader of the Hollow Men.

They listened without a word, and when he finished there were some murmurs of pleasure and approval from around the table and those standing back from it.

"That was weel done," said Sir John, his voice carrying easily through the room. "And I understand from Sir Herrac that it was only the next day ye saw and talked with the Little Men?"

"That's so," answered Jim. He was about to mention that Herrac had been with him, when he realized that the "ye" that Sir John had used, in this case, was a plural pronoun. "As you know, Sir John, and perhaps some of these other knights also, Sir Herrac was with me, as well as his Highness here, the Prince Merlion."

He paused for just a second. But there was no sound from those in the room to give him an indication of how his words were being received. He went on.

"We talked with Ardac, son of Lutel, and the five chief advisors of the Little Men. I told them everything I had done so far, and gave the date for which the destruction of the Hollow Men had been set. . . . I did not firmly set a time for a final council just before the battle," he wound up, "but I suggest it take place the night before. I will send that message to them if the rest of you agree."

He paused. Now was the time to face them with it.

"I also suggest that the meeting be made at the Castle de Mer, which I suppose to be most appropriate, as I understand that you will probably be choosing Sir Herrac here as your battle leader."

For a moment there was silence. Then there were a few scattered cries of "Yes!" here and there about the room; followed almost immediately by a flood of voices agreeing with the selection. Sir John, who had opened his mouth to speak, sank back on his bench, closing his mouth, with a slight frown on his face.

"I think," said Sir John unexpectedly, "that we have yet to hear Sir Herrac himself agree to taking that responsibility. Do you, Sir Herrac?"

Herrac's deep and powerful voice rang almost unexpectedly through the Hall.

"I am not one that likes to be a leader," he said. "I think all here know that. My duty is to my family and my heritage which is my castle and its lands. Nonetheless, in this case, where it is so important that the Hollow Men be finished once and for all, I do accept!"

A deep-voiced acclamation sounded in the room. When it had died down, Sir John turned again and Jim felt the knight's eyes upon him coldly.

"You were about to tell us the substance of your talk and agreement with the Little Men, Sir James," said Sir John. "Pray go on."

"They will come, in numbers equal to your own and perhaps surpassing it," said Jim. "Their first response was to ask how many Borderers would be at this council. I guessed eighteen— I see that I was wrong. We will have more than that. Ardac, son of Lutel, then answered me that in that case eighteen Little Men would be sent to join the council."

A clamor broke out in the room, of half a dozen voices speaking at once, with an undertone of angry mutters in the background.

"What gives them to think that we will welcome eighteen of them to our council?" shouted William of Berwick, pounding the table. "One were enough, and more than enough, to carry our decisions back to them. After all, they will be fighting under our command."

There was a silence following that, and Jim found himself glad that he was on his feet.

"But they will not be under your command. They will be under their own commander, who is Prince Merlion here—who shares some ancient brotherhood of blood with them."

"This is foolish," said Sir John the Graeme. "Two leaders will simply make a disaster of our fight. Yet I admit it is hard to ask his Highness here to serve under a simple, if noble, knight like Sir Herrac."

"I am willing." Dafydd's voice, soft as usual, still carried through the room.

"Why that, I say?" shouted William of Berwick, hitting the table again. "What need we with the Little Men at all? It is our right to destroy the Hollow Men, ours alone. And we will do it with ease!"

There was a thud suddenly in the middle of the table and every man there froze, for one of Dafydd's war arrows stood with its head all but buried to the tines in the thick, oak top of the table.

"Permit me to dispute with you somewhat on that point, Sir William," said Dafydd, gently but carryingly.

He had come into the Hall with his bow on his shoulder and his arrows on his hip, since the others were all wearing their swords, and they—living in a country where the archers were weak; and in a land and time in which all belted and armored knights looked down their noses at the commoners who bore bows—had never stopped to think what a weapon it was, and that it could be used indoors in this fashion. It had simply never crossed their minds. Swordplay between these walls, they could have envisioned. But not this.

Sir William sat silent, staring from the arrow to Dafydd.

"I wish to point out something with the arrow you see there," went on Dafydd. "Now it happened I merely plucked my bow-string so that the arrow would stand upright in the table. Let me show you how it would have gone had I plucked it a little further."

So fast that it almost seemed like a form of magic itself, another arrow was fitted to Dafydd's bow and flew from it—into and through the table until it rested against the floor beneath. Only the tips of its feathers and its notched end showing above the table top.

"You see," said Dafydd, almost kindly, "that this bow of mine is not an unworthy weapon. In fact—perhaps, Sir Herrac, you would now have summoned in to us your son Sir Giles, who was with Sir James and myself in France, that he might tell the story of the sword with which he defended the Crown Prince of England against nearly a score of knights belonging to an evil magician. Will you do so, Sir Herrac?"

For answer Herrac merely turned his head, lifted his voice and bellowed out a call that would easily have penetrated the door behind him and the servant waiting without.

"*Ho! Fetch Sir Giles—at once!*"

The door was opened almost as if on cue and Sir Giles stepped through into the room, closing the door again behind him.

"There was no need to seek me, Father," he said. "I, also, have been waiting outside to hear the results of your meeting."

"His Highness, here," said Herrac, still letting his voice roll through the chamber, "would that you tell of a sword with which you defended the Prince of England last year in France."

"Yes, Father," said Giles. He looked down the table and lifted his voice to reach everyone in the room. "The sword with which I had the honor to fight for the young Prince, was one that I got from the Prince Merlon, himself."

He turned to Dafydd.

"Noble Sir?" he asked. "What is it you wish me to tell these gentlemen about the sword?"

"All," said Dafydd. "From what I told you of how it came into my hands until how it passed into your hands."

"I will be more than willing to do so," said Sir Giles. He was probably the shortest man there. But his mustache bristled fiercely; and the large nose of which he was normally rather ashamed lifted proudly like the prow of a ship about to go into battle.

"It was before the battle of Nouaille–Poitiers; and the Prince Edward was swordless. He asked that one of us who was there present, and wearing swords, give him one of ours, for that it shamed him that he, a Plantagenet and a Prince, should be swordless on a day of battle."

He looked at Dafydd, who nodded at him to go on.

"In truth, all of us were loath to give up our swords. For what is a knight without his sword?"

There were murmurs of agreement around the room. Jim was a little surprised, then remembered that these Northumbrians were only recently included under the English Crown; and, in any case, they would not have been all that ready to give up their swords themselves.

"So we hesitated," went on Sir Giles. "And his—the Prince Merlon—said to the Prince Edward, who knew him only as a simple bowman, that perhaps he could solve the problem. The Prince Merlon then went off, and returned from his baggage with a magnificent knight's sword in a jeweled scabbard. He gave it to the Prince who half drew it, held it a moment and appeared uneasy. '*I cannot carry this sword,*' the Prince said."

Sir Giles had the room dead silent. He took a deep breath and went on.

"At this point, shame overtook me that I had not offered my own sword before," said Giles. "I stepped forward, unhooked my scabbard from its sword belt and offered it with the sword within it to the noble English Prince, saying, '*If you would do me the honor of accepting the sword of a common knight*'— and graciously, the Prince accepted it. While I took the sword that the Prince Merlon had brought and hooked it to my own belt. It was with that sword, then, that I essayed to keep the young Prince of England safe against his enemies."

He stopped speaking.

"Thank you, Sir Giles," said Dafydd. "But you have not yet told how the sword came into my hands."

"Oh. Forgive me," said Sir Giles. "I should tell you all"— he was addressing the room once more—"that Da—"

Sir Giles caught himself just in time.

"—His Highness of Merlon told us the story of how he had acquired the sword. It was at a time when he was disguised as a bowman, as he is now, but in that land that was formerly called Wales, but now is English territory. It seems that one of the English Wardens there believed in holding tournaments to demonstrate the prowess of his knights, particularly to his Welsh subjects. This day the Warden had thought of an additional entertainment."

Sir Giles stopped to take a deep breath.

"So, since he had heard of the bowman the Prince Merlon was supposed to be, as one very skilled with that instrument, he had him fetched to the tourney ground and faced with five knights in armor and lances. These five were on horseback, and he alone, afoot, with his bow. They rode upon him, but he slew them all with his arrows before they reached him; before indeed they were even close to him."

Giles paused again; but in this instance it was to give the muttering this statement had given rise to time to die down.

"He had made a request that if he should win the day, he should—like any victor in the list—win also the arms and armor of his opponents; and the Warden had laughingly agreed. As a result, he came into possession of all the armor and weapons of those he had just killed; but turned all back except this one sword, which he kept. The which he had brought with him, and later offered to the Prince. Again, it was this sword with which I essayed to defend his Grace of England."

"Thank you, Sir Giles," said Dafydd. He turned back to those in the room. "That story and those arrows in the table I have had you see and hear for a purpose. This weapon is not usual among you gentlemen, and no gentleman uses it except for hunting or sport. But it is a powerful weapon, nonetheless; and I, for one, do not feel my rank diminished by the fact that I go disguised as an ordinary man of the bow."

He paused.

"I would that you consider, therefore and likewise, gentlemen, that no gentleman ever bands with other gentles in a schiltron, on foot, with spears, to meet their enemies. Yet the Little Men do this, and do it well. May I point out they have held their borders against the Hollow Men all these centuries, which is no mean feat. You who have met scattered bands of the Hollow Men know that they are not easy to fight.

"What I am saying," Dafydd said, "is that they, by right of combat and blood and lives lost, have as much right to be there at the ending of the Hollow Men as yourselves. They have won that right on fields of battles, innumerable. I am proud to be chosen their leader, and I am not too proud to serve under Sir Herrac, as our supreme commander. But, since I know many of you feel uneasy about the Little Men, I asked that they reduce their number from eighteen to no more than five representatives at our council the night before the battle. This they agreed to. This, as their commander, I place before you not as a request but as a demand."

The room was silent.

CHAPTER 27

The silence persisted in the room. As it stretched out, a tension could be felt in the air, beginning to gather itself together, as the spring of a watch gathers itself into a smaller and smaller space when it is wound tight. Into this tightening silence, Herrac's voice broke like the prow of a ship splintering its way through new ice over freezing water.

"As the chosen commander of the Borderers in this endeavor," his powerful voice said flatly, "I accept the Prince Merlon's proposal that no more than five of the Little Men shall meet with us on the night before our battle with the Hollow Men in council for final planning. Any who wish not to follow me in this matter may now declare themselves apart from it and leave the rest of us. I would have no man follow my orders who does not do so willingly, and with a full heart."

For a long moment more nothing happened; then the tension began to dissipate, as a spring might unwind, without ever having been brought to full tightness.

No one moved to leave the room.

"I am glad so many of you will be with us," said Herrac, dominating the room again with his voice. "For it will take the strength of all of us; and the strength of the Little Men as well, to put an utter end to the Hollow Men. It will be no easy task."

He broke off for a moment to emphasize his last words.

"I have already considered some plans of battle," he went on. "I will continue to consider them; and do all of you consider, yourselves, whether there is anything that we might do that would improve our chances of winning this battle, with as little loss on our own side as possible. Then, if you think of any such, bring it to the council on the eve of battle, to be spoken there; and advise the rest of us on it. For tonight, unless there is further discussion of anything important, I will declare this meeting closed."

There was another silence; but this time it was a short one.

"I would believe our commander has the right of it," put in Sir John Graeme. "I can think of no further reason to prolong this meeting. So let us all move to the Great Hall of this castle, where I understand our host has prepared food and drink for us. To any, of course, who have business that takes them elsewhere without delay, I say farewell, and I look forward to seeing you again, before the battle."

With a sudden outburst of voices, the meeting broke up. Everyone was standing up at the table, and mixing with those behind them. The door had been opened and Herrac had led the way out, followed by Jim and Dafydd, with Sir John Graeme close behind them. The rest trailed after in an unstructured, loudly talking tail of men that wound through the short corridor outside and into the Great Hall of the castle where they had gathered.

The meeting, as was not uncommon in medieval matters, turnéd into a drinking party.

Jim, taking advantage of the pretense that he had things to do, left early so as not to befuddle himself with more wine than he wanted to drink. Dafydd chose to come with him— and, surprisingly, Herrac as well.

"I thought you might feel obligated to stay, Sir Herrac," said Jim, once they were on their horses outside and headed back toward Castle de Mer; with Sir Giles and some of the de Mer men-at-arms riding with them, on general principles of defense, considering the land and the times.

"None will miss me," said Herrac. "Also, if I had stayed, there might have been a tendency for some to try to advance some privy point with me; and others to gather perhaps around someone like Sir John the Graeme, who might still choose a separate way of his own and take some others with him."

"You were wise," murmured Dafydd. Herrac went on.

"It is my belief that a commander should be at some distance from those he commands. Since you two gentlemen are guests of mine, I can hardly distance myself from you. But I intend to either command or not command; and I think the first step in that direction is to establish the distance I spoke of."

"I agree with Dafydd," said Jim, just loudly enough to be heard over the creak of their saddles and the sound of their horses' hooves on the hard ground underneath. It was a chill, cloudless night that made the horses' breath smoke before them, and the moon was three-quarters full. Their road was bright enough, accordingly, so that none of the party were required to carry torches and go ahead. Jim found himself appreciating Herrac's position.

The knight was in fact, Jim thought, a natural leader. Only his other responsibilities had kept him from it until this moment. He wondered if now Sir Herrac was actually enjoying the fact that he had been chosen commander. Which reminded him that there was something more to be said.

"Sir Herrac," he said, "you spoke up in just the nick of time back there, after Dafydd had mentioned that five Little Men would be attending our council. None of us meant you to take the responsibility all on yourself—"

"That is my job now," interrupted Herrac. "Would you not consider it your job, if you had the command in keeping, Sir James?"

Jim thought for a moment and was a little surprised.

"I might," he said. "Yes, I might just do exactly that. Still, it was your presence and your voice that did it just now; and I doubt mine would have had that persuasive an effect on all the other Borderers there."

"They know me," said Herrac briefly.

Jim could well believe it. Herrac, with his strength and size, and even his silkie blood, could be a living legend among these Borderers. But that was hardly a point to make, right at this moment. Consequently he said nothing.

They reached the castle safely, and separated to their various bedrooms, Jim only going along with Dafydd for a short visit to Sir Brian. Brian was in his bed, because he was too tired to stay on his feet any longer. But he was chafing at his inactivity; and the fact that he had not been able to go to the meeting himself.

He listened, therefore, with interest to what Jim, Dafydd and Sir Giles—who had also come along with them—had to tell him of it. He exclaimed with delight over the account of Herrac's command that the Little Men should be accepted at the council; and applauded when Jim repeated Herrac's remark later that a commander should be a certain distance from those he commanded.

"How very right the good knight is!" said Brian. "I've yet to see a successful leader of men who did not keep his distance. Those who mix and mingle with the ones they lead are invariably liked and well thought of, but not always well obeyed. Better for all to be apart; and even—yes—disliked by those you lead; than to be too close, so that you are taken for less than you are."

"So I told him—more or less," said Dafydd.

"Dafydd was the one to bring it up," said Jim. "But I said after him and I have to say now that I agree with him, and you, Brian. Sir Herrac is a natural leader."

"We, his sons," put in Sir Giles, "have known this all our lives. You do not have any idea how much Father has seen his responsibility to his family. Not the least to my mother, who he loved most dearly; as did we all."

The last words ended on a note of sadness; which might have blighted the conversation for a while, if Brian had not burst out in a new direction.

"But you, James!" he said. "You must begin practicing immediately; and it must be well away from this castle here, so that no eyes, that should not, see that perhaps you are a little rusty, or not yet as skilled as you might be with weapons."

"That's a polite way of putting it, Brian," said Jim. "You know, and we all here know, that I'm nothing to talk about as a fighter. My great fight against the Ogre was with the advantage of the reflexes of the dragon whose body I was in. If it hadn't been for Gorbash, the Ogre would have squashed me in half a minute."

"You will get better, James, you will get better!" said Brian. "Particularly with practice and under my tutelage. Now, as I say, you must practice out of sight of anyone else in the castle here. I would counsel that not even Sir Herrac—if you will pardon me, Sir Giles—know of you and your limitations with sword and other like tools."

"You're right," said Jim thoughtfully.

"We must all go off by ourselves from the castle tomorrow," Brian went on. "All of us, that is, except you, Dafydd—unless there is some reason you want to accompany us. Then, when we are a distance from the castle that is sufficient to make sure we cannot be overseen or overheard, Sir Giles will practice with you with the various weapons; and I will stand by and order that practice, since I am yet perhaps a day or two from being able to practice with you myself."

He was a good deal more than a day or two, Jim thought. But he knew better than to mention such a thing in front of Brian. Instead he struck another note.

"It really isn't necessary, Brian," he said. "Remember, I've told you what our plans are like. I will be with Dafydd up on the ledge above the ground where everyone is fighting. I shouldn't have to fight."

"And how will you leave that ledge; and get through what Hollow Men remain between you and those pressing them inward, with your body and life intact?" demanded Brian. "You do not understand such fighting, even yet, James; forgive me for saying so. In the heat and turmoil of battle, friend can even strike friend, either through error or because the battle urge has been wakened so strongly in him. You may even have to use your shield to protect yourself from the Borderers, to pass through them to safety. No, no. You must practice; and we will do things as I suggested!"

So they did.

Following that evening, Jim left every morning with Brian and Giles; and very often with Dafydd as well. They rode off for half an hour or more until they were in some secluded, tree-hidden spot, well away from the castle and where there was room for the practice Brian had in mind. There he put Jim and—inevitably—Sir Giles as well, through a course of instruction; with all kinds of weapons from poignard up through mace.

"But I won't have a mace with me!" Jim said.

"Nonetheless, practice is practice," insisted Brian.

So, Jim practiced with the mace. Until his arms were worn out and ready to drop from their sockets by the feel of them. He called a halt.

"Dafydd," he said—for it was one of the times Dafydd was with them. Jim took off his helm and wiped his soaking wet forehead. "How would you like to take a little of this training, for a while?"

"Indeed," said Dafydd, "I have been watching with interest. But I would not venture to ask that a knight train me in a knight's way of combat; who am really, as you all know, no more than a common bowman."

"The hell with that!" said Brian, who was almost frothing at the mouth with his desire to instruct. "I'll teach you any day. Are you willing?"

"I am willing," said Dafydd. "But I will need armor, even if I can borrow weapons."

"Mine will fit you tolerably well," said Jim. "We're close enough in height. Your shoulders may be a little broader than mine, and you may be a little slimmer otherwise than I am, but I think it'll do. Want to try it?"

"I would much like to," said Dafydd.

Accordingly, it was done. And Brian ended up delighted with his new pupil; who in many ways showed much more aptitude for what he was taught than either Sir Giles or Jim—but Jim, as they all knew, was something of a lost cause. Too much of what Brian taught had to be learned starting in childhood. The surprising thing was that the disciplines Dafydd seemed to have learned with his bowmanship in his early years should help him adapt so quickly to make use of Brian's teaching. The truth was, Jim thought, Dafydd—like Brian—was a natural athlete.

It occurred to Jim that Dafydd might be very like some particularly skilled, twentieth-century professional football player of his own world; who, on taking an interest in golf, which he had never played before, in a few weeks is doing the full eighteen holes at an enviably low score.

Meanwhile back at this castle and the castles of the other Borderers, preparations for the battle continued. Jim was surprised to discover that this included a contingent from each castle bringing along extra armor and extra weapons.

It was a while before he realized, from what he had seen of the battle of Poitiers, that both weapons and armor could not stand up to many encounters. Even with the mild steel swords of the time, let alone with things like maces and morning-stars—the latter being devices which were essentially a metal rod with a steel chain at the end and a spiked ball at the far end of the steel chain—armor was soon hacked so badly out of shape it became useless, and weapons themselves were broken and dented beyond repair.

Also, in addition to his lessons, he found that he had to make at least one more trip to the leaders of the Hollow Men and one more trip to the Little Men, simply to firm up the details with each party of the meeting.

He took advantage of the opportunity to lay down very firmly once more to the Hollow Men leaders, and particularly to Eshan, himself, that the Hollow Men must all be gathered there by the time he arrived; and that any Hollow Man who tried to appear after he had come in would not be accepted and would not be paid.

He took Herrac with him on his second trip to the Little Men, and together they explained how Herrac had ensured that five of the small men, at any rate, could be present at the next council; and diplomatically broke the news that there would be more than eighteen Borderers, in fact over twenty at least.

The good side of all this, he pointed out, was that the Borderers should be bringing a total of something like eighteen hundred men with them to the fight, which took some of the pressure off the schiltrons of the Little Men.

Ardac, however, retorted that the Little Men would be there in their full number just the same—for two reasons. One was that not as many of the Borderers might show up as promised. Second was that the Little Men wanted to be sure of being equally represented with the taller humans when the battle started.

Beyond this, Ardac agreed readily enough to the fact that the Little Men should make the first attack, afterwards opening corridors to let the Borderers in through them, to deal particularly with the Hollow Men who were mounted on their ghost horses.

"I will add, Sir Herrac," wound up Ardac, "that I am pleased it is you who is going to be commander of the Borderers. From you, I hope and expect that my people who are in the battle will get fair treatment along with the Borderers."

"You have my word on it," said Herrac. "I didn't mention it before because I was not yet leader at that time; but even though I believe I know the answer, I must ask you if you, or any of your people, would demand a share of the Scottish gold, once the battle is over?"

"We have no use for gold," said Ardac. "I know it is highly prized among your kind; but we do not use money among us, nor do we fashion toys or jewelry as you people do. Also, gold is no use in the making of tools or weapons. Finally, I have to say that from what we have seen of its effect among your kind, we would rather not be touched with the desire for it. If there is gold, your Borderers may have it; and be welcome for all of us."

"Thank you, Ardac," said Herrac. "I was sure that would be your answer. But as commander I had to ask. You understand?"

"I understand," said Ardac. "Now, to other things. You plan to assemble your Borderers at some distance from the place where the Hollow Men will gather, is that not right?"

"Yes," said Herrac, "I'd have them in place early, but a mile or more distant, that we may not alarm the Hollow Men by our presence. How did you plan that your schiltrons would gather?"

"Once your people are gathered," said Ardac, "we will move in to join you. You need not ask how we are marshaled beforehand, nor where we come together, nor any other question of how we shall join you. Let it be enough for you that we are an older and more experienced people; and moreover we know those woods and rocks in a way that your people will never know them; unless they spend as many centuries among them as we have. We can be scattered and out of sight, not one of us showing, then in a hundred breaths be all drawn up in our schiltrons and ready to move. That is all that need concern you."

Herrac nodded.

"So," said Ardac, "when would you wish our two parties to join together and move forward?"

"I told the Hollow Men a little after noon," Jim said. "So let our two companies meet no later than terce, that we may be in position by sext in the woods below their meeting place. By that time also Sir Herrac, here, and the Prince Merlion—"

Ardac smiled a small wintry smile, parting his whiskers at Jim's mangled pronunciation of Dafydd's ancient name.

"We do not use your Christian time-keeping, as you know," Ardac said, "but we know that terce means late mid-morning and your noon is called sext. So you may use those terms with us freely, although we will not use them ourselves. Yes, those hours are agreeable; and we will be there, as you wish. At that time I suggest that you and I, Sir James, Prince Merlion"— he gave it the proper pronunciation—"and one or two others if must be, meet with myself and the other schiltron-leaders before we move up close to where the Hollow Men will be."

"That is agreeable to me," said Herrac. "It shall be so. With me will be Sir James, Prince Merlon and another good knight named Sir Brian who is well experienced in such armed meetings as we go to that day. Possibly one or two others—but no more. I believe you met Sir Brian Neville-Smythe."

"We did," said Ardac. "He was with us in one of our brushes with the Hollow Men. He will be welcome."

"Good," said Herrac.

He looked up at the sun.

"Now," he said, "we should be taking our leave of you. I will not see you again then, until we meet as agreed in the woods at some distance from the Hollow Men's meeting place but with both our peoples ready to move up."

"So it is agreed," said Ardac.

They turned away from each other. Jim, Dafydd and Herrac mounted their horses and rode off back to Castle de Mer. There, Herrac went off to deal with matters of his own concern, and Dafydd and Jim went up to acquaint an impatient Brian with the news of what had gone on at their meeting.

It seemed to Jim, as they talked, that Brian was much more wound up about this oncoming battle than he ordinarily would have been. Jim was a little puzzled by this; and then the realization occurred to him that fighting was the one thing that could take his mind off his newly found love for Liseth, and her constant companionship with Ewen MacDougall. Brian had been scrupulous about leaving the two to themselves.

MacDougall was very clearly falling into a real emotional attachment to Liseth—a good clue, thought Jim wryly—that, in decidedly non-medieval terms he had not got to first base with her, physically. Otherwise with someone like him, who was used to a Royal Court's sort of brief dalliance followed by a quick tumble into bed together, he would have cooled off in his enthusiasm before this.

As to whether Liseth was at all attracted to MacDougall or not, Jim became more and more puzzled by this all the time. If she was not attracted by him, then she was a most excellent actress. A most surprisingly excellent actress for a young woman who had grown up in an isolated castle next to the sea and the Scottish border in the lightly populated land that was Northumberland. There was nothing to be done about it by Jim in any case; so he simply sat back and turned his thoughts to the more important matter, which was getting ready for the fight.

He took the practice sessions in grave earnest. Now, Brian was enough recovered to work out with him, although Jim would hardly have believed that he would have been able to. Brian was still insisting—and now Jim saw that there would be no stopping him—that he would be part of the Borderer group when it went against the Hollow Men.

So the time that he had thought would travel slowly, if anything went by all too fast.

Suddenly it was the eve of the day of battle; and this evening they would hold their final council.

CHAPTER 28

It was not yet time for Jim to make himself available for the council, which would be held downstairs in the Great Hall of the de Mer castle, since Herrac was now commander. It must be the Great Hall, since there was no other room in his home that would comfortably hold the number of individuals who would be attending.

Jim, with the late afternoon sun slanting through the arrow slits let into the outside wall of his small stone room, was making a final effort to contact Carolinus by dream. He had already tried several times in the past few days; but curiously, had been unable to get through to his tutor in magic.

He had found that, if he fell asleep while wanting to have a dream conversation with Carolinus, it happened more quickly if he wrote a sleep spell on what he pictured as the inside of his forehead. He had decided to do just that, this time.

He was stretched out on his mattress. He had closed his eyes; and now he wrote on the inside of his forehead:

MESLEEP/DREAM→CAROLINUS

He fell asleep instantly. This time he was inside Carolinus's crowded little house and standing face to face with the magician.

"I suppose you've been busy," Jim said, "since I haven't been able to get through. So let me apologize for interrupting, if that's what I'm doing. But things have reached a sort of crisis point up here."

"Not at all, my boy. Not at all," said Carolinus. "I've been as eager to talk with you as no doubt you are with me."

Jim, in his dream, gazed at the thin, old man with the white beard and the bushy eyebrows that could look so fierce ordinarily, but were now gazing at him in as soothing and friendly a manner as possible.

His heart sank. It was always bad news when Carolinus was pleasant. The other only abandoned his usual irascibility when he wanted to soften the blow of unhappy news.

"I—" began Jim; but Carolinus cut him off.

"I should warn you first," Carolinus almost snapped in his usual manner, "that you now face both a dangerous and difficult time. However, since that can't be helped, we shall talk of how to best deal with it."

"What I was going to say was," said Jim, "that I've got the Little Men and the men on the English side of the border here ready to see if they can't exterminate all the Hollow Men at once, so that none will be left alive to bring the rest back to life. In other words, things seem in hand up here—depending upon whether we can win the battle or not. But I wanted to ask you—have *you* learned anything more about the Worm, and the Dark Powers' involvement in this?"

"No, and no," said Carolinus decisively, "particularly as regards the Worm. I've no idea why it's there by itself, what it's supposed to be doing and why it's appeared at all; in defiance of the usual practice of the Dark Powers of keeping such creatures close to one of their centers of power. But I'd strongly suggest you stay very much on your guard against it. Somewhere along the line it has to become involved; otherwise, there's no point in it being there at all."

He stopped and took a deep breath.

"More than that," he went on, "I haven't been able to find out. So, more than that, I can't tell you. I've no further knowledge about the Dark Powers, either; except that they're definitely still encouraging both the Scottish invasion and a French one at the same time, the French to come from the south and across the channel."

"You're not much help," said Jim.

"I'd like to be, my boy. I really would," said Carolinus. "How are you fixed with your magic account?"

"I'm going to have to use some magic to make myself a duplicate of Ewen MacDougall to hand out the gold to the Hollow Men tomorrow," said Jim. "Beyond that, I've been afraid to ask the Accounting Office just where I stand. You're sure there's no way you could lend—"

"None!" said Carolinus. "The Accounting Office was very clear about that. No loans from a Master to his Apprentice. I suggest you check with the Accounting Office yourself and find out what your account really is. You don't want to turn from looking like MacDougall into looking exactly like yourself, right in the middle of what you're planning to do, do you?"

"No," said Jim, "that's the last thing I'd want. But I may have to gamble on it."

"Well, then," said Carolinus, his mustache bristling, "if you want my advice—gamble! No one ever got anywhere by avoiding the taking of all chances. Every so often you have to put yourself at risk."

"I'm going to," said Jim. "But—I did have one idea. The Little Men say they have a certain amount of small magic; and I believe them. Do you suppose it'd be possible for me to borrow some of their magic? I haven't mentioned it to them, because I wanted to check with you first."

"Don't ask them!" said Carolinus. "In the first place, no group can lend their magic to you; although the Accounting Office did not strictly forbid that sort of a loan. But the mechanisms for it—the magical mechanisms—simply aren't there. Secondly, you'll find that they treasure their bits of magic very highly, and you'd be asking for something that you should not in decency ask of them."

"All right," said Jim, resigned. "It was only a thought, anyway. Well, then—we go to a final meeting around supper time, soon now, here in the castle. Tomorrow we meet in the woods at some distance from the place where the Hollow Men gather; and there I'll leave the group and go on with Dafydd—and Brian if he seems determined to be in it—to take the gold to the Hollow Men and start handing it out. Then it'll be up to the Little Men and the Borderers to attack as planned and close in the Hollow Men until they can all be disposed of."

He paused, then added a little wistfully:

"I wish there was some way I could contact you on the spur of the moment in the middle of something like this."

"All right!" said Carolinus suddenly. "I'm not exactly breaking the rules. I may be bending them a bit. If you really need to get in touch with me, or if you feel a tingling in your right elbow, close your eyes; and you'll see me. Don't speak out loud; but think the words at me in your head. You can do that?"

"Happily!" said Jim—and he meant what he said.

"I'm doing this on the basis not that you need me, but that I might need you," said Carolinus. "A Master may have a reason to summon or question his Apprentice if he wants, I should think? If the Accounting Office doesn't like that, they can call me on it."

"Thank you," said Jim.

"By Beelzebub and Belshazzar!" snapped Carolinus in his usual ill-tempered tone. "You don't have to go around thanking me all the time. Just do your duty as my Apprentice, that's all! Now, you'd better get going. I have matters in hand at the moment."

"I will," said Jim. "Goodbye, then."

"Good—" said Carolinus, "—bye!"

He winked out. Suddenly Jim was lying on his back with his eyes wide open, staring simply at the rather uneven raised surface of the stone ceiling overhead.

He got to his feet. He was about to leave the room when temptation got the better of him. He stopped. There was no one around to hear.

"Accounting Office," he said.

"Yes?" inquired the bass voice suddenly level with his left elbow.

Jim started. For some reason the Accounting Office voice always had a tendency to make him want to jump, whether he did or not.

"How much do I have left in my magic account?" he asked. "Enough for the slight amount of invisibility and disguise I want to do tomorrow?"

"That will depend on how long you continue in your disguise," said the Accounting Office. "Do you have any more questions?"

"No," said Jim glumly.

It was silent in the room. Jim thought grimly that he might as well never have asked the question. It left him right back where he had started. How long was too long? He did not know. Now, for the first time it occurred to him that possibly the Accounting Office did not know, since the amount of time he would have to be in the disguise depended on the amount of time that he would have to act the part of Ewen MacDougall, before the attack took the Hollow Men's attention off him.

After that he could snap his helmet's visor down over his face; and start, with Dafydd's and perhaps Brian's help, to try to fight his way off the ledge—out through the Hollow Men and the encircling Little Men and Borderers, to safety.

The sun had abandoned the arrow slits of his room; and within, it now was gloomy with a darkness like that of late twilight. He would be leaving the room in any case, so there was no point in lighting the cresset. He went to the door, opened it, and started down to the Great Hall.

He would be a little ahead of the rest of the crowd, he told himself as he descended the winding stairs; but there would be no harm in that. When he got there, however, he was surprised to find the number of others who were there before him. In fact, Herrac and all his sons, except Christopher, were already at the table; as were Dafydd and Brian. Ewen MacDougall was missing.

"Where's MacDougall?" asked Jim as he joined them.

"For the moment, he is in his room," said Herrac. "I have set a strong guard on the door. I told him flatly that I had private business and he would be kept where he was until I felt like freeing him again. He has food and drink and the cressets will keep him warm. Servants have orders to replenish the fuel, and empty his chamber pot, if sobeit needs it. Let us forget him now. The others will be here shortly. Meanwhile, I would counsel all at this table—"

He looked hard at his sons, who seemed to shrink, as they always did, when he regarded or addressed them directly. "—that we relax, take our minds off tomorrow, and appear as indifferent to what is before us as possible. We do not want to give those who come to join us here the idea that we may have been doing some planning or plotting when they were absent."

"An excellent idea, Sir Herrac," said Brian. He yawned and stretched out his legs, quite naturally relaxed. "After all, it will be a merry day tomorrow. I look forward to it!"

"I fear you have more of a taste for battle than many of us, Sir Brian," said Herrac. "Yet you set a good example. I myself will try to take my mind off why we are meeting here tonight and what is coming tomorrow."

Liseth came in at that moment and joined them, sitting down at the table.

"You may stay with us now, Beth—" Herrac rumbled. It was the first time Jim had heard her addressed by what must be a short, familiar form of her name. He liked the sound of it.

"Thank you, Father," said Beth swiftly.

"—But you will leave us as our first guest arrives—as your dear mother would have known to do without being asked," Herrac went on.

"Yes, Father," said Liseth, but with less pleasure in her voice. "Fear not. I will be the proper chatelaine and lady."

"That is all I wish for you—and for my sons," said Herrac. "That you be forever a lady, and they be forever gentlemen; and eventually knights, both worthy and brave."

"I know, Father," said Liseth, more gently. She was sitting close enough to him on the other side of the table to reach across and lay a hand for a moment on one of his massive forearms. "None of us will ever disappoint you. You know that."

"I believe I do know it," said Herrac. He broke off, suddenly, looking past her down toward the entrance to the Hall. "And here comes the first of our guests. You may stay long enough to greet him, Liseth."

"Yes, Father."

She stood up, stepped back from her bench, and turned to face the oncoming figure. It turned out to be William of Berwick, who smiled as he saw her.

"Ha!" said William of Berwick as he came up to her. "No longer the little Beth I used to toss in the air and catch again! It is good to see you grown into a beauteous woman, Lady Liseth."

"Thank you, Sir William." She gave him a small curtsy. "But I must leave you men now for other concerns. If you want for anything, the servants are close and listening." She turned her face to those at the table. "Good night to you all."

"Good night, Liseth," said her father; and she went off down the back steps from the platform that held the High Table and disappeared in the direction of the kitchen.

"Sit down and take some wine, Wullie," said Herrac. "You're welcome."

"By St. Peter!" said William, taking a bench and accepting the wine cup that Herrac poured full for him. "And I would not like to doubt it, as I see your sons have grown in equal measure as your daughter!"

He emptied the cup in one long swallow and when he set it down Herrac filled it again. William took it up and drank lightly from it, and then held it in mid-air with his elbow on the table.

"I passed none on the road," he said, "but I believe all will be here. Sir John the Graeme has been chiding into brighter spirits those who might have been laggard in joining us."

"He is well on our side in this, then?" said Herrac.

"Indeed!" William took another good-sized drink from his cup, but continued to hold it with his elbow propped on the table. "Did you think he would be jealous of your commandership? He does not think you will make a habit of it, Herrac. We all know where your heart lies, and it is not in leading other men into battle. And, beyond that, all know you to be the best knight we could have to command us."

"That is so. That is very so!" burst out William, the next youngest son after Giles. William of Berwick looked at him rather sourly.

"I spoke of the men," he said, "not of the boys."

"Do you say my brothers, the sons of Herrac," snapped Giles, his thick blond mustache suddenly bristling, "are not to be allowed to speak at this meeting, although they will fight well enough with the rest of us tomorrow? Is that your meaning, Sir William? If so, I, as one of those sons and a belted knight, do not take it kindly!"

"Ha!" said Sir William, but in a conciliatory tone. "I meant no attempt to lump you among the boys, Sir Giles. Also, you have caught me fairly. My words were unfair to your brothers. Let them speak as they will; and I, at least, will make no objection henceforward."

"Then all is well." Herrac's voice intruded on the argument and Sir William's apology. "Sir William has acknowledged that he might be in error most graciously, Giles. I bid you mark it for your own education, knight though you are, already. But look, here come others of those bidden to our meeting."

They all looked toward the entrance; and, in fact, four men were coming together down along one side of the long lower table, and another one coming through the door behind them. In spite of himself, Jim felt an alertness and a tension building in him. The meeting was about to get underway.

There seemed, Jim noticed as he sat there and watched the hall fill up, a knowledge of some sort of relative rank among those who were to be there. The seats at the high table were avoided by most of the newcomers, who seated themselves at the long, lower table. Only the upper side of the high table was occupied, so that no one would be seated there with his back to the men seated below. Herrac had his usual middle seat at the table. To his right was Dafydd, in his persona as Prince Merlon, taking that place by right of rank. To his left was Jim, then Brian. Beyond them the rest of that end of the table was filled up with Sir Giles and Herrac's other sons.

All the seats to the right of Dafydd had been left empty. Now, however, Sir William of Berwick, who had at first sat down opposite Herrac at the table when he had been the first arrival, got to his feet and came around to sit also on the upper side of it. He stopped short a few steps from Herrac.

"Now what the Devil's this?" he said, staring at the seats on the other side of Dafydd.

Jim leaned back from the table to look past Herrac himself. For the first time he noticed that the other first five benches had been replaced with some that had legs long enough to bring them almost up to the table itself. Only beyond them were the benches of normal height. Herrac turned his head to look at the other knight.

"Wullie," he said, "those are to be the seats for our five representatives from the Little Men. Take the bench beyond if you will, or perhaps leave that for Sir John the Graeme and take the one beyond it."

Sir William chose the second seat of normal height. But as he sat down he stared hard at Herrac.

"Are they all five to sit at the high table?" he demanded. "When the larger share of our own good knights must sit below the salt?"

"This side of the table is for my family and the leaders," answered Herrac. "All five of the Little Men—since their number are held down to that—are leaders equal to those who sit beside me among our own people. So, they all have their seats ready for them."

Sir William said nothing more, but he turned away, reached for his wine cup and refilled it with every appearance of disapproval.

Herrac ignored the other's reactions and the hall continued to fill up. Occasionally, one of those who came in would come up and take a seat that was open at the high table to the right of Sir William. One of these—the memory of the name came back to Jim almost by accident—was Sir Peter Lindsay, one of the Lindsays who were strong in the district.

He was only slightly taller than Sir Giles, but, like Dafydd, so well proportioned that he seemed taller. His shoulders were straight and broad, his waist narrow and his thirty-year-old face was shrewd, with bright blue eyes under light brown brows and sharp features around them.

Gradually the hall filled, and the high table filled. One of those arriving within moments of Sir William having reseated himself was Sir John Graeme, who took the seat just to the right of those reserved for the Little Men. Unlike Sir William of Berwick, he did not comment on the seats; evidently taking in at a glance who they were for, and why.

The other Borderers continued to stream in. When what Jim counted to be the last of them was inside and seated at the lower table, with general conversation and wine drinking going on, the door opened and the five Little Men came in together.

They brought silence into the hall. Within less than a minute as, one by one, the Borderers perceived them, the seated men fell quiet. As for the schiltron-leaders, with Ardac at their head they walked up the hall, around and up to the high table, saw the seats that were prepared for them there, and seated themselves.

The silence persisted. It took Herrac's voice to break it.

"His Highness, the Prince of Merlon," said Herrac, his voice reaching to the limits of the hall, "the Baron Sir James de Bois de Malencontri et Riveroak, and our allies of the Little Men, led, I believe by Ardac, son of Lutel—" He glanced for a moment at Ardac, who nodded imperceptibly. Herrac turned back to look at the hall before him. "—and all others bidden to this meeting, now seem to be here. I therefore declare all ready for discussion of our attack tomorrow against the Hollow Men."

CHAPTER 29

O nce the discussion was open, Jim was a little surprised at the businesslike air of it. A great deal of the looseness, shouted interruptions, and other elements that had gone into meetings of these fourteenth-century people that Jim had been involved in before, were absent.

It reminded him of a time shortly after he had come to this world, in his pursuit of a way to save Angie and bring her back to the twentieth century. A time in which he, Dafydd, Brian and some local people, including the wolf Aargh, were engaged in getting ready early in the morning for an assault on the enemy-occupied castle of Brian's lady, Geronde Isabel de Chaney—an assault that was to begin at sunrise. At that time it had been nothing but business for everyone concerned. To the point where Brian had politely, if definitely, suggested that Jim take himself and his dragon body outside, someplace out of their way, and leave them to their preparations.

Herrac began by announcing the time and place of their meeting in the woods short of the meeting place of the Hollow Men, and the handing out of crude, but comprehensible, maps. Those who did not know the way were put in touch with a party that did. A count was taken of the fighting men that each there could bring to the battle.

When all had been counted, Herrac himself pledged a hundred and twenty-three men, which considerably surprised Jim, since he had seen nothing like that number of men-at-arms around the castle itself. Then he reminded himself that Herrac's lands undoubtedly held a great many more who could be called to arms if needed—and were already alerted to be so on the morrow.

When Herrac had finished, Sir John the Graeme spoke up.

"We have yet to hear," he said, and his own voice reached everyone in the hall, "from our allies, the leaders of whom are here now with us. Perhaps they will tell us of the numbers they can bring and assure us that they will be there when needed."

It was not quite a challenge, considering the structure of the meeting, but its intent was clearly a challenge and everybody in the hall knew it.

Ardac turned his head and looked down along the line toward Sir John, then faced the hall.

"We will bring to the fight eight schiltrons of one hundred and fifty spearmen each," he answered, "counting also those who lead them and making a total of twelve hundred fighting men in all—which is, I believe more than the total number the rest of you have promised to bring."

Once more, Jim was impressed with the deepness of the Little Man's voice. That, and the fact that he now sat on a taller bench than that of the full-sized men around him, made him seem little different from the other leaders on either side of him.

"A schiltron is normally organized into six ranks of twenty spearmen across," he went on. "For the purposes of making sure we are able to completely encircle the Hollow Men, so that none shall escape, we will for this encounter divide each schiltron in half—giving us sixteen schiltrons of three ranks only."

"Do you—" Sir John Graeme was beginning, when Ardac cut him off.

"By your favor, Sir John," he said, "I am not yet finished. We will not meet with the rest of you at the place where you have planned all together before moving up toward the assault on the Hollow Men. But our leaders will meet with your leaders, there—once you are so gathered. Otherwise, you will not see any of us until you are up close, yourselves encircling the place where the Hollow Men are met. We have our own way of moving through the woods and its manner need not concern you. The only thing that need do so is that you can be certain you will find us in position when you move up behind us, ready for the attack on the Hollow Men."

He paused and looked down the table past Herrac toward Dafydd.

"The Prince Merlion"—once more he pronounced Dafydd's rank and name properly, so that for the first time most of those in the hall there heard the musical sound of it—"is to be our leader in this matter. Consequently we wish him to return with us tonight and set out with us tomorrow so that you will also meet him for the first time tomorrow when you have moved up into position around the place where the Hollow Men are gathered."

"Forgive me, Ardac, son of Lutel," said Dafydd. Again, his soft voice seemed to carry as it did when he wanted it to. He was clearly being heard by everyone. "I will be your leader, and represent you in all things. But I cannot go with you tonight nor move with you tomorrow. I will not be with the attackers. I will be with Sir James Eckert de Bois de Malencontri on the ledge as he begins to hand out the gold wherewith the Hollow Men expect to be paid. You have all been given your map of that clearing; and you know how there is a rocky ledge at the base of a part of the cliffs that will hold us two or three feet above the floor of the main clearing. Sir James must be there to hold the attention of the Hollow Men, and I must be with him."

"And I," said Sir Brian. "Sir James will not be on that ledge without me—I promise you!"

"And I!" said a harsh voice.

Out of nowhere a dark form materialized and leaped up onto the surface of the high table. It was Snorrl, the wolf, come from some dark shadowed corner of the hall.

He had leaped up on the end of the table in front of Christopher, the youngest of Herrac's sons; and now he moved down nearly the half length of it, to put him before Jim. There he stopped and turned to face those in the hall. "I am Snorrl, a Northumbrian wolf. Some of you may have known of me, or have heard me when I sing on frosty nights. I will be on that ledge as well; because the Hollow Men fear wolves as the rest of you fear all things of darkness. Those of you who did not know that before, know it now; because I have just told you."

He opened his jaws for a moment and laughed at them in his silent way.

"So," he went on, "now that you have been educated by Snorrl, whose people owned this land before any of your kind ever came here, I will leave you to your foolish talk. Let no one try to follow or find me. He who does will find it the worse for him!"

As he said the last words Snorrl turned around with a scratching of his claws on the table top, leaped over Jim's head to the floor behind him, and was suddenly gone.

—As suddenly as he had appeared within the building, where he had given Jim and the others to understand that he would never come.

The silence was complete within the hall. Not only the Borderers but the Little Men themselves stared in Jim's direction like people hypnotized.

"Perhaps," said Jim, when the silence had gone on so long that it was threatening to become embarrassing, "I should say a few words at this point. I am, as you all know, a magician as well as a knight. You haven't seen me working magic, because magic is not worked lightly. When you see me next, however, I'll look differently. While I am on the ledge handing out the gold, I will be dressed as Ewen MacDougall, the Scot King's envoy to the Hollow Men, is dressed, and I will be wearing his face. I may make some other small magic, but that does not concern you. I tell you about myself now, because once the Hollow Men are encircled and as soon as they've been driven in far enough for you Borderers to move in, and take advantage of the lanes the Little Men will open for you through their ranks, I will know that you are driving to consolidate the victory that they have begun."

He looked to his right and left at the persons he now mentioned.

"At that point, Sir Brian, the Prince Merlion and the wolf you just saw will come with me back through the ranks of the Hollow Men as best we can fight our way, and through the ranks of the Little Men, if they will part enough to let us by. I charge the rest of you to be on watch for us, so that you too may let us through when we come. I will have my own face back again by that time, but I will still be wearing over my armor a surcoat that belongs to Ewen MacDougall. As you leave, you will find, fastened to a pillar by the door, that surcoat; with his coat of arms upon it and his clan's war cry—'*Buaidh no Bás*'."

The gaelic words of the war cry, which meant "*Victory or death*" had been taught Jim by Giles. These Borderers all spoke the universal tongue of this world. But there would be none of them who would not understand and recognize the words Jim had just spoken with passable pronunciation.

He went on.

"I bid you note it; and remember it, so that you may let us by when the time comes. Note—when I say us, I mean all of us, including the wolf. Let no man lift weapon against any of my friends, whether these go on four legs or two. I promise on my honor as a magician that any man who does it will regret it. Again—I say this on my honor as a magician!"

He stopped speaking. The hall was still silent. He had not relieved the tension, as he had originally intended to do—in fact, he may have made it worse. But when the time came he had found words inside him that must be said. The men beside him and before him were men who had probably in their time hunted wolves when they saw them, and tried to kill them. Snorrl, effective as he might be, should not have to run a gauntlet of blood-mad Borderers.

This time, it was the voice of Herrac that broke tension and silence at the same time.

"Very well, gentlemen," the shock of his great voice brought them out of their daze, "we have heard I think from all who have anything particular to tell us. Is there anyone else who wishes to speak on any matter?"

He looked down along the edge of the table to Sir John the Graeme. Sir John shook his head. He moved his gaze back to Ardac.

"We have said what we came to say," said Ardac. "Now, we will take our leave."

He got off his stool, and the other Little Men followed him. As the rest of those in the hall watched in silence, they walked off the platform where the high table was, along the length of the room and out the door.

It was the closing of the door that seemed to finally free everyone left there from the constraint of what they had just witnessed and heard. Talking broke out all over, directed not at the assembly, but at each other or the man beside or across the table from them. Wine cups were filled and the wine in them taken in large swallows.

"In that case," Herrac's voice rolled out again over the

conversation, "this meeting is closed. We will hold a head count at the time appointed tomorrow morning, at the place appointed. Those who wish to leave now may leave. Those who wish to stay and speak, either with each other, or with one of us here at the high table, are free to do so."

With that, the outbreak of voices, which had stilled itself momentarily when he began to speak, broke out again, louder than before. Jim sat with Herrac, Dafydd and Brian at the table, waiting to see if anyone wanted to come up from the lower table with a question for him. But no one came. He heard a voice in his ear.

"How did he get in—the wolf?" Brian murmured in his ear. Jim shook his head.

"You remember Aargh," he answered in the same low tones, "how he could come and go without being seen? It looks like all wolves can do it. Why Snorrl wanted to be heard at this time is plain enough, though. Unless everyone here understood why he was on the ledge with us, they would have felt free to attack him as we came out, even if they left the rest of us alone."

"Even still," Dafydd's murmured voice joined their conversation, "there may be more than one blood-mad enough to take a cut at him with a sword or other weapon. Best that when we leave, he leaves in the midst of us; with you, James, going first, I on your right side and a little behind to protect the wolf and Brian likewise on your left."

"No one seems particularly anxious to come up and talk to us," said Jim.

"It may be the rank that Dafydd now wears," answered Brian in the same low voice, "as well as our reputation, which I do not doubt all know. These are proud men, these Northumbrians. They would not like to be seen by their neighbors as seeming to scrape acquaintance with those of fame or rank. Let us up to my room; send the servants out; and sit there with a pitcher of wine to make our own plans for what we shall be doing on that ledge tomorrow."

"A wise thought," said Dafydd.

"It is," said Jim.

Almost as if they rehearsed it, they stood up together, stepped behind their benches, said good night to Herrac and slipped off down the back part of the platform that held the high table above the others. Then it was through the kitchen and up the stairs to the room which had been Brian and Dafydd's alone;

since Jim had required separate quarters for himself.

When they went in, they found that the room had been readied for Brian and Dafydd's going to bed. The cressets were lit, but the room was only moderately smoky; and a pitcher of wine with cups were set on the table. A single servant—their number had been reduced as Brian got more and more healthy—sat on the floor in the corner. He got hastily to his feet as they came in.

"Another pitcher; and then wait outside!" Brian commanded him.

"Yes, Sir Brian—" The man hurried off.

Left alone, the three of them sat down at the table and Brian filled cups from the pitcher. Jim took a reasonable sip, then set his cup down. He had no intention of being the least bit bothered with a hangover from too much wine tomorrow morning, of all mornings.

"What think you, James?" asked Brian, after taking a healthy swallow from his own cup. "How will it go with us tomorrow?"

"I think everything should be pretty straightforward," said Jim. "The three of us, on horseback, and leading a single horse with both chests of gold strapped to it, will show up at the edge of the clearing; and I've no doubt they'll be eager to get out of our way and let us through to the ledge so that the handing out of payments can begin. I've had a look at that ledge close up, and I think we can lead the horses up on to it as well. It's not too wide, but it's easily long enough to leave them at one end, unload the chests—by the way, we must do that ourselves, and not let the Hollow Men help, or we may have one of them trying to get a handful of gold ahead of time."

"That is a danger, to be sure," said Dafydd. "Perhaps if you placed some sort of magic sign upon the chests and told them as we mounted the ledge of some dire thing that would happen to them if they tried to touch it before we had opened the cases ourselves and distributed what was within."

"A good thought, Dafydd," said Brian.

"I'll let the two of you in on a secret," said Jim. "You've both heard me speak to the Accounting Office, haven't you?"

"To be sure we have," said Brian, frowning a little. "How does that affect us now, James?"

"You should know, even if no one else does," Jim said, "that at the present time my supply of magic is almost gone. I will have just enough to change my face to the appearance of Ewen MacDougall's, and hope it lasts as long as it needs to while we're up on the ledge. Also, I need to use some of it, the magic that is, to make Snorrl look twice his size. I think that this will strongly impress the Hollow Men. Don't let it fool the two of you, however. For all his appearance of larger size, Snorrl will be the same wolf, with the same strength and no more."

There was a moment of silence from the other two.

"It is well you told us this now, James," said Dafydd.

"Very well indeed—" began Brian in agreement, and stopped talking abruptly as the door to the room swung open and the servant came in with another full pitcher of wine. Breathing heavily, he placed it on the table.

"I'll be right outside the door, Sir Brian, m'Lord and your Highness," he gasped, with a jerky bow; and slipped out the door again. Brian waited until the door had firmly closed behind the man before he tried to speak again.

"As I was saying, Dafydd is quite right. I'm not sure how I would have reacted myself to a double-sized wolf—though Aargh is close enough to it, damme; and I'm used enough to him. By the way, James, when will he be joining us?"

"I don't have the slightest idea," Jim said. "I don't believe Snorrl has any particular plans for any place himself. He'll choose a place when he gets to the point of needing to choose one; and the first we see of him is when he'll be there. I imagine outside the clearing, before we go in among the Hollow Men. He will want to be with us on the way in, as well as on the way out, for the sheer pleasure of seeing the Hollow Men shrink away from him."

"It is most strange, these men who are ghosts in all but one particular curious fashion," said Dafydd, "that they should be so fearful of a wolf."

"Snorrl said that it was because for some reason they look on him as most humans look on them—as something from beyond the grave or beyond all usual experience."

"Once he's joined us and we've gone in," Jim said, "we leave the horses as I said, and unstrap and carry over the chests ourselves. Then we begin the handing out. Two French gold coins to each Hollow Man."

" 'Fore God!" swore Brian. "These Hollow Men do not come cheap!"

Jim winced a little, himself.

"You're right," he said. "Two full-weight gold *franc à chevals*, recently minted by King Jean of France to pay for this invasion of his. It shows him on his horse on one side of the coin."

"And the Borderers will end up with it!" said Brian almost wistfully, plainly thinking of what a mere handful of such coins would mean to him and his broken-down Castle Smythe. "Ah well, we have wine and our strength—"

He looked at the other two and smiled.

"And our friends."

Both Jim and Dafydd smiled back.

"Indeed," said Dafydd gently, "and might not that be the most valuable of all?"

There was a moment of silence in the room. Jim found himself taking a somewhat larger swallow from his wine cup than he had intended. He set the cup down.

"At any rate, hopefully long before we have even as much as half the coins passed out," he said, "the Little Men will make their attack. Their first assault should catch the Hollow Men unprepared and drive them inwards, perhaps a third of the way from the edge. After that, the Little Men will probably be hard put to simply hold their ground, until the Borderers can come up and fight their way down the corridors the Little Men open for them. At any rate, as soon as that happens, I suggest we get on our horses and start to fight our way out."

"And the gold?" asked Brian.

"I suggest we don't try to take any of it ourselves," said Jim. "To begin with, it's promised to the Borderers. Secondly, if any of the Hollow Men see us coming off with what they suspect is gold on our persons, they'll make our escape that much more difficult, just to get hold of us and rob us."

"Aye," sighed Brian. "That's true enough. Very well, then. Now, another question, James. Many of the Hollow Men will probably be invisible, except for the clothes they wear, and even these could be exchanged. How are you going to know that you aren't paying one Hollow Man several times, and others none at all—and so leaving you short of gold for the last who honestly are owed it?"

"I'm counting heavily on the Hollow Men to police themselves on that," said Jim. "Every one of them has been given to understand that there's only gold enough to go around to everyone who's there. None of them is going to be happy about the idea of his share being taken by somebody else. Remember

Eshan, the leader, and some of their other leaders will be on the ledge with us. They'll also be watching, to make sure that no one gets more than his share—if only because they hope that there'll be some left over, which will come to them as leaders. But in any case I have Snorrl's nose to make sure none of them come twice."

"Still," murmured Dafydd, "there may be ways by which one may collect more than another, though we cannot think of them now."

"I'm just hoping there aren't," said Jim. "After all, our only interest is in getting them in position for the Little Men and the Borderers to deal with them—then to get out as best we can, to safety beyond the fighting lines."

"Ah, yes," said Brian, "but of course that does not mean, James, that we can't turn back once we're outside and reenter the fighting ourselves if sobeit one or more of us wishes to."

"I hope you won't do that, Brian," said Jim. "I know you're remarkably well healed considering the time that's passed since you got wounded. But you'd be very foolish to go into a battle like that, unless you're at the top of your form. Remember in that kind of a mêlée you can find yourself surrounded by four or five at once, and no one else near to help you."

"True," admitted Brian. "Still . . ."

He said no more; and Jim left it there, simply hoping that his argument had gotten through to the other man. In the end it would depend on whether Brian could hold himself back from the fighting, or not. He was like a football player who sits and twitches on the bench, watching and hoping for an opportunity that will send him in against the opposing team.

The talk had generally run down, and as far as Jim knew they had covered all the information that he had wanted to get to the other two.

"Dafydd had better bring you back up here tomorrow morning, as soon as you're up and dressed," Brian said. "Then we can all three set forth together—it will do no harm if no one else knows the way we take to the gathering place of the Hollow Men. Don't you think so, James?"

"Yes, I think you're right," Jim said.

He pushed his cup away from him, stood up from his bench at the table with the rest of them, and stretched. Unaccountably, he suddenly found himself very weary. Not so much physically tired out or even mentally tired out, but just weary. He found he had a longing to be by himself and think perhaps for a bit about Angie, before he dropped off into sleep in a room by himself.

"I'll say good night, then," he said to the other two.

"Good night, James," they answered him.

He went out the door and barely made out the figure of the servant, seated with his back against the wall in the nearly pitch dark corridor.

The man scrambled to his feet at Jim's appearance.

"Fetch me a torch, will you?" asked Jim. "Come to think of it, it wouldn't do any harm if you also fetched back someone to carry it for me and light me to my own room. There, whoever it is can use the torch to start my cresset in the room, for me."

CHAPTER 30

"A right good sword, a constant mind—"

—Sang Sir Brian Neville-Smythe, as he, Jim and Dafydd rode together through the early morning woods inland of the Castle de Mer, headed for the general area of the gathering place of the Hollow Men.

> *"A trusty heart and true!*
> *The Loathly Hollow Men shall find*
> *What Neville-Smythe can do!"*

Jim had heard the song from him before, with slightly different words, nearly two years ago. But at that time the ones who were going to find out what Neville-Smythe could do had been the dragons of the Mere; and Jim had been in the body of a dragon named Gorbash. He had also been clinging to the top of a not-too-tall tree.

It had been his first encounter with Brian; and it had been only moments after he had heard him singing before Brian was below the tree, looking up through its branches at him, and earnestly requesting him to come down and fight. While Jim was desperately trying to convince Brian that he was not a dragon; but a man who just happened to be in a dragon's body, through no fault of his own.

Sir Brian's singing, therefore, might have been thought to have brought back unhappy memories. But it did not. The whole situation then had been resolved by his being able to convince Brian that he was, indeed, a Christian gentleman, ensorceled into the dragon body.

After which Jim had descended; and—to make a long story short—Brian had ended up as the first of the Companions with whom Jim had managed to rescue Angie, who was now his wife, from the Loathly Tower in the Meres. An evil location where the Dark Powers had then held her as bait to draw Jim into their clutches.

In any case, there was no doubt now that Brian was in a good mood. He was full of cold meat, bread and wine, like Jim and Dafydd, likewise on horseback with him.

This type of food and drink was not exactly the kind of breakfast that Jim would naturally have picked for himself; but it was one that he was becoming used to; and Brian, of course, had been used to since a very early age. At that, they were lucky to have it. The lower orders had to content themselves with whatever kind of porridge could be put together at the end of a long, cold winter.

Spring might be here, but so far the only thing that had been found sprouting locally were the onions that only Sir Brian—only because he had been wounded and abed—had tasted. Jim could hardly get fresh vegetables out of his mind. He had never imagined feeling that way about them.

It apparently was quite otherwise with Brian. His stomach was full, the day promised to be bright and sunny; and there was a fine battle waiting for them all just a little later on.

Sir Herrac had been right when he had said that Brian seemed to have more of a taste for fighting than most people. Where Jim foresaw the coming armed encounter with a natural lack of enthusiasm, thinking of the various types of weapons that might end up pounding on him, armored though he was, Brian never seemed bothered by such worries. Brian's mind seemed always happily filled only with the anticipation of pounding on other people with his own weapons.

However, Brian had a pleasant baritone, and his good spirits were—as always—infectious. Jim felt his own early morning gloominess beginning to evaporate under the double attack of Brian's cheerfulness and the morning sun that was now warming them.

But Brian suddenly broke off in mid-verse. He looked across at Dafydd, who was riding on the other side of Jim. For here, away from the castle, they rode three abreast like ordinary equals.

"Dafydd—your Highness, I mean—" Brian fumbled a little with the words.

" 'Dafydd,' Sir Brian," interrupted the bowman. "Dafydd ap Hywel, with whom you're well acquainted."

"Yes." Brian still seemed to have trouble finding his words. "But—what I mean to say is—this title of Prince of Merlon that the Little Men seemed to believe you own by right. Is it true? Is it an actual title, I mean? Are you really a Prince? I mean to say, I would not wish to fail of proper courtesy in addressing you—"

Dafydd interrupted him with a laugh.

"Oh, it is real enough, Brian," he said. "But what is it to be Prince of some hundreds of miles of ocean waves; over which you have no control, and on which you never venture? Prince I am, if titles are to be counted, look you. But it is a title that long since lost any meaning; and I am much more content to be Dafydd ap Hywel, Master of all Master bowmen, than Prince of anything. In short, my being a Prince vanishes, once we leave Castle de Mer behind us."

"Well, if you say so—" said Brian, frowning. "But it seems damned unfair, somehow. Men all over the world scrambling to be named Baron, Duke, let alone Prince—and here you are, one already; but you want us to take you as we thought you were, for a common bowman . . ."

"A most *un*-common bowman," corrected Jim gently.

"Oh, as un-common as you like!" said Brian. "Nonetheless, it feels not right to me. It is courtesy and manners that make us more than brute beasts. That, and our souls, within, of course—" He crossed himself.

"But in the ordinary way of things, knowing a man's rank and behaving to him accordingly makes for a decent society," went on Brian. "Now it seems to me, Dafydd—your Highness—if you're really a Prince, you should admit to being a Prince; so that all could treat you with the proper respect."

"Nay, let it rest," said Dafydd. "It has no more real meaning than to call someone Prince of the Air. It has no real place amongst we men of the present day. Here and now, I am a bowman, and not ashamed of it. What more would I have?

You will do me the most courtesy, Brian, by thinking of me as you have always known me; and, after we leave here letting me ride behind you as usual when others are about; and so in all other things where my rank is taken to be lesser than yours."

"You really want this, Dafydd?" demanded Brian, staring at him keenly with his bright blue eyes.

"I do," said Dafydd.

"Well, there's an end on it, then!" said Brian. "The wish of a friend should be respected. You have my word on it, Dafydd. After we leave Castle de Mer—but only after then, look you, or whenever we are amongst those who have not heard of you as Prince—I will speak you and think of you only as the bowman I have known these past two years. God knows, it is a fair enough calling. I am as inept with a bow myself as Jame—" He was interrupted by an embarrassed fit of coughing. "—as many who have never picked up a weapon before."

Jim diplomatically ignored the slip of the tongue.

"I will not say it is not so," said Dafydd, smiling, "but I will wager that if you were left with nothing but a bow to defend yourself with for a year or so, you would turn out a bowman well worthy of the name."

"Think you so?" said Brian. "That is interesting. However, I have no year to spend in such an experiment."

They rode on for a moment in silence.

"Now," put in Jim, "if the matter of Dafydd's title is settled, suppose I bring up another subject? All of us want to show up at the meeting of the leaders where the Borderers are to gather, with the Little Men no doubt nearby. But after that, I think we should make a wide swing, so as to come down on the actual place where the Hollow Men will be gathered from the north, or Scottish side, so that they do not suspect anything."

He looked meaningfully at his two Companions in turn.

"In that respect, I've been worried by one thing. Without clothing they can move invisibly through the woods, and even ride invisibly upon their horses—though that would not be the most comfortable thing to do—and I'm concerned about their catching us or overhearing us under some conditions where they'll suspect what's going to happen."

"No fear!" said a harsh voice beside them and they looked to see Snorrl trotting along with them. The wolf grinned up at them.

"I have been with you almost since you left the castle," Snorrl said. "I will be with you, whether you see me or not, until we go in among the Hollow Men together. I guarantee that no Hollow Man will come anywhere close enough to see or hear you without my warning you. Now, go where and as you will. You will not see me but I will be there."

With that, Snorrl disappeared again, although Jim could have sworn, from the lack of underbrush around, that there was nothing for him to dodge behind.

"Well, that settles that," said Jim, "and also relieves my mind. Now, if we keep on as we are, we'll get to the gathering place of the Borderers early."

He paused; thinking about it for a minute.

"Probably, though, that's not going to do any harm. Our being available early can mean that the meeting of leaders can take place early; which will be all to the good for the three of us. Particularly, if we're going to circle around behind the Hollow Men before coming up on them. Don't the two of you think so?"

Brian and Dafydd both nodded.

"A wise thing to be early, and a wise move to go around behind," said Brian. "In anything involving a battle, or indeed in anything involving the lives of men, the unexpected will always happen. Best to make sure of what it is possible to make sure of."

"That is so," murmured Dafydd.

So it was that they reached the gathering spot for the Borderers before more than a third of them had shown up. The area picked contained a small clearing. But it was one not large enough for all the contingents together; particularly as the contingents tended to stay aloof from one another. As a result, most of them were out of view, among the trees surrounding the clearing.

Jim, Brian and Dafydd rode up to Herrac. The Lord of the Castle de Mer, with his sons and his hundred and twenty-three men, had taken the central spot in the clearing, as if by right.

"Hah!" said Herrac. "It is good to have you here, your Highness, m'Lord and Sir Brian," he said. "We've been waiting for you."

"But surely," said Jim, as he halted his horse before the towering commander of the Borderers, "not all of the leaders— in fact many of them—are here yet?"

"No, many are not," said Herrac. "However, I did not specify who would meet with the Little Men. I meant only that certain of the leaders, certain important ones, would meet with Ardac, son of Lutel, and his schiltron-leaders."

He frowned for a moment.

"I'm willing to wager that he himself brings only half a dozen or so of his own leaders. For our side, Sir John the Graeme, Sir William Berwick, Sir Peter Lindsay and the others who will be important in carrying the fight forward, are already with us. Moreover, there's a limit to how long we can wait, since some may not show up at all; and it were foolish to wait and wait until the noon hour had past, for someone who has no intention of coming."

"You're going to hold the meeting right away, then?" asked Jim. As far as he could read the sun, it was barely terce yet—that church hour of prayer which Jim privately translated in his head into ten o'clock in the morning.

"As soon as I can gather them together," answered Herrac. "Wait you here."

He turned to his sons and sent them off in different directions to gather some eight men whom he evidently wanted to join with him in the meeting. Jim reflected that that would make only eleven who were not Little Men, at the meeting. All to the good, he thought, with the Little Men in mind; just as long as the other Borderer leaders did not later object to being left out. He was a little relieved of this anxiety by Brian leaning toward him and speaking in a low voice into his ear.

"Things are often done this way, James," Brian said. "Do not concern yourself about it. Usually, the only reason a council is delayed is because some are not present, or an important share of those promised really do not want to go forward at all. After all, it is the one who commands who decides, when and what things are to be done; from attending councils to attacking the enemy."

Jim nodded.

"I see," he muttered.

Some twenty or thirty minutes later, the eleven full-size men were together with eight of the Little Men, Lachlan among them, looking as happy as Brian. They were situated at a distance far enough from the rest of the waiting Borderers, so that there would be no danger of anyone but those at the council overhearing what was said there.

"It only remains, I think," said Herrac, after greetings had been exchanged between him and Ardac, "to make certain that our plans of last night have not changed and all go as we planned. At what time, or at what signal, should the Borderers begin to move in?"

"I will blow my horn," said Ardac, lifting the cow horn that depended from his shoulder and putting the small end to his lips. "Listen now, for you will hear no other horn like it."

He blew; and his words proved to be perfectly true. Jim had been expecting to hear the kind of raucous blast that he had heard before from other such cattle horns converted into hunter's signaling devices. But this one sounded a high sweet note that seemed to carry away and away amongst the trees until it was lost in the distance.

Ardac lowered the horn and smiled his bushy lips.

"There are some of your men back there who will wonder about that horn-call," he said. "But they will have no notion of where to look, for the sound is one that does not give away where it comes from, as do the horns that you larger men use. At the same time, having heard it once, they will recognize it when the time comes. Finally, you may take my word for it that it is a sound that will carry over any noise of battle. That is why the horn is made as it is."

"In truth," said Herrac, "it is a fair-sounding and memorable horn. Very well, we will listen for it. At what point do you think your schiltrons will be in their attack on the Hollow Men when you blow that horn?"

"It is in my mind that our first charge, even with schiltrons at half depth, should enclose the Hollow Men there and push them inwards the distance of perhaps one quarter or more of the space of the clearing."

"By the arm of St. Christopher!" burst out William of Berwick. "But you must think well of yourselves to do that to Hollow Men; who may well be in a number of a thousand and a half men."

"Two thousand and more," said Ardac. "We know them a little bit better than you and your people, Sir William. You think what I promise is not possible? What would you do if taken by surprise by three ranks of spears, as far as you could see to your right and left, coming at you at a run? It is instinctive in a man under those conditions to back off; to run away, even. But I will say this—we can push them back perhaps a third the

Gordon R. Dickson

width of the open space. But holding them will be something
else again, once they get over their first alarm and turn to fight
in earnest. So that when I blow my horn, I pray that all of your
people will come as quickly as possible. Because the need of
you will be great. If you delay, we will be overrun; and the
advantage of having hit them unawares will be lost."

"I am commander," said Herrac grimly. "I promise you.
When your horn blows, all men under my command that hope
to face me again will come to your aid as quickly as we can get
there, whether on horse or on foot."

He did not even pause to give anyone else a chance to speak
but went on.

"I think," he said, "that should conclude this meeting. Ardac,
son of Lutel, you and your leaders will want to move up into
position. His Highness, here, with Sir James and Sir Brian, must
needs be on their way, since they must be among the Hollow
Men first before all of us. I declare this meeting closed."

He turned and began to stride away. The Borderers went
with him; almost automatically, Jim thought. Ardac looked after
them for a moment and then looked at Dafydd.

"We had hoped to have you among us, to give us heart," he
said. "I am sorry you will not be there."

"I am sorry myself," answered Dafydd. "But I have no
choice. My greater duty is with these two good knights and
on that ledge keeping the attention of the Hollow Men fixed
on us so that the rest of you can move in behind them and take
them by surprise, as you said. How would you do without me
there?"

"Sir James could not do it alone—or Sir James and Sir Brian
could not do it alone?" asked Ardac.

"No."

As usual, the word was gently said in Dafydd's soft voice,
but there was a finality about it that even Jim and Brian felt.
Certainly Ardac and those with him felt it. For their spears went
up in the salute Jim and Brian had seen them give Dafydd, on
the occasion when they had all been together in the earlier brush
with the Hollow Men. Then Ardac turned and led the way off
into the woods. He and his schiltron-leaders disappeared among
the tree trunks almost as quickly and quietly as Snorrl was
able to do.

Jim turned to the other two beside him. For once they were
together on his right and he could face them both at once.

"Do you want to appear to be leading the three of us, Dafydd?"
he asked.

"No, James," said Dafydd. "I leave that to you."

"Brian?" Jim fastened his gaze on Brian alone. "How about
you? You've had far more experience than I with battle."

"With battle, yes," said Brian, "but this other matter of going
to the Hollow Men under the pretense of being someone else
and handing out gold to them in such manner as they do not
suspect us—this I think is something you will do best of the
three of us, James. If you need me at any time, call upon me.
But with Dafydd, I say—you lead."

"Then it's settled," said Jim.

He swung up on his horse, which he had led to the place
where they had met with the Little Men; and the other two also
mounted, with Dafydd automatically leading the pack horse
carrying the chests of gold. They headed north and west of
the point where the Hollow Men were to be met.

When they had gone far enough, they did a ninety-degree
turn and now headed east. Shortly they cut the trail—or road—
where they had ambushed and kidnapped Ewen MacDougall,
though they were a good four or five miles down from where
that particular kidnaping had taken place. They followed the
trail back to a spot just a little north of the place where the
Hollow Men would be gathered.

Here they turned off the trail once more, going east again
and partly south, so that they would be generally heading for
their enemies. They were not far into the woods when Snorrl's
familiar voice spoke beside Jim.

"You'll be seen by one of their sentinels in just a little ways
now," said the wolf. "Don't you think it's time for you and I
to make the magical changes you talked about?"

"You're right," said Jim. He did not mention that he had
merely been waiting for Snorrl to appear beside them again,
feeling that the wolf would not take kindly to Jim calling him.

He reined up his horse, as did Brian and Dafydd, to wait
for him, and got off the animal. He had been faced with a
problem right from the start. Ewen MacDougall was a smaller
man than he was. If he changed himself completely into Ewen
MacDougall as he had the time before, he would have to wear
MacDougall's armor.

But if his magic wore off on him while he was at the ledge
and he had to fight his way off the ledge and through the

Hollow Men, past the Little Men and Borderers to safety, he would need to be wearing his own armor, because any armor he was wearing would simply burst and fly apart at its joints when he suddenly increased in size.

He had thought of carrying his own armor along, one way or another, and changing if he had to on the ledge before plunging into the battle before it. But there would hardly be time for that. It was not an easy or a quickly accomplished job, getting a knight into his armor.

The solution had been very simple. He would change his face only; and wear his own armor with the surcoat over it. It was unlikely that Eshan would have paid enough attention to him to notice that Ewen MacDougall was now several inches taller, wider in the shoulders and longer of limb, as long as the surcoat was the same.

Furthermore, Jim would have his visor up and the face he would be showing would be the face of Ewen. This tidy answer had the great advantage also of conserving what small amount of magic Jim had left—stretching it as far as possible, in fact.

Consequently, he had ridden out that morning in his own armor. Now, as he stood beside his horse he wrote an equation on the inside of his forehead:

$$\text{MYFACE} \rightarrow \text{FACE OF EWEN MACDOUGALL}$$

As usual, he felt nothing after writing this spell. But the reaction of Snorrl was startling. At a leap, the wolf was eight to ten feet away, crouched facing him and jaws open in a snarl.

"Stop it, Snorrl!" said Jim irritably. "It's only me, magicked to look like Ewen MacDougall. Are you ready to be changed yourself?"

The tension gradually went out of Snorrl and he rose up to his normal height.

"Will this harm me in any way?" he demanded.

"No," said Jim. "Not only that, you won't even feel a thing. You're going to have to find something like a pool of water to look at yourself in to see the difference—oh, you may notice that you're a little higher off the ground than you used to be."

"Then go ahead," said Snorrl.

Jim wrote the second equation:

SNORRL→DOUBLE HEIGHT, DOUBLE SIZE

It was not possible to see the change happen. Just one moment Snorrl was there as he normally was, then suddenly he was the size of a small pony or baggage horse. The real horses reared, and tried to bolt. Jim found himself digging his heels into the ground and being dragged along by Gorp for a moment before Brian, who had gotten his well-trained war horse under command first, came up alongside and also took hold of the reins of Gorp.

"By St. Peter!" said Brian, laughing. "If your wolf has half as much that effect on the Hollow Men, we should be able to slice our way through them like a knife through soft cheese."

Together, Brian and Jim managed to finally calm Gorp down enough so that Jim could remount the horse. Snorrl, meanwhile, had disappeared again.

"Now, where did he go?" said Jim, vexed.

Brian shrugged and Dafydd shook his head; mutual acknowledgment that Snorrl had simply pulled one of his vanishing acts. Almost as soon as the words were out of Jim's mouth, however, he appeared again.

"That was a good suggestion of yours," he said to Jim. "I did indeed find some water, still enough for me to look at myself in. Yes. Indeed, I would as soon stay this way from now on."

"Sorry," said Jim, "but you'll lose it when my magic runs out—and that may happen while we're still up on the ledge. In which case, both you and I will revert to ourselves and have to fight our way out like that as best we can with the help of Sir Brian and Dafydd ap Hywel, here."

Snorrl was silent for a moment.

"Well, if it is to be, it will," he said. "Oversize or my regular size, I promise to go through those Hollow Men, and the rest of you can follow in my path—if you will!"

CHAPTER 31

"We have been seen," announced Snorrl, a short while later; as he, the three men on horseback and the baggage horse with the gold behind them approached the area where the Hollow Men should be gathered.

Jim looked down at the wolf curiously.

"How did you scent whoever was watching for us?" he asked. "The wind's from us to them."

"I didn't scent him," said Snorrl. "I saw and heard him; both when he was waiting and as he hurried off to tell the rest we were coming. You would have heard and seen him too, except that going about on two legs has made all of you half-blind and half-deaf."

There was no appropriate answer to this, since Snorrl—like many individuals—judged everybody else by himself. Jim wisely said nothing.

"We are only a short distance from them, now," said Snorrl.

Jim looked up at the sun, which was not quite at its zenith above them. A part of his mind longed for the trusty wristwatch he had worn for fourteen years and left behind in that twentieth-century world he had come from, now undoubtedly mega-light years—and possibly mega-universes—from where he now was.

This business of alternate worlds was something he would look into someday, if he ever got enough of a rating as a magician. Certainly Carolinus was aware of the fact of multiple universes; and, among them, possible future versions of his own world. He had betrayed such knowledge from time to time, in talking to Jim. But then Carolinus was one of the three top magicians in this world. Where he was, was a long climb for a D class magician like Jim.

So Jim put aside the idea of the watch. They were clearly early, but there was nothing to be done about it. Particularly if their approach had already been sighted. They would have to go forward as they were going now, move up on the ledge, and start handing out the money. Meanwhile they could simply hope that the Little Men and the Borderers were either in place, or could be, before the gold was exhausted; or the use of the last of Jim's magic robbed him of Ewen's face and revealed his own.

Either happening, he thought, would precipitate a riot among the Hollow Men, in which he, Brian, Dafydd—and probably Snorrl as well—could be overwhelmed and killed; for all the wolf's belief in his ability to pass safely through any number of Hollow Men.

So they continued. In fact, it was not long before the trees thinned before them and they came out on the edge of the clearing.

The Hollow Men were there. They were there in remarkable numbers. The clearing was packed; and Jim had a sinking feeling, seeing them all there in their numbers. As Ardac had said, there must indeed be more than two thousand of them; for they almost fully filled the clearing, which he had estimated to be larger than necessary. It was lucky that he had not made the mistake of picking the more convenient spot Snorrl had shown him. An ideal clearing, it had been; but one which would have certainly proved to be too small.

The Hollow Men were clearly expecting Jim and those with him—with the exception of Snorrl. The outer ranks of the undead warriors wore clothing only, going from partially clad, to fully clad, to armored, invisible bodies in a final cluster around the ledge. Here, possibly twenty or thirty ranks deep, were Hollow Men in full armor. A few of these were on invisible horses. Most were on foot. But it was on Snorrl now they were all concentrating.

Snorrl moved forward as well as Jim and the others. The outside Hollow Men moved back and parted before them; almost as if an invisible wedge was being driven through the crowd to make a way to the stone ledge at the foot of the cliffs.

None seemed eager to come within ten or fifteen feet of Snorrl; and Snorrl clearly appreciated this fact and enjoyed it. He stalked ahead of Jim, Brian and Dafydd on their horses, darting his gaze right and left to watch the Hollow Men draw back from his glance, as if he identified each one of them.

In one sense, he probably *was* identifying them, thought Jim; since now that the wolf was among them, his nose would be making a note of the difference in each one's odor. So he, Jim, Brian and Dafydd moved forward along the wide corridor; until at last it was the fully armored ranks that parted before them. In a perfect silence, finally, they mounted the lower end of the ledge at a point where it came almost to the ground.

The horses balked a little, their hooves slipping on the bare rock; but they ended by coming on, and did not protest strongly at being taken up on to the ledge.

The three dismounted. At the far end of the ledge were five figures in full armor in very good shape, like that he had seen Eshan wearing. Eshan would almost undoubtedly be one of them. Their visors were up; but of course this was no help. Within, only emptiness was to be seen. But Jim could not imagine Eshan failing to identify himself, eventually.

Jim dismounted to check the lashings that supported the gold chests on the baggage horse. Snorrl paced alongside him, with Brian and Dafydd following.

Jim was only killing time. By the sun, noon was still some minutes off. But it gave him a chance for a quick glance around at part of the edge of the clearing. However, there was no sign of either Little Men or Borderers. None.

His eye was caught, however, by an unusual number of hawks and other large birds, such as ravens, circling in the sky above them.

"Why all the birds overhead?" he asked of Snorrl in an undertone that none of the Hollow Men would be able to pick up; but which would not escape the wolf's sensitive ears.

Snorrl had been grinning evilly at the five at the far end of the ledge. Without turning his head he answered. "The Little Men will have whistled them in," he answered. "They're friends to all birds, as well as animals. Has not Liseth told you how they whistle down her falcon when she sends it in search of them?"

340 Gordon R. Dickson

"They mentioned something like that," answered Jim. "But why do the Little Men want birds here?"

"The birds can see, or sense, the Hollow Men—how, I do not know—even though they are without clothes completely," said Snorrl, "just as I can smell them. They will undoubtedly help the Little Men know if any try to escape by making themselves invisible. What are we waiting for?"

"I'm using up time," hissed Jim under his breath. "It's still not noon; and I've no way of knowing if the Little Men or the Borderers are in position."

"Is that all?" murmured Snorrl. "I could have told you that the Little Men are there; and if the Little Men are there, the Borderers will not be far behind. This is a day none of them will want to miss."

Jim felt a great sense of relief.

"All right, then," he said to Brian and Dafydd, and began untying the lead rope of the baggage horse as he led it forward along the ledge.

As they went forward, Snorrl continued with them. The five armored figures at the far end of the ledge took a step or two backward; but none of them more than that. Jim led the horse to approximately the middle of the ledge before halting it.

"Come forward!" Jim called to the five. "Aren't you here to watch me hand out the wages? I expected you to be close beside me, watching me all the time."

There was a moment's hesitation and some muttering amongst the armored figures. Then they came up to within about ten feet, and stopped.

"I am Eshan," said the most forward one of the five. "Maybe you can't recognize me, but you'll remember me from our earlier meeting. Well, now you're here, get on with it! But keep that wolf back!"

Jim smiled engagingly. Almost sweetly.

"He won't bother you unless we see a need for it," said Jim.

With that he turned about, opened the nearer chest and took out a handful of the coins.

"Since I can't see you, except by your armor or clothes," he said, lifting his voice to make it carry over the crowd, "I won't know one of you from the other. But the wolf beside me will know. And if any try to take a double share, the wolf will take care of him."

There was a sort of wave motion in the front few ranks of the armored men, as if they would back away from him; but so many other Hollow Men were packed tight behind them any real retreat was impossible. Still, a sort of dimple appeared in the front rank opposite where Snorrl stood. Clearly, those there were getting as far from him as was possible.

"All of you," said Jim, speaking to the crowd and still pitching his voice so that it would be heard even by those farthest away from him, "will get two of these newly minted, full-weight *francs d'or*, freshly minted by the King of France to pay the expenses of his coming invasion of England!"

He reached into the chest and held up one of the golden coins, turning it from left to right and back again, so that it caught the sunlight and was visible to all of them.

"It's called the *franc à cheval*, because it shows the King on horseback," he said; and there was a murmur from the crowd and a movement toward the ledge from its fringes, where the Hollow Men were packed less tightly.

There was no way to stall any longer.

"All right, then," Jim shouted, "let the first come forward! After that, each one in his turn!"

There was a moment's hesitation and then one of the armored figures from the front row on the other side of Jim from that where Snorrl stood, advanced to the ledge. The figure held out a gauntleted hand and Jim placed two of the *francs d'or* into its palm. The metal-clad fingers closed upon them; and the figure backed away, to have its place taken almost immediately by another, repeating the same gesture.

So the giving out of the money began.

The gauntleted hands came one after another, their owners always approaching Jim from the opposite side of him on which Snorrl stood, and staying as far away from the wolf as possible.

Jim had not thought to expect this would be either a wearying or a dizzying task. But as the sun reached its highest point overhead and began to move on, he became conscious of a sort of daze. It began to seem to him that an endless number of hands kept approaching him; and would keep on forever, reaching out like the jaws of young vultures waiting to be fed.

It was like being in a receiving line, greeting countless guests, where he had to repeat the same action, over and over again, until its sheer repetition made it mechanical and mind-blurring.

He found himself grateful for Snorrl's presence beside him. Alone, he would long since have given up the task of trying to make out whether one of the Hollow Men was trying to get a double portion or not. Now, to him, all the hands looked alike; all the figures looked alike. Even their height and weight inside their armor, or what else they wore, did not differentiate them any more. It was as if one Hollow Man kept coming back, over and over again.

Occasionally, using the excuse of wiping from his forehead the sweat on it brought out there by the heat of the unclouded, spring sun overhead, he was able to catch a glimpse of the woods around the clearing—each time hoping to see some sign of the Little Men.

But there was none. Only the birds, circling lower and lower overhead, now crying out to each other—or against each other, for all Jim knew. He was aware that the cries of most birds were either territorial warning-off signals, or sounds of warning, anger or alarm. If they were any of them, in this case at least, they seemed to be directed more at the other birds than at the Hollow Men below.

He told himself that the Little Men must have known what they were doing, if indeed it was they who had summoned the winged creatures.

He had half exhausted the chest of gold; and now, among the armored figures were beginning some who wore only partial armor over clothing. Often it was merely a sleeve end with an apparently empty space beyond it that was held out to him.

It was an eerie, and somewhat tricky, thing to place the coins where they should go.

He got in the habit of letting go of the coins in mid-air, just beyond the upper end of the sleeve; and leaving it to the Hollow Man himself to make sure that he caught them. He took the last few coins from one of the two compartments in the chest; and called a halt while he turned the baggage horse around and opened the chest on its other side.

This move gave him his first good chance to look beyond the clearing. For a moment, he thought that he saw a wink of light among the trees; but it could have been his imagination. Inside him an unreasonable anger was growing.

It was long past the time when the Little Men and the Borderers should have been in place. What was holding up their attack? If they did not bestir themselves soon, he would run out of gold.

Then, very probably, the Hollow Men there—particularly those in armor—would simply mob him, Dafydd and Brian; and either kill them outright or keep them for some more elaborate and painful ceremony of execution.

Right now things were getting worse. A cloud of dust had been raised over the clearing by the milling around of the Hollow Men. Also, the birds had begun flying very low over the heads of them; and their shrill cries were making the Hollow Men nervous. Finally, those not already paid were beginning to have their fear of Snorrl overcome by their greed. They were crowding and fighting to get close to Jim.

The situation was worsened even further by the fact that those in armor clearly found their position closest to the ledge a privileged spot. Only grudgingly were they opening up spaces to let the ones farther back through to collect. Some of these behind, in only part armor, or completely armorless, had to struggle hard to make a way through the ranks of their iron-clad companions; and voices rose in anger.

Jim found his arm suddenly seized by a gauntleted hand, and turned to look into the empty interior of the helmet of one of the Hollow Men who had been on the ledge with them.

"You've got to do this faster!" shouted the voice of Eshan, over the rising clamor.

"There's no way to do it faster!" Jim shouted back.

He jerked his arm free of the other's grasp. But Eshan still stood beside him for several minutes more, possibly glaring at him from his invisible face, before turning and walking back to the other four.

Jim was diving into the second compartment of the chest for another double handful of gold pieces, when through the haze of dust, finally, out of the corner of his eye he caught the glint of light among the trees—not merely at one point, but at several.

He turned hastily back to the business of handing out the coins. It was his job to make sure that the Hollow Men's attention was on him; while the Little Men got started in their run across the open space toward them. He was not happy doing it, but he kept his head down; and so he did not see what was going on beyond the Hollow Men immediately before him.

He emptied his hands finally, and turned again to the chest, giving him another chance to glance out over the heads of the

Hollow Men. To his delight, this time he caught a momentary glimpse at last of a solid ring of the little spearmen, three, and sometimes four, ranks deep, advancing at a run.

He turned hastily back to those in front of him who had outstretched arms and were still clamoring for their gold; but almost as he did so, the first spearman must have hit the outer edge of the congregation of Hollow Men.

There was an immediate change and increase in the uproar. Shrieks from the most lightly armed and armored of the outer Hollow Men rose over the general noise. But all those within Jim's sight continued to crowd around, reaching out for their gold pieces. He thought it best to keep handing the gold out to these, distracting at least them, if not the others, from the fact of what had already begun to happen.

It was a minute or two, consequently, before he heard the hum of arrows, passing behind him. By now, except for those in the very forefront of the crowd, helmets and other headgear were turning to look outward.

He glanced to his right and saw four armored shapes lying still on the ledge, with the ends of Dafydd's arrows projecting from their upper bodies. The fifth armored figure there was missing. Clearly, it was time for him to go.

He filled both hands with coins from the chest and flung them into the empty faces of those before him. Turning, he sprinted toward the lower end of the ledge. Brian, riding his own war horse, Blanchard of Tours and leading Gorp, met him halfway.

Jim could not vault into the saddle as Brian could, in full armor; though, vexingly, the unusual strength of Jim's legs had always made it possible for him to leap that high. But his aim was invariably bad. Accordingly now, he scrambled aboard with the help of a stirrup, in the usual fashion; and they rode hastily toward and off the lower end of the ledge.

Dafydd, also back on his horse, joined them. His bow, still strung, was over his shoulder. A broadsword was in his right hand, a shield from the Castle de Mer on his left arm. As they came off the rock, they ran into a solid band of the Hollow Men in full armor, weaponed and on their invisible steeds, who were turning from the attack by the Little Men to battle with the three of them.

Jim felt hope start to drain out of him. They would never hew their way past this deep and solid wall of opponents.

But at that moment, Gorp's hindquarters sagged as if from a sudden heavy blow there; and the next moment a furry shape leaped over Jim's shoulder onto the Hollow Man directly opposing him.

Its long jaws shoved up under the chain camail that protected the Hollow Man's neck below his helm; and its teeth closed on the invisible, naked throat beneath.

It was Snorrl, come to the rescue; and the Hollow Men opposing them seemed to lose their appetite for fighting almost immediately.

Most of them tried to claw backward into the press. Jim's heart sank, for Snorrl was no longer or any way different than he was in his ordinary self. He felt his own face, and it felt, undeniably, familiar. The magic had worn off; and the Hollow Men crazed for gold in front of him had not even noticed that he looked differently.

His disguise must have lasted, anyway, through the moment in which Eshan came up and spoke to him. Or else Eshan would have noticed immediately that he was looking at the face of Jim Eckert, rather than that of Ewen MacDougall.

But it made no difference now. Snorrl was now making a way for them through the Hollow Men. Also, hopefully, to the Little Men and Borderers beyond. In the noise and dust and general confusion of the clearing, Jim could not see beyond the Hollow Men closest in front of him.

Blows came hard against his shield, as he literally hid behind it.

He saw that Brian, on his left, was not using his lance. Bodies of men and horses alike were pressed too close together for lance-work. Brian's shield and broadsword were both busily at work, as were Dafydd's, on his right.

Jim glanced around his shield and ventured a full-arm slash at the Hollow Man before him. The Hollow Man went down. He suddenly realized that others like him, but on foot, were trying to kill or cripple Gorp; so that Jim, himself, would be brought to the ground.

He turned his attention to these footmen, consequently; and found himself unexpectedly helped by Gorp, himself. The war horse—panicking in the uproar that was going on—had once again begun to kick out and bite at everything within reach, armored or not.

CHAPTER 32

W hat followed was a sort of timeless blur.
      Jim found himself at once frightened to the very core
of his being and at the same time strangely elated; but with
both emotions pushed into the background by the need of the
moment to thrust, to hit, to work his way forward or be helped
forward, by the attacks of Snorrl, Brian or Dafydd. The smell
of dust was clogging in his nostrils.

It seemed to go on for a time that was at once momentary and endless. In fact there was no time. It was all one
moment and it was eternity at the same time. But suddenly
the bright spear-points of the Little Men were before them,
and these were parting to let them through. They crowded
into the opening made for them, while the spears behind them
closed together once again, against those who had tried to
follow.

Suddenly, they were out of the immediate need to keep
fighting constantly. Jim found himself slippery within his armor
with his own sweat—he hoped it was all sweat, and not some
of it blood.

To his left the spears and the dust still obscured everything.
To his right there was another corridor through the spears down
which in the opposite direction Borderers on horseback were
pouring, to lock in fight with the fully armored Hollow Men

close in toward the cliffs that blocked their escape from the clearing.

Past the Little Men and Borderers, in the clear beyond the fighting at last, they reined up. Jim looked about him; and, glancing right, saw Herrac sitting still on his horse; with the mounted and armored figures of his sons horsed and around him, particularly noticeable by the smallness of Sir Giles among his brothers.

Jim had not expected to see his massive figure back here. It was not the usual way for a medieval commander in a battle like this to stand aloof. He turned Gorp toward Herrac and trotted toward him, with Brian on his right and Dafydd on his left, going with him. Snorrl had disappeared, whether to turn back into the fight or vanish into the woods about them, it was impossible to say.

Herrac not merely had his visor up; but his helm was tilted back, so that his complete head and face were clear. He turned to see Jim and his Companions as they came up.

"Now, God be thanked!" he said, as the three came within sound of his voice. They rode up to him and stopped.

"Can we charge with the others, now, Father?" asked Alan, beside his father, his helmet on but its visor up.

"In a moment," said Herrac. "I've but waited to make sure that his Highness, Sir James and Sir Brian were clear. Now that they are safe, we will join the battle." He flipped his helmet over his head, but kept his visor up.

"I will return to the fight with you, Sir Herrac!" said Brian. But his voice was weak, and Jim saw Brian sway slightly in his saddle.

Jim turned, reached out, and lifted the visor that was hiding Brian's face. Beneath it, the other's features were paper-white, once more. He swayed again, slightly in the saddle, even as Jim lifted the visor.

"You'll not return," said Jim. "I order you to stay with us, Brian!"

"And I reinforce that order, if need be!" said Herrac. "Sir Giles, you will turn aside from the battle and help these three gentlemen, in particular Sir Brian, so that he may be brought safely back to the castle and cared for. You too, Christopher!"

"Father!" protested the sixteen-year-old, youngest son.

"You heard, Christopher," said Herrac. "No more is to be said. You and Giles will take these gentlemen home. For the rest of us, down visors and follow me!"

With that he dropped his own visor, put spurs to his horse and galloped forward with the rest of his sons toward the nearest opening between the ranks of the Little Men. Christopher and Giles, their visors up and showing unhappy faces, watched them go.

"Come on, then," said Jim impatiently. "Let's get him back to the castle. One of you ride on each side of Sir Brian."

"I need them not—" feebly protested Brian.

"You'll have them, nonetheless," said Jim. "Giles—Christopher!"

The other two moved up and arranged themselves one on each side of Brian, Sir Giles putting out his arm around Brian's waist.

Jim, who had moved aside to give Christopher room to move up alongside Brian, led the horses forward at a walk. After a moment he ventured on a trot and looked back over his shoulder.

"Can he stand this pace, Giles?" he asked.

"Stand a damn gallop—" Brian made a feeble protest. But Giles nodded.

"Then go as quickly as you can, but not above this speed," said Jim.

Suddenly, however, it was as if a hand was laid on Jim's shoulder. He pulled up abruptly.

"The rest of you take Brian back," he said. "Go as fast as he can stand. Brian, are you additionally wounded? Are you bleeding someplace new?"

"Not bleeding, damn it!" Brian's voice could hardly be heard. "Just so . . . damn weak . . ."

He sagged in the saddle.

"Dafydd," said Jim, "you take charge and—"

"No, James," said Dafydd, calmly but decisively. "Giles and Christopher are enough."

The bowman turned in his saddle and went on speaking to the other two de Mers.

"The two of you check him for bleeding from his earlier wound, from time to time," he said. "If he bleeds more than a little, slow your horses, and if need be, stop. If the wound or his weakness makes it too much for him to ride, make a litter out of two small fir trees, chopped down and bound together, laying him on that to be dragged back by your horses. You understand?"

Giles and Christopher both nodded.

"If even that is too much for him," Dafydd went on, "one of you stay with him and the other gallop at full speed for the castle, to bring back Liseth and help. Giles, best you stay with him; and Christopher make the ride."

"Dafydd—" began Jim again; but Dafydd calmly turned to face him.

"You are speaking to Prince Merlion, Sir James," said Dafydd. "I also intend to stay here."

While this did not settle things for Jim, it was apparently the final argument for Giles and Christopher. Both of them, with an arm around Brian's waist now and back to moving at a walk, started away into the woods. Jim watched them go with deep anxiety.

"I hope he'll be all right!" he said, more to himself than to anyone else.

"He is a strong man, James," said Dafydd's voice in his ear. "What man can survive, he can survive—and possibly then some. But if you have reason for staying, so do I—even if that reason is not the same. I have a responsibility to the Little Men. Will we share our responsibilities, James?"

Jim looked at him. Dafydd's handsome face was calm and coldly set, so that it seemed to Jim he saw the man as he had never seen him before.

"Yes," he said. "We have to know, beyond all doubt that all the Hollow Men are destroyed, before either of us leaves the field. Then—"

He broke off.

"Then?" prompted Dafydd.

"Then . . ." said Jim.

Jim fell silent for a moment.

He did not know what he had been about to say.

"I don't know," he went on, feeling an uneasiness inside him that was not connected for the moment with Brian's state of health. "Perhaps there's something else."

"Something else?" asked Dafydd, his eyes hard upon Jim. "Tell me now, and what else should there be?"

"I don't know," said Jim, again. "At the moment, all I have is a feeling."

"Whether it will make you wiser to know it or not, I know not," said Dafydd, "but I will say, look you, that I have a feeling also. And you know that I have feelings from time to time that were best paid attention to. You will remember how, shortly after we first met, I felt the passing of something, when you made your decision to go first with Brian and the others to recover the de Chaney Castle before trying the rescue of your Lady Angela?"

He waited.

Jim nodded.

"And again, last year, you remember I told all of you— you, Brian, Giles and the young English Prince—that I had had a cold feeling when I packed to leave the wife I love for France? So that all things I touched seemed cold to my fingers?"

Again he paused; and again Jim nodded.

"—All except that sword that Giles took and the Prince would not carry," Dafydd went on. "And it was a sword that was to bring Giles to a time of death, but also to great honor. I have a feeling now; but it is about you, James. A feeling that I should not leave your side, any more than I may leave the Little Men."

"Well, I can't send you away," said Jim unhappily, but trying to smile. "As you pointed out, you're Prince Merlion."

"That is true," said Dafydd. "But I also sense that you feel something beyond what is to be seen here today. Yet it seems that the Little Men and the Borderers together are winning the field—are they not?"

For the first time in some moments, Jim's thoughts came back to where he was and what he was doing. He looked at the clearing. The dust had thinned; and he saw, indeed, that the Hollow Men, what were left of them, were mainly those in full armor. But these were pressed back against the cliff by both Borderers and Little Men, and fighting desperately. All others lay as empty clothing, or armor on the field.

"Just as long as none of them are playing dead, to be over-looked in their armor by lying still," said Jim with a new and sudden sense of alarm.

"I think both Snorrl and the birds will be watching for that," said Dafydd.

Jim looked around him.

"But Snorrl has gone," he said.

"Not far," said Dafydd. "Look yon."

Jim glanced in the direction of the bowman's pointing finger.

Through the thinning dust he made out the form of Snorrl at the clearing's far end, nosing among the recumbent suits of armor on the ground. The birds were still with them, still circling, the smaller coming down right next to the ground—and now there were some that were indeed small—no bigger than swallows or swifts.

The end was inevitable now. The living on both sides fought with a cold ferocity. What was left of the Hollow Men fought for survival. The Little Men and Borderers fought with years of hatred behind them. Curiously, none of them spoke or shouted now; and there was no noise but the sound of metal on metal itself.

Slowly, the line of armored Hollow Men pressed against the cliff grew smaller, thinner and thinner; until there were only a few scattered ones left—and then they were gone.

The Little Men and the Borderers drew back, in this one moment strangely close; the Little Men no longer in ranks and the Borderers no longer together but mixed among the Little Men. They looked at each other as if they were seeing each other for the first time, in the light of what they had just now shared.

Slowly, they pulled back from the foot of the cliff; and now Jim could see, as if they were not made of metal but something light that the wind had tossed there, the armor of the last of the Hollow Men, piled like leaves by an autumn wind against the base of the cliff.

The Little Men and the Borderers continued to move slowly back, pulling apart as they did so, and beginning to regroup into two separate peoples, Little Men with Little Men, Borderers with Borderers.

Although the battle was over, there still was silence. Jim made out Herrac's towering figure, still on his horse, still surrounded by—as far as Jim could tell—most of his sons, turning back to set up a rallying point well away from the cliff. He made it, turned about and shouted.

"Borderers! To me."

The sound of his great voice breaking on the silence seemed almost like a sacrilege. But the Borderers moved toward him like men in a dream, and the Little Men slowly reformed in their ranks, without orders, also moving back from the cliff. Jim started forward on his horse; and, with Dafydd beside him, he rode up to Herrac. The Borderers already around Herrac drew back to let him through. All the sons were there except Giles and Christopher.

Jim stopped in front of Herrac.

"You did it—you and the Little Men," he said. "It's done finally, and over with."

Herrac's glance went past him and Jim turned to see what the other knight was looking at.

It was Ardac, and five other of the Little Men still carrying their spears and shields. Jim thought he recognized some of the bearded faces from the meeting in the woods early before the battle.

"We did it with your help," said Herrac to Ardac. "We could never have done it alone. Your spears helped hold them against the cliff so that there was no escape."

"Nor could we have done it alone." said Ardac. "We know this—you and I, and many still alive here. But we will go now. This will be remembered. But, in a few days, some months, a generation, it will be forgotten again. Things will go back to being as they always have been; with you and your kind, and those who come after you, pressing against us, and we fighting back to hold our borders."

"No," said Jim, "I don't think it'll ever be the same from now on."

"Think that if you like," said Ardac to him, "but I think as I always have. There will be no changes—"

He broke off suddenly as one of the other Little Men touched him at the elbow, and turned him to look away from Jim. Ardac and all the rest were looking away from him too.

In perfect silence, coming around and down the far edge of the cliff, where the slope was small, stretching out into boulders and rubble, slowly, inexorably and massively, was a Worm larger than the one Jim had seen in the battle at the Loathly Tower.

Riding it was a man in armor, with his visor up and hollowness showing within. From that hollowness now came the voice of Eshan, shouting into the silence of all on the clearing below, who were staring at him.

"You thought you'd win!" shouted Eshan. "You can never win! I'm alive and soon all these will be again! Come kill me if you can!"

None of those below, Little Men or Borderers, moved toward him. Instead, all, and alike, they drew back, though a large distance still separated them from Eshan and the Worm. Snorrl was gone and Lachlan moved back with the Borderers.

But it was not the sight of Eshan that pushed them back; and it was not even the Worm, hideous and large enough as it was. It flowed over the rocks, leaving those over which it passed with a glistening trail upon them. Four to five feet thick above the ground and ten to twelve feet in length, it bulked, with two tall eyestalks bearing at their ends strangely blank-seeming eyes. These turned and focused from one part of the field to the other below it as it went.

In front of and below the eyestalks was no indication of a nose, but only a circular, suckerlike mouth, partially opened to show numerous rings of tiny, ivory teeth within.

There was a jingle of harness, a thud of hooves just behind and to the side of Jim; and a voice spoke.

"I am here," said the voice of Brian.

Jim jerked about in his saddle. Brian sat his horse with more firmness now. His visor was up and his face, while still pale, had lost the unnatural whiteness that had been its color before. A little behind him rode Giles and Christopher, looking embarrassed.

"Forgive me, Sir James!" said Sir Giles, pushing his mount forward until he was on the other side of Brian, and looking across past Brian at Jim. "The fault is mine. But he swore he would fight us if we did not let him return. I could not fight him, nor let Christopher do so; so we have merely come back with him. He *would* be here; and he is here."

"Indeed," came the grim voice of Herrac, "the fault is yours, Giles!"

"Blame him not," said Brian, without looking at the large knight. "No one and nothing could have kept me away. My duty is here. I did not know what that duty was until now; but now I see it clearly. There is one Hollow Man left and he is protected by a Worm; and I—I alone—have fought a Worm and know how to fight it. I must yet fight this one."

"No," said Jim, with a strangely sudden and quiet sense of finality inside him. "You can't fight him, because you could not possibly fight him and win, the way you are now. I must fight him, and you must direct me, as you have always directed me in my fighting. It's a job for both of us."

"God save us that it must be!" cried Herrac, in a voice thick with rage. "Because I cannot bring even myself to approach that—that thing; and I see that neither can anyone else here except yourselves! It is not the Worm—it is . . . it is that and something more!"

He was right. Terrible as the Worm was, something worse came with and went before it. Something like a great cold breath of wind that seemed to blow through the watchers to their very bones, that sought out in them all that they had ever evilly thought or evilly done. They retreated before it so that, little by little, they all were being driven back by it toward the edge of the clearing.

"You cannot fight it, James," said Brian, still staring at the Worm. He fumbled out his sword. "You are not capable. You know and I know you are not capable."

"I must be capable this time!" said Jim. "Brian, put that sword back!"

"Ah!" said Dafydd, on the other side of Jim. He had his strung bow off his shoulder and was running his hand almost lovingly up and down the smooth length of the tapered shaft. "My arrows may not do any harm to the Worm, if Carolinus and Brian spoke truly about its thick hide, at the Loathly Tower; but I may be able to do something about that one last Hollow Man who rides it."

Even as he spoke, he had whipped an arrow from his quiver, fitted it to the bow and pulled it back until its head almost touched the woods.

He paused a moment, then let the arrow go. It leaped through the air toward the Worm and the Hollow Man and was almost to them when, in a lightning-swift move, the Worm threw up the forepart of its body and caught the flying arrow in its mouth. In a second it had chewed it into shards with those innumerable tiny, gleaming teeth, and swallowed it.

Eshan, on the Worm, rocked back and forth with laughter.

"Shoot at me all you like, bowman!" he shouted. "No arrow of yours can touch me, while I ride this steed."

Meanwhile, the Worm was still advancing toward them.

Jim looked back at Brian.

"You see, Brian, how it still comes on?" he said. "Face what's true. You can't fight him. I must. Tell me how!"

"God help me!" Brian's features were wrung with chagrin and self-hate. He jammed his sword back into its scabbard. "There's little enough I can tell you, James, except what Carolinus told me. Try to cut off its eyestalks first, and then simply do what

you can to cut through that very thick, very tough, outer hide—
and that is like cured leather several feet through, so that almost
it can turn the edge of a blade itself—for its vital parts are deep
within it."

He took a deep breath.

"There is no help for it," he said, in a calmer voice. "Perhaps . . . perhaps, James, it may that you will do as well or
better than I, even, the time before. You have no skill as a
swordsman—forgive me, I should say you have little skill as
a swordsman. But skill is not so much called for here. Only
strength. Just be sure you get those eyestalks cut so that it is
blinded first; and then commence trying to cut your way into it,
behind the part that it just now lifted to catch and eat Dafydd's
arrow."

"At least, perhaps I can help with those eyestalks!" said
Dafydd—and with the same swift sureness he launched two
more arrows at the Worm.

Once more, the forefront of the Worm flashed up in time,
the mouth caught the arrows and ate them.

"Go back behind that front part and then reach forward to
cut the eyestalks—that is what I did," said Brian to Jim. "The
eyes can turn to see you. But their judgment is off, it seems,
looking backward, because this way I could reach and destroy
them. Also, the reason for cutting the stalks in the first place
is that there is something missing in the creature. Once it is
blinded, it knows you are hurting it, but does not exactly know
where you are doing it. So it turns about to reach you, blindly
and unsurely."

"If you can keep it busy fighting you," said Dafydd, "perhaps
then I can then put an arrow through that Hollow Man."

"I think not," said another voice, unexpected but familiar to
Jim, Dafydd and Brian at least.

They turned to see that Carolinus had appeared beside them.
The elderly magician, his white beard and mustaches blowing
in the cold wind that continued to try to suck the strength from
them, was wearing his usual faded red robe that covered him
from shoulder to ankle. He looked very frail.

"I think not, Dafydd," he repeated. He pointed. "See!"

They looked, just in time to see Eshan slipping off the back
of the Worm and disappearing as he went down on his stomach
among the boulders and rubble.

"He cannot escape unless he comes into sight on the far side of that loose rock, in order to run behind the cliff," went on Carolinus. "Watch the far side of those boulders with an arrow at your bow. That is the only way you can help James now, Dafydd."

"Yes," answered Dafydd slowly. Arrow nocked to his bowstring but not drawn, he moved to his left several paces to where he could see all the far edge of the tumbled rock.

"You see," continued Carolinus gently, his voice carrying easily to Dafydd in the utter stillness of the moment. Even the birds, though they still circled, but higher now, had fallen silent. "It isn't intended by the Dark Powers that you help James in any way. And Brian—you see that it's James who's to be tested, here. The Worm is for him and no one else."

"Cannot you tell him something more that will help, then, Mage?" Brian's tone was close to one of pleading.

Carolinus shook his head.

"I cannot," he said. "And if I could, I would not be allowed to. James, it's up to you."

The last words were addressed to Jim.

"You had best go for him on foot, then," said Brian, turning back to Jim. "Keep your sword arm as high as you can, approaching it, so that it may not trap it against your side; and keep your shield well up beside you also. Rest its top edge against the shoulder boss of your armor and its lower edge against one of your leg greaves. That way the great blow of its body's forepart back at you will not be able to drive these edges into you. It cannot break through the shield itself; and its mouth is so made that it cannot get a grip on the upper or lower edge of the shield, to wrest it from your grasp."

"Right," said Jim.

He paused and looked around.

"I'd like a drink of something first," he said. "My mouth is dry as ashes."

"Alas—" said Herrac, who had drawn close. But Carolinus was already pouring from a small bottle into a thick blue glass almost as large as the bottle; both of which had appeared without warning in his hands.

He handed the filled glass to Jim. Jim drank. The liquid looked and tasted like the milk Carolinus drank; however, it was something more. It not only satisfied Jim's thirst, but sent a fire of energy running all through him.

Suddenly he was light and strong. But then the feel of the

strange wind came back upon him as well.

He felt again the emptiness, the coldness of a fear that had come to him upon that unnatural wind; but also, together with these emotions, there was a sort of resignation, an acceptance of what awaited him. He descended from Gorp, checked the position of the shield on his arm, drew his sword and began to walk to meet the approaching monster.

CHAPTER 33

J im and the Worm had started toward each other from about
as far apart as the clearing permitted, diagonally across from
each other on it. Looking toward the cliffs from Jim's point of
view, he was at the right front edge of the clearing, just in
front of the trees there; while the Worm had come into sight
around the left edge of those same cliffs, which walled in nearly
two-thirds of the clearing.

The Worm, for all its size, and the sudden lightning movement of its upper body, came on with relative slowness, certainly no faster than Jim was walking, and possibly more slowly.

He saw now that the upper part of its body, that part that
had lifted so quickly to catch and swallow Dafydd's arrows
in mid-air, was actually held slightly off the ground. Behind
it, the Worm's body moved by a series of bones, or something
like them, underneath the skin; the way a snake moves over
the ground, except that the Worm came straight on, rather than
wriggling from side to side to advance. He had not noticed this
at the Loathly Tower fight because his attention had been all
on the Ogre that was his particular opponent.

In this moment of utter stillness, as he moved forward, Jim's
mind felt completely empty.

—No, not completely empty. Something was nagging at him.
Some old memory was stimulating him to move toward an idea

that might improve his chances of defeating the Worm. What was it?

Suddenly it came back to him. He stopped, swung about and strode, as hastily in his armor as he could, back toward where Brian, Carolinus, Dafydd, Herrac and his sons waited.

"I've just thought of something," he said breathlessly, coming up to them. "Brian, Gorp's nowhere near as imaginative and high-strung as your war horse. I think maybe Gorp will carry me up to the Worm, where Blanchard wouldn't. I just remembered how, when I was in the body of Gorbash, the dragon, how I made the mistake of flying directly against the lance of Sir Hugh de Bois de Malencontri, who held my castle before me. I'd been warned about attacking an armored knight with lance by Smrgol, Gorbash's dragon grand-uncle. But I'd forgotten it completely. You remember how Sir Hugh wasn't hurt, but his lance pierced me through and I nearly died as a result?"

"Well I remember it," said Brian grimly.

"It suddenly struck me," said Jim excitedly. "I've got nothing to lose by trying to put a lance into that Worm from horseback. At full charge, with my weight and the horse's behind it, that lance point can't miss going in deep enough to do some serious damage to the vital parts of the Worm. If nothing else, it'll cripple the creature, so that it bleeds internally, and it'll be weakened when I come to fight it on foot."

"An excellent idea! A marvelous idea!" cried Brian. "But not you, James. Not you! You know that lance-work is the weakest of your fighting skills. However, I have taken the prize at more tourneys than I have fingers on both hands. Moreover, you are completely wrong. It was not the Worm that Blanchard feared so greatly. It was the Ogre, because of his twelve feet of height. To Blanchard he looked like a mountain, and Blanchard recognized the club in his hand for what it was. No, I will take Blanchard and a lance—and I promise you I will put it in behind the front part of the body, where it will do the most damage!"

He broke off.

"A lance!" he cried, looking about him. "Who will give me a lance? Fetch me a lance!"

"You may have mine," said Herrac. "I left it behind a tree, when it became plain that there would be no room for lance-work when we went in. Alan—you know where. Fetch it!"

His eldest son reined his horse around and galloped off. In a moment he was back with the lance.

There were two bright spots of color on Brian's cheek. He sat as straight on the back of Blanchard as if there had never been anything wrong with him. He took the lance and laid it diagonally across the shoulders of the horse, pointing forward; then clasped the butt of it under his upper arm against his side, and lifted the point clear of its support.

"A good lance—a good weapon!" he said.

For a moment the point of the lance held there, steady in mid-air, its steel point gleaming. But then, it began to sag; it drooped downward, until Brian was forced to rest its weight once more on Blanchard's shoulders, to keep from it going point-first into the ground.

There was an embarrassed silence all around. Brian sagged in his saddle.

"What a wretch I am!" he said savagely. "I have strength enough for a moment, but not enough to hold it up for more than that. And to place its point properly in the Worm I would need to keep it in air far longer than that. James, I cannot do it!"

"Never mind," said Jim, mounting Gorp, who had followed the other horse, partially out of curiosity. "Give me the lance—"

He reached over and took it from Brian's now-lax grasp. The other knight was not looking at him, but staring at Blanchard's neck in utter dejection.

"You will never manage it, James," said Brian in a low, sad voice. "Forgive me! But it is, or would be, a hard task even for someone like myself to dodge the front of the Worm and still bury my point in the back part of its body."

"Still," said Jim, "I've got to try."

Simply the fact that he had made the decision seemed to give him strength. He rested the lance on the forepart of the saddle, to take its weight off Gorp's shoulders, and began to ride toward the approaching Worm.

"Wait!" shouted Brian behind him. "One second yet, James! There is a thing I can do, after all!"

He rode up level with Jim.

"Yes, James," he said almost triumphantly, reining his horse in, so that Jim was forced to stop Gorp for a second. "I need no hands to control Blanchard. He will respond to my knees. And I need strength only for a moment. In that moment I can do great damage. Hark to me a moment!"

"All right," said Jim, reining in Gorp. "But I haven't got all that many moments to waste."

"It will be no waste," said Brian. "Listen, James! I will ride Blanchard at full speed toward the Worm; and then, with a touch of my knees, direct Blanchard aside at the last moment before the creature can quite reach us. So we will go down along his side; and, as I pass, I can lean over and cut both eyestalks with a single slash of my sword. It is not even hard! It is child's play! Come you behind me if you will, James; but I ride ahead of you now to blind the Worm!"

Once more, it seemed as if he had never been wounded, never been exhausted. Brian lifted the reins and Blanchard broke into movement.

Jim lifted his own reins to send Gorp galloping after the other man; but almost immediately dropped them again. He could no more stop Brian now from what the other intended to do than Gorp could catch Blanchard of Tours. The great white horse on which Brian had spent all of his inheritance, except his lands and castle, was much faster than his size and weight indicated.

That speed had often given Brian an advantage, in battle and in tourneys, that others did not expect. In any case, thought Jim, watching Brian's figure rapidly approaching the Worm, there was no point stopping something that was pure will by something purely physical.

What he was looking at in Brian, what they were all looking at—for Herrac and his sons had now ridden up and halted their horses beside him—was a triumph of spirit over body. Brian's body, away from this instant and this clearing, could probably not walk a dozen steps without falling. But here and now, in the saddle, no one watching without knowledge of his weakness would take him for anything but a knight riding fresh to the encounter.

Brian was directing Blanchard forward at an angle to the Worm, and the Worm began to turn toward him; but at the same time Brian also turned Blanchard toward the creature. So that they seemed finally to be approaching head-on. A sort of low groan went up from all the watchers around the clearing, as the two came together; for it seemed there must be a head-on collision.

But at the last second, as the Worm's forepart flashed up, Brian seemed miraculously to slip by it on its opposite side;

and at the same time he rose in his stirrups, and with his body and arm fully extended made one quick swing out from across his body with his sword. Both eyestalks parted at mid-stem, a couple of feet above the front of the blunt head, and fell. Then Brian was putting Blanchard about on a circle and starting him back toward Jim and the others.

"Oh, magnificent!" Herrac exclaimed. "Beautifully done! Did you mark it, my sons? You will never see such horsemanship and sword-work bettered in your life—probably you will never see anything near to approaching it. He must have judged the exact moment to pull aside from the front of the beast, the exact distance at which he must pass it; so that, at fullest, safest extent, he could make his cut from beyond its reach and sever the eyestalks! And all, to return to us safely as he does now. But—hurry to him—Alan, Giles! He will not make it back without help!"

In fact, Sir Giles and Alan reached opposite sides of Brian on Blanchard, just in time. Brian had let the great war horse slow to a walk, and all but collapsed in his saddle. As they got to him, he was just beginning to fall sideways out of it. One on each side of him, they caught him around the waist, supported him, and brought him back, still at a walk, to Herrac, Jim and the rest.

"Wonderful, wonderful, Brian!" said Jim, when Brian came close. But Brian's face was once again utterly bloodless, his whole face and body were limp and his face was the face of a man in a walking dream.

"I thank thee, James, for thy most courteous . . ." he began in a thin voice. But the voice gave out, his eyes closed; and he fell heavily against Alan, who was on his left side. The other sons clustered around to help hold him, but he was completely limp. It was obvious he could not even be held upright in the saddle.

"He must be gotten back to the castle with all dispatch!" said Herrac. "I fear already it may be too late. He may have pushed himself too far."

"Never mind!" said a sharp voice; and Carolinus was amongst them again. He pointed to Giles and Alan. "I'll send him back to the castle; and you two with him to explain things. Now!"

He snapped his fingers. Brian with Blanchard, Giles and Alan with their horses as well, disappeared.

"They are now in the castle courtyard," said Carolinus after a moment, "and your Liseth, Sir Herrac, has already been called and is running through the Great Hall to come to Brian."

"Carolinus!" said Jim. "The Accounting Office will crucify you for this!"

"It will, will it?" said Carolinus, his mustaches bristling. "It may just be I'll have a word to say to it, as well!"

He turned to look across the clearing.

"But James," he went on, "your Worm is still coming. Go at it now with the lance. Remember what Brian told you. Sword high, when it's time to fight it on foot, shield against the armor boss on one of your shoulders and the greave of one leg; and be sure to attack it well back from where the front part of its body lifts from the rest. You can go at it from the side, now. It hears through the ground with its skin, so it'll hear you coming, but it can't turn quickly enough to keep you from reaching it, behind its forepart."

"Right!" said Jim, lifting his reins in his left hand, while the other hand kept the lance balanced on the high pommel of his saddle before him.

"Wait!" said Carolinus urgently. "One other thing. Once you're in position to strike it with your sword, use the weapon point-first to pierce it; then simply hack your way in. By that time, it'll have you pinned, its front part against your shield, its mouth striving to reach you with its teeth and the ability it has to suck you in if it gets close to any part of you. But your sword arm will be free. Go now!"

Jim nodded; balancing the lance on the pommel of his saddle before him, he whirled Gorp about and put the horse as quickly as he could into a gallop straight toward the Worm.

The distance between himself and the creature was not all that much now. He had time only for one thought, and in this moment it was about Angie.

Nearly two years ago, after the battle had been won at the Loathly Tower and Angie had been rescued, he had gained enough magic credit with the Accounting Office so that Carolinus had said he could use it, if he wanted, to take them both back to their own world.

Jim had assumed then that Angie would want to return; and it was a surprise to him when she would admit only to wanting to do what he wanted to do.

The truth had been then, that he, himself, had wanted to stay. He felt himself challenged by this medieval existence. It was only after he admitted as much to himself, that he understood, somewhat slowly, and bit by bit, that Angie had felt likewise challenged.

So, stay they had.

But he had realized later, after the decision was made, that he had taken Carolinus too lightly, when the Mage had told him that if they did not go back then, it was very probable they could never go. Jim had not thought to inquire why it would be so difficult.

Now he knew. He would have to become a magician of Carolinus's level to get himself not only the magical credit, but in the necessary position with regard to the factors that governed this world—Chance and History—in order to ever return them home.

Achieving both things would take him years at least—if he was lucky. Now, effectively, they were stuck here; and that meant that it was only his life and his magic that stood between Angie and being in a very bad position.

True, she would still be mistress of the Castle de Bois de Malencontri. But in this world, in this time, and without Jim's magic, it would be almost impossible for her to hold it alone.

The only solution offered by this fourteenth-century society was that she could marry again to someone who would become Lord of the Castle, and the Lord of her. Some fourteenth-century man who had no idea of all the things that she knew and remembered.

In short, if the Worm killed him now—as was somewhere from possible to likely—Angie would be the one to really suffer.

—But now the time for thinking was over. He was already all but face to face with the Worm. To be exact, he was some thirty feet away from the creature; and this was as close as he planned to get—for now at least.

He and the Worm had met out beyond the area of the main battle where the ground was fairly clear. Jim, in spite of his good reflexes and his high rating as a volleyball player back on his own world, was someone who depended more on his mind than his muscles. In this particular instance, he had seen only one hope.

The Worm moved slowly—that is, it moved its body as a whole slowly, forward. If the pace at which it was coming was about the fastest it could go—and certainly, the Worm at the Loathly Tower had moved no faster than this—then perhaps he had a chance. He turned Gorp's head away from the Worm and began to ride around the creature, in a circle.

Gorp, who on closer view had decided he did not like the looks of the Worm after all, was only too glad to turn so. The Worm turned to face them as they moved; but gradually Jim speeded up, from the trot at which he had advanced, to a canter, to a gallop—until he was circling the Worm at high speed. By this time the Worm had made several rotations in place, stopping its forward movement.

But, as Jim had hoped, he was able to circle the creature faster than it could turn to face him. He continued circling, with the Worm trying to keep facing him, but falling steadily behind in its turning, until Jim on Gorp was finally in a good position, a little behind and at a right angle to the creature's side.

"*Now*, Gorp!" Jim shouted out loud. He lifted the reins and spear; and, once more, for the second time in Gorp's experience with him as a rider, drove the sharp points of his spurs into Gorp's flanks.

Gorp literally leaped at the sudden pricks, and, having leaped, galloped directly at the middle of the Worm. Jim clamped his arm tightly around the butt of the lance, concentrated on what he was doing—and prayed.

There was nothing harder than to direct the point of a ten-foot lance while riding on the back of a galloping horse; when every movement of the horse made your point waver up and around and from side to side, like the upper tip of a flexible wand fastened upright on the edge of a turning record.

He concentrated on making sure that the point was as low as possible. Better to run the danger of driving it into the ground than have it slide over the beast's back entirely.

All this took place in a matter of seconds. Almost immediately Gorp was upon the Worm with no choice but to jump it, after his next couple of galloping strides. Jim clung to his point and aimed it directly at the rear middle side of the Worm.

The next second they hit and the spear went in.

Then Gorp was jumping over the Worm to get to open country at the far side; and Jim had had to let go of the spear as he felt its point go in, for fear of being kicked clear out of the saddle by its butt end.

On the other side of the Worm, Jim fought to slow his panicked horse. When he got Gorp under control and circled back, it was to see the lance broken off by the Worm, now rolling over and over on the ground. It was desperately trying to reach back far enough with its head to seize in its mouth the protruding end of the broken-off lance that had penetrated it. But it could not; the broken-off part had gone clear through it.

It definitely must, he thought with sudden exultation, have hit some of the vital organs within. It could not have missed at least one. Internal bleeding had already to be at work to aid him.

But now came the hard part. It was hurt by the lance, but showed no immediate evidence of being seriously hampered in fighting. Jim managed to pull Gorp to a skidding halt some thirty feet from the Worm. As the horse stopped he leaped from Gorp's back, holding his sword in its scabbard and his shield on his arm.

He drew the sword and slapped Gorp with the flat of the blade to send the horse away. Then he was running at an angle toward the back end of the Worm; to approach from its rear, as much as was possible, the place where the lance had transfixed the creature. He ran with his sword held high, the point glinting in the sunlight like one of the Little Mens' spear-points.

CHAPTER 34

He ran with all his strength. If he could just use his sword to enlarge the wound the lance had made . . . he reached the Worm, which had now stopped rolling, and hit its mottled brown skin with the sword's point, with all his running, armored weight behind it. It went in a good third of its length, only inches from the entrance place of the broken-off lance.

He tried to work the blade in deeper and was suddenly hammered against the side of the Worm with a force like that of a wrecker's swinging ball demolishing a standing wall.

His shield slammed him against the mottled side, well behind the forepart of the Worm, which had just struck at him. His left shoulder boss and leg greave kept it from doing any but minor harm. But the top metal edge hit his cheek hard enough to start it bleeding; and he could feel it also, against his teeth, inside.

With that brassy taste of his own blood in his mouth, he began to work at the sword he had put in, back and forth to push it deeper and also to enlarge the opening he had made.

The swordpoint had now gone in even farther. Mostly, this had been with the impact of the Worm's front end, slamming back against his shield; and the sword's hilt-end being driven forward from the resultant impact of his breastplate. But part of it was the result of his efforts.

The forepart of the Worm hit him again.

He kept on working.

He was aware of the suckerlike mouth champing away sideways toward his shield, unable to get past it.

Again he was struck; and again. Concentrating on his work, he finally wriggled the sword loose and drove it back down again, deeper, at an angle, striving to meet the lance-shaft. Meanwhile the image of that ugly mouth and the deadly tiny teeth within it stayed in his mind, in spite of the fact that the wound of his swordpoint was now very close to the embedded lance-shaft fragment.

Finally his blade jarred against something hard. He had reached the wood. Still working the sword back and forth in the Worm's flesh, he struggled now to slide the swordpoint down the shaft toward the vital parts far within. Meanwhile, the Worm hit him again. And again. Until his mind blurred, and he could no longer remember why he was doing what he did; but only that it had to be done.

So he worked on; and the blows from the Worm's forepart continued. Jim's helmet was knocked partly around on his head, so that he could no longer see what he was doing. But he continued to work by feel. The world was a world of sweat, struggle and the receiving of incredible blows. It went on, and on and on . . .

The shield was dented and hammered now by the terrific blows against it, until it had begun to fit itself to his body, to touch at nearly all points against the chain armor on his side and the plates upon it. He now felt the impact of every blow clear through to him, almost as if he was wearing no armor at all.

The blows seemed more and more powerful. It was incredible that the Worm, hurt as badly as it must be by the lance through it and by his sword which was now nearly three-quarters of its depth down inside it—its point must be long since through the hide to the interior parts—and continued to strike with such incredible force. The blows were damaging Jim, now. He felt his ribs on his left side give, to one of them.

The next blow smashed the broken ribs again. He felt the damage being done, he felt the shortness of breath as the lung, undoubtedly pierced in several places, began to lose its function as an oxygen-processing organ. The blows continued.

He was being killed. The Worm was being killed. It was merely a matter of which one would die first. His sword blade was almost fully buried in the creature.

He lost all sense of what he was doing. He was deaf, dumb, blind, and being hammered flat on an enormous anvil by a mad and giant blacksmith. There was nothing left in him but a relentless urgency—he had even forgotten the reason for it— to keep pushing downwards on his sword as long as he could. He pushed. He pushed. He pushed . . .

He was aware of something stopping him. Of someone unfolding his clenched hands from the hilt of his sword, to which they seemed to have grown. Somehow, the hammering had stopped, for which he was grateful.

But he was still blind and all but unconscious. Vaguely he was aware of being upheld, lifted and carried away. He wept a little inside the darkness of his helmet, for he had been kept from finishing what he had started out to do, after all.

Then the helmet was turned straight forward and the visor lifted. He looked up into the face of Carolinus seated beside him on the ground where he lay flat on his back. The faces of Dafydd, Herrac and one of his sons wavered in and out of focus at the edge of his vision. Carolinus was bending over him and holding out to his lips a blue glass.

He tried to lift his hands to push it away from him, but his hands now weighed tons. He could not move them. He felt the edge of the glass pressed against his lips and some of the liquid in it sloshed past the lips into his mouth. At the taste of it, he was suddenly aware of a terrible thirst. He gulped greedily, as Carolinus carefully tilted the glass to let the liquid flow into him.

Then the glass was empty. He sat, wanting more, but without even the strength to ask for it.

Then, slowly but steadily, the world changed. A glow seemed to spread from his stomach out through him, bringing new strength and energy. He felt his ribs pull back and the lung mend so that he could breathe deeply again. His helmet was lifted off; and his view became wide. He was half-lifted to a sitting position; and he saw that he sat in a field, with elements of empty armor and clothes scattered about it in the near distance and reaching away toward the cliffs. Twenty feet away lay the Worm.

But it lay still. The broken lance-shaft still stood out of its side; and beside the lance-shaft, driven in to the hilt, was his sword.

A magic fire was running through his veins, now, and he was waking up. It was as it had been before, when Carolinus had given him the milk to drink from a blue glass. The magic fluid was giving him back a strength he thought he had lost. Correction: a strength he *had* lost; but which was now magically being resupplied to him.

He looked up at Carolinus and tried to speak. This time his voice came.

"What happened?" he croaked. "What . . ."

"You won, James," said Carolinus gently. He produced the bottle and began to incline it toward the blue glass, then changed his mind, put the bottle away again and the glass with it, somewhere inside his robe. "I think you can stand up now, if you try."

"Help me," Jim said. His growing appreciation of the enormous difference between the magic of which Carolinus was capable, and the simple stuff that was all he had so far been able to do, lingered now with the taste of the magic milk in his mouth. Hands lifted him to his feet.

He looked around the field.

"Eshan?" he asked.

Dafydd took him by the arm and led him off to one side until he had a different angle on the end of the cliffs. Then the bowman pointed.

Jim looked. For a moment he did not make it out. Then he saw a suit of armor lying still just beyond the end row of boulders where the cliffs ceased to be. It lay on its back with just a few inches of the feathered end showing above its breastplate. He stared at it for a long moment.

"But he's still alive!" said Jim. "Look!"

They both stared, but the figure was still. Then an armored forearm moved slightly, as if it would reach up to pluck at the arrow that pierced its chest.

Without any further words, Jim and Dafydd ran toward the figure; followed more slowly by Herrac and his sons. The sons would have galloped past the two running men, but Herrac sternly called them back. They followed at a distance of about ten yards.

Jim and Dafydd reached the Hollow Man and knelt beside him. The visor of the armor was down but Jim lifted it, and looked at the emptiness within.

"Eshan . . . ?" he asked.

There was a moment's pause. Then a voice spoke hollowly out of the emptiness.

"They're all gone, then," Eshan's voice said, sounding distant and very weary. "All of us dead—but me?"

"Yes," said Jim.

A sigh came from the emptiness of the hollow helmet followed by the ghost of a brief chuckle.

"Then I am last," he said. "At least I have that honor. But now I die too—and this ends us all. It is high time."

"High time, say you?" said Dafydd.

A wordless rattle, as if Eshan was trying to clear his throat of something sounded faintly from within the helmet.

"Yes," said Eshan, "it has been a long, long time. I have been weary. We have all been weary . . ."

The voice began to fade.

"But now, at last . . . we will rest . . ."

The voice of Eshan fell silent. There was nothing to mark his dying; but to Jim it was almost as if he could feel the life passing away from the armor below him. Suddenly it was only so much jumbled metal.

Slowly, Jim and Dafydd got to their feet. Carolinus was standing beside them.

"Now they are gone, indeed," said Carolinus.

He turned away, and Jim and Dafydd turned with him. They started to walk back toward Herrac and his sons, just a short distance away.

"The last of them dead, then?" asked Herrac.

"He died as we listened to his final words," said Jim. "I think they were all tired of what they called life—all the Hollow Men. Perhaps all like Eshan, who died here, are grateful to us."

There was a long moment of silence, not only by those around Jim, but among the Little Men and the Borderers who were still at the edge of the field. A strange stillness as well as silence; then Jim suddenly realized that the evil wind had ceased blowing.

Unexpectedly, Carolinus chuckled, breaking that silence. Jim turned to look at him, surprised.

"The Accounting Office!" Carolinus explained fiercely. "They've been trying to get through to me for some time! *Now*, I'll let them reach me—soon!"

He rubbed his hands together, almost as gleefully as Brian looking forward to a battle.

"But not just yet. One more small thing to do. I suppose you want to get back to Castle de Mer and see how your friend Brian is?"

"Yes!" said Jim, suddenly conscience-stricken. He had completely forgotten Brian for the moment. "Is he all right? I mean—?"

He did not want to put into words his fear that Brian might have been somehow more badly hurt than they thought, and now be dead.

"No, no," said Carolinus testily. "Go see for yourself. Back to Brian's sick-room with you!"

There was a blink and Jim found himself standing in Brian's room in the Castle de Mer. A couple of servants were standing waiting in the corner, and Liseth was hovering over the bed. Brian was not only not dead, he was propped up and talking.

"—And wine!" he said. "As well as some meat and bread at least! I could eat a horse!"

"I don't know whether Sir James would approve—" Liseth started to answer, but found herself broken into by Brian's interruption as his glance went past her to see Jim.

"James!" he said. "You're here. You're back from the battle! What happened? What of the Worm—"

"The Worm is dead," said Jim flatly.

"How? How?" cried Brian excitedly, looking as if he would clamber out of the bed unless he got an answer right away.

"Well," said Jim, "he was killed. I was lucky with the lance—"

"You killed it!" shouted Brian gleefully. "And with a lance? I knew you would!"

"In spite of knowing how poor my lance-work was?" Jim could not resist the dig.

"James!" said Brian reproachfully.

"Well, you're right," Jim relented. "I put my lance through it, but had to do the real killing with my sword."

"Oh, I knew you'd find a way," said Brian. "Now we must have wine, you and I. We must drink together; and, Liseth, you must drink with us. The Worm is dead!"

A change suddenly came over his face.

"And the Hollow Men—" he said anxiously. "Are they all dead?"

"Yes," said Jim. "They, too. Dafydd put an arrow through their leader, Eshan, while I was fighting the Worm; and he was the last Hollow Man alive. Dafydd and I watched him finally die, a little later. They will not rise again."

"Well, we must celebrate. We really must celebrate!" Brian turned to Liseth. "How can you delay ordering someone down to the kitchen, m'Lady, on such an occasion as this?"

But Liseth had already turned to the servants.

"You, Humbert," she said. "Down to the kitchen with you; and back with a pitcher of wine and cups, plus bread and meat for Sir Brian."

She did not have to add "run." Humbert left the room with the suddenness of an arrow discharged from Dafydd's bow. It may have been, Jim thought, that he was just as eager to carry the news to the kitchen as he was to perform the service. But all that would matter to Brian was that he went and came back with the necessary items as fast as possible.

When he did come back, Brian helped himself hugely to the wine, meat and bread; meanwhile asking Jim further questions about his encounter with the Worm.

" . . . And you remembered my instructions, all the time, didn't you?" Brian interrupted when Jim was describing his attack with his lance, after circling the creature until he was in a good position to make that attack.

"A wise move, that circling," said Brian thoughtfully, over the rim of his wine cup. "I own freely I would not have thought of it, myself."

But he went on to question Jim closely about his techniques of using the weapon.

"You kept your point low as you went in?" he asked. "The way I've showed you? A lancepoint cannot simply be aimed directly at its target, the way a bowman aims his arrow at a stationary mark. It must be kept pointed loosely, in balance with the horse's movements. Only at the last moment do you grip it tightly. But you did keep the point low?"

"Yes," said Jim.

Then Brian began to question Jim about his use of sword and shield when he was in close to the Worm. Brian was interested in the fact that Jim had been battered by the forepart of the creature, even though it was blind with its two eyestalks cut off.

"My Worm did that to me," he said. "Somehow the damned thing knows, at least, about where you are."

"Not surprising," said Jim. "Close your eyes and see if you can touch the tip of your nose with the tip of your left thumb."

Brian tried it. And, somewhat to his own surprise, succeeded.

"There's something in all our bodies that lets us know where the rest of the body parts are," said Jim. "It must be no different with the Worm."

"Well, well," said Brian. "No doubt you're right—"

He interrupted himself to yawn hugely.

"I know not what it is," he said, "but I am of a sudden very tired and sleep-hungry."

Jim thought to himself that this was not surprising, seeing that Brian had been exhausted to start off with; and now was undoubtedly being hit by fatigue like an avalanche, with the alcohol in the wine, and the food and meat inside him. Brian would need a lot of sleep before he was ready to get back on his feet again.

"Best we let you rest," said Jim. He looked at Liseth, who nodded. Brian was already settling down in the bed; and, as they watched, his eyes closed and he was asleep.

"Watch him carefully now!" said Liseth to the servants, sharply, as she and Jim went out the door into the corridor.

The door closed behind them and they started off down the corridor toward the stairs and returned to the Great Hall below. For the first time Jim noticed how drawn and unhappy her face looked, now that they were away from Brian.

"Is there something wrong, Liseth?" he said, putting a hand on her shoulder.

She stopped, he stopped with her; and she suddenly clung to him, burying her face in his chest and bursting into tears.

"Oh, Sir James!" she sobbed. "I love him so!"

Jim's heart sank. All that was needed to complete Brian's awkward falling in love with Liseth, was for Liseth to fall back in love with Brian. But Liseth was going on talking.

"—And it is fated that I must marry Ewen MacDougall, whom I detest. Really *detest*!"

Her words came out chokingly.

Jim, who had put his arms comfortingly around her out of pure reflex, suddenly started and looked down at the flaxen hair on the crown of her bowed head still against his chest.

"Marry MacDougall?" he said. "You? Why?"

She lifted her head, wiped her eyes with her fingers, and stood back from him.

"There is no choice," she said. "Otherwise he will tell the Scottish King how it was my father and brothers with your help who put an end to the Hollow Men, and made his attack into England probably impossible. We must either let him go or slay him; and bad as it is, it is better to let him return to Scotland than to kill him; and have that traced to us."

"But what's this about him telling the Scottish King?" said Jim.

"What's to stop him?" answered Liseth despairingly. "He must excuse himself for losing the French gold, and allowing the use of the Hollow Men to become impossible. The King will hold him to blame, else. Far better from his point of view that he puts that blame on us. If he does, the King will send an army against the Castle de Mer. It shall be destroyed; and perhaps we shall all be captured before we can escape to the sea, and killed, if not in the battle—then afterwards and in more painful ways. And all because Ewen MacDougall will tell the truth and put the blame on us—though heaven knows he is adept enough at lying to do otherwise!"

"Oh he will, will he?" said Jim. His mind was working. His magic account had to have been replenished by his killing of the Worm. "I think I know a way of putting a stop to that!"

"How?" She backed out of his grasp and stared at him. "There is some magic you can use, Sir James—?"

"As a matter of fact, yes," said Jim. "But not quite in the way you think. I must be alone with him in the courtyard for a little while, that is all. I'd like all the rest of you to stay away, and make sure the servants cannot see me or hear me either. I'll have a little private talk with MacDougall."

"Can't you give me some idea?" she asked, staring at him. "Some idea of what you plan to do?"

"I'd rather not," said Jim, "since I don't know how well it'll work." He took her arm and started them both forward again down the corridor. "For now, let's get down to the Great Hall. The others will be along in a matter of hours."

But he was wrong about the time factor. Carolinus had brought them all back magically. Jim winced at the thought of what the Accounting Office would say to the elderly magician about all this wholesale transporting of people and horses.

When he and Liseth reached the Hall, there were voices from the courtyard; and, going there, they found not only Carolinus himself, afoot, but Dafydd, as well as Herrac and his sons, dismounting from their horses.

Ewen MacDougall was also there in the courtyard with them.

MacDougall had a slight smirk on his face; and a horse was evidently waiting for him, with a pack of provisions behind it. Clearly he was about to be turned loose. The smirk faded, rather abruptly, giving way to a look of concern, as Carolinus suddenly appeared and cast a baleful glance at him. Unlike Jim, Carolinus only needed to be looked at, to be known as a magician.

"James?" barked Carolinus. "Where's James?"

"Right here," said Jim, advancing from the doorway with Liseth beside him. The bulks of Herrac and his sons had screened him from Carolinus's gaze at first. But now these moved aside to let him come up to the older magic worker.

"Ah," said Carolinus, "just where you should be. Fine."

He turned to the others.

"Now," he commanded, "all of you gather around. I have something to say to the Accounting Office—"

"Could it wait a moment, Carolinus?" Jim interrupted him. "I have to have a small private talk with this gentleman here—"

He pointed at MacDougall.

"Is it important, James?" said Carolinus. "Because what I have to say is very important."

"This is too," said Jim. "Also I'd like a private word with you before I have the talk. If you don't mind, Carolinus. This is really extremely important."

"Well, well, I can wait a few moments more, I suppose," said Carolinus.

He beckoned Jim to follow him and led him off far enough from the others so that their low voices could not be overheard.

"What is it, boy?" Carolinus asked testily, stopping and turning to face Jim. Jim also stopped.

"Ewen MacDougall seems to be blackmailing the de Mers," said Jim. "Unfortunately he's blackmailing them with the truth. But the price is Liseth . . ."

Jim filled Carolinus in on the details of Ewen's demands and Herrac's delay and reluctant final agreement just before their attack on the Hollow Men.

" . . . I think I can change MacDougall's mind," Jim said. "But I wanted to check with you first. Do you think my magical

account now has something in it? Since I killed the Worm and
the Hollow Men are no longer a threat; pretty well blunting the
idea of a Scottish invasion of England?"

"You can count on that," said Carolinus. He grinned a dangerous grin. "But it may be nothing to what's to come."

"Oh, yes?" answered Jim, not paying this latter statement a
great deal of attention. What he had wanted to know was
whether he had magic to use or not and the beginning of
Carolinus's answer had told him that he had.

"Then it's just a matter of talking with MacDougall privately," said Jim. "Let's go back to the others."

CHAPTER 35

They started back, but Herrac met them before they had gone halfway. He drew Jim aside.

"Liseth's been telling me that she told you of her and MacDougall," said Herrac, towering over Jim but lowering his voice to keep the conversation private. "I'm not sure that I'd approve, ordinarily . . . but, do you really think you might be able to do something about the MacDougall?"

"I'm sure I can—given a private place here in the courtyard," said Jim.

"Liseth spoke of that too," said Herrac. "I have the very spot for you. In fact I've already had MacDougall taken over to it. Come with me."

He led Jim—not outward in the courtyard, as Jim had expected, but back around the curve of the tower that was the heart of the castle. They finally reached a point where they were out of sight of everyone else still standing and talking there, Carolinus included. It was also a spot where the tower backed up against the curtain wall that surrounded the courtyard. The result was a small triangular-shaped corner, in the very point of which MacDougall was standing, looking not at all pleased with the situation.

Since an expression of displeasure was common among people of this place and time when they wished to cover up uncertainty, fear or any of the other emotions that might betray them, Jim felt encouraged. He stopped about twenty feet from MacDougall, and Herrac stopped with him.

"Now, Sir Herrac," said Jim, turning to the man beside him, "if you'd leave us too? All that's necessary now is that we not be disturbed or overheard or seen for perhaps ten or fifteen minutes—maybe less."

"Gladly," said Herrac, glaring for a second at MacDougall. He turned about and left the two of them.

"And what is this mummery or nonsense you've had me brought here for?" demanded MacDougall, drawing himself up.

"I can promise you," said Jim, beginning to take off his clothes, "it's neither mummery nor nonsense."

"If you think to make an attack on me here, after the fashion of some naked highland cateran like Lachlan MacGreggor," said MacDougall, putting his hand on the hilt of his sword, which had now been returned to him and hung from his belt, "remember that I am once again armed."

"Nothing like that," said Jim. He finished disrobing. On the inside of his forehead he wrote the spell he had been thinking about ever since Liseth had told him of her being pledged to marry MacDougall.

ME→DRAGON

As usual he felt nothing as the change was made that gave him a dragon's body. Only, he suddenly found himself looking down at MacDougall from a somewhat greater height.

But the change in MacDougall himself was more of a sign that his becoming a dragon had been successful. Abandoning all pretense of contempt or indignation, MacDougall dropped his sword, fell to his knees, and signed the cross on himself; then closed his hands together, pleadingly, looking up at Jim.

"If we are to fight, cannot you at least fight like a man?" he cried. "I will fight you even as you are now, for that I am a man, myself, and a MacDougall. But what kind of coward are you that you will not come at me man-to-man?"

"There's not going to be any fighting," said Jim.

His deep and powerful dragon's voice, muted as it was, bounced off the stone walls of the small space where they stood; and, he could see, clearly further frightened the man before him.

MacDougall got shakily to his feet and picked up his sword.
"Enough of words!" he said shakily. "Come and see how
Ewen MacDougall can die!"

"Put your weapon away," said Jim, in an even more sepul-
chral tone. "I only want to charge you with a message, which
you will give to the King of the Scots."

"Message?" MacDougall stared at him. The swordpoint
wavered.

"Yes. Listen and remember," went on Jim grimly. "You will
tell him the truth, that you were robbed of your gold and that
all the Hollow Men have been killed off by some Borderers;
men you did not see and do not know. To this you will add
a special message from me, James Eckert, Baron de Bois de
Malencontri, the DRAGON KNIGHT. Tell him that if he, or
his, attempt any move against the Castle de Mer and those
within it, I will bring all the dragons of England and Scotland
against him. He and all his court will be destroyed as if they
had never been. I charge you, tell him that!"

Ewen MacDougall's sword and carefully shaven jaw both
dropped.

"Why . . . you—you can do that?" he stammered.

It was an outrageous lie, of course. Jim could no more
bring all the dragons in England and Scotland against the
King of Scotland just because he wanted to, than he could
probably recruit a single dragon—with the exception of the
mere-dragon Secoh, who hero-worshipped him—to attack anyone.

He had even failed to rouse the English dragons of the nearest
eyrie to his own castle, to support him and the English forces
the year before; when, finally, he had managed to blackmail
the French dragons into putting in an appearance over the
battlefield at Poitiers, France. It had been only by sending the
French dragons a message hinting that they would merely have
to make a sort of aerial demonstration over the battlefield—as if
they were going to attack. They would not even have considered
doing anything like this if he had not got them into a very tight
situation, indeed.

But, the fourteenth-century mind—Jim had discovered—was
willing to credit almost anything that was out of the ordinary.
Particularly, anything that was tinged by the supernatural; as
dragons—quite simple and ordinary, if large, animals, really—
were so tinged in the imagination of most humans.

Jim let his voice rise a bit in volume and rolled the words threateningly at Ewen MacDougall.

"Let him make one move toward the Castle de Mer and find out!" he said. "Now go! And do not fail to deliver the message I have sent with you!"

"I won't, m'Lord," said MacDougall. "I won't fail! I assure you I will not forget."

"Then *go*!" said Jim, moving aside slightly, so that MacDougall could leave the little corner in which he was pinned, to get past Jim in his dragon body.

MacDougall put his sword back in its sheath, and did his best to straighten up from the unconscious semicringe into which his back had curled. He walked past Jim, keeping his eyes on him until he was safely by, then turned the corner of the building and disappeared. A few moments later, Jim heard the sound of a horse being ridden rapidly out of the courtyard, through the front gate and away.

Jim changed back from his dragon body into his ordinary one, and redressed himself. Then he went back out to the others in the courtyard. He was met by Herrac before he reached the rest, however. The Lord of the Castle de Mer drew him aside and spoke to him in a low voice.

"That was well done," Herrac said.

"You heard?" asked Jim.

"I heard the stronger voice of two people in conversation," murmured Herrac. "I thought it could not be anything but you; using some magic to present yourself powerfully to him. He left as if the edge of his cloak had been set afire."

"Essentially, you're right," said Jim. "Might as well admit it now, I suppose."

He was annoyed with himself. He should have remembered the tremendous penetrating power of a dragon's voice, even when it was lowered. It was hard for a dragon not to be overheard. He decided he might as well tell the rest of it.

"I turned myself into a dragon," he told Herrac in a low voice. "—keep that to yourself, if you please—and told him to tell the King of Scotland that if he moved against the Castle de Mer or any of you that belong to it, I would bring all the dragons of England and Scotland against him and his court; and there would be nothing left after they had finished."

He was surprised to see Herrac's face blanch.

"And you can do this?" said Herrac after a moment in a shaky whisper.

"No," muttered Jim disgustedly, in answer. "That's the trouble. But if he believes it and the Scottish King believes it, you're safe. It was the best I could do."

"None could have done more!" said Herrac, in a stronger voice. "Let us return to the others, now. I'll say nothing of what you've told me; not even within the circle of my own family."

They went out together to join the others; who were still standing clustered in the courtyard, all of the de Mer family and Dafydd, plus Lachlan MacGreggor. Liseth had her arm linked through that of Lachlan, and as Jim came up she was just in the process of hugging herself against that arm, which puzzled Jim slightly. Perhaps Lachlan was leaving also, and she was giving him a warm, old-friend, type of goodbye.

"I think I talked Ewen MacDougall into telling the Scottish King that the Hollow Men robbed him of the gold—don't ask me how—" Jim said to them, "and it's not to be recovered. Because since then a band of English Borderers he didn't see wiped out the Hollow Men to the last one, and took the gold. So that none of the Hollow Men will be coming back to life again, now."

"Oh, marvelous!" said Liseth. She hugged Lachlan's arm again. "Did you hear that?"

"Of course I heard it!" said Lachlan, but more indulgently than the words indicated. "So, everything ends well for the Castle de Mer and all of us in it. There's no reason why you and I, Liseth, can't start out for Scotland tomorrow ourselves."

"There certainly is!" said Liseth, pulling her arm out of his. "I'm going to have a proper wedding here first. And that means at least a couple of months' work to get my gown made and all the preparations set up and all the right people invited in and—"

"You are marrying Lachlan?" said Jim, bewildered.

"Oh, yes," said Liseth. She took hold of Lachlan's arm again and hugged it, looking up at him. "Just as soon as we can, dear heart."

The last words were addressed to Lachlan, rather than Jim.

"But I thought—" Jim fumbled. "Up in the corridor outside Brian's bedroom I thought it was him—"

"What's this about Sir Brian?" said Lachlan, his brows suddenly joining in a dark frown and his tone changing entirely to one which rang dangerously.

"Well, I—" began Jim, but Liseth cut him off.

"It was my fault, Lachlan," said Liseth. "I told him how much I loved you, but I forgot to call you by name; and since he and I had just a moment before left Sir Brian sleeping, Sir James must have jumped to the conclusion that it was Brian I loved."

She turned her attention to Jim.

"There has never been anyone for me but Lachlan," she said, "ever since I was a little girl. We have been pledged for years. That's why he came visiting this time—as well as to bring us the news from Scotland, and concern about me if the Scottish army came this way."

"Uh—" said Jim. "I see."

Lachlan's frown had lifted somewhat, but not completely. He spoke to Liseth. "You're sure it was just a misunderstanding on Sir James's part?"

"Oh, it was," broke in Jim quickly. "I see it now. How could I have been so foolish?"

He struck his brow dramatically with the back of his right fist to emphasize the error. You couldn't *overact* with these people.

"Well, in that case—" Lachlan's frown cleared completely and he went back to a smile. "All's well—"

He frowned again, if nowhere so deeply.

"Except this business of waiting two months to get married, Liseth," he said. "Things are not done this way in Scotland—"

"I don't care how they're done up in that wild country of yours!" said Liseth. "This is Northumbria and the Castle de Mer and my home and I'm going to have a wedding the way I want it and it'll take two months!"

She all but glared up at Lachlan, who melted almost immediately.

"Weel," said Lachlan, "after all the time I've waited already, I suppose two months more isn't going to make that much difference. Still—"

"Never mind that!" said Carolinus, suddenly interrupting. He had been tapping the toe of one slipper impatiently.

Lachlan gaped at him.

"What's that?" he said. "Never mind my wedding?"

"Tut! Be silent," said Carolinus; and, although Lachlan's mouth immediately moved again, no sound came forth. "I meant only that's enough of whatever you were talking about. I have more important business here, and I wanted all of you present while it was conducted. Now listen while I hold a conversation with somebody entirely different."

"—Talk again?" Lachlan burst out suddenly, with what was evidently the end of the sentence he had begun in his voiceless state, as a result of Carolinus's magic command.

"If you like, if you like," said Carolinus with a wave of his hand, "but just not now, if you please. Don't interrupt, any of you, whatever you do. You are here as witnesses. Also, as exhibits."

"What's an 'exhibit'?" demanded Herrac.

"Never mind, Herrac, never mind!" said Carolinus, in irritation. "It'll take us all day if you people keep interrupting me. As it happens, I'm about to have a short talk with a party that's been trying to talk to me for some time. The Accounting Office."

He looked away from Herrac at empty space. A fly was buzzing around in it; but when Carolinus's eye came upon it, it took off in a straight line without hesitation.

"Did you hear that?" demanded Carolinus of the empty space. *"Accounting Office!"*

"Mage!" boomed the bass voice with which Jim had become familiar, speaking invisibly some four feet above the straw and dirt of the courtyard floor. "We've been trying to get in touch with you—"

"I know," said Carolinus. "Well, you'll have your answers now. Besides, I've a small matter to take up with you."

The others did not hear whatever the voice answered to this; but Carolinus shook his head.

"I don't care if you like it or not," he said. "I'll speak my mind, and you'll listen! Do you understand?"

There seemed to be a slight turbulence in the air before Carolinus, but still no sound.

"Well, you'd better!" said Carolinus ominously. "I've said a word or two to you on this subject, before. But evidently it's gone in one nonexistent ear and out the other. Well, we'll discuss it now, if you please! Whether you please or not, come to think of it. Now, have I or have I not spoken to you on the subject of James Eckert, my Apprentice, before this?"

A moment of silence.

"Absolutely. And I was quite correct on all five occasions," said Carolinus. "But did you pay attention? No. That's all you think of, the rules and the bottom line. You think that's the way to get things done? Well I'll tell you it's not—"

He was apparently interrupted by the unheard voice of the Accounting Office.

"Never mind that mumbo-jumbo of yours," said Carolinus. "I can indeed prove it's not the way to get things done. Take a look at most occasions when things have got done. Did the person doing them consult the rule book first? Mostly not! No, usually they made their own rules to fit the situation—and *those* worked—and as a result became part of the rule book!"

There was another moment of silence.

"Don't take that tone with me, sir!" snapped Carolinus. "You seemed to have forgotten something. Did you create the magic you keep the accounts on? No. It was created by the magicians, themselves. People like myself—and my Apprentice, here. Your only job is to keep the accounts of it in proper order; and advise the magicians of whether they need to add to their account or not. As well as answering all useful questions to which you have an answer. In short, you work for us. We don't work for you. Now, back to the subject of James Eckert again."

There was a very brief moment of silence, possibly too brief for the Accounting Office to have answered Carolinus at all, before he launched into his next spate of words.

"Here he is, a D class Apprentice," said Carolinus, "in spite of having defeated an Ogre, evicted the creatures of the Dark Powers from the Loathly Tower, managed to bring the Second Battle of Poitiers to end in a draw; and just now put an end to all hopes of a successful invasion from Scotland! But in spite of all this"—Carolinus sneered—"you've kept him still a D!"

The Accounting Office clearly attempted to say something, but Carolinus's voice overrode it.

"I don't care what the regulations are!" he snapped. "They never were supposed to be anything but guidelines to steer you in the right direction. They're not cast in bronze, you know. If I've told you once, I've told you three—no, five— times that James Eckert is not the ordinary D class Apprentice. He's attracted the attention of the Dark Powers. Consequently, he finds himself locked in contest with them time after time—

and will continue to find himself locked in contest with them. You know this; but still you expect him to miraculously win these contests with simply an Apprentice's D class account's worth of magic!"

There was a moment in which Jim and the others heard nothing.

"Yes, yes," said Carolinus irritably, "I'm well aware his knowledge of magic does not go beyond the D level, according to those regulations you talk so much about. But they make no allowance for an extraordinary case like this. Now, he's won a number of encounters with the Dark Powers, once with the help of magic I had to lend him before you put a stop to that, but mostly using his specialized knowledge, imported from you-know-where. This is putting him under an outrageously unfair burden, d'you hear? He should have been free to use as much magic as he likes to get the kind of results he gotten!"

Carolinus evidently listened while the Accounting Office protested at length.

"No, no, *no*, NO!" snapped Carolinus. "As usual you're looking at the letter of things and not at their meaning. In essence, what he's drawn upon from within himself has been the raw material of which magic is made. He has, in other words, created new magic—for which you've given him no credit whatsoever. How many times must you have it dinned into you that magic is an art, and that its practitioners create? You, sir, do not create. You are incapable of creation. If you can't do it, at least recognize it when you see it—the creation of magic. Now, I am not asking you, I am commanding you. James Eckert is to be raised to at least a full C level magician immediately; and given unlimited credit, plus the right to borrow from me if he needs it!"

There was a very slight pause this time.

"Oh, you do, do you!" Carolinus seemed to swell with rage. "Well I'll tell you what *I* intend to do. I will contact the other two AAA+ magicians—the next of the three pillars of magicdom in this world—and see if I can't enlist them to follow my example. Whether they do or not, I will withdraw myself and my account completely from your supervision. That is my right, sir! Do not tell me it is not! I will withdraw it; and you'll see how the table that is this world's magic stands on two legs. Also, once I have withdrawn, I will begin lending my Apprentice any magic I want to lend him, in any amounts of any kind, with no regard to whatever rules you have. Now is that understood?"

The answer this time could not have been more than fragmentary.

"I certainly can and will. In fact," said Carolinus, "I will do it now. '*Hear, all ye in magicdom! I, Silvanus Carolinus, do now hereby withdraw my magic*'—"

He broke off.

This time he stood listening for a long moment.

"Well, that's better. '*Magicdom, ignore what I just announced!*' " he went on in a calmer voice. "I never doubted but what you'd wake up to the facts sooner or later. I take it then that he's now C level?"

A brief pause.

"Fine. And he has access to all the magic he needs in any situation in which he is in contest with the Dark Powers?"

Another brief pause.

"Excellent. That settles that, then," said Carolinus. "Now, give me no more cause on this subject; and you'll hear no more on it from me."

A slight pause.

"I believe you," said Carolinus. "Well, I'm off for home. Thousands of things to do."

He disappeared.

CHAPTER 36

A right good sword,
A constant mind,
A trusty spear and true . . .

Sir Brian paused for a second, seeming to fumble slightly for his next line—

The Powers of Dark shall ever find

He burst out triumphantly—

What Neville-Smythe can do—

—So sang Sir Brian Neville-Smythe lustily, as he, Jim and Dafydd rode homeward, away from the Castle de Mer.

"You're in good spirits, Brian," said Jim, smiling. He was riding, as usual, in the middle; with Brian on his left and Dafydd on his right.

"And why not, James? And why not?" said Brian cheerfully. "A beautiful spring morning; and we are headed homeward at last. Giles has promised to come down to join us for the Christmas Twelvedays at the Duke's. I have promised not only to explain the fine points of jousting to him as we watch the other knights encounter; but to ride against him myself. He is most eager to improve himself. It would do you no harm, James, to join us."

"Er—no, thanks," said Jim. "My new magic responsibilities, you know."

"Well, as a matter of fact, I don't," confessed Brian.

An understandable response, thought Jim sourly, since he had pulled the excuse out of thin air on the spur of the moment.

But he could imagine Angie's reaction if he told her he was planning to joust at a tourney. Fighting when necessary was barely excusable. But to risk life and limb for *sport*—

"—However, it doesn't matter, though I know you'll be sad to miss out," said Brian, going back to being his usual sunny self. "In any case, we're headed homeward and I can hardly wait to see Geronde. While no doubt you, James, can likewise hardly wait to see the Lady Angela, once more; and Dafydd to see his Mistress Danielle."

Jim stared at him.

"You're looking forward to seeing the Lady de Chaney?"

"Why, of course!" said Brian. "Are we not deep in love, and pledged to wed? As soon as that father of hers, that old—but I must say no ill of my future father-in-law, who is a knight of renown and a debonair gentleman—returns from the Crusade that's kept him away so long."

"But—" Jim fumbled for the proper words. "I thought you'd had a change of heart and given your love—"

"—To the sweet Lady Liseth de Mer?" said Brian. "A passing fancy only, James, alas. When I learned she loved that mad Scotsman, Lachlan, I sorrowfully recognized that if it was possible for her to love such a man, she was no love for me."

"But I thought you liked Lachlan?" said Jim. "What about all those evenings you sat up drinking with him!"

"As a cup-companion and a weapon-companion I like him right well," said Brian earnestly. "He is a good fighter—'bonny,' as they say in these parts. Yet anyone who strips himself naked to go against a foe . . . how can one think of him as a gentleman?"

"But, Brian," said Jim, uncomfortably finding himself in the position of an advocate for Lachlan MacGreggor, "it's only a matter of customs. It's just the way some of the Highland Scots like to fight."

"Perhaps," said Brian solemnly, "but I cannot find it in me to agree with it."

"But if he's there when you need him? You have to give him credit for everything but choosing to do his fighting naked."

"Oh, of course," said Brian. "But you, yourself seem to be overlooking the one thing that condemns him utterly. He is no Englishman."

Brian's face was very serious as he looked at Jim.

Jim found himself speechless. It was the one argument he could never win with those on this world. Each of them, in their own minds, lived at or near the top of a social pyramid. They were the best where they were; and, by definition, the place where they were was better than any other place in the world. He could no more change this opinion of Brian's than he could have got Snorrl to accept the idea that any wolf from outside the original borders of Northumbria was really a complete and fully qualified wolf. No doubt Lachlan would point out that the one incurable flaw in Brian was that he was not a Scot.

"—You must face the fact," Brian was saying earnestly.

Jim sighed internally. "Yes, Brian," he said, "you're right. He isn't an Englishman."

"There, you see!" said Brian. "The answer to everything is always quite plain, when you look at the simple truth of it. I've always done so—and found most decisions obvious, as a result. Have you not found this to be true also, Dafydd?"

"Indeed," answered Dafydd. "Indeed I have, look you."

"You see, James?" said Brian. He reached over to lay a hand comfortingly on Jim's left hand, which held the reins of Gorp. "Life becomes so much more simple when you look at its few really important facts and ignore all those unworthy of account."

But Jim's mind was already off on another track.

"Hmm," he said thoughtfully. "You're probably right. Tell me, Brian, do you know of some place just before I reach my castle where I might pick a large bouquet of spring flowers? I'd rather like to push a bunch of them into Angie's arms as we meet—before she has a chance to say a word."